PENGUIN BOOKS

Jenny Sparrow Knows the Future

Melissa Pimentel grew up in a small town in Massachusetts in a house without cable TV and much of her childhood was spent watching 1970s British comedy on public television. At twenty-two, she made the move to London and has lived there happily for thirteen years, though she has sadly never come across the Ministry of Funny Walks. She spends much of her time reading in the various pubs of Stoke Newington with her husband (everyone thinks they're weird but they don't care) and being woken in the night by her two squabbling cats, Roger and BoJack. She works in publishing.

Jenny Sparrow Knows the Future

MELISSA PIMENTEL

PENGUIN BOOKS

PENGUIN BOOKS

UK | USA | Canada | Ireland | Australia
India | New Zealand | South Africa

Penguin Books is part of the Penguin Random House group of companies
whose addresses can be found at global.penguinrandomhouse.com.

First published in Great Britain in Penguin Books 2017

001

Text copyright © Melissa Pimentel, 2017

The moral right of the author has been asserted

Set in 12.5/14.75 pt Garamond MT Std
Typeset by Jouve (UK), Milton Keynes
Printed in Great Britain by Clays Ltd, St Ives plc

A CIP catalogue record for this book is available from the British Library

ISBN: 978–0–718–18644–9

1999

The two girls lolled on the overstuffed sofa, eyes heavy, knees knocking together, as the final credits of the movie rolled up the screen. Their teeth were furred with Pixy Stix sugar and their tongues dip-dyed bright blue from the snow cone maker Jenny's mom had bought her three years ago, for her tenth birthday. They had known they were too old to play with it now – kids' stuff, really, to be relegated to the corner of the basement, along with the jumbo tub of Barbie dolls, and the matted plush dog Jenny used to sleep with – so they'd both hidden their delight when the slush had curled out of the machine and into their waiting paper cups. They'd also rolled their eyes at each other when Jenny's mother had appeared in the doorway and asked if they wanted hot chocolate. Though Jenny had been embarrassed, she'd also been secretly relieved that she was for the moment behaving like any other normal mother, and now two chocolate-rimmed mugs sat on the floor in front of them, sunk into the deep pile of the basement's shag carpet.

'Do you want to do the Ouija board?' Isla said. Her thick mass of spongy blonde curls was piled high on her head, and her eyelids were crusted with liquid liner from a makeover session earlier in the evening.

Jenny shook her head. 'Not right now.' The Ouija board

had freaked her out ever since an incident at a sleepover with her soccer team the year before, when the arrow had jumped frenetically across the board, calling out threats to each of the girls gathered around it. When Jenny had told her mother the story, her mother had heavily suggested that the culprit was not, in fact, the spirit of Becky Tassenhoff's mean dead aunt, as suggested, but Becky Tassenhoff herself, whose parents had been going through a nasty divorce – much like Jenny's own parents had the year before – and who'd been showing signs of the strain. Still, the Ouija had said that Jenny's hair would all fall out, and she'd spent the next six months waking up in a panic, expecting to find handfuls of her long auburn hair lying limply on the pillow in great tangled tufts.

Isla threw a couple of pillows onto the floor and plonked down on top of them. Their sleeping bags were rolled out already, but it was still too early to climb into them. 'Julia Roberts is so pretty,' she said, picking at a piece of fluff in the carpet.

'You totally look like her,' Jenny said, reaching up to touch the French braid Isla had threaded into her hair earlier in the evening. It was lopsided, Jenny could feel that without looking at it. She itched to take it out and do it herself, straight this time, but she didn't want to hurt Isla's feelings.

'God, I wish.' Isla kicked idly at one of the pillows and twisted herself into a new tangle of limbs. Isla had started growing at eleven and – now five foot eight – showed no signs of stopping. She was a string bean of a girl, all elbows and knees, with long, flat feet attached to her skinny legs like flippers. On the days she came home crying because one of the boys in her class had called her Lurch or ironing board or Gumby, her mother would brush her damp curls away from her eyes and tell her that one day she'd appreciate her long legs and slim frame. Trust me, she'd say, holding her by the shoulders with her plump hands, one day they'll all be jealous of you. But Isla couldn't see how that was possible, with her flat chest and knobbly knees, and her wide-set eyes too big for her face. She wanted to be like Tina Walker, tiny and petite except for her massive chest, which she displayed to full effect in scoop-necked Abercrombie shirts. 'What do you think it would be like?' Isla said.

Jenny glanced at her. 'What would what be like?'

'Being Julia Roberts in that movie.'

Jenny thought about it for a minute. 'Pretty bad, I think. I mean, Richard Gere is old, even if he is rich and kind of good-looking.'

'But imagine being so pretty that a guy would pay all that money just to sleep with you,' Isla said.

'I guess.' The thought made Jenny deeply nervous. In fact, any mention of sex made her squeamish, and while Isla had leaned forward during the scene where Richard Gere had led Julia Roberts into the bedroom, Jenny had secretly closed her eyes. Her mother, following her father's affair and subsequent desertion in favor of his twenty-three-year-old tennis instructor, told her that sex was a drug just as bad as heroin, and that she should protect herself against it at all costs.

'Do you think our lives will be like that?' Isla asked,

flipping over onto her stomach and looking up at Jenny from underneath her curls.

'I hope not,' Jenny said. A cool sweat broke out on the back of her neck. 'I don't want to be a prostitute.'

'Not that!' Isla laughed. 'I mean, do you think our lives will be glamorous like that? And exciting?'

The thought settled between the two girls. At the moment, in Jenny's mom's basement in suburban New Jersey, it seemed unlikely.

'Maybe,' Jenny said uncertainly. And then, more firmly this time, 'Sure.'

'Seriously?'

Jenny shrugged. 'Why not?'

Isla picked at the last few chips of polish still clinging to her thumbnail. 'Sometimes I feel like I'm going to be stuck here for ever. Like Danny.' Isla's older sister had fallen pregnant during her senior year of high school, and now lived in the condos off Route 13 with her two-year-old and the father of her child, a guy called Jimmy, who had a Kawasaki motorcycle and an unconvincing moustache.

'You are not going to be like Danny. We just have to have a plan. My mom always says that you can't do anything without a plan.'

Isla eyed her doubtfully. 'Do you have a plan?'

'Sort of. In my head at least. Do you?'

Isla shrugged. 'Sort of.'

'Wait, I know what we should do.' Jenny jumped off the couch and ran up the carpeted steps in her socked feet. She returned a few minutes later holding a purple velour-covered notebook and a sparkly silver pen. She'd got the notebook for Christmas last year, but it had been too pretty for her to use – surely anything she'd write in it wouldn't match up to its beauty? But this, she decided, was important, and should be treated as such. She curled back up on the sofa and cracked open the spine. 'Okay,' she said, voice firm, 'we're going to write down all of the things we want to do with our lives.'

'All of the things?'

Jenny nodded. 'That way we'll have a plan that we can follow, and we'll both know about each other's plan, so we'll know if the other person isn't following it. It's called accountability.' Jenny had heard the word on an episode of *Oprah* a few weeks ago, and was very pleased with her use of it here.

'So, like a life list?'

Jenny nodded triumphantly. 'Exactly.'

Isla thought about this for a minute. She didn't like the idea of sharing her dream of being a doctor, even with her best friend. She'd once hinted to her father what she wanted to be when she grew up and he'd laughed and patted her on the head, and told her that maybe, if she studied hard, she could be a nurse. She looked up at Jenny's face staring down at her, her green eyes wide, and knew that if there was one person she could trust, it was her. Plus, she knew Jenny well enough to know that once she got a plan in her head, there was no dissuading her, and if Isla wanted to go to sleep anytime that night she'd better get on board with the life list idea.

'Okay,' Jenny said, brandishing her sparkly pen like a weapon. There was a tuft of pink feathers affixed to the top of it, and it bobbed gently as her pen moved across the page. 'You go first.'

Isla groaned. 'Fine. Where do we start?'

'I think we should be super detailed about it. Like, not just where we want to be when we're thirty, but where we want to be in six months, and two years, and so on. It's called mapping.' The details of the *Oprah* show had come flooding back now, and Jenny pinked with pleasure at being able to recall them.

'I want to be hot,' Isla said, 'like, psycho hot.' Jenny started scribbling in the notebook. 'Wait, you're not writing that down, are you?'

'Of course I am! It's called visualization.' Maybe she could teach a course on this, Jenny wondered. She was obviously some sort of genius at it.

'God, this is so embarrassing.'

They heard heavy footsteps on the floor above, and then a light appeared at the top of the stairs. 'Girls, it's late,' Jenny's mom called. 'Lights out soon, okay?'

'Fine, Mom!' Jenny called, rolling her eyes at Isla. 'Okay, where were we. Psycho hot . . . What's next?'

The pages filled up with the girls' aspirations and dreams, until finally, just as the early morning light began to sneak through the small, high windows, the full picture of their futures had taken shape.

I

I leaned into the mirror and swiped another slick of Fuchsia-licious onto my lips and blotted with a piece of toilet paper. It left a faint white fuzz behind, and I rubbed at it with my fingertip. Great, now I looked like a kid who'd eaten a bucket of raspberries. I sighed and wiped the whole lot off with a wet paper towel. I looked like a deranged clown in lipstick, anyway. I slid on a layer of lip balm and smiled to check my teeth for any errant pink smudges. All clear.

'Lovely dress!' I looked up to see Florence from accounts staring at me closely as she washed her hands. She looked genuinely suspicious to see my legs unsheathed from their usual smart black trousers. 'Going somewhere nice?'

'Burnt Sienna,' I said, trying and failing to sound casual. Burnt Sienna was the hottest restaurant in London at the minute, complete with a brash young hot-shot chef, and an aquarium filled with mini sharks. Christopher must have made the reservation months ago. When he told me where we were going tonight, I knew what would happen. I just knew.

'Ooh, look at you! Special occasion?'

'My birthday.' I shrugged.

Florence clapped her hands together and did a little

hop. 'I didn't know it was your birthday! We should have done cake and champers in the office to celebrate!'

I tried not to flinch at the word 'champers'. It was on my list of gross words, along with nibbles, cuddly, and the reigning champion of gross, moist. 'I'm not big on birthdays,' I said.

'Spoilsport! Well, have a lovely time tonight! See if you can get a photo with that chef – he's super hot.' She gave me a little wave before rushing out.

I stood back and assessed my reflection. I'd already redone the liquid eyeliner twice, and my left eye was still a little different from the right. Not that anyone would be able to tell unless I closed my eyes for some kind of inspection, but still, *I* would know. Tonight had to be perfect, including the eyeliner. I got the tube back out of my make-up bag and dabbed at the black swoosh that hugged my lash line. I squinted in the mirror. There. Perfect.

It was true that I wasn't big on birthdays. I'd never thrown myself a party, or taken myself away for a pampering spa day. (Pamper. Add that to the gross words list). Most years I was happy with a takeaway on the couch, and a quick splurge in H&M. This year, though, this year was different.

What I couldn't tell Florence was that this was the year I was going to marry my soulmate. I could picture the words on the list, written in the bubbly handwriting of my thirteen-year-old self. 'Number 27: Marry soulmate when thirty-one.' I was already behind (Number 25 was get engaged when thirty), but I'd always liked a challenge, and people planned a wedding in a year all the time. It was romantic! And now, on my thirty-first birthday, I was confident that everything would be back on track by the end of the night.

That's why it had to be perfect – not because it was my birthday, but because it was the night I was going to get engaged. I was sure of it.

Well, not a hundred per cent sure, but pretty confident. Christopher was definitely my soulmate – we'd been with each other for six years, and we were perfect together – and we'd need at least ten months to plan a transatlantic wedding, so that didn't leave a whole lot of time for him to propose. Sure, he didn't exactly know about my list – no one did, except for Isla – but I'm sure he could sense that it was time for us to take the next step. So when he told me that we were going to Burnt Sienna tonight I just knew: tonight was the night.

It was six o'clock on a Tuesday, so most of my co-workers were still locked into their desks, pecking away at keyboards and studying spreadsheets. I didn't want to call attention to the fact that I was ducking out early, so I grabbed my bag and coat from my cubicle and headed for the door.

The restaurant was on the South Bank, so I wound my way through Charing Cross and over Jubilee Bridge. It was early March, and the sky was dimming with dusk. The air still held the coal-edged smell of cold, and the wind cut straight through the leather bomber jacket I'd decided looked best with my little black dress that morning. Men in gray suits hustled past, and women clicked along the paving stones in their high heels. Everyone and everything seemed to have been painted in the same palette of gray.

Despite the cold, tourists still thronged the bridge, blocking the path in their threes and fours, heads tilted outwards towards the river, mouths slightly ajar. I pushed past them. I'd been in London for three years now, and the sights that I'd once only seen on postcards were now just background noise, and the people who flocked to London to see them were basically human-shaped obstacles to be hurtled and dodged.

I took a deep breath and felt my lungs fill with the cold air. Tonight, Christopher was going to ask me to marry him. My heart fluttered at the thought. Everything was working out exactly how I imagined it would. I just hoped I could work up a convincingly surprised expression when he popped the question.

We'd agreed to meet in the bar of the BFI. I spotted him as soon as I walked in. He was sitting at a table in the corner, glass of red wine in front of him, staring down at the phone in his hand with a frown. His dark hair, usually combed neatly into submission, had started to curl at the ends after the long working day, and there was a faint shadow of stubble across his chin.

Six years – six whole years! – and the sight of him still had the power to make me swoon like a heroine in a Mills and Boon novel. How could that happen? Weren't there studies that proved this sort of thing was chemically impossible? Wasn't I supposed to be inured to him by this point, as familiar as a favorite armchair or bathrobe?

He looked up, caught my eye, and smiled, and my stomach flipped.

I walked over to the table as he stood up to kiss me. 'Happy birthday, darling,' he said, before taking my coat and settling it on the back of my chair. 'I'll get you a drink. What would you like?'

'Gin and tonic, please.'

'Right, I'll just be a tick.'

Maybe it was the accent. He'd been born in Wales, but his parents had moved up to London when he was eight and enroled him in a series of expensive (and from what I could gather, draconian) private schools, which had left him with an accent that drifted between soft lilting consonants and crisp aristocratic vowels. To my American ears, he sounded like Hugh Grant, though he hated it if I said that. Despite the harsh private school education, and the fact that his best friend was called Jonno, he soundly rejected any intimation that he was posh. 'I'm from Penmaenpool!' he'd scowl, his Welsh accent surging forward. 'I'm not bloody posh!' Anyway, I still think he sounds like Hugh Grant. Just don't tell him I said so.

'Here you are.' He handed me my drink and sat down. 'How was your day? Did anyone sing "Happy Birthday" to you? Was there cake?'

I shook my head. 'I kept it pretty quiet.'

'Ah, that's a shame. Well, I've got a bit of a surprise planned that will hopefully make up for it.'

'You do? Tell me!'

He laughed. 'That would sort of negate the point of the surprise, wouldn't it? You'll just have to be patient.' I raised my eyebrows. 'I know, I know, that isn't your strong suit!'

We finished our drinks and headed back out into the cold. The restaurant was tucked down Gabriel's Wharf, a place more traditionally known for its pizza joints, fish and chip shops, and galleries selling overpriced watercolors than for fine dining. The exterior of Burnt Sienna didn't give any clues away, either. The outside of the building was clad in chipboard, and, rather than a proper sign, the name was scrawled in chalk on the window. We stood outside and looked at each other.

'This is definitely the right place . . .' Christopher said uncertainly.

I shrugged. 'The reviews said it was edgy.'

'Come on,' he said, taking my hand, 'let's give it a go. If it's awful, we could always leave and get a pizza from one of these places.'

We walked through the door and blinked into the gloom like a pair of moles. 'Can you see anything?' he asked.

'Ow!' I replied, as my foot caught on a hidden step. A maître d' appeared in front of us, and we both jumped.

'Your name?' he purred.

'There should be a booking for two under Christopher Walsh.'

'Lovely. Follow me.'

'I wish I had thought to bring a torch,' Christopher whispered as we weaved our way through the tightly packed tables. The space, now that we were inside, was less a restaurant and more a cave, with candles guttering along the walls and ceilings so low they forced you to stoop.

We arrived at our table, and the maître d' handed us menus and disappeared with a swoop. 'The guy must be half bat,' I whispered.

Christopher pulled his phone out of his pocket and shone its light at the menu. 'I hope you're in the mood for foam,' he said, scanning the choices. 'If not, there are some lovely emulsions.'

I wrinkled my nose. 'What's an emulsion?'

'I've no idea, but they seem very keen on it here.'

Our eyes met across the table. 'You know, I wouldn't mind a large pepperoni,' I said.

He nodded. 'Particularly if there's garlic bread involved.'

We got up from the table and scampered out of the restaurant, the maître d' calling a half-hearted 'excuse me' as we darted out the door and back into the night's air.

'Christ,' Christopher said, 'what a load of horseshit! Sorry, love. I should have done my research a bit more carefully before booking it.'

'Don't be ridiculous,' I said. 'It was sweet of you to go to all that trouble. I just want to know what the hell those reviewers were talking about.'

'Maybe they wouldn't let them out of there unless they gave them four stars.'

'Dungeon prisoners,' I said. 'Old school.'

'Well, it's put a spanner in my birthday plans for you, but I'm sure I can recover. Come on, let's find you a pizza.'

We wandered along the street, glancing in windows and reading menus. I tried to picture myself getting engaged inside each of the venues, but either the lighting was wrong, or the tablecloths too plastic, or the places were too empty or too full.

'Come on, birthday girl. I'm starving.'

'I know,' I said, 'I just know what I'm looking for.'

At last, we found it. Candles stuck in empty wine bottles, starched white tablecloths, almost full but not too loud. There was a man at a piano playing Sinatra classics. 'They even have dough balls!' I crowed as my eyes scanned the menu.

'Ladies and gentlemen, I believe we have a winner.' Christopher waved to the maître d'. 'Could we have a table for two, please?'

'Right this way, signor.'

We sat at the perfect table and ate the perfect meal, a thin-crusted pepperoni pizza, with a green salad and a big basket of garlic dough balls. A bottle of Chianti was uncorked and poured into two glasses, and when the waiters overheard us toasting my birthday, they insisted on bringing us two glasses of Prosecco. Christopher disappeared after the plates were cleared away, and when he came back to the table, he was carrying a tiramisu with a lit candle stuck in the middle. 'Surprise!' he sang, and then suddenly the table was surrounded by white-shirted waiters singing 'Happy Birthday'. The rest of the restaurant joined in, and, even though my face was bright red – I could feel it, hot as the sun – my cheeks ached from smiling at the end of it.

'Happy birthday, lovely,' Christopher said, as he leaned across the table and kissed me.

This is it, I thought. This is the moment. The perfect

moment. He was about to do it. I braced myself to look surprised and delighted.

'Shall we get the bill?'

We sipped limoncello as we waited for the waiter to bring the card reader over.

'So!' I said brightly. 'What's next?'

He glanced at his watch. 'It's nearly eleven on a school night,' he said. 'I was thinking a taxi home. Unless you wanted to go clubbing in Vauxhall or something? I hear it's bondage night at Torture Garden.'

I laughed as my heart sank. 'No, that's okay. A taxi home sounds good.'

He looked at me for a minute. 'How about a walk first? We could head across the bridge, pick up a taxi on the Strand?'

I lit up. 'Perfect!'

We gathered our coats and headed out into the night. Of course he wouldn't ask me in a crowded restaurant, I thought to myself. He's not a showy kind of person. He probably wants to do it somewhere private, where it's just the two of us.

'Shall we cross at Waterloo or Blackfriars?' he asked. 'There'll probably be more taxis at the Waterloo end of the Strand, but Blackfriars is slightly closer to home.'

I weighed the romantic possibilities of both in my head. 'What about Jubilee?' It's pedestrianized, I reason, so he won't risk being run over when he goes down on one knee, and the name sounds suitably celebratory.

He pulled a face. 'That's miles out of the way.'

'It's not! Plus, there's a taxi rank underneath the railway

arch at Charing Cross.' I hadn't envisioned quite so much logistical wrangling in the lead-up to the proposal, but in retrospect I should have known better: he is a lawyer, after all.

He linked his arm through mine and tugged me towards the river. 'Jubilee it is.'

Christopher launched into a story about a fraud case he was working on. Usually I loved hearing about that sort of thing – I liked predicting the verdict before it went to trial – but I was too nervous to concentrate. Every step we took towards the bridge made my throat constrict a little tighter. 'Are you all right?' he asked, shooting me a worried glance. 'You've gone awfully quiet.'

'Fine!' I squeaked. I was impressed by his cool – he didn't look nervous in the least.

'Come on,' he said, 'if we don't hurry, we'll get caught up in pub kick-out time, and then we'll never get a cab.'

We climbed the steps and made our way across the bridge. People streamed past us – commuters rushing home after late work drinks, young couples out on third dates grinning moonily at each other, a group of American college students loudly debating about the location of Bar Opal – but I refused to move at their pace. By the time we were three quarters of the way across – having stopped twice to insist on admiring the view – I was practically moving backwards.

The stairs down to the arches were approaching. I could feel Christopher's rising irritation with me. Maybe he would wait until we got back to the flat, I reasoned. Maybe that's why he was in such a rush to get back. After all, it was the place we spent most of our time together. There would be something romantic about him proposing there, in front of the sofa where we watched television most evenings, or in the kitchen where we chopped vegetables and sautéed fish side by side. It wasn't exactly what I'd imagined, but maybe if he'd put a bottle of champagne in the fridge . . .

'Hang on a minute,' he said, and I turned to find him down on one knee, hands fiddling with something. Time turned to treacle. The world was suddenly in slow-motion, vivid and beautiful and clear. And then my mouth opened and I heard words fly out, unbidden. 'Ohmygod, YES!'

He looked up at me quizzically. 'Yes what?'

'Yes I'll—' I looked down and saw that, instead of a ring in his hands, he was holding the two ends of his shoelaces, mid-knot. Panic gripped me. 'You mean you weren't—'

His eyes widened. 'You mean you thought—'

'Nothing!' A peal of hysterical laughter bubbled up from inside me. 'I didn't think anything!'

He sprang to his feet and reached for me. 'You did! Oh, Christ. Oh, Jenny.'

'It's just — it's my birthday and all, and you said there would be a surprise . . .'

'Beyoncé,' he said quietly. 'Beyoncé was the surprise.'

'Beyoncé?'

He nodded. 'I got you a pair of tickets for her show in July.'

'Oh! Wow! Great!' The words sounded flat even to my ears. 'I mean, that's a great surprise!'

We stared at each other helplessly.

'I know you want to get married, Jenny,' he said quietly, 'but you've got to stop putting so much pressure on me.'

'I'm not putting any pressure on you!' The pitch of my voice was so high now that probably only dogs could hear it.

'You are! You don't know it, but you are. Every time we go on holiday, or out to a nice restaurant, or it's your birthday or my birthday or Christmas or – hell – even a bloody bank holiday, I can feel you waiting for me to ask you.'

'I just – I thought you wanted to be with me.'

He took my hands in his and smiled at me sadly. 'I do. I am! I just don't feel ready for the whole caboodle.'

'The whole caboodle?'

'You know what I mean.'

I folded my arms across my chest. 'I really don't.'

'Marriage! Babies! Matching crockery sets! Retirement funds! Moving to the country! Commuting by train! Discussing nurseries at dinner parties with people we don't even like but are forced to socialize with because we live in the country and can't be arsed to commute into London for a night out!'

'You're being crazy.'

His eyes shone in the moonlight. 'Am I?'

I nodded weakly. 'I hate matching crockery sets.'

He threw his hands up. 'You see! But you're not actually opposed to the rest of it, are you?'

I shrugged. 'I mean, you're not exactly painting it in rosy tones, but no, I'm not opposed to it in theory. Maybe not exactly how you just described it, but I don't think there's anything wrong with a little security.'

'Jenny, our lives are mired in routine. Every day we go to work, and every night we come home and eat one of the four dinners we have on rotation, and we have the same Kung Pao chicken from the same Chinese takeaway place every Friday, followed by the same Sunday lunch at the Queen's Head. If we were any more secure, we'd be encased in cement!'

'I thought you liked our life!' I said, my eyes filling with tears.

He sighed. 'I do! I do.' So he was capable of saying those words. 'I love our life, and I don't want it to change. Don't you see? If we get engaged, things might change.'

'They might not.'

'But they might. And I'm not ready to risk that.'

I took a deep, shuddering breath. 'Do you know if you'll ever be ready for the whole kit and caboodle?'

He shook his head. 'I don't know.'

I let that sink in. He might never be ready to marry me. I was meant to get married to my soulmate this year – it had been etched in stone on the list and on my mind for eighteen years – but my soulmate was telling me it might never happen. 'I'd like to go home now,' I said. Though the thought darted across my mind, quick as a silverfish, that it might not feel like home anymore.

We were silent for the cab ride home, the driver stealing curious glances at us in the mirror until I eventually just closed my eyes and pretended to be asleep. We pulled up to the curb outside our flat, and I waited on the sidewalk as Christopher paid. He led me up the steps and into the house, his hand gently supporting my elbow, as if I were an invalid. Our footsteps echoed on the wooden floorboards as we walked into the hallway.

'You want a drink or anything?' he asked, heading towards the kitchen. I followed him. There was a frosted chocolate cake slumped on the counter next to the oven, a white envelope with my name scrawled across it propped up next to it. 'It came out a bit wonky,' he said, nodding sheepishly towards the cake.

'You baked it yourself?'

He nodded. 'Sneaked off work a couple of hours early. I think there might be something wrong with the oven though, as both of the sponges only rose on one side. I tried to even them out when I stacked them together but it's still a little crooked.'

I burst into tears.

'Shit,' he said, coming towards me and pulling me into his arms. 'I'm sorry.'

I shook my head as I wept into his chest. I could feel the material of his shirt dampen with my tears. 'It's not your fault,' I wailed. 'You're perfect!'

He stroked my hair and led me to bed, where I lay down and cried myself into unconsciousness while he rubbed my back with the flat of his hand.

2

I woke up the next morning feeling as if I'd gone nine rounds in the ring and lost, badly. My throat ached from crying, and my eyes had swollen to slits. Christopher was already showered and dressed when my eyes fluttered open, and he leaned down and kissed the top of my head. 'Maybe you should call in sick today,' he said, taking in my puffy face and the black circles underneath my eyes.

I shook my head. 'I've got a meeting at half ten.'

'Better get up then. It's nearly eight, sleepyhead. I'll see you tonight, okay? Maybe we could go for a little post-birthday drink?'

I attempted a smile. 'That would be nice.'

He paused in the doorway and opened his mouth as if about to say something, but instead he just shook his head and blew me a kiss. 'Have a good day, love.'

I heard the door shut behind him, and pulled myself out of bed with a groan.

I showered and shaved my legs and washed my hair, and then applied various creams and unguents to my face before daring to look in the mirror. Here's a truth that should be universally acknowledged: eye creams that promise to 'de-puff' and skin creams that promise to 'brighten' summarily fail to de-puff or brighten anything following a two-hour cry-fest. It's just a physical impossibility. I would look like hell for the rest of the day, and there was nothing on this earth that could stop it. Not even in Space NK.

I pulled on my coat, slung the little leather J.Crew bag I'd splurged on last month, and the supplementary canvas tote bag that actually held most of my belongings over my shoulder, and headed for the Tube. Christopher had bought the flat in Dartmouth Park just after the 2008 crash, thanks to a combination of squirreled-away savings and what his parents had described as 'early inheritance'. It was a ground-floor two-bed, with high ceilings, crown moulding, and a little rectangle of green out the back. Every once in a while, after too much red wine, we'd look up the value of the flat and fantasize about selling up and moving to Lisbon or Barcelona, but we both knew it wasn't going to happen. Christopher loved the flat and loved London, and I loved him. I'd known the choice I was making when I boarded the plane with my work transfer papers three years ago. My mother's face flashed in front of me, and I pushed it out of my mind. I couldn't think about that. Not now.

It was a crisp spring morning, blue-skied and gentle-breezed, too beautiful for my current state of mind. I wanted low gray clouds and persistent drizzle, maybe even a hailstorm. But, as usual, the English weather refused to cooperate.

I joined the huddled masses at Tufnell Park Tube and let three packed trains pass before hurling myself onto the fourth. Despite the fact we were pressed together, nose to shoulder, like a pack of breadsticks, the compartment was silent apart from the occasional sneeze and muttered chorus of bless-yous. I pulled out a paperback and tried to lift it past my waist, but a man in a tan overcoat kept pressing his back against my arm, pinning it to my side, and I eventually gave up and just closed my eyes.

I replayed the previous night's conversation as the train rocked between stations. Maybe it wasn't as bad as I'd thought. He hadn't said never, right? Then again, he hadn't said some day.

I knew he loved me. I knew that that should be enough. It was 2017, for God's sake. Marriage was a dying tradition! The divorce rates were sky high! The wedding industry was a sham! I should embrace the fact that he was essentially freeing me from the shackles of a patriarchal institution. Why couldn't I just be happy that we were together? Why did I need a piece of paper to prove it?

I shook my head, jostling the arm of the woman holding onto the pole next to me. I don't know why I needed it, but I did. I didn't care about a big white wedding – I'd never been one to stage Barbie and Ken nuptials as a child, preferring instead to enact elaborate kidnapping plots – but I did care about the piece of paper. I thought Christopher had known that. I thought he'd been on the same page.

My throat ached and I felt the tears start to build behind my eyes. Maybe he just doesn't love me enough. Maybe I bore him. I thought of the distracted way he half-listened to my stories sometimes, the long pauses in conversation over pints at the pub, the way his gaze would sometimes drift to a point slightly to the left of my head. I blinked rapidly to try to fight it off, but it was too late. A tear fell from my eye and sploshed on the arm of the man in the tan overcoat. A darkened circle appeared on the material. After that, it was like a tap had been turned on. I tried to reach up and brush them away but I couldn't extract my arms from the crush of the crowd.

'The next station is . . . Camden Town.'

A few people got off, but even more pushed on. The man in the tan overcoat's arm was now dotted with wet splashes. I willed him not to look down. Maybe I should get off, I reasoned. Maybe I should go and sit on one of those iron benches on the platform and put my head in my hands until I got myself together. But then someone might ask me if I was okay, and there was no way I would be able to respond without losing my shit completely.

The stations whizzed by. The man in the tan overcoat got out at Euston, and I breathed a sigh of relief. The compartment had emptied slightly, enough for me to wipe the mascara from under my eyes and apply a futile swipe of lip balm. People were staring at me, I could feel it.

I changed to the Victoria Line at Kings Cross and let it whisk me to Green Park. I could have stayed on until Victoria – our offices are in a cold gray building a few blocks from the station – but most days I preferred to walk through the park.

The fresh air cleared my head a little, and I arrived at work feeling more human than I had all morning. I showed my security pass to the guard at reception and weaved my way through the labyrinthine halls to my cubicle.

I work at an insurance company. I can't say it was the exact profession I'd planned for myself – 'I want to be a claims adjuster!' said no thirteen-year-old, ever – but

Number 9 on my list was a good, steady job with a good, steady salary, and that had been the logo on the banner for Jameson Hardwick Insurers at the college job fair. Literally: 'Jameson Hardwick Insurers: A Good, Steady Career Path'. Not a particularly catchy motto, but it had appealed to me. It promised security and stability, the two things I craved the most. The nice people manning the booth had asked if I'd like to take a quick aptitude test – 'Sure!' I'd said brightly, sweating profusely in the polyester pantsuit I'd bought from The Express – and I'd aced it. They'd offered me a job straight out of graduation with full benefits, and a salary that was more than double the national average.

It turned out that I loved it, too. I know that everyone thinks that working in insurance must be boring – I can't tell you how many people fake-snooze or make loud snoring noises when I tell them what I do – but it's actually pretty interesting. No, seriously, it is. All day long, I get to read little stories about people's lives and decide whether or not they're true. Did the chip shop really burn down due to a grease fire, or did the owner's brother-in-law have it in for him? Did the woman really suffer from third-degree burns because the coffee lid was faulty, or was she looking for an easy pay-out? Did the neighbor's tree really fall on that man's car because of an act of God, or was he trying to get him back for sleeping with his wife? See? Interesting, right? It's like being a private detective without the need to wear a trench coat, chain smoke or talk out of the corner of my mouth.

'Here she is!' I arrived at my desk to find my cubemate,

Ben, standing arms akimbo, hands on his skinny jeans-wearing hips. 'It's the BIRTHDAY GIRL!'

'Shhh!' I said, eyes darting around. 'Someone might hear you! Anyway, it was yesterday, so you're too late.'

'Ah, that's what you think. But I wasn't in the office yesterday, which means I get a bonus celebration day.'

'What kind of rule is that?'

He shook his head. 'Don't question the birthday rules or you won't get any cake.'

My ears perked up. 'There's cake?'

'Not just any cake.' He reached under his desk and pulled out a small lurid-green cardboard box, which he presented to me with a flourish. 'This is the motherload.'

I leaned in to take a closer look at the box in his hands. The top of the box was covered in cellophane, and inside lay a cake in the shape of a caterpillar. 'The caterpillar cake!' I'd told Ben during one of the long, meandering chats that seem to emanate from cube-sharing that I'd always wanted a Tesco caterpillar cake. Something about its stubby little face really tugged at my heartstrings. And now here it was, staring up at me with its edible little eyes. I shook my head. 'I genuinely can't believe you remembered.'

'I couldn't let the occasion pass without celebrating it properly. It's unthinkable that you've been in this country for three whole years and have yet to sample the delights of the Tesco caterpillar.'

I lifted the top off the box, and Ben produced a plastic knife. 'I feel bad cutting him,' I said.

'Actually, caterpillars lack nociceptors, so aren't actually capable of feeling pain.' I raised an eyebrow and he shrugged. 'I watched a lot of David Attenborough as a kid.'

I hesitated for a minute, and then plunged the knife into the back of the caterpillar's neck. Its little face flopped forward in a single slab, for ever severed from its body. This thought proved too much for me in my delicate state, and I felt the knot re-form in the base of my throat.

Ben took one look at me and slid our cube door closed. 'Are you all right?' he asked, handing me a frosting-smudged napkin. 'I know you said you weren't a birthday person, but I thought you'd be pleased about the cake.'

'I am!' I wailed. 'It's great! I'm great!'

'You don't look so great to me, if you don't mind me saying.' He studied my face closely. 'In fact, you look like shit.'

'Gee, thanks,' I said, wiping mascara and frosting around my face.

'Come on, let's sit you down.' He pushed me gently into my office chair, and I rolled backwards to the edge of my desk. 'Now tell Uncle Ben what's the matter.'

I pulled a face at him. 'Uncle Ben? Gross.'

'Call me whatever you want, then. Just tell me what's happening.'

'It's Christopher,' I said, breath coming in stuttered bursts. 'He's— he's—'

'He not shagging someone else, is he?' I took that moment to burst into tears, which Ben took as an affirmation. 'He is, isn't he! What an absolute cock-end. I knew it from the minute I saw him, with his stupid slick hair.'

'What's wrong with his hair?' I squeaked.

'I don't know – it's all shiny, or whatever. Cock!' He

reached across the cube and handed me another tissue. 'Don't you worry about him. He's an arsehole and you're better off without him. Arsehole.'

I managed to shake my head. 'It's not that,' I said. 'He's not cheating on me.'

Ben looked oddly disappointed. 'He's not?'

'No. It's just — I thought he was going to propose last night, and then he didn't, and then we got into a big fight, and then— and then—' A fresh flood of tears exploded out of me. Where had I been storing all these tears, anyway? How did I have so much saline stashed inside my skull?

'Ah, I see,' Ben said, nodding sagely. 'You women. Always looking to pin us down.'

I looked at him through a swollen gimlet eye. Ben was twenty-five, and his dating history, to my understanding, consisted of three years spent in unrequited love for a woman called Amanda at university, and the occasional drunken house party hook-up. 'Some people want to settle down,' I said, sniffing defensively.

He rolled his eyes. 'Look, if a bloke doesn't want to get married, he doesn't want to get married. You should tell him to fuck off and then go out and sow your wild oats. I've got a couple of mates who are into older women — I could set you up!'

The older woman comment smarted more than I'd like to admit. God, imagine dating again. Surrounded by twenty-five-year-old idiots like Ben, who would think of me as some kind of cougar — if I was lucky. I tossed the crumpled napkin in the trash and leaned down to switch on my computer. 'Thanks but no thanks.'

'Suit yourself,' he said. He pointed to the slab of caterpillar face resting on the table. 'You going to eat that?' I shook my head and watched as he took an enormous bite. 'Look, the last thing I'll say on the matter is this: you're gorgeous, and any man would be lucky to have you. If Christopher can't get that through his shiny head, you're better off without him.'

I felt the tears threatening again and jumped up from my seat. 'I'll be back in a minute,' I said, and I grabbed my bag and ran to the ladies' room.

3

The tiled wall at the back of the bathroom stall was cool, and I leaned back and let my head rest on it. A ball of wadded-up toilet paper rested in my open palm. I'd been in here for fifteen, maybe twenty minutes now, listening to the morning rush of women emptying their post-commute bladders and blotting off excess blush and swiping on lipstick. I waited them all out.

Sitting fully-clothed on a toilet while locked in a bathroom cubicle at work wasn't a high point, and sooner or later Ben would send in a search party to rescue me. I took a deep breath and stared at the little silver latch that was keeping the outside world at bay. I knew I couldn't stay in there for ever. But I wasn't quite ready to leave my little bleach-scented cocoon.

I reached up and into my bag, which was dangling from a hook on the back of the door. I might be going through an existential crisis, but I wasn't about to let my bag touch the bathroom floor. I rummaged around until my fingers curled around my phone. I checked the time: 10.07. The case assignment meeting started in twenty-three minutes. That gave me time.

It was 5 a.m. in New York, but I knew Isla would be up, either patrolling the hospital corridors where she was a last-year neurosurgery resident or being ferried home from a BDSM club in an Uber. She was a rainbow of contradictions, my best friend.

I unspooled a fresh length of toilet paper as I listened to the phone ring out. She picked up right before the voicemail clicked in.

'Duuuuuuuuuuuuuuuuuude!' I could hear the sound of surgical equipment beeping and whirring in the background. Work, then. At least that meant she wouldn't be on a come-down from anything. 'How was your birthday? Did you play shot roulette like I told you to?'

My throat tightened. 'Not exactly,' I whimpered.

'Shit.' She heard it in my voice instantly. That's what twenty years of friendship gets you. 'Hang on a minute.' There was the sound of clipped footsteps and a door opening and closing. 'Okay, what's going on?'

'It's Christopher.'

'Has that motherfucker cheated on you? I swear to fuck, I am getting on a plane and I am going to kick his stupid English ass.'

'He's Welsh,' I croaked, 'and no, that's not it.'

'What then? He's obviously done something wrong, the little shit. Honestly, the plane ride isn't that long. I could be kicking his ass by dinnertime.'

I balled up the tissue and pressed it into my eyes. 'He doesn't want to marry me.'

'What? How do you know?'

'He told me!'

'He told you that on your *birthday*? What kind of a sick fuck—'

'Okay, he didn't exactly say it. But he intimated it.'

31

'What do you mean, he intimated it? How do you intimate something like that?'

'I thought he was going to propose last night. Because—'

'Because of the list.' I could practically hear her eyes rolling back in her head.

'I'm thirty-one now! You know this is the year I'm supposed to—'

'Marry your soulmate – I know! I know! I was there when you wrote it, remember?'

'Exactly. Which means you should understand.'

She sighed. 'So you thought he was going to propose . . .' she prompted.

'He booked us into this super fancy restaurant – which turned out to be terrible, by the way—'

'Never eat in a restaurant outside New York,' she said. 'That's just basic common sense.'

'But we ended up going to this Italian restaurant and there were candles and garlic bread and a man playing the piano—'

'Very *Lady and the Tramp*.'

'Exactly! Perfect, right? And the whole time I was just waiting for him to do it.'

'Willing him.'

'Waiting, willing – whatever. Anyway, we were crossing over the Thames, and there was moonlight, and water lapping, and sparkly city lights, and all of a sudden he dropped down on one knee, and I thought, this is it!'

'But it wasn't it.'

'His shoelace was untied.'

'Fucking shoelaces. Velcro should have made them obsolete. Oh, babe, I'm sorry. What a goddamn headfuck.'

'I know. And then we ended up getting into this huge fight, and he was basically like, I'm not ready! And I was like, Why not? And he was like, I don't know, and I don't know if I'll ever be.'

Isla heaved out a long sigh. 'Where are you now?'

'Crying in the bathroom at work. Obviously.'

'Obviously. Okay, well, here's how I see it. In times like this, there's only one solution.'

'Nunnery?'

'Vegas.'

'Vegas? What do you mean, Vegas?'

'I mean we go to Vegas. You and me. It'll give you a chance to get drunk and blow off some steam, and it'll give him a chance to miss you. You know how men are. They don't realize how much they need something until it's threatened to be taken away from them. Like toddlers and their pacifiers. Or Americans and Obamacare.'

'I don't know ... When were you thinking? Next month?'

'Next weekend.'

'Next weekend! What about work?'

'Jenny, you live in Europe. Well, what used to be part of Europe. How many vacation days do you guys get over there? Fifty? A hundred?'

'Twenty-five,' I said quietly.

'And how many of those days did you take last year?'

I hesitated. 'Twelve.'

'Jesus. Who are you, Bob Cratchit? "Oooh, please Mr

Scrooge, may I have Christmas day off so I might eat a speck of goose?"' Isla's British accent was terrible.

'Whatever. What about you? Don't you have brains to operate on?'

'Bobby Miller owes me a favor. Also, he's desperate to get in my pants. He'll cover for me.'

I searched my mind for more roadblocks. The thought of a spontaneous trip to the grocery store was enough to make me break out in hives, never mind a weekend in Las Vegas with the human hurricane that is Isla. 'The flight will cost a fortune.'

'Ah, there's where you're wrong. I have, like, a billion Air Miles thanks to all those boring pharma conferences I've been forced to attend. Thanks to Pfizer, I can totally swing your ticket and mine.'

'Oh.' That was it. Not a single obstacle in sight. 'What will I say to Christopher?'

'The man told you he didn't want to marry you on your birthday. Do you really give a single flying fuck what he thinks?'

I thought about it. 'No,' I lied.

'Good. Go talk to your boss now and email me when you have the all-clear. I'll start researching hotels. I'm thinking penthouse suite.'

'Is that somehow covered by Air Miles, too?'

'No, it'll be covered by one of my many little plastic card-shaped friends.'

'Isla . . .'

Jenny . . .' she mimicked. 'I'm going to qualify as a fully-fledged neurosurgeon next year. Do you have any idea how much money people are going to pay me to cut their heads open?' I felt momentarily queasy, though I couldn't pinpoint if it was stemming from the thought of Isla operating on someone's brain or of her being super rich. 'Just let me do this, okay?' She sounded serious. I knew it was pointless to argue.

'Okay,' I said. 'Thank you.'

'Ohhhhh my God, amazing. Amazing! We are going to have so much fun. Vegas isn't going to know what's hit it.'

The queasiness returned. I wasn't someone who dropped everything and jetted off to Vegas. I was someone who planned a vacation a year in advance, researched the best options for travel insurance, and checked the Home Office website to make sure the threat level wasn't above a sunny yellow. But these weren't ordinary times, and I knew if I stayed in London, I would just stew. I had to get out. And there was no one I'd rather see at that moment than Isla.

After we hung up, I let myself out of the bathroom stall and spent a few futile minutes trying to mitigate the damage to my blotchy, swollen face before returning to my cube.

Ben looked up when I came in, concern etched across his face (along with a little dab of frosting – my grief hasn't stopped him from polishing off the caterpillar's face). 'You okay?' he asked.

I blinked. 'I'm going to Las Vegas,' I said, and then I sat down heavily in my chair and spun around to face my computer. It was time to get to work.

4

Things came together quickly. My boss was surprisingly relaxed when I asked him if I could take a last-minute long weekend. In fact, he'd been delighted. Apparently HR had made enquiries about my unused vacation time and were about to open an investigation into whether or not I was being bullied in the workplace. Ben agreed to cover my cases while I was away and even promised to keep a running tally of the number of times Jim and Christine – an office romance just on the verge of ripening – made vaguely sexual overtures towards each other at the tea station.

Christopher, for his part, looked completely stunned when I told him. He'd actually asked if I felt all right, as if I'd told him I had a rash rather than vacation plans. I'm fairly sure he would have rolled a glass across my arm if I'd let him. He adapted pretty quickly, though, and was helping me pack within the hour. 'Are you sure a long weekend is enough?' he'd asked as he'd tossed me my bathing suit. 'Maybe you should take the full week.'

Isla sent me an e-ticket for my flight and a link to a website – she'd booked a suite at the Paris Hotel in the hope that it would make me 'feel at home' because it was 'like Europe only baller' – and before I knew it, Christopher was driving me to the airport in our little Peugeot, my case shoved in the back seat.

He sailed past long-stay parking – extinguishing the small hope I'd been harboring of him seeing me off at security – and pulled up to the drop-off lane outside Terminal 5. He kept the engine idling. 'I've been thinking,' he said, tossing an arm around the back of my seat. 'Maybe this break is a good thing.'

'It's not really a break,' I said, checking my reflection in the flip-down mirror. I looked borderline undead. 'It's just a long weekend.'

'What about – just a thought here – but what if we did think of this weekend as a break?'

I watched the hinge of my jaw go slack. 'You mean, a break from us?'

He put his hands up in the air, as if the idea was something that had flown out of his head of its own volition. 'It's just a thought, but – well, things have been a little heavy between us recently, and with you going off to Vegas like this, it just feels like a natural sort of . . . sort of . . .'

'Sort of what?'

'Break, I suppose.'

I thought briefly about screaming, but I'd never liked causing a scene. So instead I just sat there, knees shoved against the glove compartment, and stayed silent.

I couldn't believe it. Christopher being unsure about marriage was one thing, but now it seemed he was unsure about me, too. About us. I could see our life together starting to crumble, like a sandcastle at high tide.

He caught the desolate look on my face and grabbed my hand. 'Look, just forget it. Forget I ever said anything. You go and have fun.'

A man in uniform knocked on the window and gestured for us to get a move on. 'I've got to go,' I said. I opened the car door and stepped out onto the pavement. Christopher got out too, pulled the suitcase out of the back, and settled it next to my feet. Around us, families were saying their goodbyes, hugging each other and wishing them safe journeys. A tall man held a young woman as she sobbed in his arms. 'It's only for a month,' he said into her hair, but this only made her cry harder. Christopher and I exchanged looks. It hadn't been that long ago that we'd been that couple, living in two different countries, our hearts pulled across the Atlantic like saltwater taffy.

Now, he leaned down and tried to kiss me. I gave him my cheek. 'Have fun,' he said. 'Send my love to Isla.'

I nodded and walked through the wide glass door of the terminal building, my suitcase bumping against my heels as I went. I didn't turn around.

Soon I was folded like an origami crane into seat 34B, sandwiched between a teenage boy munching his way through a bag of pickled onion Monster Munch (Why, God, why?) and a middle-aged man in a fedora whose foot had already migrated into my leg room. The air-conditioning vent blasted cold air directly at my center parting, and I could already feel my contact lenses soldering themselves to my eyeballs. A voice came over the loudspeaker. 'Ladies and gentlemen, please be advised that this flight is full, so do store any handbags and coats under your seats rather than in the overhead compartments. Please make your way to your seats as quickly as possible as our flight is scheduled to depart in ten minutes.'

I pulled out the paperback I'd brought with me, but the words swam in front of my eyes.

What was it he'd said exactly? A break. That we should take a break. How long had he felt like this? This was the man who I was supposed to spend my life with. I'd moved across an ocean for him, to a country where everything smelled like wet wool, and people put vinegar on French fries. I'd left a whole life behind for him. I thought of the couple standing outside the terminal, devastated by the thought of a few weeks apart. That had been us once. Now he couldn't wait to shove me on a plane.

I felt the engine rumble to life underneath us. 'Cabin crew, please take your seats for departure.' The plane lurched forward and began accelerating down the runway. The nose lifted, and soon we were airborne. I leaned forward and tried to see past the teenager and out the window to the ground below. The teenager responded by pulling down the shade and settling a pair of enormous headphones over his ears.

I lay back and closed my eyes. In eleven hours, I'd be in Las Vegas. But more importantly, I'd be with Isla. And Isla, however crazy she might seem, always knew exactly what to do.

It had been dusk when I'd left London, and now, an eleven-hour flight plus an hour winding my way through immigration and baggage claim later, I stepped out of McCarran International Airport to find myself at the beginning of the same night I'd left behind. The sun had set a few hours ago, but the heat still punched me in the chest as the glass door slid closed behind me and left me stranded on the sidewalk. My eyes were grainy with tiredness and my feet felt like a pair of water balloons strapped to stiff legs. I wanted, briefly and very badly, to turn around and get straight back on the plane, but then I remembered that I wasn't sure I still had a home in London. Judging from the lack of texts from Christopher, probably not. And then I thought about crying.

'Jenny! Over here!' I looked up to see Isla standing up in the front seat of a bright red convertible, waving her arms like a maniac. 'Hurry, before the goddamn Gestapo come back!' She jerked a thumb towards a frowning traffic warden.

I waved back and wheeled my suitcase over to the car, heaving it onto the back seat next to Isla's duffel bag. She was still standing up inside the car, waving her arms around excitedly and jigging up and down. Her white-blonde hair was a Medusa's nest of curls, the dark roots just peeking through. She'd kept her natural blonde until her sixteenth birthday – after that, it had been all peroxide. 'Hurry! Hurry!' she shouted, one eye on the traffic cop. 'Come on, get your ass in here!' I opened the door and threw myself inside and she floored the accelerator and peeled out of the lot.

I'd forgotten about Isla's driving.

'Motherfucker!' she screamed as she cut off a minivan. She turned to me and beamed. 'I'm SO happy to see you. How are you? How was your flight? How goddamn baller is this car? How bad do you want a drink?'

40

She merged onto Paradise Road and a pickup truck blared its horn as it sailed past. 'Isla, watch the road!'

'It's fine!' She swatted the thought of our impending death in a fiery inferno away like a gnat.

'What time did you get in?' I asked as I double-checked that my seat belt was securely fastened.

'A couple of hours ago. I picked up the car and drove down the Strip before I came to get you, just to get the lay of the land. Wait till you see it – it's completely insane. It's like Disney Land on ketamine. Speaking of which . . .'

I shook my head. 'Absolutely no ketamine allowed.'

'Whatever, MOM,' she pouted.

I'd spotted the Strip from the airplane as we'd come in to land. The vast empty black of the desert and then the gridded lights of the suburbs punctuated by the singular, spectacular color of the lights. Even the surly teenager had gaped at the sight.

'What do you want to do first?' Isla asked. 'You probably want to take a shower, right? Wake yourself up after the flight? So let's check into the hotel, unpack over vodka tonics, and then get dinner.'

'Perfect.'

We were on the Strip in no time. Turns out the airport is basically in the middle of Las Vegas – that's what you get when you plan an entire place around tourists, I guess. Particularly tourists who are there to do nothing but gamble, see strippers, and get drunk. Although, as the pamphlet I'd picked up at the airport pointed out, it was also the home of the Pinball Hall of Fame, so . . .

'We're here!'

I looked up to see the Eiffel Tower looming above me, lit up in the night sky by thousands of golden bulbs. 'Wow,' I muttered.

Isla was already out of the car and tossing her keys to the valet. 'Come on!' she urged, charging through the gilded revolving doors. I scrambled to catch up, briefly squashing my suitcase between the door and the wall until the doorman came to my rescue and I was flung, at speed, into the marble lobby.

Isla was already at the front desk haggling with the check-in clerk about an upgrade, so I took a minute to look around my surroundings. There was gold, a lot of it, and a lot of marble, too. Ornate chandeliers gleamed from the corniced ceiling, and every five feet, an elaborately-plumed historical figure glowered out from an oil painting. Imagine Louis XIV had decided to jazz things up a little, décor-wise, and you've got the idea.

'Got it!' Isla brandished two plastic card keys in her hand. We sped through the lobby, past the Swarovski boutique and the shop selling high-end cigars, and sailed into an elevator. Isla pressed the button for the thirty-third floor, and then reached over and hugged me. 'I'm so glad we're here,' she said, giving me a squeeze.

I inhaled the familiar smell of her – Marlboro Lights, LA Looks and Shalimar – and felt myself relax. 'Me too.'

The elevator doors opened and Isla led us down the hallway to a door marked with a gold plaque. 'The Marie Antoinette Suite?' I read.

She shrugged. 'I guess they don't have much of a sense

of irony in Paris.' She zipped the card key through the sensor and the door clicked open.

The door swung open to reveal not a hotel room, not even a hotel suite, but basically a hotel mini-village. Red-flocked hallways led to door after mystery door. The living room had a full three-piece suite, complete with a television the size of my entire flat back in London. There was a formal dining room. Each of the two bedrooms were furnished with heavy wooden wardrobes, elaborately-carved writing desks and so many throw pillows I briefly worried for the goose population. There were two bath-rooms, one with a Jacuzzi. 'Well,' Isla said, flicking on the bidet. 'It's good to know we can wash our assholes while we're here. Drink?'

I nodded and watched her head over to the bar. That's right, the bar. There was a bar inside the hotel room. 'Vodka or tequila,' she asked, brandishing a bottle in each hand.

My stomach turned at the mention of tequila. 'I think I'll start with a beer.'

'Suit yourself,' she said, pouring herself a shot of neat vodka and tossing it back. In case you hadn't clocked it yet, Isla is not a health freak. In fact, she seems to actively go in search of new and innovative ways to kill herself. She told me once, after taking a long drag on her ciga-rette, that carving up so many bodies in med school had done something irrevocable to her sense of mortality. 'Basically,' she'd said, 'I realized we're all fucked, so I might as well enjoy myself before I get fucked for good.' It hadn't been a particularly comforting conversation.

'How did you swing this?' I asked, gesturing around the suite. 'You're not paying for this, right?'

She laughed and handed me a cold Heineken. 'Nah, I did the old twenty-dollar bill trick.'

'The twenty-dollar bill trick?'

'You know. When you slide a folded up twenty-dollar bill in between your credit card and your driver's licence at check-in. Works like a charm.'

I shook my head in disbelief. I'd forgotten what it was like to live in a country fueled so nakedly by capitalism. In London, it would never occur to me to bribe someone like that. People either did things for you or they didn't, and their reasoning seemed propelled entirely by their own personal preferences rather than outside incentives. Christopher had tried to explain the rules to me a thousand times, but they never quite sunk in. Sometimes, out of some deeply ingrained sense of duty and guilt, I'd stick a pound coin on the drip mat at the pub after buying a round. It would disappear without acknowledgement, like it was some kind of contraband substance rather than a tip.

'Okay,' Isla said, curling herself precariously on top of a bar stool. 'Tell me everything. What's going on with Christopher?'

As soon as she said his name, I was hit with an enormous wave of exhaustion. 'Can we talk about it tomorrow?'

'Of course. We have three whole days, remember? Whenever you're ready, we'll talk.' She studied my face for a minute. 'Just make sure you don't leave it too long. Remember what happened after the day of the flying ants.'

I took a sharp breath. She knew better than to mention the day of the flying ants, especially when I was at such a low ebb. She saw the stricken look on my face and reached out to rub my arm. 'Sorry. I promise I'll leave you alone, okay? You don't want to go out to dinner now, do you?'

I shook my head. 'Is that okay?'

'Jenny, you've been awake for — what? — twenty-six hours now?'

I counted in my head. 'Thirty, actually.'

'I think I can let you off for wanting to crash tonight. Let's just order a shit ton of room service and watch a movie.'

I took a shower in the gold-tiled bathroom while she ordered burgers and fries. I turned the water up as hot as it would go and watched the glass cubicle fill with steam.

It was tomorrow morning in London already. Christopher would be waking up and heading to work. The Tube would be emptier than usual — it always was on a Friday — and his co-workers would be asking him about his weekend plans. What would he tell them? What did he have planned for his first weekend as a possibly single man?

'I ordered cheesecake, too!' Isla hollered through the door.

'Great!' I shouted back, and then pushed my face under the water and let the tears be washed away as quickly as I cried them.

5

'*Bonjour!*'

I emerged from the bedroom, hair askew, eyes still seeded with sleep, silent phone held limply in one hand, to find Isla wearing a beret and holding a platter of croissants. 'What the . . .'

'Breakfast — sorry, *le petit déjeuner!* — is served!'

'Where did they come from?'

'Standard breakfast, apparently.'

'How many people do they think we have squirreled away up here?'

Isla shrugged. 'Not enough by my standards, that's for sure. Must do better tomorrow.'

'And the hat? Is that standard, too?'

'It's a beret, actually,' she said, touching it lightly. 'A gift from the bellboy.'

'A gift?'

She shrugged. 'More like a hostile takeover.'

I plucked a croissant off the plate and took a bite. It was flaky and buttery and still warm from the oven. Delicious.

She linked arms with me and pulled me into the living room. 'So today, I thought we could take a trip around the globe!' Her voice reverberated off the high ceiling.

'What do you mean?' I took another bite of croissant.

'Um, hello! In case you haven't noticed,' she said, waving a croissant in the air, 'we're in France! And Venice is just next door, and New York, and Italy . . .'

'I genuinely have no idea what you're talking about,' I said through a mouthful of crumbs.

'The Venetian, the Big Apple, the Bellagio – the whole world is literally at our goddamn fingertips. And it serves complimentary champagne.'

The thought of moving more than ten feet filled me with a deep sense of ennui, never mind traipsing around a bunch of themed hotels trawling for free booze. 'Can we do something a little more low-key?'

'Okay, fine.' She plucked a guidebook off the coffee table and started leafing through it. 'How about the Atomic Testing Museum? Ooh! Or the Mob Museum! I wonder if they'll have a statue of Frank Sinatra in there . . .' She clocked the look on my face and shook her head. 'Okay, forget the museums. We could go see a show! There's got to be some Cirque du Something around. At any time of the day, someone is contorting themselves on an aerial ribbon in Las Vegas, probably painted as a zebra. Or Britney! We could go see Britney!'

I swallowed the last bite of croissant and sighed. 'I'm pretty beat. Do you mind if we just hang out by the pool today?' All my best-laid plans to party like it was 1999 (or, more accurate for me, 2004) were out the window. I was jet-lagged and emotionally drained: it was an effort just to remain vertical.

'Of course!' Isla said. 'This trip is all about you. Whatever you want. Also, that means I can check out dudes in bathing suits, which is always a good thing. I'm pretty sure I saw a lacrosse team check in last night . . .'

'Well, that settles it.'

She leaned over and nestled her head on my shoulder. Her curls tickled my neck. 'You feel like talking yet?'

I thought back to the dream I'd had the night before. Picture it: me walking down the aisle in a white Marchesa wedding gown holding a hand-tied bouquet of peonies and white roses. The guests stood and smiled at me as I sailed past. Former mean girls from high school burned with jealousy from the pews, ex-boyfriends wiped away tears of remorse. Christopher was waiting for me at the end of the aisle, dashing in a dark blue suit. His face was luminous with love. So far, so straight from my perfect wedding Pinterest board. And then, just as I was reaching out to take his hand, a Mac truck blared through the church and ploughed him into the tabernacle. No one ever accused my subconscious of being subtle.

'Not really,' I said. 'Sorry.'

She nodded towards my phone. 'Any word from him?'

I shook my head. 'Nothing.'

'Well,' she said, thumbing the crumbs off the plate, 'fuck him.'

'Isla!'

'No, seriously! Fuck him! That is going to be the motto of this trip – I decree it. You don't have to talk about him if you don't want to, but if you don't start thinking in a "fuck him" kind of way, you're going to spend the whole time staring at your phone and no time doing what you're supposed to be doing, which is getting drunk and flirting with cute boys.'

The thought of flirting with anyone made me feel sick. 'I don't want to flirt with cute boys.'

'That's because you haven't adopted the "fuck him" attitude. Look, you're here for a reason, right? I'm not saying you should sleep with some random guy—'

'Oh my God!'

'—but I *am* saying you should let yourself have a little fun. From what I can gather, you've been living like a 1950s housewife over there, cooking him dinner and darning his socks—'

'I definitely do not darn,' I said, defensive. Okay, there was the time I sewed a button back on his coat, but that doesn't count as darning. Does it?

'Whatever. All I'm saying is you should let yourself have a little fun. Look at you – you're shit-hot! Let yourself be reminded of it.'

I sighed. 'Fine. I'll try.' Isla threw her arms around me, upending the plate and sending a shower of pastry flakes into the air. 'But I am not making out with anyone.'

She rolled her eyes. 'What are we, thirteen?'

'And I am not doing any body shots off your belly button.'

'We'll see, my friend. We'll see. Come on, let's go out to the pool. London has turned you into a tub of paste. A cute tub of paste,' she hastened to add when she saw the appalled look on my face.

I stared down at my forearm. 'I'm not that pale, am I?'

'You look like you're about to contract rickets.'

We changed into our bathing suits and headed out to the pool, flip flops slapping on the tiled floor. I had a bag stuffed with sunscreen and paperback books and extra towels and a bottle of water slung over one arm, the pressure from the straps digging rivets into the soft skin on my shoulder. Isla, on the other hand, had nothing but a pair of sunglasses, which she'd perched atop her tangle of curls, and a glossy magazine.

'Don't you want something more substantial to read?' I asked.

She looked at me like I was crazy. 'Back home, I spend every second of my free time reading medical journals.' She waggled her issue of *Us Weekly* at me. 'This is all the substance I can handle right now.'

Isla was not the most obvious candidate for a neurosurgeon, but it was the Number 1 thing on her life list: Be a doctor. Number 2 was: Be psycho hot. There wasn't a Number 3. But writing down her dream of being a doctor seemed to do something to her – she hadn't been a very strong student before, but after the list, she buckled down and was soon acing every test. She started telling people that that's what she wanted to do, and the more she said it, the more people took her seriously. Her dad even took her to the Body World exhibition when it came through New Haven. (I tagged along and had to run out to be sick when we got to the case with all the brains.)

Still, she'd refused to settle into the medical mould. She went pre-med at Tufts and graduated from Johns Hopkins with honors, but it hadn't stopped her from dancing on top of bars, flashing random strangers, and popping pills like they were Tic Tacs. Even now, at the ripe old age of thirty-one, she regularly told stories about her sex life that made me feel as if I needed an advanced anatomy class to understand them.

We pushed open the door to the pool area and stood stunned in the entrance, the sun temporarily blinding us. When the spots finally cleared from our vision, we found ourselves at the edge of a wide patio encircling an enormous azure-blue swimming pool. It was still early, but most of the loungers were already taken up by bronzed sun-worshippers, oiled and glistening like Christmas turkeys. The Eiffel Tower loomed above.

'This place is insane,' I whispered.

Isla nodded and lowered her shades onto her nose. 'Come on, I see a couple of free ones over there.'

She picked her way through the sea of bodies until we arrived in front of two empty sun loungers sandwiched between a pair of elderly women in sunhats and a middle-aged businessman with the *Financial Times* tented across his face, paunch pointed towards the sky. 'Not exactly what I had in mind,' Isla muttered as she pulled her cropped T-shirt over her head and slid her cut-offs down to her ankles. She was left wearing a small tangle of string.

'What are you wearing?' I hissed.

'Uh, a bathing suit? What do you think this is?'

'A cobweb?' I said. 'A skein of yarn you stole from a kitten?' I tugged at the neckline of my one-piece. Despite my best efforts, I'd never managed to cross Number 4 off my list: grow breasts. Isla seemed to inherit my share of the world's cleavage, with change to spare. Just looking at her pneumatic chest, covered by two minuscule triangles of material and calling Newton's law of universal gravitation into serious doubt, made my own pair of anthills ache with envy.

'Relax! We're in Las Vegas, for God's sake! There are strippers and people dressed like Elvis everywhere! This is not the time to be a prude.'

'I am not a prude!'

'Are too. Remember when you wouldn't French kiss Kevin McMann?'

'That was in eighth grade!'

'A leopard doesn't change its spots.' She shrugged. For a second, I worried that something might get jarred loose.

'I Frenched Chip Trumble underneath the bleachers that time.'

'We were sophomores by then. It was different!'

'AND I let him feel me up!'

The middle-aged man lifted the paper an inch off his face and peered at us with a rheumy eye.

Isla burst out laughing. 'Okay, okay. You win. You're basically Belladonna.'

'Who's that?'

She shook her head and sighed. 'Never mind.'

The two of us stretched out on our loungers. I slathered myself in sunscreen, lay back, and closed my eyes. I could hear the honk and rumble of cars roaring up the Strip, and the rowdy shouts of bachelor parties getting a start on their day's drinking, and the gentle but firm enquiries of the cabana boys as they upsold liquor. The air smelled of chlorine and gasoline and coconut and rum.

I thought of the phone lying silent at the bottom of my bag and flipped over onto my stomach. I could feel the backs of my thighs start to sizzle as soon as the sun hit them, but I couldn't bring myself to apply more sunscreen. What did it matter, anyway? I might as well let myself burn.

'Holy shit,' Isla said, inspecting my blistered back.

'Does it look really bad?'

'I mean, it doesn't look great, but it'll be fine in a couple of days.'

'A couple of days!' I wailed. 'I'll be back in London by then!'

'Well, you should have asked me to put sunscreen on your back. Who were you kidding, anyway? You know you burn like goddamn Snow White.'

'Can you not right now?'

'Okay, hold still.'

I inhaled sharply as she pressed a cold pack against my skin. 'Jesus Christ—'

'I know, but it will help. Trust me, I'm a doctor.' She shot me a cheesy grin in the mirror and I rolled my eyes at her. 'You should probably take some Advil, too. And I don't think we should venture too far from the hotel tonight, just in case you start showing signs of sunstroke.'

'Sunstroke! I was only out there for a couple of hours! And it's March!'

'In case you hadn't noticed, we're in the middle of the desert.'

I considered this for a minute. 'Still.' I peered around

my shoulder and tried to catch a glimpse of my back. All I could see was a sea of angry red. 'I'm sorry.'

'Sorry for what?'

'I'm being totally lame. You fly me all the way out here, and all I've done is mope around and then get burned to a crisp. I suck.'

'You don't suck.'

'I do! I totally suck!'

'Look, I'd be lying if I said I hadn't hoped that being in Vegas would make you want to cut loose and go crazy, but only because I thought it might good for you. But if you're not feeling it, that's totally fine with me. The dudes here are all spray-tanned bros or middle-aged pervs, anyway. I came here to hang out with you, which is what I'm doing. There is zero need to apologize.'

'I still feel lame.'

'Well, you've always been a little lame. It's a quality I've come to love about you.'

'Thanks for that.'

'Tell you what, you go take a cold shower. I'm going to go downstairs and see if they have any aftersun in the gift shop, and then maybe we can go down to the hotel casino and roll a few dice or whatever. You never know, maybe red's your lucky color . . .'

I showered and dressed in a billowy linen dress I found at the bottom of my suitcase. It made me look like a middle-school art teacher (the weird kind, not the sexy kind), but it was the only thing I could bear to let touch my skin. My hair was still damp – the idea of blowing hot air anywhere near me anathema at this particular moment – and the smell of the hotel shampoo (lemon and mint, surprisingly nice) clung to it. I looked, in short, like a hot mess, and my resolutely silent phone wasn't boosting my mood. Still, I forced myself to slap a smile on my face as we headed down to the casino – despite Isla's protests, it was her vacation, too, and I didn't want to ruin it completely.

The doorman's eyes lit up when he saw us coming. Well, saw Isla coming. I don't think his eyes actually made it to me. Why would they, really, with Isla looking like Isla? She was wearing a deep purple mini-dress and sky-high silver heels that made her legs look about eight feet long. Her mascaraed eyelashes framed her huge blue eyes, and she'd painted her lips a deep berry pink. The day in the sun had left her a golden tan – how did she not burn? How? She was three-quarters Irish, for Christ's sake! – and she'd liberally coated herself in some kind of shimmery oil so her skin glistened like that of a post-race thoroughbred. In short, she looked like sex on legs.

That was the thing with Isla: she always looked like sex on legs. She was, without a doubt, the sexiest woman I had ever met. You could almost see the pheromones pumping out of her pores. She was the type of woman other women immediately tried to find fault with. You could see them, methodically scanning her for flaws. Is that a tiny ripple of cellulite? Are her hips a little thick? Is the skin underneath her chin sagging a touch? Is that a nose hair peeking out from her nostril? And then, every time, you saw the disappointment in their eyes as they discounted each one. Nope, they would realize, she really was perfect, and then she'd open her mouth and they would fall in love with her despite themselves.

Everyone did. Men – I mean, Jesus. When we were teenagers, she'd gone from awkward pre-teen to super-model practically overnight. Guys would follow her through the halls like she was the Pied Piper of John F. Kennedy High. One guy bought her a car – an actual goddamn car! – because he'd overheard her saying she was tired of bumming rides off people. God knows where he got the money from – he was only seventeen. Isla didn't even have her driver's license.

As my mom once memorably said to me, 'You must have really high self-esteem to be friends with someone that beautiful.' I'm not sure I could attest to that, but the truth was it had never really bothered me. Isla had the beauty and the body and the brains, but I had something, too. Something only she and I knew about. I had a plan.

The doorman opened the door with a flourish and we walked through into the casino. A man in a shiny dark suit swooped on us immediately. 'Would you ladies like a glass of champagne? It's on the house,' he added, and we both nodded enthusiastically.

'Make sure you bring this one a water, too,' Isla said, jabbing a thumb towards me.

'Thanks, Mom,' I said, flushing even more red than I already was.

She shrugged. 'Gotta keep you hydrated. So, where to first? Le craps table or le slot machines?'

I looked around and laughed. The place was done out like a Disney-fied French boulevard, complete with quaint little road signs pointing the way *en français*. 'When they commit to a theme, they really commit.'

'This is Vegas,' she said, hooking her arm through mine. 'They don't do anything by halves.'

A cocktail waitress in an extremely short skirt and extremely high heels appeared with a tray full of champagne flutes. 'Here you go, girls,' she said, handing us one each.

'What about the water?' Isla asked. I nudged her in the ribs.

The waitress twisted her lips. 'We don't serve water here, but I think there's a water cooler by the ladies' room.'

She turned on her heel and stalked off towards le poker table. I worried briefly for the state of her feet – imagine working all night in those shoes! She'll have trouble when she's older, poor woman. Bunions and everything.

We bought a handful of chips each and made our way to the blackjack table, glasses balanced delicately in hands. 'Fifty dollars on black!' Isla shouted as soon as we sat down.

The croupier raised an eyebrow, but then the full force of Isla's beauty took hold and he smiled indulgently at her. 'Would mademoiselle like to place a bet?' he asked in an overblown French accent.

'*Oui, monsieur!*' she cried, pushing a pile of chips his way.

'Very good,' he said, hooking them with his special little hook and pulling them into the middle of the table.

'Do you even know how to play twenty-one?' I whispered.

She shrugged. 'I can count, can't I?' She nodded to the

dealer. He slapped two cards face up in front of her and then dealt himself a pair, one up one down. I had a look at her cards. A three of clubs and a six of diamonds. Not good. The dealer had an ace showing.

'Hit me!' she cried

A four of spades went down on the table.

'Again!'

A five of diamonds. She was at eighteen now.

'Maybe you should stop now,' I whispered.

She shook her head. 'Again!'

A three of hearts. Twenty-one. I couldn't believe it. And from the look on the dealer's face, neither could he. He flicked over the face-down card in front of him. An eight of spades. Eighteen. He shook his head and pushed a pile of chips towards Isla, who scooped them up and hugged them to her chest. 'Let's hit le roulette table,' she said. She scooted off her chair, necked the dregs of her champagne, and gave the dealer a wink. I saw the blush spread just above his collar.

'Your turn!' she announced when we arrived at the roulette table. There was a crowd of men packed around it, and we had to wiggle our way through to place the bet. I placed a single five-dollar chip on the green felt table. Lucky number thirteen.

'Whoa, look out for the high roller!'

I looked up to see a tall man grinning at me from across the table. He was wearing a zip-up fleece and those cargo pants with too many pockets (what are these people doing that necessitates so much portable storage?), and his hair was a mess of artfully mussed blond curls. He arched an eyebrow at me and nodded at my chip. Isla dug an elbow into my ribcage. 'He's cute,' she whispered. I rolled my eyes and ignored them both.

The dealer spun the wheel. As soon as the ball was in motion, I understood the thrill of gambling. There was so much hope as it bounced from slot to slot. Everyone at the table collectively held their breath. The wheel slowed, and we all craned forward, eager to see where it landed. There was camaraderie in that moment. For a second, we were all bound together in anticipation. And then the ball landed on twenty-four, and the dealer placed a marker on the winning number and swept all of the losing bets towards him. A stack of chips was pushed towards the blond man, who rubbed his hands together with glee. The atmosphere deflated.

'Let's go,' I said to Isla. Gambling was definitely not my forte. Too much uncertainty. Why risk something you already have in the hope of getting more? Particularly when the odds were stacked against you.

'Give it another try.' It was the blond man again, hand tucked jauntily into one of his many pockets. 'You always need a little time to warm up.'

Isla jabbed me in the ribcage with an oiled elbow. I hesitated before plucking out another five-dollar chip and placing it gingerly on the table. This was it – if I lost this time, I was done for sure. Lucky thirteen again – at least I hoped this time it would be lucky. The wheel spun and the ball bounced as we waited with bated breath.

'Number six!' the dealer cried, and I watched as he pushed a stack of chips towards the blond man.

'Again?' I said. 'Seriously?'

The blond man shrugged. 'Looks like I'm on a hot streak.'

'Jesus Christ,' I muttered. 'Come on,' I said to Isla, 'Let's get a drink.'

'Don't go!' the blonde man shouted as we edged away from the table. 'You're my lucky charm!'

'What a jackass,' I said to Isla as we made our way towards the bar.

'I thought he was sexy,' she said with a shrug.

'Please. Did you see what he was wearing?'

'It's America, Jenny. All men dress like that.'

'That doesn't mean it's a good thing. And his hair! It was so – so – pouffy! *Yeuch*. I can't believe you thought he was cute.'

She leveled an appraising eye towards me. 'Sounds like you're protesting a little too much.'

'Am not.'

'Come on – a cute guy was trying to flirt with you! You don't have to act like he was trying to infect you with herpes.'

'Whatever. Let's just get a drink.' We sat down at the bar and ordered a couple of vodka tonics. The chill that had followed me into the casino was stronger now, and I hugged my arms across my chest for warmth. 'They're not kidding with the AC in this place,' I said. 'Aren't you freezing in that dress?'

Isla shot me a worried look. 'I was actually thinking it was pretty warm in here. Are you feeling okay?'

'Fine!' I said. I locked my jaw to stop my teeth from chattering. 'Just a little chilly.'

'Jenny, your lips are blue. I'm pretty sure you have sunstroke. Come on, we should get you back up to the room.'

'No!' I cried. 'I'm fine, honestly!' My teeth were now banging into each other so hard I was worried I'd shake loose a filling. 'I've ruined enough of your vacation. Let's stay out! Let's have another drink! Mai Tais this time!'

She shook her head. 'There is no way I'm going to sit here and drink a goddamn Mai Tai while you shiver your ass off. Come on, let's go.'

She hauled me to my feet and we started making our way out. 'I'm sorry,' I whispered. She threw an arm around my waist and pulled me towards her, and, to my horror, I started to cry. Not just a little, either. Huge, plopping tears, shuddering breaths, snotty nose – the works.

Isla took my face in her hands. 'Sweetie, talk to me. Are you okay?'

'It's fucked,' I cried. 'Everything's fucked!'

A security guard moved towards us, and Isla put up a hand to stop him. 'It's okay,' she said. 'We're on our way out now.'

I could feel everyone's eyes on us as we walked through the casino. Men in suits exchanged glances, women whispered in hushed tones. They probably think I'm drunk, I thought to myself. They probably think I'm crazy. They definitely thought I was a mess.

'Do you need any help with her?' Through the film of tears, I could vaguely see the outline of a man blocking our way.

'We're good, thanks,' I heard Isla say.

'Is your hotel close by? I could give you a ride, or call a cab?' The man's solicitude only made me cry harder.

'We're staying here,' she said. 'Honestly, we're fine. Thanks, though.'

Out of the casino and into the lobby and up in the elevator and through the door to our suite, Isla holding onto me the whole time. When we got inside, I went straight to my room and lay down on the bed and commenced soaking the pillowcase with my tears. I was like a spigot whose valve was broken – I didn't know how to stop.

Isla kicked off her heels and lay down next to me. 'Shh,' she soothed, stroking my hair. 'It's okay. It's going to be okay.'

But it wasn't okay. Not really. Everything I'd planned on – everything I'd been so sure of – was suddenly laid out on that green felt table. The wheel was spinning, and, for the first time in a long time, I had no idea where the ball would drop.

6

Isla appeared in the doorway of my room, mug of coffee in one hand and pain au chocolat in the other. 'C'mon,' she said, setting the mug down on the bedside table and pulling open the curtains. 'Time to wake up!'

Sunlight streamed into the room and I batted my eyelids in a futile attempt to defend myself from it. 'What time is it?'

'Almost noon,' she said. 'You've been asleep for twelve hours.'

I sat up and rubbed my eyes, which were puffed up like a pair of hamburger buns. The previous night came flooding back: the gambling, the sunburn, the crying . . . 'Oh God,' I said, pressing the heels of my hands into them. 'How bad do I look?'

'Here,' she said, reaching into her back pocket and pulling out a tube of hemorrhoid cream. She tossed it onto the bed and I picked it up between thumb and forefinger.

'Gross. Why are you giving this to me?'

'It's the best thing for swollen eyes. Which makes sense, if you think about it.'

'I don't want to think about it,' I groaned, unscrewing the top and patting the thick lotion under my eyes. 'Does it have to be so bright in here?'

'Come on, look at that sky! Not a single cloud! I've got

to go back to work tomorrow, which means twelve-hour days without so much as a glimpse of sunshine. I've got to get my vitamin D in while I can. You too, by the way. Although . . .' She peered at the blistered red skin covering my back. 'Maybe you should stay in the shade.'

It was only then that I realized I was just in my bra and underwear. 'Did you undress me last night?'

'Of course I did! I couldn't risk you getting strangled by that weird linen muumuu you were wearing. Where did you get that thing, anyway?'

'Greece!' I said defensively.

'Well, it looks like you stole it from my Great Aunt Mabel. Which I don't recommend you do, by the way, because that woman has one hell of a temper.' She threw herself down onto the bed and cupped her head in her palms. 'So, are we going to talk about it or what?'

My hand reached for the mug of coffee and nudged my cell phone off the table in the process. I stared down at the lit screen. No new calls or messages. 'Talk about what?' I asked, taking a sip. The coffee was hot and strong and furred the tip of my tongue.

'The NAFTA agreement. What do you think?'

I rolled out of bed and wrapped a terrycloth robe around me. 'I'm going to take a shower.'

'Fine,' she said, lying back on the pillow and taking a bite out of her pain au chocolat. I watched as flakes of pastry fluttered across the duvet. 'You take a shower, but don't think we're not going to talk about what's going on, because we absolutely one hundred per cent are.'

I shut the door to the bathroom and turned on the

64

shower. The water was only lukewarm, but on my scorched back it felt as if I was being pelted with boiling-hot water. Tomorrow, I thought with some relief, I'd get on a plane and go back to London. What a mess this weekend had turned out to be. Three days with my best friend and I'd wasted most of it miserable and sunburned. And I still hadn't heard a word from Christopher. What could he be doing? Was he even thinking about me? Maybe he was in the flat right now, packing up his things. I'd come home to find the place cold and empty, filled with that strange musty smell of abandoned spaces.

Wait, he owned the place. It would be my things he'd be packing. Shit.

I closed my eyes and pictured our flat – the enormous cast-iron radiator that hissed and spluttered, the separate cold and hot water taps in the bathroom basin that meant I had to alternate between the two when washing my face, the front door that always stuck no matter what the weather. The battered leather sofa that Christopher and I curled up on every night. The old brass bed we slept in together. What would I do if it stopped being ours? Where would I call home?

Nothing was turning out the way it was supposed to.

There was a knock on the door. 'You okay in there?'

'Fine!' I croaked. I hopped out of the shower, toweled off and ran a comb through my hair. The mirror was fogged up, so I wiped a circle clear with the flat of my hand and peered at myself in the glass. My eyes were puffy and bloodshot, my skin blotchy and pale, and I could see nests of blisters cresting on the tops of my shoulders.

'Jesus Christ,' I muttered. I slathered myself in moisturizer, but it didn't make much difference. I wrapped the robe around me, trudged out of the bathroom, and flopped back onto the bed, where Isla was reading *People* magazine and drinking Diet Coke through a straw.

'Feel better?' she asked.

'Not really.'

'Okay, well, I have a plan. First of all, we're going to sit down and you're going to tell me all about the existential crisis you're having, because let's face it, not talking about it doesn't seem to be working for you.'

'I really don't think—'

'Did I mention this plan is not optional?'

'Fine,' I grumbled.

'After we've figured out what you're going to do with your life, we're going to go downstairs to the spa and you're going to have a facial and a massage and whatever else it takes to get you feeling better.' She squinted at me. 'And looking better, too, no offense.'

'None taken.'

'And then we are going to have a full-on, knock-down, drag-out crazy last night in Vegas. It's going to be like *Girls Gone Wild* except for the creepy guy with the camera. Okay?'

'Okay.' It wasn't, not really, but I could tell I didn't really have a choice in the matter.

'Okay.' She tossed the magazine off the edge of the bed and shifted herself around to face me. 'Tell me what's going on.'

'You know what's going on. Christopher doesn't want to marry me.'

'Look, I know that Christopher said that thing about getting married, but he loves you – I know he does. If now isn't the right time for him, that doesn't mean it won't be someday.'

I swallowed, hard. 'It's more than that. When he dropped me off at the airport, he said we should go on a break.'

'A break? What do you mean, a break?'

'Like, a break as in a break from each other, obviously.'

'What did you say?'

'I didn't say anything.'

'Well, what did he say?'

'He told me to forget it.'

'So you're not on a break?'

'I don't know! I haven't heard from him at all since I've been here. Not once.'

'Have you called him? Texted him?'

I stared down at my hands. The pads of my fingertips were still shriveled and pruney from the shower. 'No.'

'Okay, so maybe he thinks *you* want a break.'

I sighed. 'All I know is it's not working out the way I'd planned. He's the love of my life, Isla. We're supposed to get *married* this year!'

'Oh my God!' Isla threw herself back on the bank of pillows. 'Jenny, you have got to let go of that stupid life list!'

'It's not stupid – it's important! You're a doctor now, aren't you?'

'I'm not saying the list wasn't helpful. I know for sure that it gave me focus when I was a kid, and you're right, maybe without it I wouldn't have become a doctor.'

'See?'

'But we were thirteen when we wrote it. We didn't understand what it meant to be an adult. Life doesn't come neatly packaged the way we thought it would. You know that more than most,' she added gently.

'There's nothing wrong with having goals,' I muttered.

'I'm not saying there is,' she said. 'I'm saying that it's not healthy to let something you did when you were a teenager hold you hostage like this.'

'It's not holding me hostage. It's guiding me. I mean, look at this.' I picked my bag up off the floor and rummaged around until I found it. 'Here,' I said, handing a piece of paper to her.

'Wait,' she said, holding it up to the light, 'you laminated it?'

I nodded. 'It was getting torn and frayed in my bag.'

Her eyes widened in disbelief. 'You carry it around with you?'

'Of course! I need it to keep me on track. Remember this one?' I leaned over and pointed to Number 6 on the list: Live in a foreign country before turning twenty-one. 'Without it, there's no way I would have gone to Colombia junior year.'

'Didn't you end up with dysentery?'

'That's not the point! The point is, I was super scared of leaving home, and the list made me do something I normally wouldn't have done.'

Isla tapped a fingernail on the list. 'How'd this one work out for you?'

Number 17: Have an affair with an older man. 'Professor Michel was a gentleman.'

68

'A gentleman who had sex with you during office hours and then gave you a C in French Literature?'

'He could recite Molière from memory! Doesn't that count for something?'

Isla wrinkled her nose. 'Not when his ass is saggy, no.'

'Okay, fine. What about this one?' Number 13: Sing with a band.

'You have never, ever sung with a band.'

'You're forgetting the freshman year talent show. Remember? I was Jem, and a bunch of girls from the soccer team were the Holograms?'

'That does not count. My point is, there are things on that list that you might never accomplish, and that's okay. There also might be things on that list that you no longer want to accomplish, and that's okay, too.'

I folded my arms across my chest. 'There is nothing on that list I don't want to accomplish.'

'Seriously? How about number 11?'

I looked down at the list. Number 11: Make out with James van der Beek. 'Still valid!' I said triumphantly.

Isla sighed. 'I just feel like you're putting too much pressure on yourself for no reason. I know that you want to get married this year, but honestly, I don't know if it's because of the list or because you actually do want to get married.'

'Of course I want to get married!' I said defensively. 'I love Christopher and I want to spend the rest of my life with him.'

'Are you really sure about that?' She shifted over to be closer to me. 'Look, I like Christopher. He's a nice guy and he's good to you, and like I said, I think he really does love you. But you haven't seemed all that happy since you moved to London.'

I shrugged. 'It takes time to adjust to a new place.'

'You've been there for three years now. Do you have friends over there? A support network at all?'

'I have Christopher,' I said. 'And my colleagues are nice. I guess I'd consider Ben a friend.'

'I just worry about you, that's all. I worry that you're chasing after a future that you've decided is fated for you without taking the time to consider whether or not it would actually make you happy.'

I hugged myself more tightly and fixed her with a steely gaze. 'Marrying Christopher would make me happy.'

'I'm not saying you shouldn't marry Christopher. I'm just saying that the sky won't fall in if you *don't* marry Christopher. Nothing bad will happen to you if your plans change.'

'I know that!' I spluttered. But somewhere deep inside my chest ached as if a very soft bit of me had been prodded with a very sharp stick.

Isla hesitated. 'Jenny, what happened with your mom . . .'

'I don't want to talk about it,' I snapped. That was the problem with friends you'd known their whole life: they'd known you your whole life, too. It made you vulnerable.

She held up her hands. 'Okay, okay, I'll leave you alone. I just want you to remember that there's a whole world out there, my friend. Let yourself consider the options it gives you.'

'All right,' I said quietly. I didn't believe a word of it, but

I was sick of sitting in this damp robe and I wanted the conversation to be over.

'Good. Whatever happens when you get back to London is going to happen – there's nothing you can do about it right now. We've got one night left in Vegas. I want you to forget about Christopher and marriage and the whole fucking life list and just have fun. Okay?'

I nodded sullenly and plucked at an errant piece of thread unspooling from the cuff of my robe.

'Not exactly a ringing endorsement, but I'll take it.' She hopped off the bed and bounced towards the door. 'Meet me in the living room in fifteen,' she sang. 'It's spa time, bitches!'

We were rubbed. We were buffed. We were scrubbed. We were steamed. We were painted and polished and blow-dried and fluffed. And finally we emerged, groomed and purring like a pair of Siamese cats.

'Okay,' Isla said, tilting her iPhone to get the best angle on her cherry-red lips. 'What do you want to do first?'

'Umm . . .' The truth was, I was still feeling a little woozy after the massage, and my neck ached from the weight of the elaborate up-do the hairdresser had fashioned on the top of my head. What I really wanted to do was drink a bottle of priccy coconut water and take a nap, but one look at Isla's expectant face told me that wasn't an option. 'Get a drink?' I offered.

'Yes! But we should get changed first. They won't let us in anywhere in these clothes.'

I glanced down at my terrycloth shorts and my

newly polished toes hanging over the edge of a pair of dollar flip-flops. 'Good point.'

'Pre-party!' Isla sang when we got through the door of the suite. 'Vodka or tequila?'

'Uh . . . maybe I'll start with a glass of wine or something.'

'No way. Wine will make you sleepy. Vodka will perk you up. That's just science.' She poured two neat shots and handed one to me. 'Bottoms up!'

The liquor burned as it made its way down my neck. It occurred to me that I should have eaten more than half a chicken salad wrap that day, but the thought was swiftly pushed aside by Isla charging past me towards my bedroom.

'What are you doing?' I called after her.

'Seeing if you have anything other than giant linen tunics to wear!'

I followed her into the bedroom and found her already elbow-deep in my suitcase. 'You brought a turtleneck to Las Vegas?' she asked, holding up the offensive item.

'I thought it might get cold in the evenings!'

'It's the desert, dude. Okay, what have we got here? Jeans. Jeans. Maxi-dress. Mom shorts.'

'They are not mom shorts!' I cried, snatching them out of her hands.

'Jenny, you could fit two of you in those things.'

'They're meant to be slouchy!'

She tossed the remaining few scraps of clothing onto the bed and threw up her hands. 'We're going to have to go to plan B.'

'What's plan B?'

'My suitcase, obviously.'

I was seized with panic. Visions of myself squeezed into Lycra like so much sausage meat danced in my head. 'There is no way I'm going to fit into any of your clothes.'

'Of course you will – look at you! You're tiny!' She took my hand and pulled me towards the door, but not before my eye caught the silvered gleam of my phone charging on the nightstand.

'Wait one second,' I said, straining to reach it. 'I just want to check—'

'No!' she shouted, launching herself onto the bed and snatching the phone away. She unplugged it and shoved it in the back pocket of her shorts. 'You'll get it back tomorrow.'

'Come on . . . !'

'Tonight is about you and me having all of the fun and giving zero fucks – remember? And that means you not mournfully checking your phone every five minutes to see if Christopher has been in touch.'

'Can you at least see if he's texted me?'

She slid it out of her pocket and pressed the home key. The screen lit up her face as she frowned into it. 'No,' she said softly. My heart sank. 'I'm sorry.'

'It's okay.'

'No, it's not. He's being a douche. But you know what?'

'What?'

'Fuck him. Zero fucks, remember? Tonight we give zero fucks. Say it with me now.'

'Zero fucks,' we chorused. Mine was a little less heartfelt than hers.

'That's right. Now, let's go get you all sexed up and then let's get a motherfucking DRINK! This town isn't going to know what hit it.'

After a long and lively debate – punctuated with vodka shots and the occasional creative curse word – Isla managed to convince me to squeeze into a little black dress of hers that even I had to admit didn't look half bad. (She wore a silver jumpsuit slashed to the navel, and a pair of platform heels: standard). We headed down to the hotel bar, ordered two espresso martinis, and sat tall on the bar stools as we plotted out the rest of the night.

'Apparently there's a bar with mermaids,' Isla said, sliding an olive off a toothpick with her teeth.

'Mermaids?'

'Yeah. They swim around in a giant fish tank.'

'How do they breathe?'

'I think there's some kind of central breathing tube they can take breaths from,' she said with a shrug.

'I think I'll pass.' I was a nervous swimmer, and the thought of being trapped in a fish tank with a fake tail strapped to my feet was enough to make me break out in a cold sweat.

Isla signaled to the bartender, who took one look at her and hurled himself across the bar to get to her. 'Can I help you?'

'You sure can,' she said, flashing him her best smile. 'It's our last night in Vegas, and we were hoping you could point us in the direction of a few great bars.'

The bartender picked up a cocktail shaker and started

spinning it around in his hand. 'Sure thing, beautiful,' he said, tossing the shaker in the air and catching it behind his back. 'What's your poison?'

'Just somewhere fun where we can drink and maybe dance a little.'

'Gin? Tequila? Bourbon?'

'All of the above,' she announced.

'Center Bar is pretty great – Drake was in there the other night – or the Apostrophe Bar. It's guest list only, but I have a friend who works the door.' He tossed two limes in the air along with the cocktail shaker and juggled them for a few minutes.

'I think we're looking for someplace a little less fancy,' she said. 'Maybe even a little dirty. We like to get dirty, don't we, Jenny?'

He lost his grip on the shaker and it bounced off the marble bar top with a clang. 'Shit,' he said, scrambling to recover it. I saw Isla's shoulders start to shake from laughing and mouthed the words STOP IT at her.

The bartender jumped back to his feet and swept his hair back with his hands, strategically flexing his biceps in the process. 'Sorry about that. Uh, let me think . . .' He started juggling the shaker again. Brave man. 'The Bourbon Room is pretty cool. They play a lot of 80s' rock – Bon Jovi, and that kind of thing. Or – wait, I know exactly where you guys should go.'

'Amazing! Where?'

The bartender flashed a triumphant grin. 'Benny's! They do these huge fishbowl drinks, and after 10 p.m., all they play is 90s' hip hop.'

Isla's eyes widened. 'It literally sounds like nirvana.' She turned to me. 'What do you think?'

I nodded. 'Let's do it.'

'Benny's it is! Thank you so much!' Isla reached across the bar and high-fived the bartender, who did a passable job of hiding his delight.

'Glad I could help. You know, I get off at eleven tonight. I could meet you guys over there, if you were into it . . .' He reached up into a tactical stretch, revealing a slice of toned midriff in the process. He was unassailably hot, I'd give him that. I nudged Isla and tried to catch her eye, but she ignored me.

'Sorry,' she said, 'it's kind of a ladies-only thing.'

The bartender cast an appraising eye over the two of us and nodded approvingly. 'Oh, I get it,' he said, though it was pretty clear that he didn't. 'Cool. Well, if you change your mind, here's my number.' He grabbed a cocktail napkin out of the holder and scrawled down a set of digits. 'Drinks are on the house, by the way.'

'You're too sweet,' Isla said, folding up the napkin and tossing it into her bag. She leaned across the bar and kissed him on the cheek. I swear I saw the man go weak at the knees.

'I will never get used to being out with you,' I said as we waited for our Uber to arrive. It was dark out, but the night air was still steamy, and I felt sweat begin to pool underneath my bra.

'What do you mean?'

'I mean the way that men fall all over you. What's it like, wielding that kind of power?'

She rolled her eyes. 'They do not fall all over me.'

'Isla, I just watched that bartender perform circus tricks to get your attention. They absolutely do fall all over you.'

She sighed. 'Well, it's nice, I guess. I mean, it can get annoying sometimes, but I'd be lying if I said I didn't like the attention.' She gestured towards her silver jumpsuit. 'As if I need to explain to you that I'm attention-seeking.'

'I wouldn't call it attention-seeking,' I said. 'More like confident.'

'Thanks. But just for the record, men fall all over you just as much as they do me. You just don't see it.' She rummaged around in her bag and pulled out a cigarette and a bright pink Bic. She lit up and took a deep drag.

I frowned at her. 'Those things will kill you, you know.'

'Honestly, babe, when you've seen the kind of shit I have, you stop worrying about how you're going to die. The other day, I had a woman come in with an arrow in her head. A goddamn arrow! She'd been in her backyard – which happens to back onto an archery center – and a stray arrow got her right in the parietal lobe.'

'Oh my God,' I said. 'Is she alive?'

She took another drag and puffed out a series of perfect smoke rings. 'We managed to get it out without too much damage, but now she can't taste anything and she keeps talking with a Spanish accent. Can you imagine?'

'Jesus. That's awful.'

'I know, right? So really, in the grand scheme of things, there's no point in wondering what will kill you in the end. The main point is that something will. Or it will at least fuck up your life pretty good.'

We were silent as we let this thought sink in. Isla took a final drag and stubbed out her cigarette underneath her heel. 'Come on,' she said, grabbing my hand. 'That's our guy in the black Prius.'

Driving down the Strip at night was surreal. The lights glinting off the windows, the people streaming past, the moon shining above, casting its glow across this vast desert. I let myself wonder about Christopher, just for a minute. Like Fievel the mouse, I wondered if he was sleeping underneath the same big sky. Then I remembered that it was 7 a.m. in London. He was probably up already and off on his Sunday run. I forced myself to push the thought of him aside. I couldn't allow myself to become maudlin, at least not this early into the night. I owed Isla that much. From the way she was just talking, I suspected she needed a carefree girls' night out just as much as I did.

Besides, he was probably having a whale of a time on his own in London. The vodka coursed steadily through my veins. Maybe he wasn't out for his Sunday morning run. Maybe he was still in our bed, a tiny blonde called Tiffany wrapped around him like a baby monkey. Maybe he hadn't thought about me this whole weekend. Not even once. Maybe he was glad I was gone. I leaned back and watched the night sky sail past.

Benny's, it turned out, wasn't on the Strip at all. It was tucked behind a Walmart supercenter, the only clue of its location a small, worn wooden sign illuminated by a single flickering lightbulb.

'Are you sure about this?' I asked Isla. Even the Uber driver looked nervous about leaving us there.

'If it sucks, we'll just go someplace else,' she said, climbing out of the car.

The driver and I exchanged a look. 'I'm not coming back here,' he said firmly. I nodded my understanding and closed the door.

I followed Isla out of the car and the two of us linked arms as we headed for the door. The ground pulsed beneath our feet as we approached. 'Well, at least they have a decent sound system,' Isla said.

She pulled open the door and we were both hit by a wall of thundering noise. 'Holy shit,' I whispered.

'WHAT?' she yelled.

'I SAID HOLY SHIT!'

We made our way down a flight of stairs and into the cavernous bar. Cavernous wasn't just an adjective in this case – the place was literally a cave. It seemed as if it had been hulled out of the rocky desert floor, the ragged stone walls sweating gently from the heat of a hundred or so bodies pressed tightly together, the only light coming from a few fringed chandeliers hanging dangerously close to the dance floor.

'This place is insane!' I shouted.

She nodded and tugged me towards the bar, where a tall, muscular man with a tattoo of a snake curled around his neck was doling out shots. Isla propped her elbows on the bar. 'Bourbon or tequila?' the tattooed man asked her.

She turned around and repeated the question.

'Um, do they have any beer?' I asked.

She glanced back at the bar, which was stacked high

with bottles of Maker's Mark and Jose Cuervo. 'I don't think that's an option.'

'Bourbon, then. On ice, please. Just a small one!'

The man poured out four fingers into each glass and pushed them across the bar. 'Ten bucks,' he said, and Isla handed him a twenty and told him to keep the change. 'Just make sure you keep them coming.'

'Bottoms up,' she cried, though I could see the fear on her face as she lifted the glass to her lips. She sank it in two gulps. 'Jesus, that burns!' she shouted, and then turned back to the bartender. 'Another, kind sir!'

'Don't you think we should slow down a little?' I asked, taking a tentative sip. She was right, it did burn, all the way down my esophagus and into my too-empty stomach.

'Are you still thinking about Christopher?'

I shrugged. Of course I was thinking about him.

'Then it's not time to slow down.'

I wasn't sure if it was the bourbon or the thumping bass shuddering through my ribcage, or the image – stubbornly vivid – of his limbs entwined with Tiffany the tiny blonde's, but a sense of righteous indignation suddenly roared through me. My life, as I'd known it, was quite possibly over. I might as well enjoy myself. 'You're right,' I said, tossing my head back and swallowing the contents of the tumbler in one go. 'Fuck it. Let's get fucked up.'

'That's the spirit,' she said, and handed me a fresh glass. I made short work of that one, too, and then pulled her out onto the dance floor.

The night, from there, took on the quality of a stop-motion film. Dancing beneath the flashing disco lights.

Isla's face beaming at me. More bourbon. Pushing my sweaty hair out of my face. Reapplying my lipstick in the dingy bathroom mirror. More bourbon. The music pulsing through me as I twirled and twirled.

And then the gaps in my memory become longer until it's just one long blank expanse. Scene missing. Scene missing. Scene missing.

7

I woke up in a vast tangle of 400-thread-count white cotton sheets, a feather from a down comforter stuck to my lower lip. My mouth was cottony and filled with my parched, swollen tongue, and a hundred marbles pinged themselves against the walls of my skull. I opened an eye and squinted into the bright daylight.

I was in a hotel room. I picked my head off the pillow gingerly and gazed dazedly at my surroundings. It wasn't my room. It wasn't Isla's room, either. A floor-to-ceiling window looked out across the Strip, and I flinched at the sunlight that glinted off the various highly-polished surfaces. An enormous flat-screen TV stared at me with its blank black eye. I noticed a pile of clothes thrown haphazardly across an armchair. A blue button-down shirt. A brown leather belt. A pair of jeans.

Oh God.

I lifted the covers and looked down at my body. I was wearing an oversized gray cotton T-shirt featuring a bright orange bull's skull and the word LONGHORNS written across the chest. I shoved a hand down into the sheets and felt a wave of relief: I was still wearing underwear.

I heard noises coming from the next room. A toilet flushed and a shower turned on. A man cleared his throat and I leaped out of bed like a startled wild animal.

'Shit,' I whispered to myself. I searched the room for my things. My bag was shoved in a corner next to a pair of men's sneakers – 'SHIT!' – and my clothes were in a tangle next to the coat rack. I pulled on Isla's dress and shoved my aching feet into my heels, all the while trying to distract myself from the increasingly urgent need to throw up. The man in the next room started to sing, a deep, warbling bass. I heard the shower turn off just as I shut the door behind me.

I stared at my reflection in the mirrored cocoon of the elevator. It wasn't pretty. Dark smudges encircled my bloodshot eyes, and my hair sprang in unruly tufts from the top of my head. I'd say I looked like a prostitute, but I suspected prostitutes were better groomed. In truth, I looked like what I was: a thirty-one-year-old woman who'd just woken up from a bender in a strange man's hotel room.

The thought was too much for my delicate stomach, and my throat burned with bile. How could I have let this happen? Regardless of what had been happening with us, I loved Christopher. He was the man I was destined to spend my life with! And yet apparently half a bottle of bourbon was all it took to get me into bed with another man.

I fumbled around in my purse until I remembered that Isla had confiscated my phone. This was all her fault, really. She'd been the one to drag us to that stupid bar and pour liquor down my throat like it was going out of style. A vague memory of her pushing a glass of water in my hands surfaced, but I pushed it away. So what if she'd given me a glass of water? She'd still got me into this mess.

I charged through the marble-floored lobby, ignoring the smirks and arched eyebrows and heading straight for the taxi rank. 'The Paris Hotel, please,' I told the driver in my most dignified voice. The driver looked at me in the rear-view mirror. 'Lady, it's not worth the fare,' he said, and pointed across the street to where the Eiffel Tower loomed over us.

'Oh,' I said, opening the door and climbing out with as much dignity as I could muster. 'Thank you.'

I had no way of telling what time it was, but I knew it must be close to midday – the sun was so hot it made the pavement sing. I crossed the street and walked through the foyer and into the elevator and down the hallway and opened the door to the suite, where I found Isla, ashen-faced, with her ear pressed to her telephone. 'Hang on, she's just walked through the door,' she said, before hanging up and tossing the phone across the room. 'Oh, thank God!' she shouted, charging towards me and gathering me up in her arms. 'I've been so worried about you!'

I extricated myself and folded my arms across my chest. 'I hope you're happy,' I said.

'Are you fucking kidding me? I've been going out of my mind here! I was just on the phone to the police to report you as a missing person! Are you okay? What the hell happened to you?'

'You mean you don't know?'

'Of course I don't know! One minute you were talking to that guy, and then the next minute, I turn around and you're both gone!'

'What guy?'

She looked at me closely. 'The guy from the casino.' I blinked at her. 'You know, the blond guy with all the

84

pockets?' she prompted. My mind remained stubbornly blank. 'You really don't remember?'

I shook my head.

'He showed up with his friends and they bought us a round of drinks. Remember? One of them was wearing that sheepskin jacket and we were all calling him Lamb Chop?'

I shook my head again. My brain was in place-holder mode. 'We're experiencing technical difficulties. Normal programming will resume shortly.' At least I hoped it would.

'Well, you and the blond guy with the pockets were totally loving each other.' She caught the look on my face and frowned. 'Not like that. It's not like you were making out or anything – I wouldn't have let you do that. You were just having fun, that's all. It was nice to see. Until you pulled a disappearing act on me, and then it sucked.'

'What did you do?'

'I ran out of the bar and looked for you, of course. His friends did too – they were calling him and calling him, but he didn't pick up. That's a lie – he picked up once, yelled something about you two going to see Elvis, and then the phone cut out.'

I couldn't believe any of it. Me and the pockets guy loving each other? Us running away together? The Elvis bit was the weirdest part. I hate Elvis.

'So where were you?' she asked.

'I don't know,' I said, 'but I woke up in a hotel room that wasn't mine. I'm guessing it was his.'

She let out a low whistle. 'Do you think you two . . . ?' She made a circle with her thumb and forefinger and poked her other forefinger through it.

'OH GOD!' I wailed. And then, sheepishly, 'I don't know.' The admission made me wince.

She threw an arm around me. 'Oh, honey.'

A thought occurred to me, and a fresh wave of panic washed over me. 'What time is it?'

She checked her phone. 'Quarter to three.'

'Oh my God!' I leaped to my feet. 'My flight is in two hours!'

'Shit! Okay, don't panic. You get in the shower, I'll pack your stuff.'

'I don't have time to take a shower!'

She shot me a look. 'I'm saying this because I'm your friend. You do not want to travel looking like you do now. They will escort your ass off the plane for the fumes alone.'

We drove to the airport at breakneck speed, Isla leaving a chorus of honks and curses in her wake as she screeched into the departures lot. 'You've got an hour and fifteen,' Isla said, peering at the dashboard clock. 'You might have to throw some elbows going though security, but you should be fine.'

'Thanks.' I opened the car door, but couldn't bring myself to get out. 'I'm sorry,' I said finally.

'For what?'

'For ruining this vacation by moping around the whole time and then disappearing with a stranger on our last night together! What do you mean, for what?'

'Jenny, stop. I had a great time! Anytime I get to spend with you is great time, even if you're moping or shitfaced on bourbon. Honest.'

I nodded. 'I love you, you know.'

She reached across the armrest and pulled me in for a hug. 'I love you, too. Now you better bust your ass or you're going to miss your plane.'

I thought about what might be waiting for me at the other end of the flight. 'Would that be such a bad thing?'

'Well, not for me, because it would mean I could kidnap you and bring you back to New York with me. But I don't think it would be great for you.'

'I really fucked up, didn't I?'

'No, you didn't. Whatever happened last night, just forget about it. It doesn't matter. It's Vegas – nothing that happens here counts.'

'I don't think Christopher would think that way.'

'Well, Christopher doesn't need to know about it. Anyway, you guys have bigger fish to fry than some drunken night out in Las Vegas.'

I nodded.

'Just keep an open mind. Whatever happens when you get off the plane, remember that you have a choice. I know you want to believe that everything's set in stone, but it really isn't. You're in charge of what happens in your life. Now go!' she said, shooing me out of the car. 'Call me when you land, okay?'

'Okay.' I pulled my suitcase out of the back seat of the car and made one final check that I had my passport. 'Thanks, friend.'

'Anytime,' she said, and then with a blown kiss and a rev of the engine, she peeled out of the parking lot, leaving the faint smell of burned rubber in her wake.

I braced myself as I headed into the airport. The fluorescent lights, the smell of industrial floor polish, the endless lines snaking away from the check-in desks: none of them did my hangover any favors. I walked up to a woman in a Delta uniform who was standing at the end of the rope maze. 'I'm on the 16:55 to London,' I said. 'Am I screwed?'

She looked up at the clock and back at me. 'Almost, but not quite. Do you definitely need to check that?'

I looked down at my little wheeled suitcase. 'I have liquids in here.'

'How badly do you need those liquids?' She saw me hesitate – my Kérastase! – and folded her arms across her chest. 'Let me rephrase that. Do you need those liquids so bad you're willing to miss your flight and pay for another one?'

I tossed the liquids. I gave the woman in the Delta uniform the Kérastase and she told me to ask for Duane when I got to security. 'Tell him Tina sent you,' she said. 'He'll speed you right through.'

As I pushed my way through the crowds, I was quietly grateful I was in America – where such pushing was frowned upon but not forbidden – rather than England, where queuing is an ancient and sacred art. Sure, a couple of people called me an asshole, or yelled at me as I squeezed by, but no one shook their heads and tutted. It was the tutting I dreaded the most.

There was a sprint finish down the people-mover, and I twice clipped my Achilles with my wheeled suitcase, but I made it just before the gate closed. People whistled as I hurried, shamefaced, down the crowded aisle and took my seat. Middle of the row, back of the plane, right next to the bathroom. I rooted through my bag, found a Xanax, and closed my eyes.

When I woke up, we were circling London, the gray mist clearing just enough for me to spot the Thames snaking its dark way through the city below.

I was home. At least it was home for now.

8

I studied my face in the bathroom mirror. Bloated. Patches of dry skin flaking from my cheeks. And was that . . . ? Yes. That was a trail of drool caked on my chin. I looked like the last crumb-covered scraping in a tub of discount margarine.

I splashed water on my face and rummaged through my bag for my moisturizer, until I remembered that I'd jettisoned all of my liquids back in Vegas. I uncapped a tin of Vaseline and rubbed a dab into my lips, which only highlighted the cracks.

'Jesus,' I muttered to myself. There was no way I could face Christopher looking like this. This was not the face of a woman you wanted to marry. This was the face of a woman you paid ten dollars after she gives you a hand-job in the back of a station wagon. I splashed my face with cold water before I realized that there were no paper towels available, only hand dryers. I stooped down and let the hot breeze blast me.

There was a Boots in arrivals. I could buy a few emergency supplies and try to do some damage control on my way home on the Piccadilly Line. I grabbed my suitcase and wheeled myself out of there, careful not to look in the mirror again.

I made my way through the customs door and the sad

little duty free display, and out into the harsh light of the arrivals lounge. I was always filled with free-floating anxiety when emerging from the bowels of the airport. The barriers lined with the patiently waiting, their faces upturned in expectance, their eyes scanning for loved ones. Even the cab drivers holding signs with passengers' names misspelled on them made me strangely sad. I wasn't who they were looking for, so my very presence was a disappointment. I was a walking let-down.

This time, I forced myself to keep my head tilted towards the ground. Don't stop. Don't even think about looking around. There wasn't anyone waiting for me here.

And then I heard it.

'Jenny!'

There are lots of Jennys in the world. Keep going. Don't embarrass yourself by looking up hopefully. It will just make everyone feel uncomfortable.

But it was my name being called again, louder this time, and then the sound of footsteps rushing towards me. I stopped and looked up just in time to see Christopher, arms laden with the biggest bouquet of red roses I'd ever seen, about to descend on me.

'Jenny!' he said, and then he wrapped his arms around me and hugged me tightly. The bouquet's cellophane wrapping crinkled noisily between us, and I felt a stray thorn graze my cheek, but I didn't care. I dropped the handle of my suitcase and heard it fall with a thud behind me as I hugged him back.

'What are you doing here?' I mumbled into his shoulder.

He pulled back and studied my face. 'God, I've missed

you. I've been such a massive cock – can you ever for-give me?'

'What do you mean?' Thoughts of tiny blonde Tiffany danced in my head. Then I remembered the man's voice singing in the shower. I wasn't be in a particularly strong position to judge.

'I can't believe I said that thing about going on a break. I've been going out of my mind this weekend.'

'You have?' I asked incredulously. 'But you haven't called or texted . . . I haven't heard from you at all.'

'I wanted to give you space,' he said, running a thumb across my cheek. I wondered if he could feel the scaly patch. 'I thought you deserved a weekend with Isla with-out having to think about me. So when you didn't get in touch . . .' He shook his head. 'Look, I know I've been selfish. After seeing my parents be so unhappy for so long, I wasn't sure if marriage was for me.' He sighed. 'But I know how important it is to you, and I want to make you happy, so . . .'

He dropped to one knee and I heard someone gasp. I'm pretty sure it was me.

As if in slow motion, he reached into his back pocket and pulled out a tiny black velvet box. 'I love you, Jenny Sparrow. Will you marry me?' He lifted the lid and an enormous red candy ring shone out enticingly. 'This is just a temporary ring, of course,' he added hurriedly. 'I didn't want to choose the real one without you.'

It was really happening. Here, underneath the unfor-giving lights, teeth gently furred, breath stale, eyes grimed with sleep. I was being asked for my hand in marriage by the man I was destined to be with. 'Yes!' I cried. 'Of course I'll marry you!'

He slid the candy ring on my finger. My nostrils filled with the scent of artificial cherry, and, just like that, it had happened. The fogged memories of the past weekend cleared and I beamed like the sun. It was really happening.

Christopher sprang to his feet and kissed me, one of those big dramatic swooping kisses you see in old movies. I even kicked up a foot. A burst of applause rippled around us, and I looked up to see the patient-waiters cheering us on. Even the bored taxi drivers were smiling. Christopher and I exchanged a shy glance and took a bow. 'Come on,' he said, taking hold of my suitcase and wheeling it towards the parking lot. 'Let's go celebrate.'

And just like that, I had my future back.

Reactions to the happy news were mixed. My mother cried. 'Happy tears!' she insisted, but years of experience had taught me when she was on the edge. My aunt took the phone away from her and told me how happy she was for me, but I could hear the strain in her voice. Marriage meant I wasn't coming home any time soon. Before we hung up, I promised to send money soon. I didn't promise to visit.

My dad cleared his throat and said Christopher was a lucky man. 'I hope he's a better husband than me,' he'd added, which I'd smoothly transitioned away from by asking after the tricky carburetor on his pickup truck.

Ben gave me an awkward hug and left a little bouquet of tulips on my desk the next morning. 'It's an occasion, isn't it?' he'd explained, waving away my thanks.

Isla paused for a pulse too long before squealing with excitement, but then called me a week later and asked if I was sure. 'What about your options?' she asked. 'I don't want options,' I told her, 'I want Christopher.'

And Christopher . . . well, Christopher was great. After I got back, he cooked me dinner every night for a week. He brought me coffee in bed every morning. He let me choose the movie on Saturday night, and didn't flinch when I put the disc of *The Philadelphia Story* into the DVD player. He was perfect. He was amazing. He was my Christopher, and he was going to be my husband.

And yet. And yet. I couldn't quite seem to give myself over to the wedding. Appointments at bridal boutiques were made and cancelled. Pinterest boards were left blank. I couldn't even bring myself to choose a venue. I would see places I liked – an adorable farmhouse in Wiltshire, a beautiful beach in Devon, an old music hall in Hackney – and I'd find fault with every one of them. I told myself it was because I wanted it to be perfect – but after I rejected a lighthouse in Sussex – a lighthouse! – I started to wonder if I'd ever commit.

The truth was, a vague sense of unease had been building since the car ride home from the airport. I couldn't understand it. I was engaged to the man I loved. We would be married before the end of the year. My happiness should have been pure and crystal-clear, but there was something muddying it. A sense of discomfort I couldn't seem to shake.

As soon as he dropped to one knee, I'd decided not to tell Christopher about what had happened that night in

Vegas. What was the point? It would only hurt him, and besides, I wasn't even sure what had happened. Maybe nothing! Maybe it had been as innocent as a sleepover party. No, I wouldn't tell him. I couldn't. The guilt was something I'd just have to carry with me.

A month passed, and things returned pretty much back to normal, with added flourishes of wedding talk. I started working on a case about a man who'd crashed his car into his ex-wife's house, ploughing through the bay window and sailing halfway into the living room before finally settling on the sofa. The photographs made it look as if the car had just stopped by to watch TV. The man claimed his brakes had failed.

I was in the middle of researching brake failure in 2007 Honda Civic XLs when I had a call from Bethany on reception.

'Your husband's here to see you,' she trilled. I told her I'd be down in a minute, and twirled around in my chair.

'Christopher's here to see me!' I announced to Ben, who managed to glance up briefly from the sheaf of papers spread out in front of him and smile.

I practically skipped down the hallway. How sweet that he was calling himself my husband! And Bethany obviously thought Christopher was cute – she sounded all breathy and excited over the phone. Granted, she always sounded breathy and excited. Ben called her Shirley Temple. But she sounded even more breathy and excited than usual. My chest swelled with pride. Tonight, we'd sit down and pick a venue. No more stalling. It was time.

I walked into reception to find Bethany pink-cheeked

and beaming. She shook her head and pulled her mouth into an exaggerated moue when she saw me. 'I can't believe you've been hiding him from us all this time,' she chastized. 'I didn't even know you were married!'

I shrugged my shoulders and smiled. I'd barely exchanged a half-dozen words with Bethany over the past three years, never mind details about my romantic life, but it didn't matter. What mattered was Christopher. Speaking of which . . . 'Where is he?' I asked.

She nodded towards a man standing with his back to us, staring at one of the godawful motivational prints the office manager had put up to 'freshen up the space'. I stared at the back of his head and froze.

Bethany cleared her throat. 'Here she is!' she announced.

The man turned around and grinned. He was tall, with shaggy blond hair and unsettlingly white teeth. He was wearing a worn gray T-shirt peppered with holes, and a pair of baggy cargo pants held up with a braided leather belt. He took a step towards me, arms outstretched. 'Sweetheart!'

I stumbled back into a large potted fern.

It was him. The man from the casino. And, if Isla was right, the man whose hotel room I'd spent the night in. I blinked rapidly in the hope he might dematerialize. But no, he was still standing there looking at me, that same stupid grin on his face.

'Come on, baby – don't be shy!' He turned to Bethany and shook his head. 'She's not big into PDAs.'

I managed to work up enough saliva to speak. 'What are you doing here?'

He put his hands on his hips and swayed back on his

heels. 'What? Can't a man visit his wife at work?' I recoiled further into the fern. The man was clearly insane.

'You have absolutely no right to barge into my place of work like this,' I said, with as much authority as I could muster.

Bethany's eyes bulged. I could hear her mind compiling a list of people to tell about her rude American co-worker.

'Please forgive my wife,' the man said. 'Jenny's just not good with surprises. Isn't that right, sweetheart? Maybe a little fresh air would help.' He raised his eyebrows at me and nodded towards the elevator door.

I had two choices. I could follow this madman into the street and risk him murdering me in broad daylight, or I could risk causing a scene at work. I'd lived in England long enough to know which would be frowned upon more.

'Okay,' I said, 'but it better be quick.'

'Don't worry,' he said, lips quirking into a grin. 'I know you're always in a rush.'

He pressed the button to call the elevator, and we stood and waited for it in silence. Finally, after what seemed like an eternity, the doors opened and we stepped inside. 'Very nice to meet you!' he called to Bethany as the doors closed in front of us, and I watched her cheeks flush with renewed pleasure.

The elevator descended. He began to hum. My mind continued to unravel.

I dragged him through the lobby, out of the building, and down a urine-and-bacon-scented alleyway.

He looked around at the discarded industrial-sized

drum of mayonnaise lolling on its side and the heap of black bin bags stacked against the wall, and smiled. 'It's not where I imagined our reunion, but it's nice to see that you want to get me alone.' And then he winked at me. I fought the urge to slug him.

'Will you please tell me what the hell you're doing here? Seriously, this could qualify as – as harassment or something. And why on earth did you tell Bethany that we're married? Do you know how awkward it's going to be when I have to go back inside and explain that was just some sick joke played on me by a guy I met once in Las Vegas?'

'Twice. We met twice.'

'Fine! Twice! That still doesn't give you the right to come to my work and spin some kind of *genuinely insane* yarn about being my husband!'

His grin faltered for a minute. 'Don't tell me you don't remember.'

'Remember what? That you're an asshole? Because yeah, I'm remembering that pretty clearly.'

'The little white chapel? The guy dressed as Elvis? The two old guys who agreed to witness the papers for a fifth of whisky?' I stared at him blankly, and he let out a low whistle. 'Shit. What about the Hells Angels who serenaded us on our way out? Do you remember that?'

'I don't know what you're talking about,' I said, more weakly this time. The truth was, I could feel the kernel of something in the back of my mind slowly popping. It wasn't quite out of its shell yet, but it was there.

'They sang that song from *Top Gun*,' he prompted. 'You know – "Take My Breath Away".'

The song filled my head, and as I reached the soaring chorus, it suddenly became clear. Him dropping to his knee in the crowded bar, us hurling ourselves into the taxi, both of us doubled over with laughter as it careened down the Strip. Somehow, a bottle of champagne was produced. Then we were getting out of the cab and . . . yes, there it was, the Little White Chapel, with its wedding-cake gazebo and enormous neon sign, and a group of burly Hells Angels serenading us.

'I'm going to throw up,' I said, and true to my word, I did. To be fair to the man, he held back my hair as I retched into a pile of garbage.

'I'm guessing you remember now?' he asked, as I wiped my mouth on the back of my hand.

I nodded weakly. 'A little.' I looked up at him, appalled. 'The hotel room . . . did we?'

He shook his head. 'We were both too far gone. We watched an episode of *Cheers*, and then passed out.'

I breathed a sigh of relief. I might be married to another man, but at least now I knew that I hadn't cheated on Christopher. 'Thank God.'

'I don't know if I'd be thanking God if I were you. You missed out on an earth-shattering experience.'

'I'll have to take your word on that. Look, how do we fix this?'

'What do you mean?'

'We need to get a divorce as soon as possible, obviously. Do we need lawyers, or is there some kind of form we can fill out online, like when you renew your driver's license?'

He held a hand to his heart. 'I can't believe you'd compare the sanctity of marriage to a trip to the DMV. Just what kind of monster have I married?'

'Stop! I don't have time for this! I'm getting married this year – married for real, to the man that I love – which means I need to make this whole thing disappear.'

He groaned. 'Don't tell me you're marrying that Christopher guy.'

I looked at him sharply. 'How do you know about Christopher?'

'Jesus. I guess your memory is still a little patchy. You don't remember telling me about him in the bar that night?' I shook my head, and he sighed. 'You told me the two of you had broken up and that you were glad because you hadn't been sure you wanted to be with him anyway.'

'I did not say that.'

'Trust me, you did. Many, many times. You told me you were happy you were free, and that you were better off alone, and then you sang "I Will Survive", but you couldn't remember how most of the lyrics went, so you just kept yelling the words "I Will Survive" over and over again until the bouncer came over and told you to stop.' He studied my face. 'Not ringing any bells, huh?'

'No, but even if I did say those things – which I seriously doubt – it doesn't matter because I was *obviously* not in my right mind at the time. I married *you,* for Christ's sake!'

He pulled a face. 'I'll have you know that I was voted prom king both my junior *and* senior year in high school.

You ask any of the girls back in Texas, and they'll tell you that you got yourself a helluva catch.'

I winced. 'You're from Texas?'

He tipped an imaginary hat. 'Yes, ma'am. A little town called New Deal.'

'God, it just gets worse,' I muttered. I checked my watch – I'd been gone from the office for nearly twenty minutes. Ben would notice any moment, and I didn't want to have to answer any more questions than were strictly necessary. 'So are you going to help us get divorced or what? Or did you just come here to torture me?'

He tilted his head and pondered for a minute. 'Tell you what. I haven't been to London for a couple of years, and I could use someone to show me around.'

'You want me to be your tour guide?'

'That's right. I'm only here for a week. You keep me company, show me a good time, take me to your favorite places, and when it's time for me to leave, we'll shake hands and say nice knowing you and I'll get you your divorce so you can marry good old Christopher. What do you say?'

'When you say "show you a good time" . . . you do know that absolutely nothing is going to happen between us, right?'

'Sweetheart, I just watched you throw up. I promise you I'm not itching to get in your pants at this particular juncture.'

I considered his offer. A week wasn't that long in the grand scheme of things, and if he was true to his word, all of this would be over, and I could forget the whole mess had ever happened. There was one thing that was nagging me, though. 'I don't get why you're doing this,' I said finally.

He grinned his wolfish grin and shrugged. 'Same reason we decided to get married, I guess. I thought it'd be fun. And you, my darling wife, look like you could use a little fun in your life.'

'My life is actually really, really fun,' I said, folding my arms across my chest.

He looked at me and laughed. 'Yeah, I can tell. I'll pick you up outside your office at six tonight – I won't risk going back in the building in case they set security on me or something.'

I blinked at him. Tonight? We were starting tonight? 'What am I supposed to tell Christopher?' I asked.

'That's your problem, I reckon,' he said, sauntering away. 'And make sure you've got something good planned for us!'

He was halfway down the block when a thought occurred to me. 'Hey!' I shouted. 'What's your name?'

'Jackson! Jackson Gaines!' And with that, he tipped that goddamn imaginary hat again, spun on his heel, and disappeared into the crowd.

9

'Jenny, you're going to have to breathe.'

'How – can I – breathe – at a time – like – this?' I gasped down the phone. I was locked in the disabled toilet at work while Isla listened to me have a panic attack from the on-call room at Mount Sinai.

'Slow down, buddy. Deep breaths.' I forced myself to block out the voice screaming inside my head and listened to Isla's instead. 'That's it,' she coaxed. 'Good girl.'

I took one last deep, shuddering breath and exhaled. 'Okay,' I said. 'I'm okay.'

'Good. Now tell me what the fuck is going on.' I brought her up to speed, leaving out the part where I threw up in the alleyway. 'Holy fucking shit,' she said when I'd finished. 'I can't believe you guys got married! That is some badass Vegas behaviour right there.'

I let out a strangled groan. 'I can't believe it either. I'm screwed.'

'You are not screwed. Jackson told you he'd give you a divorce, right?'

'Yeah, after I spend a week acting as his personal London Beefeater.'

'Okay, so that's a little weird, but it could be so much worse. What if he hadn't told you, and then you'd married Christopher? You'd have had to move to Utah. Instead, you spend a week with a guy who you don't completely hate – at least you didn't when you guys were in that bar together – and you take him to see Big Ben or whatever, and then he goes back to America, you get a divorce, and you never see him again.'

'What if Christopher finds out?'

'He's not going to find out. Men don't just randomly start researching their fiancée's marriage records for shits and giggles. The only way he'll find out is if you tell him, so just don't tell him. Simple.'

'I'm married to a stranger, Isla. This is definitely not simple.' I bit at a patch of skin around my cuticle until it bled. A thought struck me like a lightning bolt. 'I'm going to be a divorcee.'

'That's the spirit!' Isla trilled. 'See, before long, this will all be behind you. You might even find it funny one day!'

'No, you're not getting it!' I felt my chest tighten and my throat begin to close. My tongue felt like a great slab of concrete in my mouth. 'Isla, I'm going to be divorced.'

'Don't even think about it,' she cautioned. 'You are not your mother.'

But it was already in my head. It was always there, really.

'Jenny? Are you there?' I became suddenly aware of Isla shouting at me down the phone. 'JENNY?'

'I'm here,' I said softly, but I didn't feel like I was here at all.

'Listen to me,' she said sternly. 'This is different. This isn't a real divorce, this is—' I could sense her casting around for the right word. 'Admin!' she announced triumphantly.

'Admin,' I murmured.

'Exactly. You spend a week with a guy you don't know, sign on the dotted line and then the whole thing is over. It's basically like getting your driver's license, only without the three-point turn.'

Could I really see it as admin? I guess it wasn't a real marriage – according to Jackson, we hadn't even come close to sleeping together, and Christ knows we didn't have any of the normal trappings of a marriage, like a joint bank account or a shared home or an intimate knowledge of each other's failings. My mind raced. 'What am I going to tell Christopher when I'm out showing Jackson around?'

'Make something up! Tell him you're having a crazy week at work.'

'He knows my hours are super regular.'

'Then tell him a friend of yours is having some kind of personal crisis.'

'He knows I don't have any friends here.'

'Tell him you have a friend visiting from back home,' she said. She sounded exasperated, not that I could blame her. I was a little exasperated myself. 'It's not that far from the truth if you think about it.'

'Jackson is *not* my friend.'

'Sorry, you're right. Tell him your accidental husband is in town, see how that goes over.' I didn't say anything. 'Jenny, I know you don't like to lie, but right now, the truth is not your friend. You're going to have to bend it a little until this whole shitshow blows over.'

I sighed. 'I know. I know! It's just . . .'

'I know,' she said. Her voice was gentler now. 'Look, I've got to go – they're paging me here. It really will be okay, I promise.'

I nodded, but my reply caught in my throat.

'Jenny? Are you there?'

'I'm here,' I said finally.

'I love you. You need anything, you call me. Okay?'

'Okay.' I listened to the phone go dead, and sat in the cold stall for a few minutes, listening to the sound of the faucet dripping into the basin and feeling my chest tighten with dread. I forced myself to breathe again and tried to imagine Isla's voice in my head. It will be fine, I chanted under my breath. It will be fine. But the tightness in my chest refused to loosen.

Ben took one look at me when I got back to my desk and immediately reached for his coat. 'Pub?'

I shook my head. 'I've got too much work.' I also wasn't sure drinking was the best solution, considering it's what got me in this mess in the first place. Besides, how was I supposed to explain what had happened to Ben? To anyone? They'd think I'd lost it. They'd think I was crazy. My heart thudded in my chest and I felt my throat begin to close.

Breathe, I chanted to myself. Breathe.

Ben gave me one last look of concern before turning back to his computer. We typed in silence for a few minutes, though I didn't get too far in my case notes. The cursor blinked at me accusingly. Finally, he sighed and swung his chair around towards me.

'Whatever's happened between you and Christopher,

just try not to worry about it too much. When my sister was planning her wedding last year, she and her fiancé fell out all the time. Because of the stress and everything,' he added with a shrug.

I swiveled my chair. 'Why do you think I'm in a fight with Christopher?'

He looked at me, puzzled. 'That's who was in reception, wasn't it?'

'Oh.' My mind spun. 'Yeah.'

'All I'm saying is that it's probably over something stupid, that's all. My sister once threw her fiancé out of their flat for three days because he said the bridesmaids' dresses she'd picked out looked like old tablecloths. And then *he* threw *her* out because she told him he couldn't ride to the church on his motorbike. Weddings are seriously mental.'

'Ben, it's fine, honestly.'

'I read somewhere that weddings are the third most stressful experience a couple can go through, behind buying a house and having a baby.' He shook his head. 'It can really turn you into a nutter. The way I see it is—'

I sighed. 'No offense, but you're the last person I would take relationship advice from, considering you haven't made it past a first date with a woman in the three years I've known you.' I felt the air go out of the room, and I knew I'd really hurt him. I couldn't bring myself to look him in the eye.

'Right then,' he said quietly. 'Right.' He spun back around in his chair, and I heard the typing start up again, sharp thwacks on the keys. We didn't talk again for the rest of the afternoon.

*

I found Jackson leaning against the side of the building opposite, hands shoved in his pockets, staring out into the street. He waved when he saw me and headed across the road, only narrowly avoiding collision with a black cab and an irate cyclist.

'Why's everyone always in such a rush in this town?' he asked as he hopped onto the sidewalk.

I shrugged. 'It's London. Also, word to the wise, it's always good to look both ways before you cross the street. Or did your mother not teach you that?'

'My mom taught me a lot of things,' he said, grinning. 'Sometimes it's hard to keep track. So where are we heading?'

I'd spent the afternoon racking my brains trying to think of somewhere suitable to take him, and finally settled on that venerable British institution, Claridges. I figured it was the kind of place that would strike awe in most Americans, particularly those who hadn't traveled much outside of the US. The checkerboard marble floors in the lobby, the heavy crystal chandeliers, the high, straight-backed chairs and similarly straight-backed waiters darting between tables. It was just what I'd imagined England would be like before I moved here. I'd brought my aunt there when she'd come to visit, and she'd spent the whole time nudging me under the table and asking if various glossy brunettes were 'Princess Kate'. Jackson, I assumed, would be suitably impressed.

But now that I was standing in front of him, I wondered if I'd be able to sneak him past the doorman. He was wearing a beat-up denim jacket, jeans so worn the knees had all but given up, and a pair of cowboy boots. This was not a joke. The man was wearing cowboy boots. 'Are you dressed?' I asked finally.

He looked down. 'This sure as hell isn't what I look like naked.'

'That's not what I meant.'

'I take it I'm not dressed the way you were hoping I'd be dressed?'

'No! I don't care how you dress! How you dress is none of my business at all. Whatsoever.' I was still rattled by him invoking the specter of his naked self. 'It's just – the restaurant, I think it might have a dress code.'

He tilted his head and smiled at me. 'What restaurant is that?'

'Claridges.'

He let out a low whistle. 'Damn! I had no idea my wife had such fancy tastes!'

I folded my arms across my chest and glared. 'You told me to take you somewhere special!'

'Sure, but I didn't tell you to take me to a mausoleum full of old rich people.'

'It's nice there,' I said lamely.

'It's so far up its own ass it hasn't seen daylight in forty years.'

'Fine! We won't go there! Any suggestions on where you want to go instead?'

'How do you feel about spicy food?'

I wrinkled my nose. 'I hate it.'

'I know just the place.'

I hesitated. Why should I trust him? I didn't know him,

not even one bit. For all I knew, he might chop people up and stuff them into freezers as a hobby. I might be next.

'C'mon,' he said, gentler this time. 'Trust me. Please?'

'Fine,' I said. 'But I am definitely not taking your arm.'

'Suit yourself!' He set off at a rapid clip, and I had to hurry to keep up, the click of my sensible heels on the pavement echoing in my wake. We snaked our way through the quaint cobbled yards of Westminster School and down to the Embankment, where black cabs and Ubers and Addison Lees hurriedly sped Londoners to dinners and dates across the city.

A man in a dark suit clutching a worn briefcase shouldered me as he passed. Jackson caught me as I stumbled. 'You all right?' he asked. I nodded. 'What a jackass,' he said, shaking his head.

Sometimes, walking around this city, I felt like a moving target. Men with briefcases, scuffed white vans, pigeons . . . all of them seemed set on a collision course with me. And if I wasn't dodging out of the way of someone, I was invisible. Everyone's eyes on the Tube, staring at worn paperbacks or glowing screens, never looking at each other, never connecting. There were times when Christopher had gone away for the weekend to run across some hilly stretch of countryside, and I'd reach Sunday evening and realize I hadn't spoken to a single soul since Friday afternoon. You could do it, in this city. You could just . . . melt into the background. Even when a pigeon was dive-bombing your skull.

'It's a left up here,' Jackson called, steering us down a narrow alleyway.

'How do you know your way around?' I asked, trying to ignore the rising dread in my stomach. I could be home right now, I thought. I could be curled up on the couch watching a rerun of *Gilmore Girls*, waiting for Christopher to get home, rather than careening down an alleyway that reeked of piss, trying to keep up with a man who may very well be a psychopath.

Jackson threw a grin over his shoulder but didn't answer. I scowled and doubled my pace. We rushed across Vauxhall Bridge, minnows caught in the stream of commuters, and then down into the arches below, where he stopped in front of an unpromising-looking doorway.

'Still here!' he announced, shooting me an excited glance.

A single flickering bulb hung above the rotten wooden door. Mounted on the wall to the left was a laminated menu featuring pictures of various ambiguous-looking brown foods. 'What is this place?' I asked.

'It's only the best curry house in London,' he said, eyes gleaming with excitement.

'God, Jackson! I literally just told you I don't like spicy food!'

'Everybody likes spicy food! It's just that some people haven't discovered the right spicy food. And you, my friend, are about to discover the right spicy food.'

As if that settled the matter, he opened the door with a swoop and ushered me inside.

It was a dank, dark little room, the walls stained with streaks of yellow. A ceiling fan moaned ineffectually above. There were only six tables in the place, all of them crowded together so closely that people had to synchronize their eating so as not to elbow their fellow diner in the face when lifting their forks to their mouths. Incredibly, all of the tables were full.

'I can't believe this,' I grumbled.

'Neither can I! I haven't been here in years – it hasn't changed a bit!'

A disgruntled-looking waiter approached us and thrust a pair of menus at us. 'Half hour wait,' he grunted, before turning on his heel and disappearing into the kitchen, which was hidden behind a tattered floral curtain.

I scanned the menu, but nothing looked even remotely familiar – or appetizing. 'Are you sure you want to eat here?' I whispered, eyes scanning the grimy laminate floor and cheap paper tablecloths. 'It looks like it might give us food poisoning.'

'I've eaten here a dozen times and have never had so much as a hiccup afterwards. Trust me, you're going to love this place. Just give it a chance.'

I shot him a sceptical glance. 'Fine, but if I throw up, tomorrow night's dinner is cancelled.'

'Not going to happen . . .'

'Do we have a deal or not?'

He held out a hand. 'Tell you what. If the food here makes you puke, you never have to see me again.'

We shook on it. For the first time in my life, I was praying for botulism.

'So where did you tell Christopher you were tonight?' he asked, leaning against the presumably-once-white-but-now-brown wall.

'Work,' I said tersely. The truth was, I'd told Christopher that I was taking Ben for a drink because he was having 'relationship problems', a lie that Christopher had accepted with a kindness that nearly killed me.

'What sort of work do you do? Your office looked like a law firm or something.'

'Insurance.'

'Damn. You see, I knew you needed a little fun in your life.'

'I actually really enjoy my profession,' I snapped. I knew I was being rude, but I couldn't seem to help myself. Yes, this mess was my fault, but it was his, too, and he wasn't helping matters by making us spend time together. I was damned if I was going to let that time be pleasant.

'Well, good for you.' He paused, clearly waiting for me to ask what he did, but I just stood there, arms folded across my chest, and scowled. Jackson scratched the back of his neck. 'So,' he said finally, 'I guess you're wondering how I found you.'

'Not really.' I was desperate to know.

'Well, it took a little sleuthing on my part, I'll tell you. I had your name from the marriage certificate' – I flinched at the mention of it – 'so I started out by just Googling you. Turns out there are a lot of Jenny Sparrows out there!' he chuckled.

I stayed silent.

'So then I started thinking about the things you'd told me about yourself. I remembered you'd said you were from New Jersey—'

'I did?' This was not a fact I readily volunteered normally.

'Yeah, you told me all about growing up on the shore. You even did your accent for me.'

I wondered if this would be an ideal moment to cause a distraction. Shout 'Fire!' maybe, or pretend to have a stroke. Anything to get me out of there.

' . . . So I had New Jersey, and I had that you lived in London – you did your British accent for me too, by the way – and that narrowed it down to two. Then I saw the photo on your Facebook profile and I knew I had the right girl. I always remember a face,' he said, nodding to himself approvingly.

'Why?'

He tilted his head quizzically. 'Why what?'

'Why go to all the trouble to find me?'

He shrugged. 'Seemed only right to find my wife.'

It was a fair point. 'Yeah, but . . . why now? Why not straight away? Or a year from now? Or when you met a woman you actually wanted to marry for real?'

The waiter appeared. 'You want drinks while you wait?' he barked. We ordered a couple of beers and watched him storm off. He came back with two bottles of ice-cold beer. The caps were still on.

'Excuse me,' I said, gesturing towards my beer. 'Could you open this?'

A look of disgust crossed the waiter's face. 'It's twist off!' he shouted.

'Give me that,' Jackson muttered. I passed him my bottle and he covered the top with the edge of his T-shirt and eased the cap off. 'Here.'

'Thanks.' I took a long slug of beer and spilled some down my shirt in the process. I cursed, dabbing at the stain.

'Look, I get it,' he sighed. 'You're pissed that I showed up like this, but I didn't know what else to do. I thought a phone call would be a little weird – "Hey, it's me! Your husband!" – and after your little stunt in the hotel room . . .'

'Stunt! What stunt?'

'You left when I was in the goddamn shower! And don't tell me you don't remember that, either, because while I know you were drunk the night before, I'm damn sure you'd have been sober by the morning.'

I took another sip, more carefully this time. 'I freaked out.'

'I'll bet, but that still doesn't give you the excuse to just run away like that. I didn't come here to give you grief. The reason I waited until now to find you is I knew you might not be thrilled to hear from me, so I thought it'd be better to do it in person.'

'And you just happened to be in London . . .' I said, eyeing him suspiciously.

'I told you, I'm here for work.' He saw the look on my face and threw his hands in the air. His beer burped out a little foam. 'Scouts' honor!'

'Whatever,' I muttered moodily. Something about the guy brought out the thirteen-year-old in me.

Forty-five minutes later, a table freed up and we were pushed into chairs before the detritus of the previous diners had been cleared away. 'Do you know what you want?'

the waiter barked as he crumpled up the dirty tablecloth and set out a fresh one.

I looked down at the menu uncertainly. 'Uh . . . do you have anything plain? Some grilled chicken or something?'

Jackson snatched the menu out of my hands. 'Ignore her. We'll have two of the specials, and two more Kingfishers, please.'

The waiter wordlessly collected the menus and disappeared into the kitchen.

'What's the special?' I asked.

He shrugged. 'Dunno.'

'You mean you don't know what we're about to eat? Jackson, it could be anything! It could be – I don't know . . .'

He raised an eyebrow. 'What? What could it be?'

'I don't know. Something gross.'

'Trust me, it won't be gross. I might not know what it is, but I know it'll be delicious.'

'Do you always live like this?' I asked.

'Like what?'

'Like all . . .' I waved my hands around in the air. 'Crazy?'

He raised an eyebrow. 'You think I'm crazy?'

'Well, let's look at the evidence, shall we? You married a stranger in Las Vegas—'

'So did you!'

'And then you turned up at her place of work unannounced and forced her to eat an unidentified curry with you.' I folded my arms across my chest and leaned back in the chair. 'I'd call that pretty crazy, wouldn't you?'

'Where's the gratitude? The respect? I travel all the way across the ocean to stop you from becoming a polygamist, and then, out of the kindness of my own heart, I take you for what will soon be the best meal of your life.' He shook his head. 'Some people are just never satisfied.'

'Ha ha,' I deadpanned. 'I'm serious, though. Are you usually this . . . this . . .'

He gave me a bemused smile. 'Charming? Handsome? Debonair?'

'Chaotic?'

He considered this for a second. 'I don't think there's anything wrong with being spontaneous.'

'Well, I do. The one time I decided to be spontaneous, I ended up married to you.'

He leaned across the table and pushed his hair out of his eyes with his hand. 'Are you telling me that you've never done anything else spontaneous in your life? Ever?'

I shrugged. 'I like to have a plan.' I didn't mention the 87-step laminated life plan currently sitting neatly in the pocket of my bag. 'Plans are good.'

He waved the thought away. 'Plans are boring! How are you supposed to experience anything new if you're always sticking to a plan?'

'Uh, plan for it?'

He shook his head. 'I mean something really new. Something completely unexpected. Doesn't that idea excite you at all?'

'Like I said, the last time I did something off-plan, I

married you, and that doesn't excite me in the least. The opposite, in fact.'

He clutched at his heart. 'Ouch.'

'Planning is absolutely the way forward,' I said firmly.

'Yeah, well, not all plans work out the way they're supposed to,' he said quietly. He stared down at the table, a faraway look on his face. All at once, the energy drained from him.

I reached across the table and lightly tapped his hand. 'Are you okay?'

Before he could answer, the waiter appeared with two steaming plates in his hands. He threw them on the table in front of us and stalked away.

Jackson's face lit up and he rubbed his hands together. Whatever strange mood had overcome him a minute ago cleared instantly. 'I hope you're ready to have your mind blown.'

I gazed down at the mound of brown, lumpen meat sitting in front of me and felt my stomach try to flee the building. I picked up my fork and gave an exploratory prod, but what I found underneath – more brown, lumpen meat – wasn't particularly reassuring. I looked at him doubtfully. 'You're absolutely, one-hundred-per-cent sure this isn't going to kill me?'

He was already shoveling it in faster than I'd previously thought possible. 'Dig in!' he said through a dangerously full mouth. I briefly reminded myself of the steps involved in the Heimlich maneuver. I had a feeling I might be called upon to act before the meal was finished.

I speared a small fleck onto my fork and lifted it to my mouth. The smell was . . . actually not revolting. In fact, it smelled pretty good. I opened my mouth and took a bite. Immediately, my eyes started to water. The heat was intense, but there was more to it than that. There was sweetness, too, and richness, and tenderness from where the meat had been cooked to the point that it almost melted.

'Oh my God,' I muttered.

Jackson looked up at me, beaming. His mouth was ringed with reddish oil, and there was a splodge of sauce on the front of his shirt. 'Good, huh?'

I nodded and took another bite, bigger this time. My upper lip began to sweat. The heat worked its way through me, warming me through to my skin. Before I knew it, I was wiping up the last of the sauce with a hunk of peshwari nan and wondering if it would be impolite to ask for a separate jug of it for dipping.

Jackson was watching me from across the table, a huge, messy grin stretched across his face. 'You liked it?'

I sat back in my chair and sighed. 'That,' I said, 'was maybe the most delicious thing I've ever eaten in my life.'

'And the spice? It wasn't too much?'

I shook my head. 'It was genuinely fantastic.'

He clapped his hands together and hooted. 'I knew it! You see, everybody likes spicy food! It's just some people haven't eaten it right yet.'

I gave him a begrudging smile. 'You were right. I'm a convert.'

'I'll say you are. I thought you were going to pick up that plate and lick it at one point.'

I picked up the paper napkin and tried to mop the grease off my chin as delicately as possible. 'So how do you know about this place?'

'I lived here a while back.'

'You lived here? In London?' My head spun.

The waiter deposited another two cold, tall bottles of beer on the table and Jackson picked his up, tilted it in my direction, and took a long pull. 'That's right.'

'If you lived here, why the hell did you tell me you needed me to play tour guide?'

He shrugged. 'I thought it would be fun.'

Indignation bubbled up from my ribcage. 'You thought it would be fun?' I pushed back from the table and tossed my napkin next to my plate. 'You're nuts.' A hysterical laugh escaped. 'You're nuts!'

'Hang on a minute . . .'

Everyone in the restaurant was staring at us now, but I didn't care. 'No! You're a crazy person, and I refuse to spend any more time with a crazy person, even if we are married.' There was the clatter of a knife dropping, and I turned to see a man sitting dumbfounded next to us, his fork halfway to his mouth, his eyes wide. 'Oh, eat your food,' I hissed.

'Jenny, will you calm down for a second?' Jackson was hovering a couple of inches off his seat. He had the look of a man who'd got too close to a grizzly bear and was trying not to get mauled. 'Please?'

I lowered myself reluctantly back into my seat. 'You have three minutes to explain, and then I'm out of here.'

He plucked sheepishly at his napkin. 'I don't like being on my own in this town.'

I rolled my eyes. 'You're going to have to do better than that, buddy.'

'I've got some bad memories here,' he shrugged. 'I like to have company to distract me. I love London, but it can be a lonely place.'

I felt a twinge of sympathy. I knew the feeling all too well. 'So I'm the distraction?'

That grin of his reappeared. 'Well, you *are* my wife . . .'

'Oh God,' I groaned. 'How long ago did you live here?'

He paused to consider this. 'Nearly ten years ago now. I came over when I was twenty-four.'

'How come?'

Jackson started peeling the label off his bottle of beer in long, clean strips as I drank from mine. 'A girl.'

'You moved to London for a girl?'

He shrugged. 'I was young and in love.'

'And I'm guessing she's the reason for the bad memories. Did she break your heart?'

'Something like that.' He folded his arms, and I could tell he wasn't going to say any more about it. 'What about you? How long have you lived here?'

'About three years.' Saying the words aloud made my heart sink.

'Three years in London, and the only restaurant you know is Claridges?'

'I know other restaurants!' I cried indignantly.

'I'm sure you're a walking, talking *Time Out* guide.' He nodded towards my almost-empty beer. 'You want another of those?'

I hesitated. It was a week night, and I'd already had

three bottles. A fourth would mean a foggy head the next day, and I had that early meeting . . .

I looked up and saw that Jackson was already signaling the waiter to bring us another round.

'So how do you like it here?' he asked.

'Where, Vauxhall? I'm not much of clubber, so . . .'

'Not Vauxhall specifically. London in general.'

'Oh.' A series of words popped into my head. Lonely. Isolated. Overwhelmed. I forced a smile. 'It's okay, I guess.'

'Only okay?'

How could I explain how small the city made me feel without seeming totally pathetic? And why would I want to tell him, anyway? I shrugged. 'I guess I haven't explored all that much of it.'

'Why's that?'

I took another sip of beer to stall for time. 'Well, Christopher and I both work, and on the weekends he's got his training, so we tend to just stay around home—'

'What's he training for?'

'Triathlons, marathons . . . that kind of thing.'

Jackson sat back in his chair and placed his hands behind his head. 'I'm impressed. Not much of an exercise man myself.'

I eyed the sliver of soft stomach where his T-shirt had ridden up. 'You don't say.'

'Nah, I can't be doing with all that stuff. Life's too short.'

'Especially when you don't exercise.'

He let out a laugh then, a huge, growling guffaw, and I

jumped in my seat. 'You're funny,' he said. 'I remember that from our night in Vegas.'

I groaned. 'Please, can we not talk about that night?'

'Suit yourself. You were funny as hell, though.'

I was mortified to find myself blushing, and moved swiftly to change the subject. 'So how come you left London? Something happen with the girl?'

The same faraway look stole across his face. 'You could say that. That's not why I left, though.'

'Then why did you? You obviously like it here.'

He shrugged. 'Like I said. Plans change.' He emptied the rest of his beer and banged it down on the table. It was pretty clear that the subject was now closed.

I decided to change tack. 'You haven't told me what kind of work you're in.'

'I'm a camera man.'

'As in lights, action . . .'

He nodded. 'You got it.'

'That's so cool! What sort of stuff do you work on?'

'All sorts, I guess. Television, feature films, a few documentaries. Last March I was in Fallujah doing a film for *Vice* about the aftermath of the war in Afghanistan.'

'That sounds . . . terrifying.' The waiter plonked two fresh beers down on the table, and this time I unscrewed my own cap. It gave way beneath my palm with a satisfying hiss.

Jackson nodded and took a long pull from his beer. 'It was, at times. At one point, our convoy came under sniper fire.' Suddenly my work at the insurance agency seemed a lot less exciting.

My eyes widened. 'What happened?'

He laughed again. I was starting to notice how often he laughed, and how easily. 'We got the hell out of there as fast as we could. I got some great footage, though.'

'How could you remember to film when that was happening? Weren't you scared?'

'Sure I was. I was scared shitless. But it's part of the job. You can't let yourself get rattled and forget why you're there.'

I shook my head in disbelief. I couldn't imagine being so unperturbable. 'Where else have you been?'

'You name it, I've probably been there. I'm on the road pretty much all the time – have been for the best part of a decade.'

The thought of him living out of a suitcase, spending his life in airplanes and anonymous hotel rooms, filled me with sadness. 'Aren't you lonely?'

He grinned wickedly. 'There's plenty of company on a shoot, I promise you.'

'Oh God,' I groaned. 'I really don't want to hear about that.'

'Sorry, am I making you jealous, sweetheart?'

I resisted the urge to reach across the table and punch him. 'In your dreams.' In a matter of minutes, we'd devolved into twelve-year-olds. 'So, how often do you get to go back home? Where is home, anyway?'

'Technically, it's still in Texas. I've got a little house in New Deal, right near my parents. But really, it's just a glorified mailbox. I get back there probably once every couple of months, and even then it's usually only for a couple of days, though I'll be there for a stretch after I leave here.'

I shook my head. 'I don't know how you do that.' Not having a routine, no security, not knowing where I'd be from one day to the next . . . well, it was enough to give me night terrors. In fact, I'm pretty sure that's what my last nightmare was about. All of them were about that, really.

He shrugged. 'I prefer it that way. I don't like being in one place too long. Gives you too long to think.' I was about to ask what he was so keen to avoid thinking about when a funny look came over his face. He leaned over the table towards me. 'C'mere,' he said, 'you've got a little bit of sauce on your—' He reached out and wiped the corner of my mouth with his thumb.

His touch was like an electric current shooting through me. Every nerve in my body was suddenly singing.

I flinched and pulled away. Our eyes met, and we stared at each other for a minute, some wordless charge connecting us. I raised my hand to my face and touched the place where his thumb had been.

'Did you get it?' I said finally.

'What?' he asked softly.

'The sauce,' I said. 'Did you get it?'

'Oh.' He sat back in the chair and shoved his hands in his pockets. 'Yeah, I got it.'

'Good. Should we get the bill? It's getting late, and I've got to be at work early tomorrow . . .'

'Sure, sure. Of course.' He raised his hand and signaled to the waiter.

We didn't speak again until we left the restaurant. The warmth had gone out of the evening, and a sharp breeze blew through the night, cutting through my thin leather jacket.

'So,' he said, rocking back on his heels.

'Where are you going now? Back to your hotel?'

'Nah, I think I might take a walk. I like walking around cities at night, when it's quiet.'

I nodded. 'Well, my Tube station's just over there, so—'

'I can walk you to the Tube if you want—'

'I'm fine,' I said quickly. 'You go enjoy your walk. Thanks again for dinner. It really was delicious.'

'Well, I'm just happy I could introduce you to this place. Maybe you can take Christopher here sometime.'

I tried to picture luring Christopher into a cramped Indian restaurant under Vauxhall Bridge. 'Maybe,' I said doubtfully. The wind picked up and I hugged my arms to my chest.

'See you tomorrow?' I knew it wasn't really a question, but there was a note of uncertainty in his voice. I realized he was worried I'd say no.

I looked up at him. His blond curls had been blown around by the wind and were sticking up at haphazard angles from his head. There was a boyishness to his features in the dim half-light. 'Sure,' I said. 'I can book somewhere . . .'

'No way,' he said, shaking his head. 'I think tonight has proven that I'm the better plan-maker out of the two of us. And there was no puking, either, which means our deal still stands.'

I smiled. 'I know when I'm beaten.'

'That's what I like to hear. Give me your number – I'll

text you the plan tomorrow.' I read out my digits and he tapped them into his phone. 'You get home safe, okay?'

'You too,' I said. 'Enjoy your walk.'

He smiled and raised a hand as he walked away. I could hear his footsteps fading behind me as I made my way to the Tube.

10

I woke up the next morning with a heavy sense of dread. It didn't take long for it all to come flooding back – Jackson turning up at my office, the news that I was married to him – God, I couldn't even think it without feeling sick – our crazy dinner. And tonight, I had to do it all over again. I rolled over and shoved my face in the pillow.

'Get up, sleepyhead!' Christopher leaned over the bed and pulled the covers off me. I groaned and buried my head more deeply into the pillow. Christopher climbed into bed next to me and kissed the back of my head. 'Come on, you'll be late.'

I rolled over and shielded my eyes from the sunlight currently streaming through the bay window. Just my luck – of all the days, this would be the one that London chose to be sunny. 'What time is it?'

'Half seven,' he said.

'Shit,' I muttered.

'Told you. I'll put the kettle on.'

I rolled out of bed and poured myself into the shower, studiously avoiding my reflection in the bathroom mirror. The truly heroic amount of spiced meat I'd consumed the night before had caught up with me, and I felt bloated and heady.

I was toweling off my hair when Christopher appeared

with a cup of coffee. 'How was Ben?' he asked, setting the mug on the dresser.

It took me a minute to figure out what he was talking about. 'Oh, fine!' I said eventually. 'It was just a stupid little thing.'

'Good.' He leaned down and kissed the top of my head. 'I've got to shoot off. Are you in tonight?'

'Yep,' I said automatically. I took a sip of coffee and felt the gears in my head grind slowly into motion. 'I mean, maybe. I might not be. I might be late.'

He tilted his head. 'What are you up to?'

'Spin class!' I blurted out. 'I said I'd try this new spin class with this woman from work. It doesn't start until eight, and then we might get a drink after, so . . .'

'Hey, that's great! I've been trying to get you on a bike for ages – maybe this will convince you.'

'Maybe,' I said weakly. Oh God. Now I was going to have to ride a bike, too. And it wouldn't be just a leisurely pedal up to Hampstead Heath. Christopher was a 'cyclist', which meant he wore a spandex onesie and owned a bike that cost almost as much as a compact car. This goddamn Vegas nightmare was going to result in me careening down a hill in a spandex onesie too. I could just feel it.

'Just make sure you drink plenty of water afterwards,' he continued. 'Spinning can seriously dehydrate you.'

He was so nice. Look at him standing there, hair still damp from the shower, tie knotted around his neck, jacket slung over his shoulder. He was gorgeous. Even in a spandex onesie, he was cute. And so, so nice. And me?

What was I? I was a monster. A married, lying, almost-certainly-crazy monster.

I plastered a smile across my face. 'Will do!'

I heard the door shut behind him and stood deflated in front of the mirror. 'You stupid, stupid woman,' I hissed at my reflection. How was I supposed to get through a whole week of lying to him like this? The guilt was already chewing me up inside, and besides, I was a terrible liar. Always have been.

In tenth grade, my friend Tara decided to throw a party. Her dad worked night shifts and her mom let kids drink in her house and even offered to buy it for them – one of those 'they're going to do it anyway so I'd rather it be under my supervision' moms who actually just wanted some company while she sank two bottles of white Zinfandel at her kitchen table. I knew my mother would never let me go to a party at Tara's house because she once saw Tara's mom offer Tara a drag from her cigarette, but I had to be there, because Jimmy Sangillo was going to be there, and I'd decided that he was going to help me achieve Number 8 on my life list (fling with a bad boy) because he wore a leather jacket and kept a pack of Camels tucked up the arm of his T-shirt.

Anyway, I told my mother that I was going to stay at Isla's house, knowing that she wouldn't call there because she was convinced that Isla's mother hated her and gossiped about her behind her back. (She didn't.) Of course, no more than ten minutes after leaving the house, my mother discovered that I'd left my retainer behind and – in one of her moods – called Isla's house to tell me to come get it, which led to Isla's mom telling her that she thought Isla was staying at ours that night, which led my mother to spin out, go through my emails, find out about the party, and show up at Tara's house in her nightdress holding my retainer, the police trailing close behind. The party was broken up, and Jimmy Sangillo called me brace face for the rest of the year, even though technically a retainer and braces are two entirely different things. (We still ended up making out during a field trip to an apple orchard in my senior year, so I got to cross Number 8 off the list, even though by that point I suspected that he wasn't so much a bad boy as a kid who'd watched *Rebel Without a Cause* too many times.)

All of this is a long-winded way of saying I'm a terrible liar and would never last a whole week. But somehow, I had to.

I flicked on a little mascara, scraped my hair back into a ponytail, and took one last sip of my now-tepid coffee before heading out the door and down to the Tube. After a half hour contorted like a circus performer (head lodged in armpit of middle-aged cyclist, leg twisted awkwardly to avoid his fold-up bicycle, back in spasm after holding it at a 45 degree angle to avoid the newspaper he consistently flapped in my face), I emerged at Green Park to find a glorious spring day. The sky was a faultless bright blue, the daffodils sprouted in riotous bursts of yellow, the air sun-warmed and sweet. It all felt like an affront to my fraught nerves and cottony brain.

Ben was waiting for me when I got in, coiled like a snake in his ergonomic chair. He sprang on me as soon as I tossed my bag on the floor.

'Thank God you're here. I need your help.'

I looked at him closely. His hair, normally pomaded into submission, was unruly and wild, one particular lock standing straight in the air from his forehead like an antenna. His eyes were red-rimmed, and his face was pale. But the really worrying thing was his shoes. He was wearing sneakers. And not trendy sneakers, either. Big, clunky sneakers that dads wear to go running on Sundays. 'What's going on?' I asked, alarmed.

'I think I'm having a nervous breakdown,' he said, chewing at a cuticle.

'Jesus. Why?'

'I can't think straight, my heart is racing . . . Maybe I'm having a heart attack.' He looked up at me, eyes filled with panic. 'Do you think I'm having a heart attack?'

'I don't think you're having a heart attack, but I do think you need to slow down. Just breathe for a minute.' I waited as he inhaled and exhaled deeply. 'Now walk me through what's happening.'

He exhaled one last time and stared up at the ceiling. 'I met a girl last night.'

'Okay . . .'

'We went to a bar, and then we went to dinner—'

'On the first date? You never eat on a first date!' I was well-versed in Ben's three golden rules for first dates, the first of which was 'no dinner'. He thought it signified too much commitment.

'I know! But we were having a good time, and she said she was hungry, so we went for dinner.'

I shook my head in disbelief. 'Incredible.'

'And then after dinner, I told her there was this great bar near my place, so—'

'Wait, what?'

He nodded. The look of shock on his face mirrored mine. 'After we went for a drink, I took her back to my flat.'

I threw myself into my chair. 'But you never—'

'I know!' Ben's second golden rule was 'never tell them where you live'. If he took a girl home on the first date – and he did, often – it was always to her place, not his. He hid his flat like Bruce Wayne hid the Batcave, only his flat contained a PlayStation 4 and several pairs of limited edition Adidas trainers rather than a butler and the Batmobile. As far as I knew, at least. I'd never been to Ben's flat. Or the Batcave, for that matter.

I shook my head. 'This is unbelievable.'

'It gets worse. In the morning, I didn't want her to leave. She said she was hungry, so I . . .'

'You didn't.' Rule number three: no shared morning after breakfast food or beverage of any kind.

'Scrambled eggs on toast,' he said gravely. 'I even let her use my Italian espresso machine!' He put his head in his hands. 'All three golden rules, out the window in one night.'

We sat there in silence for a minute, letting the enormity of the situation sink in. 'And now you think you're having a nervous breakdown?' I said finally.

'I can't think of any other explanation.' A wave of realization washed across his face. 'Unless she's drugged me. Come to think of it, this does remind me of the time I ate half a tin of hash brownies at college . . .'

I rolled my eyes. 'I don't think she drugged you. You know what I do think happened?'

He looked at me beseechingly. 'Please, tell me.'

'I think you might be in love.'

He scoffed. 'Are you mad? I am absolutely *not* in love. I've only just met the girl!'

'You only just met her, and yet you broke all three of your rules for her, and now you're sitting here like a heart-sick puppy. I'd say you're in love.' I couldn't believe it. The day after I lie to Christopher about Ben having some sort of romantic entanglement, and here he was, entangled.

'Honestly, I came to you for genuine help and assistance, and this is what you offer me.'

I shrugged. 'I call them like I see them. What's her name, anyway?'

'Lucy,' he said, slightly dreamily. 'Lucy Claremont.'

'Ooh, good name. Show me a photo!'

He shifted uncomfortably in his seat. 'I don't know that I can find one.'

'Ben, we live in the age of Google. You can find a picture of anything, anytime, anywhere. Right now, if I wanted, I could show you a picture of my fourth-grade teacher's beagle. That's part of technology's terrifying charm.'

'Maybe in a bit,' he said shiftily. 'I should really get back to work.'

He spun around and hit the space bar on his keyboard, and his formerly dark computer screen lit up. I peered around his shoulder and saw a photo of a pretty, pixie-ish blonde with a dimple on one cheek. 'That's her, isn't it? Aha! You've already looked her up!' I crowed.

He looked mortified, as if I'd just caught him looking at Furby porn. 'I just wanted to see if I remember what she looked like!' he cried.

'You only saw her an hour ago!'

I could see the blush surging up past his collar. 'I wanted to double-check, that's all!'

'She's very pretty,' I said gently.

He turned around and gave me a shy smile. 'Isn't she?' He turned back and gazed at her for another moment. 'She's lovely.' He paused for a moment and cleared his throat. 'Who was that bloke you were with last night?'

My heart lodged in my windpipe. 'What guy?' I asked.

'I saw you meet him outside the office. Tall guy, blond. Looked a bit like a sort of cowboy Captain America.'

'Oh, him? He's just an old friend from home.' I wondered, briefly, whether I was going to be sick.

'Here for a visit?'

God, who was this guy? Perry Mason? 'Yep! Just for a week!' My voice went up by an octave – always a telltale sign that I was lying.

'That's nice,' he said. He peered at me closely. 'He doesn't have anything to do with your fight with Christopher, does he?'

Columbo, I thought to myself. He's like Columbo. He even owns a trench coat. 'I told you, I didn't have a fight with Christopher!' I snapped.

He held his hands up. 'Forget I said anything!'

I spun around without saying another word and started clearing my inbox with thunderous speed, the keys clacking beneath my fingers. I felt bad about shutting Ben down like that, but I couldn't bring myself to talk about what was really going on. Not only was I worried about another person knowing about Jackson – I trusted Ben, but another mouth was another mouth – but I needed work to be a place where I didn't think about it. Until Jackson showed up again, that is.

There was a message from Isla waiting for me in my inbox. I double-clicked and it flashed up on my screen.

Soooooo how was your first date with your husband?

I let out a shriek of horror.

'And I thought I was the one having the breakdown,' Ben said over his shoulder. 'What's wrong now?'

'Nothing!'

I hit reply:

1. It wasn't a date 2. Don't use the h-word over email!!!

I hit send and leaned back in my chair. What was wrong with everyone? Had the entire world gone insane?

Isla's response flashed up.

Sorry! From now on will refer to him as Agent Albatross. So how was your date with Agent Albatross?

My fingers flew across the keyboard.

Why Agent Albatross? Also, I hate you.

Agent because it's a secret, Albatross because you can't get rid of him. Aren't I goddamn hilarious? Soooooo . . . ? Are you in LOOOOOVE?

GOD NO. He's just some dumb hick from Texas.

I felt mildly disloyal as I typed out the message, but I couldn't risk her writing stuff like that to me, not even as a joke.

> Well, don't rule him out without giving him a fair shot. You
> know what they say . . . they grow them big in Texas.

> FFS ISLA!

There was a knock at the door of the cubicle. I quickly x'ed out of our email conversation and turned to find my boss leaning against the flimsy plastic wall, hand tucked rakishly in one pocket of an expensive wool blazer. Jeremy was in his late fifties, but was still clinging to the last vestiges of youth almost as tightly as the last few strands of hair artfully combed across top of his head.

'Knock knock,' he said, even though he'd already knocked and I'd already responded by turning around to face him. 'How's my favorite duo doing in here?'

Ben and I beamed up at him like a pair of schoolchildren. 'Good!' we chorused.

Jeremy hitched up his pants and cracked his neck. The sound made a shiver run up my spine. It wasn't that Jeremy was a bad guy. He was actually a nice guy, and a decent boss, too. But there was something about him that was slightly off-putting. His shoes were too shiny. His teeth suspiciously white and even. His skin an unnatural shade of mahogany, despite us just emerging from the long, dark months of an English winter. In short, he looked like he'd been assembled in a factory before being discarded for being slightly irregular.

'I've got a big case coming up,' he said, pointing a pair of finger guns at me.

I sat up straighter in my chair. I relished big cases. 'Really? What is it?'

'An old East End gangster is trying to pull the wool over our eyes with a phony claim.' Whenever Jeremy talked about a case, he sounded as if he was in a Chandler novel. I secretly loved it.

'Ooh! That sounds exciting!' Christopher and I had just watched that Tom Hardy movie about the Krays, so I felt I was up to speed on the whole East End gangster thing. It seemed to involve a lot of mumbling and mindless violence.

'You bet it's exciting. We're talking major property fraud.' He rocked back on his heels. 'And I need my best investigator on the case.'

'Me?' I feigned surprise. The truth was, I knew I was his best investigator, not least because he said as much every time he got a few sherries into him at the Christmas party. Plus, nobody enjoyed snooping around as much as I did. Speaking of which, why hadn't I looked up Jackson yet? I zoned out as Jeremy spoke. He'd told me his last name, hadn't he? What was it again . . . Grant? Gray? Gaines! I had his name and his home town – that should be plenty to dig up some dirt on the guy. Maybe enough so he'd agree to just give me the divorce without all the forced hospitality.

'So you're up for it then?' I momentarily drew a blank. Jeremy stared at me expectantly.

'Jenny, the case . . .' Ben prompted.

'Yes! Sorry! Of course!' I practically shouted.

'Love your enthusiasm, Sparrow. I'll send the details over tomorrow. I can't wait for you to nab this bum!'

He swooped out of the office, leaving a cloud of Aramis behind. Ben and I exchanged a look. 'Christ, I haven't seen old Jezza worked up that much in ages,' Ben said. He cleared his throat and put on a cheesy American accent. 'Looks like you're about to hit the big time, kid.'

'Promise me you will never, ever talk like that again,' I said, dissolving into giggles.

'Hey, what's the idea? Can't a guy talk straight to his dame?'

'God, stop!' I cried. 'It's genuinely painful for me to hear!'

He shrugged and shot me a grin. 'Suit yourself,' he said, spinning back around to his desk. 'Some people can't appreciate talent even when it's being wafted under their nose.'

I rolled my eyes and turned towards my computer. Okay, now to find out who this Jackson guy really was. I opened a new browser, typed his name into Google, and hit return.

I scrolled through the results and my heart sank.

Nada. Zip. Zilch. Not a single match.

Sure, there were a few Jackson Gaines out there. One was a teenager from Southern Florida who seemed to have an unhealthy interest in *Call of Duty*. Another was a man in his sixties whose Facebook feed was peppered with photos of small, intricate wooden animals he'd whittled. Another still was a bearded orthopedist from

Seattle. Absolutely none of them was the man who was now my husband. He was completely off the grid.

A text flashed up on my phone. It was Jackson.

> Have you got gym gear with you?

I stared at the duffel bag under my desk.

> Why?

> I thought we'd do something a little different tonight. If you don't have anything with you, I can run by the shop and grab you something. What size are you?

My fingers flew across the keypad.

> No! I have my gym stuff!

> Great! Meet me in your finest Richard Simmons gear at the Rose and Crown in Stoke Newington at 6:30.

A loud gurgle emerged from my gut.

'You all right over there?' Ben asked, snickering.

'I think I'm going to make myself a cup of tea,' I said. 'Do you want one?'

'Yes please. Not too much milk!'

The tiny alcove that served as the company kitchen was, as ever, covered in the detritus of fifty people's lunches, teas, snacks and coffees. Half a loaf of a sad-looking fruit cake languished on the side table, and I picked at the crumbs as I waited for the kettle to boil.

There was a health and safety poster tacked up to the wall, and I read it for the hundredth time. At the bottom corner was a drawing of a man demonstrating the correct technique for using a fire blanket. Something about him – the smoothness of his brown hair, the straightness of his nose – reminded me of Christopher.

Christopher. The thought of him made my heart ache, and my stomach gave out another plaintive gurgle.

The switch on the kettle flicked up. I stuffed teabags into a pair of mugs and poured hot water over them, watching as it turned a murky brown. I sloshed in some milk and carried the mugs back to our cube.

Ben assessed his tea with a critical eye. 'How long have you lived in this country?'

'Three years,' I said, knowing what was coming next.

'Three years, and you still don't know how to make a decent cup of tea. Honestly, they should make tea-making lessons compulsory for all Americans who move here.'

I rolled my eyes. 'That, and queueing etiquette, I know, I know. I genuinely don't know why I still offer to make you tea.'

He batted his eyelashes at me and smiled. 'Because you love me?'

I sighed. 'Because I'm a glutton for punishment.'

It turns out, Stoke Newington is one of those pretty, leafy parts of London that is virtually impossible to get to. I lost count of the number of transfers I had to make, but by the time the 73 chuntered up to Church Street and deposited me unceremoniously on the doorstep of the Rose and Crown, I was twenty minutes late and in a decidedly terrible mood.

Jackson was leaning against the bar chatting with

the scruffy bartender when I pushed through the door. He gave me a wave, ordered me a beer, and then stood back to take in my outfit. 'Now that is some high performance gear,' he said, taking in the oversized T-shirt I'd got free with a magazine six years ago and the pair of H&M leggings I'd washed so many times they were practically translucent. 'Are you sponsored by Nike or something?'

'Shut up,' I said, swatting him on the arm. 'You don't exactly look like Usain Bolt.' Jackson was wearing a pair of paint-flecked cargo shorts and a marl-gray T-shirt with a ripped neck. 'What is up with you and cargo pants, anyway? Who needs that many pockets?'

'Always be prepared,' he said, giving me the three-fingered Boy Scout salute. The scruffy bartender clocked it as he set my pint down on the drip mat and shot him a quizzical look.

'So what are we doing here, anyway? Why are we having a drink in our gym stuff in the middle of nowhere?'

'Dutch courage,' he said, eyes twinkling irritatingly.

I paused, my pint halfway to my lips. 'Why do we need Dutch courage?'

'You'll see!' He tapped the side of his nose with his finger and I fought the urge to slug him.

We finished our drinks and headed out to whatever fresh hell Jackson had waiting for us. We threaded our way through a park still full of post-work picnickers sipping warm Prosecco and tucking into Whole Foods bags. Joggers huffed past people walking their dogs, and little kids pedalling their first bicycles. 'Where are we going?' I kept asking, but Jackson would just ignore me and point out another cute dog. Distraction tactics.

Finally, we spilled out of the park and onto a main road. 'There,' Jackson said, pointing ahead. 'That's where we're going.'

I followed his finger and found myself staring at what looked very much like a castle. It was a squat, hulking, medieval-looking thing, built in red brick and topped with what was indisputably a turret. All that was missing was a moat and a drawbridge. My geography wasn't great, but even I knew that it was a little odd to find a castle in the middle of North London. 'What the hell is that?' I asked, eyes wide.

'Crazy, right? I think it used to be a pumping station.'

'But . . . why is it built like a castle?' Another, more pressing question occurred to me. 'And why are we here?'

'It's a climbing center!' he announced gleefully.

I stopped dead in my tracks. 'Absolutely not.'

'Come on!' He laughed and tugged on my arm.

I leaned back on my heels. 'There is no way I'm climbing anything. Period.'

He turned and looked at me. He must have seen the fear on my face because he stopped laughing. 'Hey. What's the matter?'

'I'm scared of heights,' I admitted. That was an under-statement. I held my breath when I crossed a bridge. I refused to climb past the first rung of a ladder. Even step stools made me a little nervous.

'Hell, most people are scared of heights,' he said.

'Not like me.'

'I promise you this is totally safe. You're strapped in the whole time, and it's not even that high up.'

'I'm not doing it.'

'All right,' he sighed. 'I can't force you. But now that we've come all the way here, do you mind if I have a quick climb? There are sofas inside, so you can just sit there and read your book or whatever. I'll even buy you a flapjack.'

'Fine,' I grumbled. Really, though, I was just relieved that I was off the hook.

I followed him in and watched him pay admission for the two of us. 'Just in case you change your mind,' he said as he handed me my ticket.

The inside of the castle smelled like chalk dust and sweaty feet and testosterone, but not in an entirely negative way. Jackson sat me down on one of the beat-up sofas upstairs that faced the tall climbing wall, got me the promised flapjack, squeezed his feet into a pair of what looked like skin-tight galoshes, clipped into a harness that put a little more emphasis on his groin than I was strictly comfortably with, and promptly skittered up the wall like a squirrel.

He'd clearly done this before.

He belayed back down and landed elegantly. 'You sure you're not tempted?' he asked, nodding up towards the top.

I shook my head and held up my half-eaten flapjack. 'I'm good, thanks.'

He shrugged as he clapped a little more chalk dust onto his hands. 'Suit yourself.'

He did a couple more runs up the wall before hefting himself down on the sofa next to me. I could smell the sweat on his skin mixing with his aftershave. 'I'm about ready to go,' he said, wiping his hands down the front of his T-shirt. 'Unless you want to give it a try?'

I shook my head and folded my arms across my chest. 'I told you already. No.'

'What's got you so scared, anyway?'

My heart pounded just thinking about it. I could still remember it so clearly. My fingers losing their grip. The breeze lifting the hair around my face. The feeling of weightlessness. The sickening thud. 'Nothing,' I said quietly.

He sighed and leaned back into the cushions. 'I know about the tree.'

He said it so quietly that at first I thought I'd misheard him. 'What did you say?'

'I know you fell out of that tree when you were little.'

That was impossible. No one knew about that other than my mom and Isla, and I'd sworn Isla to secrecy at the time. 'I don't know what you're talking about.'

'Come on, Jenny. Cut the crap. You told me about it that night in Vegas – about how you were climbing that big tree in your front yard, and your mother—'

'Stop.' I didn't want to hear it. I already knew the rest. We were silent for a moment. 'I told you that?' I asked finally.

'Yeah, you did. That's why I brought you here. I thought . . .' He shook his head. 'It was stupid.'

'What did you think?'

'I thought I could help you get over your fear. Show you there's nothing to be afraid of.'

'There's always something to be afraid of,' I snapped. Then, more softly, 'When it comes to heights, I mean. You could fall. Break something.' My hand went instinctively to my wrist. I could still feel the little spur of bone sticking up from where it had healed badly.

'That's the thing,' he said. 'You can't break anything here. You'd be strapped into a harness, and I'd be spotting you the whole time. If you fall, I'll catch you.'

I rolled my eyes. 'No offense, but I can't say you're the most trustworthy guy I've ever met.'

He looked genuinely offended. 'What's that supposed to mean?'

'I mean . . .' I struggled to find the words and failed. What did I mean? How did I know the guy wasn't trustworthy? I'd told him about the tree. That had to count for something, even if I'd been ninety-five sheets to the wind at the time. And he had made climbing up that wall look kind of fun. Maybe I could do it. Maybe I could at least try. 'Be brave for me, Jenny.' That's what my mom had said to me. Maybe it was time I tried to be brave for myself. I looked him in the eye. 'You promise I won't kill myself up there?'

He grinned. 'Scouts' honour.'

The process of putting on a harness was mildly humiliating, and the new climbing shoes Jackson had produced from his backpack pinched my pinky toes, but I still felt a flutter of excitement as I placed my hand on the first hold. 'Like this?' I asked, looking back at Jackson.

'That's right,' he said, nodding encouragingly. 'Just go for it. Do whatever feels comfortable. I got you.'

146

It was hard. Jesus Christ, it was hard. By the time I'd grabbed onto the fifth hold, my fingers were screaming and my left foot was lodged precariously into a crack on the ledge. But there was something beautiful about it, too. It was like trying to solve a logic puzzle with your body. There wasn't room to think about anything other than where you were going to next place your hands.

I made it three-quarters of the way up when it happened. My hand reached up for the hold, but I couldn't get a grip on it, and suddenly I was falling. That same sickening feeling of weightlessness from all those years ago. I opened my mouth to scream, but before I could, I felt a tug on my harness. I stopped mid-flight and started soaring instead. 'I got you,' Jackson hollered up at me. 'Don't worry, I got you.' I looked down to see him holding the rope. He started lowering me down slowly.

'You okay?' he asked, when my feet finally touched the ground.

I was a little shaky, but elation quickly overtook my nerves. 'I did it!' I beamed. 'I can't believe it, but I did it!'

Jackson winked at me and smiled. 'I knew you would. Now, what do you say we go back to the Rose and Crown and have a celebratory drink?' He saw me hesitate. 'Unless you want to call it a night? I can order you a cab from here . . .'

'No,' I said, shaking my head. 'I think we deserve a drink. But do you mind if I do another run up the wall first?'

His laugh echoed around the room, and a few of the more solemn-looking climbers shot us disapproving looks. 'Lady,' he said, clipping me back into the harness, 'you can climb that wall as many times as you like.'

I crept into the darkened flat, wincing as the floorboards creaked beneath my weight. My head felt fuzzy from all the post-climbing celebratory beer, and I wanted, very badly, to crawl into bed, close my eyes, and lose myself to sleep.

'Jenny? Is that you?' I heard the sound of a light being switched on in the other room and then Christopher's footsteps as he padded out to the hall. He appeared in the doorway, squinty and rumpled from sleep. He was wearing a pair of boxer shorts and an old Arsenal top he'd had since he was a kid. I knew that because he'd told me the story of his grandfather buying it for him before a match one day, the same day that his grandfather allowed Christopher to try a pint. More importantly, I knew that because it was the sort of thing you knew about someone you'd shared six years of your life with and lived with for the past three. The guilt made my stomach clench, and I wondered whether Jackson wouldn't lose yesterday's bet after all.

'Hi!' I said brightly. I could feel the strain in my voice.

'You're home late,' he said, leaning in to kiss me. His chin was sandpapery with stubble and he tasted of toothpaste.

'Sorry, I didn't mean to wake you.'

He made a face. 'You stink.'

I pulled away from him. 'I told you I was sorry.'

'No, I mean you actually, literally stink.' He leaned in and took a sniff. 'Is this from spinning?'

'Spinning?' Shit. I'd told him I was going to a spin class.

'Oh, spinning! Yeah, probably. We really worked up a sweat.' I wiped a hand across my metaphorical brow.

He frowned. 'You smell like something else, too. Like old cheese or something.'

'Gee, thanks.'

He leaned in for another sniff. The man was a lawyer. He would not be deterred when he sniffed something funny. Even, apparently, in the most literal sense. 'Why do you smell like a blackboard?'

'Let's go to bed!' I shouted. We both started at the sound. 'Sorry,' I said, more quietly this time. 'I'm just totally wiped out.'

'From all the spinning,' he said, arching an eyebrow.

'Exactly.'

'Well, can you at least take a shower before you get into bed? Seriously, I don't think I can stomach a night of that smell.'

The bathroom floor was icy, and I shivered as I waited for the water to heat up. The air still carried the faint smell of Christopher's aftershave, and I breathed it in. I stared at the contents of the open cabinet. Deodorant. The three-step Korean skincare routine I spent a fortune on and never use. The face wipes I actually use. The toothpaste. The tweezers. The floss.

The anti-fungal cream.

I checked the water temperature: finally warm. I stepped into the shower. We'd replaced the shower head a few months ago, but the water still came out at a pathetic trickle, and once I'd lathered up it took for ever to rinse the suds away.

As I waited, my mind returned to the anti-fungal cream in the cabinet. Poor Christopher and his chronic athlete's foot. Living with someone wasn't always glamorous. There were blenders coated with the remains of a wheat-grass smoothie, crusted socks balled up in the laundry, sly gas in bed that stank up the sheets . . . But there was security, too, and comfort, and that's what I wanted more than anything. I had to remember that.

I thought about Jackson and his freewheeling lifestyle. Rootless, sure, but exciting. But I'd already had my wild years – I had to remember that, too. I'd had it marked out on my list. And from the age of nineteen to twenty-one, I'd been the party girl in short skirts and thigh-high boots doing shots with frat boys. Twenty-two through twenty-four were about frivolous dating in New York, which turned out to be slightly less fun than my thirteen-year-old self had envisioned. (Have you heard the thing about there being two single women for every single man in NYC? Have you also heard that all of those other women are basically supermodels? Because from my experience, they are.) But those years were mine to waste. That's what my aunt and I had worked out. She could give me those years, but she couldn't give me for ever. I had until I was twenty-five to be young, and after that I'd get serious and settle down. She needed help with my mom, and I had to give it to her.

Twenty-five was when I'd met Christopher. Like clock-work, really. There I was, standing on a street corner in the West Village trying to hail a taxi on a Saturday night, when a cab pulled up a block away. I'd bolted down the street, arms waving wildly in the hope of catching the driver's attention, but my heel caught on a subway vent, and suddenly I was flying through the air. I landed, hard, right outside the taxi's door, and out stepped Christopher, face etched with concern.

'God, are you all right?' he'd asked in that perfect accent of his, and in an instant I'd forgotten about my bloodied knees and the taxi and the blind date who was waiting for me uptown.

'I'm fine,' I'd said, but I knew that I was better than fine. I was on the threshold of crossing another thing off my list. Number 19: Meet the man of my dreams at twenty-five. And here he was, twinkling down at me as I lay on the sidewalk. And British, too! Number 17 on my list popped into my head: Live in a foreign country. This guy was a stone capable of taking out multiple birds. I canceled my date, and, after a quick trip to Rite Aid for band-aids, the two of us went out for drinks, and that, basically, was that.

And now, here I was, living with him and about to marry him. (Number 25: tick! Number 27: almost tick!) Forget about the goddamn anti-fungal cream – this was everything I'd wanted! Besides, it was time. I was thirty-one. It was in the plan. An unstructured life was one step away from chaos, and I'd spent my entire life avoiding chaos.

I turned off the water and toweled off. My legs goosepimpled as soon as I stepped back onto the cold bathroom floor. I wondered what time it was. Late, probably. Nearly midnight. I had to be up early, too. If I was lucky, I'd get six and a half hours of sleep that night. Really, I needed eight. Mild anxiety hummed through me as I thought about how tired I'd be tomorrow.

Jackson wouldn't keep track of the hours he slept, counting them out and hoarding them like a miser. The thought popped into my head, unwelcome as a boil. I shook it away. Who cared what Jackson would do?

I threw my damp hair up into a bun, pulled on a T-shirt and a pair of shorts, and climbed into bed. Christopher was already fast asleep, his chest gently rising and falling, a light whistle emanating from his nose with every exhalation.

I pulled up the covers and tucked myself into his side, wrapping my arm across his chest. 'You're freezing,' he murmured, taking my hand in his.

Yes, I thought, as I drifted off. This is where I'm meant to be.

11

The next morning, I arrived at work early thanks to last night's shower and a mercifully quiet Northern Line, and by nine o'clock, armed with a strong cup of coffee and a biscuit stolen from the tea-point tin, I was ready to dig in to the new case files Jeremy had left on my desk. Ben wasn't in yet, so the office was quiet, with just the dull hum of the comfort cooling system for company.

I scanned through the basics of the case. A cobbler's in Columbia Road had burned down, gutting the shop and causing serious damage to the flat above. It was an owner-occupied building, the cobbler living upstairs and coming down each morning to work in the shop. Along with re-heeling the soles of Hackney's hipsters and bankers, he also cut keys and repaired leather goods. He was claiming that the fire had been caused by an electrical fault, but the initial case manager had suspicions that he'd set the fire on purpose to collect the money. Cobbling wasn't exactly a booming trade these days, and with property values being what they were in London, he was set to get a healthy pay-out. Whether he deserved that pay-out was the question I had to answer.

I clicked on the cobbler's biography and scrolled through it. Full name: Edward Bryant. Age: 63. Pretty close to retirement age. He'd been born in Hackney, and from the looks of it, he'd lived there his whole life. He'd bought the shop forty-one years ago and had been there ever since. I checked his marital status. Widowed. Poor old Edward Bryant, all alone in his shoe shop. Still, it could be another reason to cut his losses. Maybe he had an eye on a nice place in Spain. A new life in the sun for himself.

I flicked through the photographs Mr Bryant had sent through as evidence. The extent of the damage was pretty clear – the shop had been gutted entirely, just a blackened skeleton remaining, and the flat upstairs was grayed and grimed from smoke damage. Definitely uninhabitable. Probably a tear-down.

The next set of photographs showed what the flat had looked like before and . . . I had to say, it wasn't exactly a bed of roses. The shop looked musty and tattered, and the flat upstairs was locked firmly in the 1970s, down to the avocado-green bathroom suite. If he'd put it on the market before the fire, he would have got below market rate. People looking to move to Columbia Road had serious money these days, and they wanted something that was already modernized and high-spec. The laminate kitchen cabinets alone would be enough to send most of them screaming towards the nearest artisanal bakery for a soothing turmeric latte.

If he'd wanted to make serious cash, the fire made sense. Burn the place down, collect the money, rebuild and sell it to the highest bidder. Or sell the land to a hungry developer . . .

I drummed my fingers on the desk. I glanced through his file again. Widowed. He was widowed . . . I typed his wife's name into our database and a record popped up. Mrs Victoria Bryant, died aged fifty-seven from bowel cancer, poor woman. She'd held a life insurance policy with the company for nearly thirty years, and the full pay out – a whopping £150,000 – was paid to a single benefactor. Mr Edward Bryant.

I leaned back in my chair. Well, he sure didn't need the money. At least he shouldn't need it. Maybe he had a gambling problem? I'd need to do more research before I could draw any concrete conclusions.

I was planning my next step when Ben slid open the cubicle door and sloped inside. He grunted at me, threw his rucksack in a corner, and slumped into his chair with a long, pained sigh. With his tufty hair and big, sad brown eyes, he was a double for Eeyore.

'Nice to see you, too,' I said, stifling a laugh. 'Long night last night?'

He shook his head, morose. 'Just went to football. I was home by ten.'

'Then why do you look like someone's just peed in your cornflakes?'

Another protracted sigh. 'She's ignoring me.'

I looked at him. He really did look awful. His eyes were red-rimmed and rheumy, and his hair disheveled. He was even wearing a pair of regular fit, medium-wash jeans – a clear sign that he was not in his right mind. 'You just saw her yesterday morning, didn't you?'

He threw his head back in despair. 'I know!' he cried. 'God, it feels like it was ages ago. She's probably forgotten all about me.'

'Ben, get a grip. How can she already be ignoring you?'

'Because,' he said, exasperated, 'I sent her a text on my way to football yesterday, and she still hasn't replied.'

I shook my head. 'Jesus, you really have lost it over her.'

He shot me a dark look. 'I appreciate the sympathy.'

'No! I mean, I get it. You obviously like her a lot. But . . . it's only nine thirty in the morning. Give the woman a chance to have a cup of coffee before you assume she's ditched you.'

'She could have texted back last night!'

I shrugged. 'Maybe she was busy.'

'With WHO? That's what I want to know.' He ground his fists into his eyes. 'Why is she doing this to me?'

I wheeled my chair over to his and put my hands on his shoulders. 'Ben! You seriously need to calm down right now, because you are acting crazier than a box of frogs. I know you like her, and it sounds like she likes you, too. Just cut her a little slack, okay? Maybe she hasn't texted you back yet because she doesn't want to seem too keen.'

'But why would she want to do that?'

I sighed. He was so young, and had so much to learn. 'Because women are basically trained that the only way a guy will like us is if we pretend not to like them.'

His eyes widened. 'Seriously?'

'Of course! We spend our whole lives hearing that no man wants a woman who's too available, that we should "treat 'em mean and keep 'em keen". Hell, Sleeping Beauty had to be knocked unconscious before Prince Charming noticed her!'

Ben shook his head, causing an avalanche of curls to fall into his eyes. He really needed to get some product in that hen's nest of his. 'I would never be interested in a woman just because she didn't seem interested in me. That's so shallow.'

My jaw dropped. 'Please do not tell me you just said that.'

He looked at me, eyes wide with innocence. 'What? I wouldn't!'

'What about the time you went on a date with a woman and she asked what your last name was?'

His face darkened. 'Why did she need to know? I ask you!'

'And the time you deleted a woman's number because she had the audacity to ask if you wanted her spare ticket to The Black Keys?'

He scowled. 'She was practically stalking me.'

'Ben, she wasn't even asking you to go to the concert with her. She was just asking if you wanted to buy the ticket off her.'

'That's what she said,' he grumbled. 'Who knows what she was planning?'

'You see?' I hooted. 'You're totally put off by a woman who shows interest in you!'

He shrugged, pouting slightly. 'Fine, maybe I do like a bit of a chase usually. But not when it comes to Lucy. I don't want to have to chase her. I just want her to . . . be with me.' He looked so sweet then, like a little boy asking Santa for his Christmas wish.

'I'm sure she feels the same way,' I said gently. 'But you might have to do just a little chasing before you two can go full-on Netflix-and-takeaway.'

He gave me a withering look. 'It's Netflix and chill.'

I gave him a withering look right back. 'Which one of us has been in a serious relationship before? Trust me, Netflix-and-takeaway is the more accurate description.'

'Thanks for that searing glimpse into your personal life,' he said, rolling his eyes. 'Trust me, with Lucy it'll be all chill and very little takeaway.'

'Go ahead,' I said, 'think whatever you want now. But don't think I won't say I told you so when she pulls out the de-elasticated sweatpants.'

His eyes filmed over with a faraway look. 'I bet she'd look ace in sweatpants . . .'

I shook my head in disbelief. 'You really are a lost cause.'

I was scribbling notes about the case on my yellow legal pad when a message flashed up on my phone. It was Jackson.

> Meet me outside Westminster Abbey at 7:30 tonight. I've
> got a plan.

I groaned inwardly. Every Londoner knew what an absolute tourist clusterfuck it was around Westminster Abbey and the Houses of Parliament. The sidewalks were clogged full of people staring open-mouthed at Big Ben or unfolding enormous maps and staring at them ponderously. I'd been once, when my mom had come to visit during my first year here, but the experience had been enough to convince me not to return.

> Can we meet literally anywhere else?

I hit send and heard the text whoosh off into the ether. My phone beeped straight away with his response.

I let out an involuntary cry of despair and threw my phone into my bag.

Ben glanced at me over his shoulder. 'You all right?'

'Fine,' I muttered.

'Of course you are,' he said, sighing deeply. 'You're loved.'

'Oh my God,' I cried. 'Stop! I told you this morning, she'll text you when she's ready!'

'I might be dead by then,' he said glumly.

It went on all day. Every time Ben's phone chirruped – which, considering he was an active user of every form of social media available, was often – I'd hear him scrabble to grab it, followed by a long, deep sigh of despair when he realized it wasn't Lucy. Frankly, it was a medical miracle that he hadn't collapsed a lung with the amount of air he was forcefully exhaling.

The rest of the day passed in a blur, though not a particularly productive one. Between fielding Ben's bouts of melancholy, and frequent 'Knock knocks!' from Jeremy, asking about progress on the case, I'd barely had time to take a breath before I heard the rustle and murmur of people around us shutting down for the day and asking each other about evening plans.

It was in the process of shutting my own computer off when I realized I hadn't told Christopher that I wouldn't be home for dinner. I was racking my brains for an excuse – work event? Spontaneous tennis match? Trip to the emergency room? – when a text flashed up on my phone. It was Christopher.

I'm out with my running club tonight so don't wait up. xx ps
can you defrost the pack of salmon in the freezer?

My body sagged with relief. Nights out with his running mates tended to be extremely boozy. I think they convinced themselves that downing pints of lager served as carb loading. Regardless, it meant he wouldn't be home until at least midnight, at which point I'd be back from whatever crazy dinner Jackson had planned for us and safely tucked up in bed.

I sent a treacherous frowny-faced emoji as a response. Did it fill me with guilt? Yes. But I didn't have time to dwell on it. I had to meet my husband at Westminster Abbey.

The crowds were as thick as I'd expected. A horde of Italian teenagers almost pushed me into oncoming traffic, and I was very nearly impaled on a series of errant selfie sticks. I sighed and tutted my way through it all. No matter how long I lived here, I'd never get used to the crush of tourists that descended on us year-round. New York was bad enough – Times Square notably the ninth circle of hell – but at least you could avoid most of it if you wanted to. Here in London, thanks to the constant barrage of beautiful and historically significant buildings, there was no escaping. Bloomsbury, Piccadilly Circus, Regents Park, Camden Town, Borough Market: all up to their eyeballs in poncho-wearing slow-walkers. It was maddening.

As if to punctuate my point, I was about to cross Great Smith Street when I ran smack into a bunch of middle-aged

Japanese men in bright-yellow rain slickers (chance of rain today: zero per cent), all of them rooted in place, heads tilted up towards the sky. I was about to shove past, when my gaze followed theirs and I stopped dead in my tracks.

The lights. My God, the lights.

The front of Westminster Abbey was a riot of luminous color. Strips of blue ran up either side of the building's face, framing the illuminated figures of the statuettes mounted above the great doors. The muted gray stone figures of the saints were now painted in vivid purples and blues and reds, their heads ringed in glowing gold. It was breathtaking, like Christmas on steroids. The sort of vision that makes you believe in miracles.

One of the Japanese men turned to me and beamed. 'Pretty incredible, huh?'

I nodded mutely.

I felt my phone vibrate in my bag. It was Jackson.

I'm under the column with the lady on top!

I threaded my way through the Japanese men, apologizing as I went, and dashed across Dean's Yard and over to the column, where Jackson was holding an expensive-looking camera and looking out across the crowd.

'Isn't it incredible?' he shouted as I came closer.

I couldn't stop myself from smiling at him. 'It's amazing!'

We stood there for a minute, mute, and let the lights wash over us.

'You ready?' he asked. I nodded. 'Come on,' he said, tugging at my arm. 'There's more to see.'

We pushed our way through the thronging crowds and made our way onto Westminster Bridge. The morning had kept its promise, and the evening still held a residual sweet warmth even though the sun had set. The crowds made it impossible to have a conversation, so Jackson led the way and I followed, the memory of the lights still dancing behind my eyes.

The good mood didn't last long. We were halfway across the bridge when he stopped abruptly, sending me flying into the back of his denim jacket. 'What are you doing?' I asked, rubbing my shoulder.

'Will you look at this?' he said, pointing at something across the Thames.

A passing woman lodged a sharp elbow into my ribcage. The familiar rage returned. 'It's too busy to stop,' I snapped. 'We can look on the other side.'

He shook his head. 'You've got to look now.'

I sighed and stared out over the sparkling black water. 'What am I looking at?'

'Wait a minute. It'll come back.'

I sighed again and folded my arms across my chest. 'Honestly, only tourists stop here—' And then I saw it. A brilliant green flash coming from underneath the water's surface. 'What is that?'

'Just watch.'

The green glow grew more intense, more distinct, until we were both staring down at the glimmering outline of a mermaid swishing through the Thames.

'Are – are you seeing what I'm seeing?' I stuttered.

'I sure am. Beautiful, isn't it?'

162

'This is genuinely insane. Isn't this insane?' I looked at Jackson for confirmation that yes, what we were looking at was insane, but he was too caught up in the moment to take any notice. 'How is this happening?' I said finally.

'The lights,' he said, nodding back towards the abbey. 'They're everywhere tonight, all across London. I'd heard that there was going to be something in the Thames, too, but I didn't expect it to be so . . .'

'Magical.'

He looked over at me and smiled. 'That's right,' he said. 'Magical. You hungry?'

I nodded. 'Starving.'

'Great. How do you feel about tacos?'

'I feel good about tacos.'

We headed down to the South Bank, where the London Eye had been lit to look like . . . well, like an actual eye, complete with glowing purple iris in the center. The Royal Festival Hall had been made to look like an enormous cruise ship, with iridescent waves licking at its hull. Outside the BFI, huge stalks of green LED lights reached up to the sky, capped with brilliant petals in oranges and reds and pinks.

'This is incredible,' I murmured as we ducked under the illuminated frame of a flying angel.

'It's an incredible city,' he said, shooting me a grin. 'You just have to look out for it.'

The taco place was less a restaurant and more an old silver Air Streamer parked up behind the Hayward Gallery. Jackson rubbed his hands together as he looked at the menu scrawled on a chalkboard next to the service hatch. 'You know what you want?' he asked.

I scanned the options. 'Maybe the chicken?'

He shook his head. 'No way are you getting some lame chicken taco on my watch.' He turned to the man in the stained apron waiting to take our order. 'We'll take two pulled pork tacos, extra jalapeños, extra crackling, extra cheese.'

I thought of how long it had been since I'd made it to the gym. 'No cheese for me,' I piped up.

Jackson gave me a withering look. 'No self-respecting taco eater asks for no cheese.' He turned back to the man in the apron. 'Ignore her, she doesn't know what she wants.'

Anger flared inside me. 'Actually, I do know what I want, thank you. I'm a grown woman and I can order a goddamn taco without your help.' The man in the apron's eyebrows shot up. 'I'll have a chicken taco, please, no jalapeños, no cheese, extra lettuce and avocado.'

Jackson rolled his eyes. 'That's just a salad in a taco shell.'

'Well maybe I like salad in a taco shell! Did you ever think of that?'

The aproned man's head receded back into the Air Streamer. 'Your tacos will be ready in five,' he called.

Jackson and I stared at each other, our arms folded tightly across our chests, our breath coming out as steam in the cold evening air. 'You have got some nerve,' I fumed.

Jackson heaved out an irritated sigh. 'Here we go . . . You know, what's so wrong about me trying to feed you something delicious?'

'Because you're steamrolling over what I want, that's what! I mean, look at the other night – I told you I don't like spicy foods, and you take me to a curry house.'

'You liked it, didn't you?'

'That's beside the point! You knew I was scared of heights, and you took me to a climbing center!'

'Which, again, you liked! I'm just trying to get you out of your comfort zone a little, that's all.'

'Well, maybe I don't want to get out of my comfort zone!' We glared at each other. 'The point,' I said finally, 'is that you seem convinced that you know what's best for me better than I do, and that's patronizing.'

'Well, I don't know that you do know what's best for you,' he said quietly.

'Excuse me? I am a grown woman. I have a great job, a growing pension, a degree from a very good college, and a successful, attractive fiancé, all of which I managed to achieve without your help.'

'"Successful, attractive fiancé." Man, the passion just pours off of you in waves, doesn't it? How is Christopher, anyway?'

'I told you, I don't want to talk about Christopher.'

He tilted his head up to the sky and blew out his cheeks. 'I didn't come here to fight. Look, I'm sorry I was steamrolling you on the taco front. Please just accept my apology and let's get back to having a nice time tonight.'

He looked pained, and, I had to admit, genuinely remorseful. I felt a jolt of sympathy for him. 'Okay,' I said reluctantly. 'But no more ordering for me. I'm not some mail-order bride you can boss around.'

He grinned. 'You're right about that. If I had a whole catalog of brides to choose from, you can guarantee I wouldn't pick one who's as big of a pain in the behind as you are.'

I reached out and whacked him on the arm. The tension between us cleared as quickly as it had gathered, like the thunderstorms we used to have in New Jersey at the height of summer. 'Did you take lots of photos of the lights?' I asked, pointing at the camera swaying around his neck.

He nodded. 'Want to see?'

He tilted the screen of the camera towards me and clicked view. A photo flashed up of a young couple, arms wrapped tightly around each other, faces tipped up, looks of absolute joy stretched across their faces. I looked up at Jackson. 'Who are they?' I asked.

He shrugged. 'No idea.' He clicked on the next one, this time of a man carrying his small son on his shoulders. They were both wearing identical plaid button-downs, and both of them had the same look on their broad, round faces – that same absolute, uncomplicated joy.

I took the camera from his hands and started flicking through. All of the photos were the same – people in the crowd looking up, faces beaming and awestruck and childlike in their happiness. 'Didn't you take any of the lights?'

'I sure did.' He took the camera from my hands, clicked a few times on one of the buttons, and handed it back to me. It was the little boy from the second photo, but Jackson had zoomed in so that all you could see now were his

166

eyes. And in his eyes was a perfect reflection of the kalei-doscopic color of the lights.

'Incredible,' I murmured.

'Order up!' called the man in the stained apron. He held two tinfoil-wrapped parcels through the hatch. 'That'll be eight pounds.'

Jackson peeled off a ten-pound note and handed it to him. 'Keep the change,' he said, and then handed me my taco. 'Cheers,' he said, clinking his taco to mine.

I unpeeled a corner of the foil and took a bite. It was good – the chicken was juicy and blackened from the grill, the avocado creamy, and the lettuce nice and crisp – but something was missing. I turned back to the aproned man. 'Excuse me, do you have any hot sauce?'

'On the side,' he said, nodding towards a condiment station set up on a little metal folding table.

'Am I seeing things?' Jackson asked as I shook a few drops of Mexican Devil on my taco. 'Have I died and gone to I Told You So heaven?'

'Shut up,' I said in between mouthfuls. 'I don't want to hear another gloating word out of you.'

'Just hang on one second,' he said. 'Here, take a bite.' He held out his taco, and I grudgingly pulled a little bit off the end with my fingers and stuck it in my mouth. It was infuriatingly delicious, way better than my chicken taco (which did indeed look like just a salad in a taco shell compared to his, even with the Mexican Devil's help). I tried to mask my enjoyment as I swallowed. 'So? What do you think?' There was a triumphant glint in his eye. Dammit. I'd been outed.

'It's not bad,' I shrugged. 'A little greasy.'

The man in the apron leaned his head out of the window. 'Did you just call my tacos greasy?' He looked very angry.

'No!' I demurred. 'Of course not! They're delicious!'

'You're damn right they are,' he huffed, before turning to clean down his grill.

Jackson smirked at me. 'You really do know how to make friends, don't you?'

'Just call me Miss Congeniality.' I polished off the rest of my taco, crumpled up the foil, and tossed it in the bin. 'Well, dinner's finished. So what's next?'

He licked the last of the hot sauce off his fingers and winked. 'What comes after all good meals?' he asked. 'Dessert!'

We hailed a taxi at Waterloo and hurtled our way through Covent Garden. The theatres hadn't yet emptied, so the streets were fairly quiet, peopled with the occasional strolling couple or group of colleagues making their way back to the Tube after a post-work session in the pub. I stared out the window at the passing shops, each one lit up like a stage and filled with mannequins striking poses in shorts and flimsy dresses.

Summer would be here before I knew it, and by the end of it, I'd be married. I tried to picture myself walking down the aisle in a long white gown, clutching a bouquet and beaming at a waiting Christopher, but my mind couldn't quite make it real. I'd envisioned marrying him for so long, but now that it was close, I couldn't bring myself to do anything about it. It was as if I was stuck in a state of suspended wedding animation. Maybe I'd waited too long. Dwelled on it too much. And now we were so behind with our plans . . . I would get on it tomorrow, I promised myself.

The cab sped up through Seven Dials, around the little roundabout filled with people standing outside bars, smoking cigarettes in their shirtsleeves, and pretending they weren't cold. I looked over at Jackson, who was also staring out of the window, lost in thought. 'Where are we going again?' I asked, though he hadn't told me in the first place.

He started at the sound of my voice. He really had been zoning out. He recovered himself quickly and shot me a wink. 'Cool your jets,' he said. 'We'll be there in a couple of minutes.'

We pulled up to a café on Frith Street. There was a green awning stretched across the front, under which sat a line of small metal tables and chairs. A clock jutted out from the side of the building, the name of the place – Bar Italia – picked out in neon lights above it, and on the street in front, a row of candy-colored Vespas sat patiently awaiting their riders. It looked like a café you'd find down a backstreet in Rome, or in a Fellini film. Definitely not in the middle of London.

'What is this place?' I asked.

'It does the best macchiato in the city,' Jackson said, opening the door and ushering me in, 'and a tiramisu that will make you go weak at the knees.'

The inside of the café matched the exterior – all 1950s

169

Italian charm. The room was long and narrow, with tables packed closely against one side. The walls were covered with framed photographs and newspaper clippings and mementos from the old country. Above us, a huge Italian flag hung across the length of the ceiling. The main event, though, was the long marble bar, at the end of which an enormous red Gaggia hissed and banged and whizzed as the white-shirted bartenders made endless perfect espressos.

One of them looked up at us and cocked an eyebrow. 'Inside or out?'

'Out,' Jackson said, before looking over at me nervously. 'I mean, if outside's okay with you . . .'

'Sure.' I appreciated that he'd finally asked for my opinion, but after the taco incident I was starting to suspect that he really did know better than me when it came to these things.

The bartender pouted artfully and thrust a pair of laminated menus at us.

'We don't need those,' I said, pushing them back across the bar. 'We'll have two macchiatos and a tiramisu to share.'

'Make that two tiramisu,' Jackson added. 'Trust me, you won't want to share.'

The bartender nodded towards the tables outside. 'Sit. I'll bring to you when ready,' he said.

We nabbed the last available table and sat down with happy sighs, tucking our bags by our feet. Jackson raised an eyebrow at me. 'You don't need to look at the menu, huh?'

I shrugged. 'You said the tiramisu was good.'

'And now you're taking my word all of the sudden?'

'Don't get a big head about it.'

All of the chairs were arranged so that they looked out on the street, so we sat side by side in silence and watched the parade of people stream past. The light festival had bled into Soho, and above us huge illuminated clouds seemed to float between the Georgian terraces. Even though it was a Wednesday night, the streets were thronged with people tumbling out of restaurants after a boozy meal, or huddled against the side of pubs, smoking cigarettes and clutching pints in plastic glasses.

It was too cold for it, really – back in New York, you'd never find people desperate to stand outside in fifty-degree weather – but Londoners took any dry, non-frigid night as an invitation, and the light festival had brought even more people out than usual. Couples and groups of friends wandered past, fingers entwined, gazing up at the brightly lit clouds, and smiling as though they couldn't believe their luck.

In the distance, we heard the beat of drums and the faint chime of bells, and as it grew closer we saw that it was a band of Hare Krishnas, heads closely shaved, dressed in bright shades of orange and white, dancing up Old Compton Street and chanting at the top of their lungs. A few passers-by joined in with them, clapping their hands and stomping their feet as their friends took photos with their phones. Suddenly, out of one of the pubs charged a man dressed in an enormous Bart Simpson costume, complete with inflatable skateboard, who took his place at the head of the parade. His friends appeared in the doorway of the pub and shouted encouragement, and soon the Hare Krishnas had gathered around him, arms thrown around Bart's plush shoulders, and they made their way singing and dancing up through to Shaftesbury Avenue.

I glanced over at Jackson's face and saw a look of pure delight etched across it. He turned to me and shook his head. 'Only in London,' he said.

'What do you think that guy was doing in a Bart Simpson costume?'

He shrugged. 'Bachelor party, I guess. You know how nuts the Brits go for those things. I once went to one—' he stopped himself. 'Nah, never mind.'

'What were you going to say?' I prompted.

He shook his head. 'It's not for polite company.'

I hooted with laughter. 'I am hardly polite company. C'mon, tell me! I promise I won't judge.'

He hesitated for a minute before leaning towards me conspiratorially. 'Let's just say that it ended with a guy straddling one of the lions in Trafalgar Square.'

I wrinkled my nose. 'So what? People do that all the time.'

'Ah,' he said, eyes twinkling, 'but do they do it at ten a.m. on a Sunday morning, naked as the day they were born, off their heads on ketamine?'

'I see your point. God, I genuinely can't imagine anything worse. I'd rather stick my tongue in a toaster than subject myself to anything like that.'

He raised his eyebrows. 'So no bachelorette party before your big day with Christopher?'

'What, and be forced to drink pink drinks out of penis straws while a bunch of women who can barely stand each other play pin-the-cock-on-the-naked-guy? No thank you.'

'You know, men are meant to come with those. They aren't supposed to be pinned on.'

I rolled my eyes. 'It's like pin the tail on the donkey, only—'

He let out a belly laugh. 'I was just pulling your leg! I'll be damned if you aren't the most literal woman I have ever met.' I wasn't entirely sure, but I didn't think he meant that as a compliment. He sighed and leaned back in his chair. 'What about your folks?' he asked.

I looked over at him. 'What about them?'

'I don't know – are they married?'

I shook my head. 'Divorced,' I said curtly. This was not a conversational path I wanted to venture down. There were too many ghosts hiding in the woods.

'I'm sorry to hear that,' he said. 'How old were you?'

'Eleven. Is this table wobbly?' I jiggled the edge and the legs scraped on the pavement. 'Hang on a minute,' I said, digging around in my purse. I pulled out a bunch of napkins and dived under the table, wedging them under one of the legs. I surfaced hoping he'd forget all about the whole divorce thing. 'There,' I said, giving the table another shake. 'Perfect.'

'Nice work, MacGyver,' he said, nodding approvingly. 'So you were saying about your parents?'

I ducked back under the table. 'I think this chair is uneven, too,' I muttered.

He grabbed me by the elbow and hauled me back up. 'The chair's fine.'

We sat there in silence for several minutes, the noise from the crowd washing over us. Finally, I opened my mouth, and something surprising came out. 'My mom got sick after my dad left.'

He looked at me. 'Man, that's tough. Was it serious?'

My heart thudded in my chest and, to my horror, I felt myself well up. The day of the flying ants came flooding back. It was like I was living it all over again. The wail of the ambulance. The hushed voices of the doctors. The neighbors lining the lawns, straining to get a closer look while pretending to mind their own business. The fear I'd felt. The shame.

Jackson didn't say anything. He just reached over, patted my hand, and turned back towards the street. He wasn't going to push me on it. He was going to leave it be.

My heart ached from the kindness of it.

A waiter appeared and silently deposited two perfectly-poured macchiatos, and a pair of plates threatening to shatter beneath the weight of two enormous slabs of tiramisu. He tucked the bill discreetly under Jackson's plate and left without a word.

I took a few deep breaths to recover, and slowly the dark thoughts edged offstage. That's how it was – they were never gone completely, but I could hide them from plain sight. I forced a smile on my face. 'Just so we're clear,' I said, picking up the delicate little espresso cup and raising it towards him, 'I'm getting the bill.'

'Afraid not,' he said, shaking his head. 'It goes against my chivalric code.'

'Didn't you hear? Chivalry's dead.' I took a sip. The coffee was smooth and creamy and ever so slightly bitter. Delicious.

'Not in Texas it isn't.'

I tucked a fork into the tiramisu and pushed it through the layers of sponge and mascarpone. I lifted the fork to my lips, closed my eyes and savored the taste. Jackson was right again – their tiramisu was enough to make you weak at the knees. And tight at the waistband, if I was right about the amount of cream involved. I would definitely, absolutely, go to the gym tomorrow, I vowed as I took another bite.

'You okay over there?' I looked up to see Jackson watching me eat, a smile playing on his lips. 'You don't seem to like that tiramisu one bit.'

I scraped the final morsel of cream from the plate with the side of my fork and licked it off. 'It was disgusting,' I agreed.

He finished the last of his coffee and put a few notes on the table. 'Come on,' he said, scraping back his chair. 'Time for a nightcap.'

'I really shouldn't . . .' I began, but I knew it was pointless. I'd lost all control over the evening. For once, though, the thought of being out of control didn't terrify me.

We wound our way through the streets, dodging tipsy revelers as they weaved down the sidewalk, and ended up in front of an unpromising-looking blue door that led to an even less-appealing stairwell. 'What is this place?' I asked as we trudged down the steps.

'You haven't lived until you've been to Trish's,' he called over his shoulder.

A burly man met us at the foot of the stairs. 'You two members?' he asked gruffly.

'Of course we are,' Jackson said.

The burly man eyed us suspiciously. 'I don't think I've seen you in here before.'

'C'mon, buddy. I'm sure you remember me,' Jackson said, risking life and limb by giving the guy a playful pat on the shoulder. I readied myself to run.

He was not buying it. 'Where's your membership card?'

Jackson grinned widely. 'C'mon, don't tell me you don't remember me!'

I was about to tug on Jackson's arm and suggest we cut our losses and head to All Bar One when, incredibly, the burly man returned Jackson's smile. 'Sorry to give you hassle, mate,' he said, ushering us in. 'My memory's been playing up. Can't remember shit these days.'

'Don't worry about it,' Jackson said, giving him another playful tap. 'It happens to the best of us.'

'Do you really know that guy?' I whispered as we hurried past.

Jackson shook his head. 'Never seen him before in my life.'

We pushed through a red velvet curtain and found ourselves in what appeared to be my uncle's rec room from 1987. The place was lit more brightly than Wembley, and my feet stuck stubbornly to the tacky linoleum floor. A few scattered tables were filled with brawny Italian men arguing over the Serie A match playing on the flat screen tacked up to one of the walls, while over by the bar, a middle-aged woman wearing a Karen Millen skirt suit was arguing with the bartender over the amount of Jack in her Jack and Coke. 'I can't even taste it!' she slurred, while a younger, nervous-looking co-worker tugged at her arm. A wizened old man played a mournful tune on a fiddle in the corner.

I turned to Jackson, eyes wide. 'This place is nuts.'

He looked at me uncertainly. 'Do you hate it? We can go if you do.'

'It's like we're in Superman's Bizarro World Soho,' I said, gazing around in wonder. Where were the exposed brick walls? The tattooed struggling actor asking if we wanted to try the Bergamot small batch gin? The pouty fourteen-year-old taking photographs of her mac-and-cheese-stuffed lobster?

'Is that a good thing, or . . .'

I nodded enthusiastically. 'A good thing. A very good thing.'

Jackson looked as if I'd just given him a gold star. 'Phew! What would you like to drink?'

I looked over at the bar, which appeared to stock solely Moretti or whisky. 'Jack and Coke for me, please,' I said. My eye snagged on a tall brown bottle tucked high up on the back bar. 'Wait! I changed my mind. I'd like a Frangelico, please.'

He pulled a face. 'I thought only little old ladies drank that stuff.'

'Yeah, little old ladies with great taste. On ice, please!'

I stood back and observed the room, while Jackson sidled up to the bar. I would never in a million years have known this place existed. It definitely wasn't somewhere Christopher and I would have ended up on our own. He had a general phobia of bouncers, and I tended to be too intimidated to approach them.

I didn't use to be like that, though. There was a time in my life (between the ages of nineteen and twenty-one) when I would march to the front of any nightclub line, show the bouncer my cousin's expired driver's license, hitch up my pleather miniskirt and sail through the front door. And another (between the ages of twenty-two and twenty-four) when a Saturday night would begin at midnight, with Isla and me sailing over the Manhattan Bridge in a yellow taxi, the lights of the city twinkling just for us. We used to play this game where we'd compete to see who got the most phone numbers. Isla always won, but that wasn't the point.

The point was that, back then, everything was expendable. Time. Sleep. Brain cells. Men. None of it mattered. Especially since I knew that it would just be for a finite amount of time, before I was called back to reality and forced to concentrate on more serious things. And then, just like that, the crazy nights out were packed up and pushed out of sight, like Christmas decorations in January. Only they weren't ever meant to be seen again.

Jackson returned clutching a bottle of beer in one hand and a glass filled to the brim with a sticky-looking caramel-colored liquid. 'Bottoms up,' he said, handing the glass to me, and we clinked and sipped as we gaped around the room.

'Honestly,' I said, shaking my head in disbelief, 'I have never seen a more random group of people gathered in one room before.'

'I know,' Jackson agreed. 'And all of them look like they're about to brawl, SummerSlam style.'

He was right. Everywhere we looked, people were making terrible choices. The thin man with the glasses glaring murderously at a man twice his size, insisting he spilled his drink: terrible choice. The Jack Daniel's-loving skirt-suit wearer now running a hand up her nervous co-worker's thigh: terrible choice. Even the surly bartender – questionably sober – was making a terrible choice by hitting on the bouncer's girlfriend.

'Must be the Jack Daniel's,' I said, taking another sip.

'Or the Frangelico. How is it, anyway?'

'Honestly? Sort of disgusting. But in a good way.'

'How can something be disgusting in a good way?'

'You know the way that cotton candy, or marshmallow fluff, when eaten in huge quantities, can be both delicious and disgusting? Like that.'

He laughed. 'Thanks for clarifying.' He looked around and shook his head. 'My dad would love this kind of place.'

'He would?'

'Oh, sure. The man loves a dive bar. A genuine connoisseur. Whenever I'm home, he takes me to this place called Bucky's he's been going to since he could sneak a drink. You should see it – I swear you can smell the

asbestos in the pipes. Bucky's a real son of a bitch, too —
never gives you a free drink, never smiles, never gives you
the right change.'

'Sounds awful.'

He grinned. 'Oh, it is. But awful in a good way.' We
exchanged a glance and laughed.

A man in a waistcoat and suit jacket, bow tie loosened
around his throat, appeared in the doorway and silently
made his way to a dark corner of the room, where a grand
piano had been unceremoniously shoved. 'Do you think
he's going to play?' I whispered.

Before Jackson had the chance to answer, the man sat
down at the piano, cracked his knuckles with a flourish,
and started banging out the opening bars to 'New York,
New York'.

'I guess he's a Sinatra fan,' Jackson said with a wink. 'So
tell me, how did you end up in London? Don't tell me it
was just because good old Christopher lives here.'

I opened my mouth to protest, but was immediately
drowned out by a rich baritone crooning about spreading the news. We looked back at the dark piano corner
and found that both a microphone stand and a classically
trained singer had appeared.

'What in the—' I looked at Jackson, goggle-eyed. 'Did
you know about this?'

He attempted a casual shrug, but couldn't suppress the
smirk. 'Now that you ask, I seem to remember that actors
from the West End sometimes come here after their curtain call, and sometimes turn this place into open mic
night . . .'

We stood in awed silence as, one after another, people got up to the microphone and knocked it out of the park. The regulars barely even glanced up, and each performance was greeted with a smattering of applause and the occasional half-hearted whistle. Except for Jackson and me, of course. By the end of one woman's performance of 'All That Jazz', my feet ached from stomping them and Jackson's face looked like it was about to split down the seams under the pressure of his smile.

After a rousing final chorus of 'Something Stupid', Jackson excused himself and slipped off to the bathroom. When he reappeared, he had an odd look on his face, and kept tapping his foot anxiously against the back of the bar. 'You feeling okay?' I asked.

'Me? Sure, I'm fine.' He attempted a smooth smile, but I could hear the ice rattling in his glass as he held it to his lips.

I peered at him more closely. 'Seriously, you look a little—'

A deep voice boomed across the room. 'Is there a Miss Sparrow in the house?'

I spun on my heel and found the pianist leaning over the microphone, shielding his eyes from the light as he scanned the room. Fear gripped my ribcage and squeezed. I turned back to Jackson, eyes wide. 'What does he want?'

Jackson winked. 'I think he wants you to get up there and sing us a song, sweetheart.'

The bottom dropped out of my stomach and I wondered briefly if I'd be seeing that tiramisu again very soon. 'What do you mean, he wants me to sing?'

Jackson couldn't keep the grin off his face now. 'You told me that night in Vegas that you'd always wanted to sing with a band. Well,' he said, gesturing towards the pianist, now sighing impatiently into the microphone, 'now's your chance.'

'But—'

'I know it's not exactly a band,' he said, taking me by the elbow and steering me towards the microphone, 'but I figured a piano was better than nothing.'

'But – but—'

'Don't worry, sweetheart,' he whispered as he delivered me to the pianist. 'You're going to knock them dead. This good man here is already cued up with your song. Isn't that right?'

The pianist nodded solemnly and returned to his seat at the piano.

I was wild-eyed with fear now. What had I told him was my song? 'My song? What song?' My brain sped through the likely suspects. God, please don't let it be a Beyoncé number. I'd never be able to hit the high notes.

The pianist tapped out the opening bars to 'The Man Who Got Away'. 'Good luck,' Jackson whispered in my ear, and then he placed the microphone in my hand and disappeared into the crowd.

It felt like a dream, as if I was watching it happen to me from the other side of the room. I opened my mouth on the cue, and there it was, my voice, clear and high, and, if not good, at least not terrible. I closed my eyes and let the moment take me. The words came to me without thought, ingrained in my mind from hearing them so many times over the years. It was muscle memory, really. Pure and simple. No different from the hundreds of times I'd sung that song in the shower or in the kitchen or in my head as I pushed past angry fellow commuters. But at the end, when I'd sung my last note and the first wave of applause washed over me, I opened my eyes and realized, no, this wasn't like every other time. This was a singular moment, and it was perfect.

I placed the microphone back in the stand with shaky hands and made my way across the floor to where Jackson was waiting, arms open and drinks waiting. People patted me on the back as I passed, and murmured the occasional nice word. I knew I wasn't half the singer most of the people in there were, but it didn't matter. What mattered was how I'd felt when I was up there.

'I can't believe you did that to me!' I shouted as I ran up to Jackson. I tried to sound outraged, but I couldn't wipe the enormous grin off my face.

'Yeah,' he said, placing a shot of tequila in my hand, 'you really seemed like you were hating it up there. C'mon,' he said, raising his shot glass in salute, 'bottoms up.' I sunk it in one as he watched, astonished but impressed. 'You didn't even ask for salt and lime!'

I tried to shrug casually through the burn racing down my esophagus. 'Your turn,' I crowed, nodding to the still-full shot glass in his hand.

He tipped it towards me in salute before sinking it in one neat swallow. 'Christ,' he said, wiping his mouth with the back of his hand. 'I hate tequila.'

'Me too.'

'You know,' he said, putting his empty upside-down on the bar and signalling the bartender for a couple of beers, 'you were pretty good up there.'

'I was?'

'In fact,' he said, brushing the hair away from my face, 'you were amazing.'

I froze as his fingertips grazed my neck. 'How did you know?'

'How did I know what? That you wanted to sing? I told you, you told me that night in Vegas.'

'No,' I said, catching his arm. 'About the song. How did you know that was my song?'

He smiled. 'You told me that, too.'

'I did? But—'

'I know,' he said softly. 'You told me you didn't tell anyone that it's your song.'

I was silent for a minute. 'It's my mother's favorite. On Sundays, if she was having a . . .' I hesitated, unsure of how much to say. He nodded his encouragement. 'If she was having a good day, she'd make a big batch of popcorn and we'd cuddle up on the couch and watch old movies. *A Star is Born* was one of our favorites. Every time Judy Garland would get up to that piano and start to sing, she'd squeeze me and say, "That's my song," and then we'd sing it together. And then I guess it became my song, too.' I looked up and saw that his eyes had filled with kindness and . . . yes. Understanding. I could feel it then, the words building inside me, pushing up my throat and easing my mouth open. I don't know why, but something inside me wanted to tell him. 'I took care of her for a long time,' I said quietly.

He reached out and placed his hand lightly on my shoulder. 'That must have been tough.'

I nodded. 'I should still be taking care of her. I send money every month, but my aunt, she does most of the work now. Sometimes I think . . .' I trailed off. I could see my mother's face then, as clearly as if she were standing in front of me. The look in her eyes when she would sing that song, the way her smile never quite made its way up to her eyes.

Jackson bent down and cupped my face in his hand. 'You're a good daughter,' he said quietly. 'Your mother knows how much you love her.'

I felt a knot deep inside me ease. I waited for him to say more, but he stayed silent, just kept the steady pressure of his hand on my shoulder, and I felt almost weak with gratitude.

Jackson watched me closely. The adrenaline from earlier had worn off and had left me feeling brittle and tired. He put an arm around me and started guiding me towards the stairs without waiting for an answer. 'Come on,' he said, 'let's get you home. It's a school night, after all.'

I nodded and let him lead me up the steps and back onto the Soho streets. It was the height of the witching hour now, and the scene was shaping up to look like something out of the zombie apocalypse. People staggered stiff-legged down the pavement, veering wildly to avoid passing bikes and taxis and lampposts. A woman in a red mini-dress and high red heels was singing a Rhianna song at the top of her lungs while her friends clapped along. A guy in his twenties wearing a shiny suit and sporting an elaborate quiff (Foxtons, almost certainly) was leaning against the side of a Pret A Manger, retching like a cat with a hairball.

Jackson raised his hand to flag a passing taxi. The night was over, and rightly so – like he'd said, it was a school night, and I had to be up early for work the next day. I couldn't bring my self to look at my phone to check what the time was – I just knew that it was later than I'd thought. But something inside me, some treacherous, unhelpful little nugget buried deep in my chest, was disappointed. I didn't want it to end, not yet. It had been too much fun.

'Well,' he said, as he opened the taxi door, 'I guess this is goodnight.'

'Do you want a lift? I could drop you off at your hotel . . .'

He waved the offer away. 'I think I'll walk for a little while. It's not too far from here.'

'You sure do love your walks.'

He nodded and gazed wistfully out over the Soho carnage. 'Best way to remember this city is to walk it.'

'At this rate, you'll be Samuel goddamn Johnson by the end of this week.' I looked at him for a minute, uncertain of what to do next after a night like we'd just had. Should we shake hands? Were we on hugging terms now? In the end, I sidestepped him and hurled myself lengthwise into the taxi. 'Okay,' I called, straightening myself up in the seat. 'Well. Bye.'

He leaned into the taxi and laughed. 'You're not too good at this whole human interaction thing, are you?'

'I'm a little rusty,' I admitted.

He stepped halfway into the cab and bent down to kiss me on the cheek. 'Goodnight. Sleep tight. Don't let the bed bugs bite. I'll call you tomorrow with a plan.' He shut the door behind him and I felt the taxi jerk into motion as it sped off down the street.

I glanced at him in the rear-view mirror. He was checking his phone, lifting it to his ear . . . the penny dropped with a thud. Of course he wasn't just going for a walk. He was probably going to meet someone. He'd lived here before, he probably knew loads of people. I wondered, idly, if any of them were particularly pretty.

'Where to?' The taxi driver's voice shook me out of my thoughts.

'Oh. Um. Tufnell Park, please.' I leaned back in the seat and let the night wash over me. I felt as if I'd seen a whole new London, one I hadn't even known existed. What had I been doing these past three years? I couldn't blame Christopher for it, either. My first six months in London, he'd bombarded me with links to gigs and theatre events and hot new bars, but I always said no. I'd rather stay in, I told him. But really, I just wanted to hide. Going out like that was in the past for me. Now that I was settled down, that meant home-cooked meals and cosy duvets and smug nights in watching Saturday-night television.

Stop it, I chastized myself. I was being ridiculous. Jackson pours one decent macchiato down my throat and thrusts a microphone in my hand and suddenly I'm Virginia goddamn Woolf, yearning for a room of my own. Anyway, didn't I have enough excitement on my plate at

the minute, what with the possibility of polygamy wink-
ing at me in my future?

Still, I couldn't believe I'd told him about my song. And
I definitely couldn't believe I'd got up in front of a room
full of strangers and belted it out like that! It suddenly
occurred to me that I'd checked something off my list that
night. Number 13: Sing with a band. I couldn't believe I
hadn't clocked it right away. Usually, checking things off
my list was my main motivator. But it had just slipped my
mind.

What was it about Jackson that made me behave so . . .
unlike myself? All the years carefully building order to
protect myself from chaos, and he comes along and suddenly my whole life is careening out of control. I could
feel myself slipping. Maybe this was the moment when
the great fissure inside me would appear, and I would
finally fall through.

The familiar panic had started to return. Get a grip,
Jenny, I scolded myself. Deep breaths.

I pulled out my phone and pressed the home button, the
screen lighting up in my hand. Oh God. It was almost two
o'clock in the morning. And not only that, but I had missed
calls – a whole ream of them. And all of them bore the
same smiling face in a little circle next to the number.

Christopher.

I tried to ease the door gently into the lock behind me, but
it still clanged like a klaxon. Jesus Christ. There was no
way I was getting away with this.

'Jenny? Is that you?'

'Hello!' I trilled. My voice sounded thick in my ears. 'I'm sorry I'm so late!'

Christopher charged into the hallway, eyes bloodshot. 'Where have you been? I've been going mad!'

My mind raced. Think, Jenny, think! 'I – I was out with Ben!' The look on Christopher's face suggested that this was not the correct answer. 'He's been having women troubles again.' Women troubles. Oh God. I'd just insinuated that Ben had his period.

'I don't see why Ben needs your help sorting out his "women troubles" until two o'clock in the morning.'

'Well, he's been having a rough time . . . this girl he likes hasn't texted back . . .' I faded out listlessly. 'I thought you were out tonight.'

'Jonno's wife went into labour, so we canceled at the last minute. Anyway, what does that have to do with anything? I'm out with my friends, so you run off with Ben for the evening? Is that it?' He shook his head in disgust. 'I never liked the look of that Ben bloke. Too – too shiny! He's like a bloody Christmas bauble!' He clenched his fist on the word 'bauble'.

'Christopher, please.' I gently rubbed the top of his arm, as though he was a spooked colt and not my fiancé. 'You're overreacting. There's nothing going on between Ben and me.' Even saying the words made me feel slightly nauseated. 'Honestly, he just wanted a woman's opinion about it all, and time got away from us, and . . .' I sighed 'Look, I'm sorry I didn't answer my phone, and I'm sorry I worried you, okay? But I don't think I should be raked over the coals for having a night out with my friend.'

Christopher's face dropped. 'Oh God. I'm being a pillock, aren't I? I'm acting like some kind of 'roided up bro who smashes beer cans against his forehead.' He pulled me towards him and I buried my head in his shoulder. 'I'm sorry. It's just, you're never out in the evenings, and when I couldn't get through to you, I immediately thought the worst and—' I felt his ribcage shudder as the breath went out of him.

'You don't have to apologize,' I mumbled. 'It's okay.' I was hit with a wave of guilt so thick I thought I might stumble over. Here he was – lovely, perfect Christopher – apologizing to me when I'd just lied to his face. Again.

'Come on,' I said, gently lifting my head from his chest, 'let's go to bed.' I reached out and took his hand as we walked to the bedroom. I looked around the flat – the framed print in the hallway we'd picked out together, the dove-gray throw pillows that his mother had given us plumped on the sofa, the little geranium-scented tea lights I'd bought in a multi-pack from Sainsbury's – and thought, what the hell am I doing? This is my life – here, in this place. Not in some skeezy Soho bar or sipping espressos on a sidewalk with a relative stranger.

'I'm just going to brush my teeth,' I said. I slipped into the bathroom and shut the door behind me. I stared at my face in the cabinet mirror. My eye make-up had smudged and my mascara had flaked, and beneath it all, my eyes looked haunted. 'What am I doing?' I whispered to my reflection, but for once, I didn't have an answer.

I rested my forehead on the cool glass and watched my breath make a foggy circle below.

I couldn't take another risk like tonight – I just couldn't. I'd call Jackson tomorrow and tell him that I couldn't see him for dinner. Now that I knew him a little better, I could see he was a decent guy – he wouldn't punish me for trying to keep my relationship together. Maybe he'd forget the whole week-of-entertaining-him thing entirely. I remembered him checking his phone. He didn't need me to entertain him, anyway.

I splashed my face with cold water and dried it with one of the plush little red towels I'd bought from TK Maxx. You see? I'm the sort of person who buys plush little face towels from TK Maxx. I was not the sort of person who went gallivanting around town with another man behind her fiancé's back, even if that man was her husband.

No, tomorrow it would be over. It had to be. I could always suc him for a divorce if he kicked up a fuss. We hadn't slept together anyway, so we could probably get one of those fake divorces that Catholic people get sometimes. An annulment. Maybe I could do that without Jackson's approval. I'd look into it tomorrow.

I turned out the light and climbed into bed next to Christopher. He turned to face me in the half-light. 'Goodnight,' he said, pecking me on the mouth. 'Sorry again for being a knob.'

'You weren't a knob.'

'I was.' There was a pause. 'I thought you were going to brush your teeth.'

In the middle of my existential crisis, I'd neglected my oral hygiene. 'I forgot. It's late.'

'I know. Goodnight,' he said again, and this time he kissed me on the cheek.

I lay back on my pillow and stared up at the swirls on the ceiling. 'Goodnight,' I said softly. 'Sleep tight. Don't let the bed bugs bite.'

12

The next morning, Christopher and I were tentative around each other, speaking in soft, gentle voices, touching each other as though worried we might hit a bruise. Normally I stayed in bed while he got ready, but I got up instead and made him a cup of tea while he was in the shower. I wanted, more than anything, to be kind. I placed a chocolate digestive next to the mug of tea and left both on the nightstand for him. He walked in, toweling off his wet hair, saw the biscuit and smiled. 'You're too good to me,' he said, picking it up and dunking it in his tea.

'That's not true,' I demurred, thinking, buddy, you don't know the half of it. 'Why don't we do something tonight?' I said. 'Just the two of us.'

'Like what?' He had a smudge of dried toothpaste at the corner of his mouth. I tried not to focus on it.

I flopped back on the bed. 'I don't know. Go out to dinner? Go to the theatre? I could sneak out of work early and try to get ten-pound tickets for that show at the Old Vic?'

He wrinkled his nose. 'What's on?'

'Something about middle-aged despair,' I said, gesturing vaguely. 'It's meant to be great.'

'Yeah, it sounds it.' He leaned over the bed and kissed me on the cheek. 'Why don't we just stay in? Maybe get a pizza or something.'

My heart sank slightly. 'Sure.' I gestured towards the side of his mouth. 'You've got a little—'

He wiped his lips with the back of his hand. 'Better?'

'Still there.' I licked the tip of my thumb and reached up to scrub it off. We both realized what I was about to do and froze.

'Thanks, Mum, but I can clean my own face!'

Apparently not, I thought meanly. 'Sorry,' I said. 'That was a little gross of me.'

He pulled a face. 'Just a bit.' He pulled back and started frantically rubbing at the corner of his mouth. 'Gone now?'

I could still see a faint trace of it – toothpaste really was a stubborn adhesive, someone should talk to NASA about it – but I smiled and nodded. 'All gone!' I knew that scrubbing toothpaste off someone's face with saliva was a little disgusting, but I didn't think it required the level of horror he'd expressed. I was his fiancée, after all. I had watched him pick his toenails in bed and said nothing.

'Right, I'm off. I'll see you back here tonight – unless you decide we should go out clubbing or something.' He pronounced the word 'clubbing' as though it were 'Mars' or 'dogging'.

'I don't think that's likely.' I tilted my chin to accept his kiss. 'Have a good day.'

'You too. Say hi to Ben for me. I hope his lady troubles ease up.'

I was touched by the olive branch. I reached for him and pulled him towards me again, kissing him properly this time. He tasted of mint and chocolate and tea. 'I love you.'

194

'You too,' he said, pulling away and straightening his tie. 'See you tonight.'

I heard the door shut behind him and threw myself off the bed and into the shower. Today, I decided, would be a clean slate. I would tell Jackson that dinner was off, focus on the cobbler case at work, get back here at a reasonable time, and have a night in with Christopher. Maybe I would even cook. My mind whirred at the possibility. Lasagne? No, that would take too long. Maybe a stir-fry? Too healthy. Something Christopher would like. A pie, maybe. Could I make a pie?

I rinsed the suds out of my hair and hopped out to towel off. Yes, today would be a fresh start. I'd wear underwear that matched. I'd light candles in the living room. I'd make an effort.

I boarded the Tube with a spring in my step. I felt lighter than I had in ages. I had a plan now. I would wrest back control over my life. I would look into wedding registries and embossed stationery and jam jars for the centerpieces. I would call my mother.

I would be good.

The train chugged along the Northern Line, its doors opening at each stop to expel a few passengers and cram, Tetris-like, a few more in. I was wedged next to a group of suited-up businessmen comparing the merits of cosy pubs in the Cotswolds.

'The Plough and Stars in Withington is brill for a dirty weekend,' the man clutching a rolled-up copy of the *Telegraph* brayed into my ear. 'I took Jasmine there last February. Once she got a load of the fireplace, she practically threw her knickers at me.'

'Not half as good as the Old Bell in Bibury,' the bald man in the suede driving loafers shouted into the top of my head. 'The exposed beams alone had Tamara gagging for it as soon as we walked in.'

I shut my eyes and tried to imagine I was somewhere more pleasant, like a wildflower-strewn meadow, or an abattoir.

'How about the Crowne in Chipping Norton?' cried the man wearing a scarf I was fairly sure could be classified as a cravat. 'A magnum of champers, a ploughman's lunch, and a David Cameron sighting, and I thought Ambrosia would never come up for air!'

The men burst into a fresh round of eardrum-shattering laughter. I felt a morsel of pity for Jasmine and Tamara and poor airless Ambrosia. Surely no plate of cheese and pickle was good enough to endure this trio of chucklenuts.

It was moments like these when I felt most like a stranger in a strange land. I didn't understand these men shouting at each other about their ability to bed women who had willingly gone away with them for the weekend. I didn't understand the Cotswolds – what they were, where they were located, why everyone seemed so eager to go there to have sex. I'd overheard a woman discussing her weekend in the Cotswolds at work one day, and had gone home and suggested to Christopher that we go there, too, only to be told that the Cotswolds were full of red-trouser-wearing twats who said words like 'totes' and liked horses better than their own mothers.

I didn't understand that, either.

I thought of the easy shorthand I had with Isla. If I made a *Facts of Life* reference, she understood it. She appreciated the subtle difference in Slush Puppie flavors. She knew the etiquette around ordering a hotdog at a baseball game. Not that we ever went to baseball games, but the thought of it still made me ache with homesickness. Even with Jackson, there was an ease that comes with a shared nationality, a shared culture. Even if he was from Texas.

No. I was not going to let myself go down that particular slip'n'slide.

By the time I arrived at work, my previously good mood had been restored. The daffodils were out in full bloom in Green Park, despite the persistent mizzle falling from the gray sky, and I'd had to pause when walking over the little bridge in St James's to make way for a gaggle of geese. The clouds couldn't hide it: it was spring.

Today was a fresh start, I reminded myself as I threw my bag on the floor underneath my desk and slid into my chair. Today I was going to take back my life.

There was a cup of coffee cooling at my elbow and my favorite pen was uncapped and in hand: I was ready to make a to-do list for the day.

God, I love a list. For me, there is no greater pleasure than crossing something off a list. There were times when I'd added something I'd already done to a list, just so I could cross it off. It's a sickness, I know. But I don't care.

I wrote out the list carefully on one of the yellow legal pads I ordered specially from the US.

- Tell Jackson
- Wedding venues!
- Tax forms for Cobbler case
- Expenses to Accounts
- Go to gym
- Make dinner for Christopher – pie??

I tapped the pen against my mouth and considered the list. And then I added one more thing.

- Make coffee

And crossed it out with a thick blue line. Heaven.

Okay, first things first: I had to call Jackson and tell him dinner was off. I dug my phone out of my bag, scrolled through to his number and hit the green call button. A swarm of butterflies decamped to my stomach as I waited for it to ring.

'You're through to the voicemail of . . .'

I breathed out a sigh of relief. I wouldn't have to bite the bullet. Just nibble it a little. 'Hi Jackson,' I said in my brightest voice, 'I'm really sorry, but I won't be able to make dinner tonight. And, actually, maybe not tomorrow night either. Or the next. I'm sorry, but it's just proving a little complicated with Christopher and . . . I hope you understand. Let me know if you need money for the divorce papers. I don't know how these things work.' To my horror, I added a laugh – a stupid, insane-sounding little titter – to the end of the sentence. 'Anyway. Sorry. Bye.'

I pressed end call and sat back in my chair. My heart was pounding in my chest and I thought I might be sick, but I'd done it. I reached out and crossed Jackson off the list. Thankfully, I was distracted from the heavy feeling in the hollow of my stomach by Ben, who chose that moment to lope through the door like a wounded sloth.

I took one look at him – he was wearing a pair of chinos today, baggy ones, and a thick sweater featuring, unseasonably, a jaunty reindeer – and knew. 'Still haven't heard from Lucy?'

He shook his head and collapsed into his chair with a huff. He was wearing thick white athletic socks with his All Stars – things were even worse than I'd thought. 'Honestly, what's the point?' he howled. 'This is exactly why I don't let women know where I live. If you get too close to them, they'll only break your heart. Women,' he said, shaking his head ruefully. 'How do you live with yourselves?'

'I don't think there's any need to dismiss a whole gender because someone didn't answer your text right away.'

'Two days!' he cried. 'Two whole days, and not a single word out of her! Oh God, this is a disaster. A humiliation!'

'Calm down! Look, why don't you tell me what you said to her, and we'll work out what to do next.'

'Other than join a monastery?'

I eyeballed him across the room. 'You'd last about thirty seconds in a monastery before you'd start begging alcohol off the monks and chatting up the statue of the Virgin Mary.'

'Honestly, Jenny, I don't know how you've come to have such a warped view of me.'

'Three years of close observation. Are you going to read me this text of yours or what?'

He made a big show of taking out his phone and

scrolling through his messages until he found it. He cleared his throat. 'Hey.'

I waited for a minute. 'Hey what?'

'That's it. Just, "Hey".'

'Did you think about expanding on that a little? Maybe saying you had a nice time the other night, would she like to meet up again . . . something like that?'

'A wise man once said "Brevity is the soul of wit". I can't remember who – maybe Keith Richards? All I know is that he was wise, and that's why I said what I said.' He caught the look of disbelief on my face. 'What?'

'It's just . . . it's not a lot to go off, you know?'

His face crumpled. 'Oh God, it's a disaster, isn't it? Christ, I'm an idiot. A stupid, stupid idiot.'

'You are not an idiot. It's a perfectly fine text message to send.'

'Then why hasn't she responded?'

I thought for a minute. 'Maybe she hasn't read it yet?'

'Of course she's read it! It says it right here!' He jabbed a finger at the small print under the blue bubble. READ. Whoever invented the technology that allowed someone to see when a text message had been read was a cruel and insensitive soul. Poor Ben was in full freefall now. 'Shit shit shit! What do I do now?' He ran his hands through his un-pomaded hair. 'I've blown it, haven't I? Oh, Christ, I'm an idiot.'

'You're not an idiot,' I repeated. 'Look, we can fix this. Why don't you send her a text that involves a question?'

'What sort of question?'

'How about "What do you think of that Mussolini

guy?" What kind of question do you think, Ben? Maybe ask her on another date?'

He turned pale. 'I can't. It's too much! I can't bear the humiliation.'

'You texted a woman "Hey" and freaked out about it for two days. If you can withstand that humiliation, you can withstand the humiliation of asking her out on a date like a normal person.'

He took a deep breath and steadied himself. 'Okay. What do I say?'

'Well, first we need a plan for a date. A good one. Not just a trip to the pub followed by a shared carton of chips. A proper date, like cocktails and dinner.'

'Oh God . . .'

'Wait, I have an idea.' I scanned through my deleted items and fished out the latest Urban Junkies round-up. I'd signed up when I first moved here, but soon became intimidated by the club nights held by bingo-playing drag queens and immersive theatre experiences that involved the audience undressing and rolling around on a canvas swimming in blue paint. I still read the round-ups every week, though my interest had become more anthropological than practical. 'Observe the DJ/Model/Coder in her natural habitat . . .' 'Okay,' I said, scanning through the listings. 'There's a really cute Portuguese tapas bar that's opened up in Borough. You could take her there?'

He pulled a face. 'And fend my way through swarms of hen-dos cycling the streets on those pedi-bars? No thanks.'

'Fine. What about this? "Speakeasy cocktail bar hidden

down a back alley in Chinatown . . ." That sounds pretty good.'

'Ugh. Chinatown is always mobbed with tourists.'

'French bistro in Spitalfields?'

'Filled with Wanker Bankers.'

'American-style diner in Notting Hill?'

'Every man in there will be wearing at least three polo shirts with all the collars popped.'

I looked at his current ensemble and bit my tongue. 'What about this? Cocktail bar at the top of a car park in Peckham.'

He stirred. 'Peckham's not totally shit yet.'

'Ooh, and they're doing an outdoor screening of *Casablanca* on Saturday night! With blankets!' I felt a frisson of jealousy. I'd always wanted to go to a bar where they gave you a blanket.

He twirled his phone idly in his hand before nodding reluctantly. 'Fine. God, it all sounds so – so—'

'So much like a date?'

He looked as if I'd invited him on a tour of a fish cannery. 'Exactly!'

I rolled my eyes. 'That is exactly the point. Right, are you ready to send this text?'

'I don't know . . . are you sure I won't seem like a desperate loser?'

'You might, but better to be a desperate loser than the guy that just says "Hey".'

He groaned. 'Fine, fine. Just tell me what to say and I'll say it. I'm ceding total text control to you.'

'Excellent.' I rubbed my hands together with glee.

There was nothing I liked better than being given total control over something. It didn't matter what.

'Ah,' he said, raising a finger in the air pontifically, 'Remember what the great Winston Churchill once said: "With great power comes great responsibility."'

'That was Spiderman.' I snatched the phone out of his hands and my fingers flew across the screen.

I combed through Mr Bryant's audited accounts while trying to ignore the near-constant barrage of Ben's moans and sighs. 'Two hours and thirteen minutes,' he updated me, 'still no reply.' Then, twenty minutes later, 'Two hours and thirty-three minutes. Radio silence.' I eventually put my headphones on and blasted Death Cab for Cutie so I could concentrate.

The rest of the morning flew by, though not with any great revelations about the Bryant case. The cobbler shop brought in a modest income every year – not much, but enough to keep the lights on – and he paid himself an even more modest salary out of the company earnings. There was an anomaly with his wife's insurance pay-out – I couldn't find any trace of it in his bank account – but maybe he'd invested it, or given it to his children as an inheritance. He seemed like a man who led a frugal existence. I pictured him standing in front of the discount section in Tesco, selecting a nearly off shepherd's pie and a tin of rice pudding for dinner, and had to force the image from my head when my eyes started to well up. Rule number one of insurance investigation: don't let your sympathies sway you. The guy could still be running an underground gambling ring out of the back of his shop, or have a bathtub full of ice and Estonian kidneys in his upstairs bathroom. You just never knew.

Before I knew it, it was lunchtime, and both my phone and Ben's had remained resolutely silent. He sloped out to the pub—'A pint and a sausage roll are the only things that will sort me out now' – and I forced myself to go to the gym, if only so I could cross it off my list when I got back. Besides, Body Pump always emptied my brain of unpleasant thoughts (even as it filled my body with unpleasant amounts of pain).

I walked into the chlorine-and-sweat-scented atrium and swiped my card through the turnstile. A tiny blonde woman sporting a tight ponytail and an even tighter smile handed me a stiff cotton towel and advised me that Body Pump – sorry, 'Reps and Revs' – was fully booked. So was the spin class. So much for my lunchtime blitz. I changed into pilled leggings and an oversized T-shirt and headed up to the fitness area. The spin class was about to start on the raised platform in the middle of the room, and I looked longingly at the rows of bikes filled with spandexed asses adjusting themselves on their perilously narrow seats. 'Okay, riders, are we ready to ROCK?' shouted the instructor, a florid Spanish man wearing a full-8os Sweatin' to the Oldies ensemble. The opening strains of 'Let's Get Physical' filled the air, and I crammed my earbuds further into my ears.

I spent a desultory fifteen minutes on the elliptical machine, watching incomprehensible music videos on the wall-mounted TV as the calorie counter slowly ticked upwards, all while trying to ignore the sweat flywheeling off the spinners nearby. When I reached 250 calories (the equivalent of a handful of Cadbury's Mini Eggs and a single piece of hot buttered toast) I took myself off to the steam room (today's scent: lavender) and lay still on the damp wooden bench as my skin wrinkled up like a scotch bonnet.

When I got back out on the street, I checked my phone. Still nothing. I guess Jackson had accepted what I'd said in my message and wasn't going to question it. I tried to ignore the mild fug of disappointment that descended, and called Isla instead.

'So let me get this straight,' she said over the whir of the staffroom coffee machine, 'you have a great night out with the guy and then tell him you never want to see him again. What is this, a Danielle Steele novel?'

I was standing in Pret, phone pressed to my ear, dithering over which bread-based mayonnaise conductor I was going to eat for lunch. 'It was the right thing to do,' I said, picking up a tuna and cucumber.

'For who, exactly?'

I tapped my card on the reader and bundled my sandwich into my bag. 'For me, for Christopher . . .'

'For Christopher, I'll buy. For you, not so much.'

'Well, I've done it now, and Jackson hasn't exactly put up a fight about it, so maybe it's best for everyone.'

Isla sighed. 'It's just a shame, that's all.'

I stopped on the edge of the sidewalk to let a cyclist whizz past before crossing. 'What is?'

'It sounds like you've been having a good time with

him. And I know you had a good time with him when we were in Las Vegas, because I saw it with my own eyes.'

'I was drunk! Really, incredibly, liver-destroyingly drunk!'

'That doesn't mean you didn't have fun.'

'Isla, in the state I was in, you probably could have left me alone in a room with a pack of chewing gum and a dictionary and I would have had fun.'

'Not as much fun as you had with Jackson.'

I let out an exasperated groan. 'Look, just drop it, okay? Jackson will be gone soon, and I'll have my life back, and then I can get on with the business of getting married. Speaking of which, I'm going to start looking at bridesmaids' dresses for you.'

'Don't forget that puce is my color,' Isla deadpanned.

'I was thinking more of a vomit-orange, but I'll keep an open mind. How are you doing, anyway? Are you okay?'

'Oh, fine,' she said breezily. 'About to remove a tumor the size of a dill pickle from a guy's head.'

'The party never stops with you, does it?'

'It definitely won't tonight. I swung by Rick's on the way to work' – Rick was the name of her long-time dealer – 'and once I finish this shift, I don't plan on being sentient again until Sunday.'

Worry bloomed in my chest. 'Just be careful.'

'Caution is my motherfucking watchword.' I heard a muffled voice in the background. 'I've got to run – the dill pickle will see me now. Just promise me that if Jackson does get in touch again, you won't completely shut him down. Okay?'

'Fine. But I'm pretty sure I'm rid of him for good.'

'We'll see,' Isla trilled. 'If you ask me, he sounds like a guy who doesn't give up that easily. After all, he did marry you.'

'Goodbye, Isla!' I hung up the phone and walked into the office, bag swinging. I was ready for the afternoon, whatever it brought.

Turns out, the afternoon brought very little. The minutes stretched on into hours. I did my expenses. I added a few more things to my to-do list and then crossed them off, but the satisfaction this usually brought proved elusive.

At four-thirty, there was a 'Knock knock!' at the door of our cubicle, and Jeremy appeared clutching a mug that said 'Da Man'. Ben and I had, at that moment, both been cradling our iPhones like troublesome newborns, but at the sight of him we both dropped them on our desks as though touching them might trigger a nuclear launch.

Still, Jeremy shook his finger at us. 'I hope you two aren't Snapchatting or sexting.' He made the air quotes gesture around sexting, which made me wonder if he knew what it was, and, if he did, if he thought it didn't exist in real life. Although, I suppose, in my life it didn't exist, and I doubted very much that it existed in Jeremy's life, either. At least I hoped for the sake of humanity it didn't. From the deep beetroot shade Ben's face had now taken on, it looked like it definitely did exist in his.

'How's the Bryant case coming along?' Jeremy perched his left buttock on the edge of my desk and loomed over me. I tried not to flinch.

'Good,' I said, reaching out and patting the Manila

case file. 'I've been going through his accounts today, and there's nothing suspicious so far, but I'll keep digging.'

'Yes, keep digging, Sparrow! I'm sure that old shark has got a trick or two up his sleeve, and I'm relying on you to flush him out.'

I disentangled myself from the mixed metaphor and plastered a confident grin across my face. 'I'll do my best!'

'I'm sure you will, I'm sure you will. You're our ace in the hole! If anyone can reel in this fish, it's you.'

Right . . . 'I thought I'd maybe go down there in person tomorrow,' I said. 'Talk to a few of his neighbors, see if they know anything?' I hadn't realized I'd been planning on doing this until the words came out of my mouth, but judging by the look on Jeremy's face, it was a good thing.

'Excellent plan! Go undercover, grease some palms, smoke him out of his hole.'

'Uh, sure,' I said uncertainly. I imagined the look of incredulity on Ben's face at that moment and was careful not to catch his eye in case we both lost it. 'I'll let you know what I find.'

He took a sip from his mug and nodded approvingly. 'Good work, Sparrow. I look forward to hearing what skeletons you unearth from the old bobcat's closet.' With that, he raised two fingers to his forehead in salute and sauntered out of the cubicle. 'Markson!' I heard him call to one of the poor unsuspecting client account managers down the hall. 'What's the low-down on those invoices? Have you shaken them down for the dough?'

Ben turned around slowly in his chair. 'Bobcat?' he whispered incredulously.

I shook my head. Jeremy had shot so many random words at me at once, I'd almost missed the bobcat comment. 'Honestly, who knows where he gets these things.'

'Your idea about going on site tomorrow was genius. Jeremy lapped it up.'

I grimaced. 'Can we please not talk about Jeremy lapping things?'

'Fair enough. Seriously, though, do you think you'll be able to get anything out of his neighbors?'

I shrugged. 'Who knows? Maybe he said something to one of them about his plans, or one of them saw something on the night of the fire.' I considered this for a minute. 'Or maybe it'll be a huge waste of time, but at least it'll get me out of the office.'

'I knew it!' Ben crowed. 'You're totally just using it as an excuse to bunk off work for the afternoon.'

'I am not!' At least, not entirely. Though the idea of a Friday afternoon wandering around Columbia Road rather than staring bleary-eyed at spreadsheets and being berated by Ben about substandard cups of tea did have a certain appeal.

I was about to defend myself further when the trill of an incoming text cut through the cubicle. We both scrambled to our mobiles. 'It's me!' I cried, a little too triumphantly. Ben's face sank. I swiped the screen and opened the message. It was from Christopher.

> False alarm with Jonno's wife last night – still no baby, so
> the lads are back on for drinks this eve. Hopefully won't be
> too late xxx p.s. don't forget the salmon this time pls x

I blinked at the words on the screen. So much for a romantic night in. I couldn't believe I'd spent a whole day fighting the urge to winch a lace G-string out of my cervix for nothing. Well, at least I wouldn't have to think about what I was going to cook for dinner. I reached over and crossed it off my list. Pasta with jarred pesto for one, please, with a side of *Grazia* magazine, and a healthy dash of ennui.

I tried to think positively. Normally, I loved an evening in by myself. Unfettered carb consumption, a glass of red wine the size of a beach ball (okay, three) and unlimited reruns of *Say Yes to the Dress*. What wasn't to love? But somehow, the idea of a night marooned on the sofa like a beached sea otter didn't hold the usual appeal. It didn't feel cosy or indulgent. It felt . . . lonely.

'What are you doing tonight?'

Ben looked at me, surprised. 'I'm out with some of my uni friends. Why?'

'I just wondered if you wanted to go for a drink, that's all.'

His eyebrows were nearly lost in his hairline now. 'But . . . you never want to go for a drink.'

'I know,' I said, 'I just thought it might be . . .' I shook my head. 'Just forget it.'

'Why Jenny Sparrow,' he said coyly, tucking his fists into his ribcage, arms akimbo. 'Are you asking me on a date?'

'Oh my God!' I spluttered.

'I can't say I'm not flattered, but you know my position on ladies who are *enfianced*.' He waggled his eyebrows suggestively on this last word.

'Ben, stop!' I groaned.

'Look,' he said, serious now. 'Come to these drinks tonight, if you fancy it. It'll be a bunch of blokes in their mid-twenties discussing Arsène Wenger and wanking – separately, that is, not together – but you're welcome to come along. I'm sure the lads would be delighted to have an *older woman* in their midst, though I can't promise one of them won't ask you to show him your tits.'

I was strangely touched by the offer. Sure, I spent more time with Ben than anyone else, thanks to our close cubicle quarters, and it was clear from the start that we got along, but you never knew if an office friendship expanded outside of the office. It was nice to see that with Ben it might. Still, the idea of being surrounded by a bunch of his uni mates while they sank pints and argued over *Football Focus* didn't exactly appeal, even if it was the best (and by best, I mean only) offer I'd had all day. 'Thanks,' I said, 'but I think I'll pass.'

He nodded approvingly. 'I always knew you were a wise woman.'

I turned my attention back to the Bryant case and, before I knew it, Ben was packing up for the evening. 'You sure you don't want to come along?' he asked as he slung his messenger bag over his head.

'I'm good,' I said, 'honest. Have fun tonight. I hope you hear from Lucy.'

'Don't!' he wailed, shoulders sagging theatrically. 'It's hopeless!'

'It's not hopeless, I promise. Some things just take a little time.'

'Yeah, like the Ice Age, and look how that worked out

for the mastodon.' I shot him a quizzical look. 'Discovery Channel,' he shrugged. 'Goodnight. Don't stay too late.'

'I won't,' I said, waving him out the door.

I tried to keep working after he left, but the fight had gone out of me for the day, and I ended up aimlessly refreshing Twitter, hoping someone would say something interesting. The office was quiet now, only the faint clacking of fingers on a keyboard somewhere, and the whir of a vacuum cleaner as it worked its way through the hall.

Eventually, I logged off and started slowly gathering my stuff. I planned my journey home in my head. I could stop by Tesco on the way, pick up some supplies. I glanced at the time: 7.15. The Tube should be quieter by now. It would still be light out, so I could walk through Green Park on the way. Maybe sit and read my book for a few minutes.

I suppressed a sigh. Nothing I'd planned was getting rid of the sinking feeling that filled me when I imagined walking into the empty flat. The truth was, I didn't want to go home yet. Everyone else was out there living their own lives, surrounded by their people. What about me? Had my life really become this small?

No. I could do better than this, I was sure of it. I thought of Jackson prowling the streets on his own, scouting out all the best places, wringing every drop he could out of life. I could do that, too. I didn't need him to do it, either. I didn't need anyone. I was a grown-ass woman in London, and I could do grown-ass things on my own.

I picked up my bag and charged out the building, lit up by a new sense of purpose.

I threaded my way through St James's Park, across the Mall, and up the steps of the Queen Mother's memorial. The streets around St James's are lined with the sort of stately cream-colored buildings you could imagine filled with visiting dignitaries, all classical pillars and porticos. A string of trailers were lined up in front of Prince Philip House, and a group of people in black T-shirts and jeans gathered around an enormous camera while two actors in period dress rehearsed their lines.

I dug my phone out of my bag and dialed. My aunt picked up on the third ring.

'Hey there, baby girl,' she said in that gravelly voice of hers that was courtesy of a thirty-year Marlboro Reds habit. 'How're you holding up?'

'Okay,' I said. I ducked down a side street lined with parked cars and leaned up against the wall of one of the tall stuccoed buildings. 'How is she?'

'Oh, you know.' I heard the flick of her lighter and then a long inhale. 'Pretty much the same.'

'Did the money get to your account okay?'

'Of course it did, honey. Thank you.' She took another drag. I could picture her standing on the screened-in porch, cigarette tucked into the corner of her mouth, blondish-gray hair piled on top of her head, eyes a washed-out watery blue.

'Does she need anything else? I could order some clothes . . .'

'Don't waste your money,' she said. 'She's got plenty of clothes. If she needs anything, I'll let you know.'

'Okay.' A car rolled by, a sleek Jag, the engine purring.

'I'm sorry I haven't called lately,' I said. 'It's just, with the wedding and work and everything . . .'

'Jenny, you don't have to apologize. I know you have a life to lead – you can't be expected to call every fifteen minutes. We're doing fine here, I promise.'

'Can I talk to her?'

There was a pause and the sound of the lighter sparking up again. 'She's not having a great day today, honey,' she said gently.

I nodded. 'Tell her I love her.'

'Of course. But she knows you do without me saying so.'

'I'll make plans to come visit soon,' I said, knowing this wasn't true.

'We'll be here,' she said. 'There's no rush. You just live your life, honey.' There was a commotion in the background, the murmur of the television punctuated by someone shouting. My mother. 'I've got to go,' my aunt said. I could hear the tension in her voice. 'Send our love to Christopher. Bye, baby girl.'

The line went dead.

I needed a drink, badly. The thought of going back to the flat seemed impossible now.

It was a clear, crisp evening, and the air was filled with the spring smell of mulch and grass. I headed up Lower Regent Street and turned onto Shaftesbury Avenue, the screens of Piccadilly Circus flashing ads for fizzy drinks and fast food above me. I spotted the enormous Waterstones and a plan started to form. I ducked inside, picked up a paperback I'd been wanting to read, and paid for it at the till. Tonight, I decided, I'd take myself out for dinner.

I know, this isn't exactly revelatory. People go out to dinner on their own all the time. I'd see them sitting at a bar or in the window, one hand holding a book or a newspaper, the other a fork, and I'd feel the same way about them as I would someone who ran into a burning building to rescue a goldfish. Brave, sure, but was it strictly necessary?

But tonight, that brave idiot would be me.

There was a little Italian place on the corner that looked nice, so I screwed up my courage, pushed open the door, and asked the maître d' for a table for one. He escorted me to the bar, handed me a menu, and disappeared without a word.

My eyes flicked across the page without taking much in. The bartender appeared and took my order – a glass of white wine and a plate of *cacio e pepe* – and then, just like that, I was on my own.

I tried, very hard, not to panic.

I dug the paperback out of my bag and cracked the spine. It was a literary affair – something about a middle aged man having an amorphous life crisis – and the words swam in front of me. All I could hear was the clink and scrape of silverware on china, and the murmured rush of good conversation flowing around me.

Deep breaths, I chanted to myself. Deep breaths.

But it was no use. The confidence that had buoyed me into the restaurant deserted me as quickly as it had arrived. It was as if I could feel everyone's eyes on me, watching me, discussing me, pitying me. I half expected to turn around to find a gaggle of pitchfork-wielding townsfolk pointing at me and shouting SHAME! SHAME! The bartender delivered my wine with a small smile. He's probably laughing at me, I thought. Probably off in the backroom now, laughing with the barback about the sad, wizened spinster out front.

I could feel myself spiraling, the black maw opening up inside me. And just like that, I was back in the day of the flying ants.

It was a normal Saturday in late August. My mother was in the kitchen, the papers spread out on the kitchen table, her half-drunk coffee cooling beside her elbow. I had come downstairs for a Diet Coke and a sleeve of Chips Ahoy! My mother raised an eyebrow at that, but didn't say anything. She didn't have to. I raised my hand to my cheek, felt the irritated constellation of pimples that had bloomed since my eleventh birthday, and quietly put the cookies back in the cupboard. Years later, I would read an article stating that there was no link between junk food and acne – it was mostly hormonal, apparently – but at that point, everyone thought you got pimples from eating chocolate. And I had a lot of pimples.

I was sloping my way back up the stairs, cursing my terrible skin and knobbly knees and flat chest and red hair and every other aspect of my general appearance, and, while I was at it, personality, when it happened. The phone rang.

I jumped. I remember that clearly: I nearly jumped out of my skin when it rang. To this day, I don't know why. The phone rang all the time in my house, particularly that summer, when Isla was trapped at home with a broken leg, and phoned me constantly to discuss the latest episode of *Dawson's Creek*. She had it for Pacey, bad, though I never understood the appeal.

Still, when the phone rang this time, and when I heard

my mother get up out of her chair, pick up the phone, and say hello in that cool, slightly removed voice she used for the telephone, I was seized with fear.

'Who is this?' I heard her ask. There was a pause as she listened, and then she said, not in her normal telephone voice, but something sharper, shakier, 'No, I'm not interested. I told you never to call here again.' The phone slammed back down on the receiver, and then there were footsteps running towards the front door and my mother was screaming my dad's name over and over. 'Kevin! Kevin!' I froze in the stairwell. My dad had been gone for three months.

I ran outside after her. She was standing on the lawn in her robe, screaming and crying and wrenching at her clothes. There were red marks on her arms from where she'd torn at the skin with her fingernails. She saw me coming out the front door and wheeled on me. 'That woman keeps calling me!' she was shouting. 'Your father's little whore!'

My father's girlfriend never called the house. She wouldn't have. She was too scared of my mom.

That's when I noticed the flying ants.

They descended like a great black cloud, covering the grass and the pavement, zooming into our open eyes and getting stuck to our eyelashes. I swatted them away, but there were too many of them. All the while my mother was screaming, flying ants were swarming all around her as she stood on the front lawn, her mouth open, her eyes screwed shut, her face wet with tears.

I tried to get my mother to calm down, but I couldn't. She kept screaming and crying, and then, finally, when I'd managed to coax her back into the house, she started destroying things. Everything, really. She threw pictures and vases and ornaments. A mirror smashed. She pulled apart pillows, feathers floating through the air. She moved into the kitchen. I pulled on her arm, tried to block her way, but I wasn't strong enough. She was filled with what seemed like a superhuman strength. And she was not going to stop.

Eventually, a neighbor called the police, and a cruiser and an ambulance pulled up to the house. I let them in and pointed up the stairs, and the EMTs trudged wordlessly through our living room and up to my parents' bedroom, which, I realized, the thought hitting me like a bolt of lightning, was just my mother's now. They wheeled her into the ambulance and took her away. One of the officers stayed behind until someone could come and look after me. I begged him to take me to the hospital so I could be with my mother, but he just shook his head and offered me another Mentos from the roll he kept in his pocket. Looking back on it, he was only a kid, too, really — no more than twenty-two, a rookie cop stuck with the job of babysitting the crazy lady's kid. When I started to cry, he put the TV on to the Cartoon Network and poured me a glass of milk. It was sweet, really. But it didn't help. I knew then that I was on my own.

My mother was hospitalized. I went to stay with my aunt while she was away. My father called every day but I wouldn't speak to him. He had left us, and now my mother was broken, and it was his fault. At least that's what I believed for the first few years, when it was just her and me on our own. He even turned up on my aunt's doorstep, clutching some stupid teddy bear like he'd already forgotten that I was almost twelve and not some little girl that could be placated with a stuffed animal. My aunt chased him out of her driveway and then came back in and handed me a whole package of Chips Ahoy! I ate the lot.

After three weeks, my mom came home, and I moved back in with her. She tried hard to make it seem like everything was back to normal, but it wasn't. She would hug me and smile and laugh at my jokes like she always did, but there was something missing from her after the day of the flying ants. She looked like someone who'd had the blankets permanently ripped away from her on a cold morning. Haunted.

I took a sip of wine. The taste of it on my tongue – cold and crisp and delicious – was enough to shake me out of the moment. My shoulders dropped half an inch, and I heard myself let out a tiny little sigh. The bartender appeared again with my plate of pasta, and set it down in front of me. Steam curled up towards me.

'Do you need anything else?' he asked.

I shook my head. 'I'm fine, thanks.' I placed the napkin in my lap, took another sip of wine, and stole a quick glance around the room. There was a group of professionally dressed thirty-somethings in the corner, one of them raising his glass in a toast. An elderly couple held hands across their table. Two middle-aged women, both dolled up to the nines and with bulging shopping bags resting at their feet, were in peals of laughter. And not a single one of them was looking my way.

I twirled a few strands of pasta onto my fork and

popped it into my mouth. The spaghetti was al dente, the sauce creamy and cheesy and peppery. Perfection. I washed it down with another swig of wine and signaled to the bartender for a refill. My shoulders dropped another half an inch.

I stuffed the book back into my bag. I didn't need a shield, or a distraction. I was here on my own, and that was okay. No one had turned up with a pitchfork and judged me. In fact, no one gave a single flying fuck what I was doing at that particular moment. I'd pushed myself to do something outside of my comfort zone, and I'd survived. In fact, I'd enjoyed it, the same as I'd enjoyed the spicy food at that restaurant the other night, and climbing up that wall, and singing to a full room. I'd taken a step out into the unknown, and I hadn't lost myself in the process.

I finished the pasta and the second glass of wine, and asked for the bill. The bartender presented it to me alongside a tiny glass of limoncello and a plate of chocolate truffles, and I sank the drink and ate all the truffles, and left with a smile on my face. And then I went to the movies on my own, and saw a film that I actually wanted to see rather than one that I thought Christopher would at least tolerate, and I was so caught up in this incredible rush of sistas-are-doing-it-for-themselves freedom that it was only when I was walking to the Tube that I realized I still hadn't heard from Jackson. It really must be over. The twin feelings of relief and sadness accompanied me all the way back to my still-empty flat.

13

I was asleep by the time Christopher came in, and in the morning he still had the red-eyed, rumpled look of a man who'd had a dinner of six pints and two packets of cheese and onion crisps. 'Plus some peanuts,' he added when I handed him a glass of water.

'Good,' I said, dropping two ibuprofen capsules in his upturned palm. 'I was worried about your protein levels.'

He smiled. 'That's funny,' he said, but he didn't laugh. For once, I wished he'd laugh at something I said. Him telling me he thought it was funny didn't have quite the same effect.

'How was everyone?' I asked, pushing my irritation aside.

'You know,' he said, swallowing down the tablets. 'The usual. Jonno's panicking about the baby, Crispin's boss is riding him like a Shetland pony—'

'I thought Shetlands were more decorative than functional.'

He waved me away. 'Figuratively speaking, then. Steve's got a new girl on the go – blonde, apparently, and quite young.'

'Obviously.'

'Says he's found the one, but I think we both know how that's going to go.'

'I won't buy a fascinator just yet.' I plucked the damp towel off the bedroom floor and hung it across the bedframe to dry.

'And then Spanner brought out his bloody deck of cards and started doing his whole "pick a card, any card" shtick at the poor group of lasses next to us, and he ended up chucking the whole deck at the window.'

I looked up, aghast. 'Why the hell did he do that?'

He shrugged. 'Said he'd seen David Blaine do it once, and thought he knew the trick.'

'But he didn't know the trick?'

'Does Spanner ever know the trick? Three years of magic classes, at vast expense, plus God knows how many hours watching instructional videos on YouTube, and the man still wouldn't be able to pull off a trick if it was Halloween and he had a roll of toilet paper and a carton of eggs.'

I laughed. It was true, Spanner was hopeless at magic, despite his enduring belief that he was Houdini incarnate. He'd once tried to pull a pound coin out of my ear, and instead got tangled up with my earring. He nearly severed the lobe.

Christopher set his glass of water on the bedside table and pulled me towards him. 'C'mere,' he said, kissing me lightly. The sweetly stale smell of old booze still clung to him. 'I missed you last night.'

'Me too.' It was nice being together like this, the old shorthand flowing between us, the sheets warm from the heat of his body. Even in his hungover state, he still looked adorable – like the dissolute-but-ultimately-charming-Englishman-who-turns-out-to-secretly-be-a-prince in a Lifetime Christmas movie.

'What did you get up to? Just stayed in?'

I shook my head. 'I went out to dinner,' I said.

He raised his eyebrows. 'Not with bloody Ben again, I hope.'

I felt a swell of anger rise inside of me. What did it matter if I had gone out to dinner with Ben? I'd explained a hundred times that Ben was just a friend. I didn't nag Christopher when he went out with his friends, even that girl Becky he'd gone to uni with who I knew still harbored a crush on him. She called him 'Toph' in a tittering voice and shot me murderous looks when his back was turned. I opened my mouth to say something when I remembered that I'd lied about seeing Ben, anyway, and that maybe right now wasn't the time to go around righteously defending my right to interact with the opposite sex, seeing as the last time I'd done that I'd ended up married to one of them.

Instead, I smiled and said, 'No, on my own, actually.'

He scrunched up his face. 'You went out to dinner alone?'

'And to the movies.'

'Oh God,' he groaned, pulling me in closer. 'I'm sorry. I had no idea you were so keen to go out last night. You should have told me!'

'Why? Would you have canceled your plans?'

He pulled back, surprised. 'We were wetting Jonno's baby's head – a bit of a tradition – so probably not, but I would have invited you to tag along. It was a bit of a lads' night, so not sure how much you would have enjoyed it, but at least you wouldn't have had to go sitting in a restaurant on your own like a saddo.'

'It's okay,' I said. 'I actually had fun.'

'You don't need to say that just so I won't feel guilty.'

'I'm not.' I saw the look of horror on his face and laughed. 'Seriously, it was nice! I sat at the bar and had a drink and then I went and saw a movie that you would never in a hundred years have wanted to go to. It was actually kind of great. I might do it again soon.'

He still looked dubious, but managed to shrug his shoulders. 'As long as you're all right. Still, we should arrange something with the other couples soon. Once Jonno's wife's recovered from the birth, maybe. It would be good to give you an airing.' I wondered briefly at the idea that I was a cupboard, or a wound. 'Speaking of couple things, Crispin said he went to a cracking wedding the other week and thought the venue might be good for us. I thought we could go down this weekend, take a look?'

'Where is it?'

'I don't know – Somerset somewhere. Durleigh? Thurloxton?'

The words meant nothing to me, but I thought of uncrossed items on my to-do list and nodded enthusiastically. 'Sounds great!'

'Perfect. Maybe we could stay in a little B&B nearby, make a night of it.'

I nodded. 'Sure!'

'Great. Actually, I'm swamped today – would you mind having a look at places? I'll send you a link to the venue when I get into work. Speaking of which . . .' He hauled himself to his feet with a grunt. 'I should get going. Do me a favor and put the kettle on? There's no chance I'm getting through this morning without a brew in me. I've got Ken the Shredder at 9.30 wanting to go over the McMannon case.'

'Of course!'

He bent down and kissed me on the lips, and I watched his slim, muscular back retreat into the bathroom.

I padded into the kitchen and flicked on the kettle. A weekend away might be nice. Get some fresh air, some space from London, check out this wedding venue . . . Yes, it would be good. Christopher and I could have some time together, just the two of us, and start getting our heads around the idea of the wedding. I plonked a teabag into the mug I'd got Christopher last Christmas – a chipped blue affair with GOTTA RUN! emblazoned across the front (get it? Because he likes to . . . oh, never mind) – and poured in the boiling water. Maybe I could find a place with one of those big roaring fires.

My mind flashed back to the men on the Tube talking about weekends away in the Cotswolds. I couldn't shake the image of a room full of bloated jackasses pouring schnapps down the throats of their giggling mistresses. I shook my head, hoping to dislodge the thought. No. The weekend away would be nice. A little getaway.

Maybe it was just what I needed.

The journey to work was blissfully without incident – no noses buried in armpits, no accidental-or-otherwise gropings, and no braying pack of idiots pontificating about shagging or cricket or both. I arrived just after nine, made myself a cup of coffee, and settled in to do some groundwork before I set off for Columbia Road that afternoon.

Jeremy seemed convinced that Bryant had been up to something, but so far I couldn't find any concrete evidence of wrongdoing. His accounts were in order. He paid his taxes on time. Sure, he wasn't answering his phone, and no one knew where exactly he was living now, but his house had just burned down. Who really felt like chatting over a cup of tea and a slice of Victoria sponge after a thing like that? Maybe he'd just had a really bad string of luck.

I pulled out the formal police report on the fire, along with the sheaf of photographs documenting the damage. The forensics all seemed to check out – the electrics were old, and the conclusion was that one of the fuses had blown and a spark had caught on the curtains in the back of the shop. I glanced at the photograph – a tattered, blackened piece of canvas hung limply from the metal rings. I held it up to the light. There, through a tear in the fabric, was what looked like a small silver dial ringed with black numbers. My heart lurched. It looked like the lock on a safe.

Maybe Bryant had left something in there. A will, or bank documents that might point to his wife's life insurance money. There was no guarantee that it would lead anywhere, but there was the possibility, and that was enough to spur me on.

I was congratulating myself for being so eagle-eyed when Ben bowled into the cubicle, shouting good morning at me.

I started in my seat and stared at him. He was wearing a pair of dark denim turn-ups so tight I worried for the future of his unborn children, an artfully distressed

T-shirt, and a pair of box-fresh Jack Purcells. His hair was styled within an inch of its life, and the cubicle immediately filled up with the scent – sorry, 'oud' – of Dior Homme. 'He's alive,' I cheered. 'ALIVE!'

He rolled his eyes, but couldn't quite manage to wipe the cat-that-got-the-cream-and-the-salmon-and-hell-why-not-even-the-caviar look off his face.

'Soooo,' I said, grinning at him moonily. 'I take it you heard back from Lucy?'

He shrugged. 'She rang me last night.'

I couldn't believe he was going to try to style this out all nonchalantly. 'Annnnnnd?' I prompted.

Another shrug. He'd somehow become French overnight. 'We're going out tonight.'

'Tonight?!' I crowed. 'I thought you'd asked her out for Saturday?'

He blushed, a proper, deep crimson. 'She said she couldn't wait.'

'Holy Mary Mother of God! This is great!'

He broke now, finally, like a flood against a dam of twigs. 'I know! It's so weird, because when she called I was all like, maybe she's calling to tell me to leave her alone, you know? But then she was all like, hey, sorry I didn't get in touch with you sooner, I was in Luxembourg.'

'She was in Luxembourg?'

Another shrug. As if a jaunt to Luxembourg was a normal, everyday occurrence. As if it was almost surprising that we ourselves were not currently in Luxembourg. 'She works in finance, so . . .'

'Wow. She must be a high-flyer if they're sending her to

Luxembourg.' I heard my father's voice come out of my body, and yet I was powerless to stop it.

He smiled shyly. 'Yeah, I think she's quite senior. Anyway, she was all, sorry I've been MIA, let's go for drinks tomorrow, and then I'll stay at yours, and we can go out for brunch or whatever on Saturday.'

'And you said yes?' I gripped the arms of my chair. This woman was not pulling any punches. I scanned Ben's face for signs of The Fear. The old Ben would have changed his phone number and deleted his Snapchat if a woman had proposed they share a cab, never mind a weekend. But the new Ben was just smiling idly at two interlinked paperclips on his desk, as though they were representative of the powerful cosmic nature of true love.

''Course I did,' he said, clasping his hands behind his head and leaning back in his swivel chair. 'Why wouldn't I?'

And that, my friends, was the moment that hell froze over. 'Well,' I said, reaching over and catching him on the shoulder. 'I'm really happy for you.'

He shrugged again. Seriously, he'd gone so Gallic that at any moment he was going to throw a string of onions around his neck and declare that he was going on strike. 'It's cool,' he said casually. 'I figured it would work out.'

'Sure you did.' Poor little Satan and his minions, so very, very cold down there.

'How's it going on the Bryant case?' he asked, tipping back in his chair.

I opened my mouth to tell him about the safe in the photograph, but decided against it. Best to wait until I had concrete evidence. 'Nothing new,' I shrugged. 'Hopefully one of his neighbors will have seen something.' Or, I thought, I'd see something for myself.

The rest of the morning sped by, and before I knew it, I was finishing up my Pret sandwich, brushing the crumbs from my chair, and gathering up my belongings.

Ben glanced up as I slung my bag over my shoulder. 'You off to do your sleuthing?' he asked through a mouthful of All Day Breakfast.

I nodded. 'I'll probably be back before the end of the day,' I said. 'I have to file a few things for that hit-and-run claim.'

He rolled his eyes. 'Christ, you're such a spod.'

I shot him a saccharine smile. This was only half-true. I was definitely a goody-two-shoes when it came to work, but I'd also failed to look into a single B&B for the weekend, and I knew Christopher would ask when I got home. I figured I could come back to the office and do a quick Internet search so I'd at least have something to offer over dinner tonight.

I waved goodbye to Ben and shot out of the office. I checked the time on the way out: ten past two. My mind whirred with mental calculations. Fifteen minutes on the Victoria Line. Change at King's Cross or Highbury and Islington? Getting the Overground might take a little longer, but it would save me the walk from—

I heard a low whistle, and a deep voice call out to me from across the street. 'You look like you mean business.'

I looked up to find Jackson leaning against the wall opposite, jacket slung over one arm, booted foot cocked against the bricks. He gave me a sly grin, and made his way across the street towards me, neglecting – as ever – to look out for traffic. A car beeped as it swerved to avoid him. He didn't so much as blink.

'What are you doing here?' I asked as he arrived safely on my side of the street.

'We had a deal, didn't we?'

'I know,' I spluttered, 'but I left you a message –'

He waved me away. 'I never listen to my messages.'

'That's very irresponsible,' I asked. 'What if it's important?'

'My theory is that if someone has something important to say to me, they'll call back.' He reached up and plucked a bit of fluff from my hair. My mind flashed to the feeling of his palm cupping my chin in the bar the other night. It had seemed so clear-cut the night before, but now that he was standing here in front of me, holding a biscuit crumb he'd fished out of my hair between his thumb and fore-finger, I was wavering. 'Anyway,' he said, blowing the bit of fluff from his fingertip, 'I know how much you hate talking on the phone, so I figured I'd show up in person and save you the agony.' He smirked at me. 'So what was your message about?'

'Nothing,' I muttered. 'It wasn't important. And what makes you think I hate talking on the phone?' Not that it wasn't true. Phone conversations, even with people I knew – even with Isla! – made me break out into a sweat. I always ended up pacing around the room like a panther, talking in a too-loud voice usually reserved for football matches, or trying to communicate with people who didn't speak your language. If I was forced to call the gas company or book a doctor's appointment, I would mentally rehearse what I was going to say before I dialed. I don't know what I thought was going to come out of my mouth if I didn't – a confession about a sexual deviance? Some sort of strange verbal tick? – but attempting to apply logic to the situation was pointless. Still, I didn't remember telling Jackson as much.

'You told me about it in Vegas.' He shook his head. 'I still can't believe how much you don't remember from that night.'

'Don't remind me,' I groaned.

'It seems like I don't have much of a choice. Anyway, you told me how much you hated the phone, so I figured it was futile to try to talk any sense into you that way.'

I bridled at this. 'What do you mean, talk sense? I'm the one who's being rational here, not you.'

'Hey there, no need to get all defensive.'

It was enough to spin me off into another dimension of irrational rage. 'And what exactly do you think you're doing, just showing up at my office like this? I get that you don't have a normal job – that you like to "live free" or whatever, like a poor man's bongo-playing-era Matthew McConaughey, but some of us actually take our jobs seriously, and it is totally inappropriate of you to keep turning up like this.'

He gave me a long, even look. 'You done?'

I huffed. 'Yes.'

'Glad to hear it. Now where are we off to?'

My stomach clenched. 'We?'

'Sure. We missed our dinner last night, which means we've got time to make up.'

'I'm not having dinner with you tonight,' I blurted out.

'Even more reason for us to spend the afternoon together. Come on, where to? Anywhere you're going, I'm going.'

'What if I said I was going to get a bikini wax?'

He raised his eyebrows. 'I'd say I'll buy you a whiskey now and one when you're done. But that's not where you're going, is it?'

'It's a work thing,' I said. 'I have to go to Columbia Road and try to get this guy's neighbors to tell me he's a crook.'

'Sounds like fun. Besides, I'm great at getting people to tell me stuff.'

I looked at him sceptically. 'You are?'

He crossed his arms. 'You want me to tell you what your nickname was in high school?'

Oh God. I couldn't have! There was no way I would have told him. Only Isla knew the story about Brad Tompkins stumbling over my soccer cleats in the middle of a make-out session. Even today, the humiliation of it was enough to make my gorge rise. Whatever a gorge was.

He winked at me then, the bastard. 'Let's go, Garbage Feet. We've got neighbors to grill.'

I groaned. 'What the hell else did I tell you that night?'

He tapped the side of his nose with his finger. 'That's for me to know and you to find out. You thinking of changing at King's Cross or Highbury and Islington? The Overground will take longer but—'

'It will save the walk,' I said, 'I know, I know.' We set off towards the Tube. 'So you didn't have to work again today?'

He shrugged. 'They don't need me much.'

'Pretty sweet gig. What did you say the movie you were working on was?'

'I didn't,' he said. 'It's some big budget dystopian thing. They're still scouting locations and they wanted me to come along to check out possible camera angles. Anyway, let's not waste our time talking about boring stuff like work. Why don't you tell me about the time you tried out for the cheerleading squad?'

I stopped short. 'Oh my God! I didn't.'

'Relax. I'm sure they thought you had tissues stuffed in your bra because of your hay fever.'

'Shut up,' I hissed.

'Just a shame you didn't think of it before you did that cartwheel . . .'

'Arghhhh! You know, some people might class this as harassment.'

'Some have,' he reached over and tucked my hand in the crook of his elbow, 'but the charges have never stuck.'

We ended up taking the Northern Line. We emerged at Old Street, the traffic of the roundabout drowning out our conversation even in the middle of the day, and gazed up at the enormous cranes lifting steel beams into place on flashy new blocks of flats called things like The Apothecary and The Old Printing Press.

Jackson shook his head as he took it all in. 'Things sure change fast. When I lived here, it was all council flats and artists' squats.'

I shot him a sceptical glance. 'Didn't you say you lived here ten years ago?'

'That's right.'

'I'm pretty sure Old Street wasn't exactly a shanty town back then.'

He laughed. 'Okay, you got me. Maybe I'm looking back with rose-colored glasses.'

'More like a rose-colored telescope,' I said.

'Still,' he said, gesturing towards a skyscraper built like a jackknife, 'all this glass and steel wasn't here, and I'm damn sure there wasn't a fancy coffee place in the middle of the roundabout.'

I tugged on his arm. 'C'mon, gramps. Let's go before you start telling me about how you used to walk three miles to school every day.'

'In the snow,' he added.

'Uphill both ways.'

We grinned at each other before setting off down Old Street. We passed glass-fronted cafés stacked with people pecking away on MacBooks, pubs with late lunchers sneaking in a pint before returning to their flexible work space, and boutiques displaying collections of what looked like extortionately priced sticks.

He stopped short when we got to the intersection with Curtain Road. 'Do you mind if we take a little detour?'

I checked the time. It was ten to three. 'Sure,' I said, and we hooked a right.

He shook his head and *tsk*ed as we passed former dive bars that were now fancy tapas places, skate shops that were now salons, and a pub that was now a Foxton's. 'At least the tattoo place is still there,' he said as we looped around on ourselves, 'but I don't think I'm ever going to get over that American Apparel.' He stopped outside of Rivington Street

and pointed up at the top floor of a nondescript brick building. 'There,' he said. 'That's where we used to live.'

I followed his gaze. 'We?'

'Me and my girl,' he said quietly. We both stood there for
a minute, staring up at the building, before a man with a
handlebar moustache pushed past and stirred Jackson out
of his reverie. 'Come on,' he said, shaking his head. 'No use
standing around here looking for things that are long gone.'

I wanted to ask him about this girl – his girl – but the
look on his face told me not to push him on it. At least not
right now. We walked the rest of our journey in silence,
crossing the melee of Kingsland Road and into the relative quiet of Hackney Road. I stopped him just before we
got to Columbia Road.

'Okay,' I said, brushing the hair back from my face. 'So
here's the deal. I'm going to go knock on some doors and
hope that one of this guy's neighbors wants to invite me
in for a cup of tea and a chat.'

'The lonely old woman ploy,' Jackson said. 'I like it.'

'What I need you to do is to not talk.'

'Hey now!'

'I mean it! This case is a big deal at work, and I can't
have you going around ruining it.'

He folded his arms across his chest. 'Are you calling me
a ruiner?'

'Based on evidence to date, yes, I am calling you a
ruiner. Why don't you go have a cup of coffee or something?' I spotted a café done out to look like a 1950s tea
parlor and pointed to it. 'There! Go sit in there and have
a piece of Victoria sponge, and just don't – don't—'

'Do anything?'

I nodded gratefully. 'Exactly.'

He rolled his eyes. 'Fine. But if you get into any trouble, just let me know. I'm telling you, I can charm the birds out of the trees if necessary.'

'Leave the birds in the trees and the snakes in the grass and all other animals exactly where they are. Got it?'

'Got it.' I watched as he walked, whistling, across the street and pushed open the door to the café. A bell chimed his arrival and I heard him calling out a greeting to the waitress. God help her.

I decided to take a walk down the street to get the lay of the land before approaching anyone – or, as Jeremy would say, to case the joint. Victorian terraces lined the street, most of them with shopfronts painted in pretty shades of blue and green and pale yellow. There was an old dairy on one side, its ground floor now a posh bakery, and a school set back from the road and guarded by a wrought-iron fence. Most of the windows on the houses were lined with flower-boxes overflowing with blooms in bright reds and pinks.

In short, it looked like a postcard of a place rather than a real one, and I was certain I'd never been in the vicinity of so many artisanal throw pillows in my life.

It was gorgeous, of course, but there was something about it that didn't feel real, and it was smack dab in the middle of it that I found Mr Bryant's shop, its boarded-up remains sandwiched between a shop selling upscale baby knitwear and a gluten-free crêperie. Even before the fire, his shop would have stuck out like a pair of Clarks at a Louboutin sample sale.

I doubled back on myself and headed towards the Hackney Road end. Here, the façade of pleasant gentility wore away to reveal its original, slightly grittier incarnation. The park was beautifully kept, but thankfully full of people who didn't look like they'd fallen out of a Boden catalog. A bunch of schoolkids chased each other, squealing, as their mothers looked on impassively. A teenaged girl with Coke-can headphones on walked past clutching a cardboard box full of chips, the tinny thud of bass surrounding her like a cloud. And there, on a park bench, sat a pair of old men, hands resting on top of canes, heads angled in towards each other, just taking it all in.

They would be as good a place to start as any.

'Excuse me,' I said, striding over to them. 'Do either of you know Edward Bryant?'

The two men exchanged glances. 'Sorry, darling, never heard of him,' the man in the flat cap said.

'He owns the cobblers,' I said, pointing down the street. 'There was a fire there a few weeks ago?'

The man with the white moustache scratched his chin. 'Doesn't ring a bell . . .'

I sighed. 'Do you live around here?'

The man in the flat cap gave me a long appraising gaze. 'That's a very personal question, young lady.'

'Yes,' the man with the moustache piped up. 'Why should I tell you where I live? I don't know you from Adam.'

'You might follow us home,' the flat cap man said.

'Knock us on the head and rob us blind,' the moustache man added.

'I'm not – I'm just—' I spluttered.

The two men looked at each other and broke into laughter. 'We're only joking, love,' said the man in the cap. 'Of course I know the cobblers. I've lived here nearly twenty years.'

'He's still settling in,' said the moustache man, jerking his thumb towards flat cap. 'I've been here since I was just a nipper.'

'Great!' I said brightly. 'So can you tell me—'

'Now where's your accent from?' The man in the flat cap rested his chin in the cup of his hand and smiled up at me.

'America.'

'Ah, America! Lovely place. Always wanted to go. Where in America are you from?'

'New Jersey,' I said reluctantly. I was always reluctant to admit to Brits I was from New Jersey. First of all, because they were always hoping for somewhere more glamorous – New York, Los Angeles, even Florida had a strange allure. And second –

The man in the flat cap lit up like a casino at Atlantic City. 'Baddabing! New Jersey! *Sopranos*, right?'

I nodded wearily. 'Right.' The only things most British people knew about New Jersey came from *The Sopranos*, which meant that as soon as they heard I was from there, they assumed that I owned a fur coat and understood that pointing-at-the-nose gesture, neither of which was true.

'Brilliant program, that,' said the man with the moustache. 'My son got me the DVD for Christmas one year and I watched the whole series in a month.'

'Lazy git!' hooted the man in the cap.

'Yes, it's a great show,' I said, 'James Gandolfini was an amazing actor. Now, about the cobbler shop—'

'Such a shame he popped his clogs, isn't it?' The man in the cap looked positively mournful. 'So young, too.'

'True, but you can't live like he did and not suffer the consequences,' the man with the moustache said, gently caressing his own sizable stomach.

'The fella did look like he loved a bit of steak, God bless him.'

'Nothing wrong with that!' The two men dissolved into laughter again. It was becoming increasingly clear that I wasn't getting anywhere with them.

'Look,' I said, a little too impatiently, 'I don't have much time, so I'd really appreciate it if you could tell me a little bit about the cobbler shop.' I saw the eyebrows shoot up on the two men, but ploughed on regardless. 'Were you there the day of the fire? Did you see anything? Did you speak with Mr Bryant at all?'

The man with the flat cap rose to leave, leaning heavily on his cane for support. 'Sorry, love,' he said, 'I'm afraid I can't help you there.'

The man with the moustache joined him. 'His mind's not so good these days,' he said, placing a steadying hand on the back of the bench. 'And neither is mine. Good luck.'

They nodded at me curtly and shuffled towards the exit of the park. I suppressed the urge to scream.

'Not going too well, huh?' I turned to find Jackson smirking at me. He held out a paper takeaway cup. 'Thought you could use a coffee.'

'Thanks,' I said, snatching the cup from him. I took a sip. The coffee was hot – I felt the tip of my tongue sizzle on contact – but delicious. 'I thought I told you to stay in the café.'

'It's exactly that sort of charming attitude that got you so far with those two gentlemen,' he said, nodding towards the now-empty bench. 'You sure you don't need a hand? I'm telling you, I'm good with people.'

I sighed. 'Fine. But only because I know you're not going to leave me alone anyway.'

He fell in step as I walked back towards the street. 'Great! Where to next?' He rubbed his hands together. 'This is like being a private eye. I always wanted to be a private eye, didn't you? All those Chandler novels . . .'

I glanced over at him. 'You read Chandler?' Somehow Jackson didn't strike me as the Chandler type. He was too . . . glib. Although, frankly, he didn't really even strike me as the reading type.

His eyes lit up. 'Oh, man, I love Chandler! *The Big Sleep. The Long Goodbye.*'

'*Farewell My Lovely,*' I added.

'That's my favorite.'

'It is?' It was mine, too.

'Absolutely! It has the best character name in fiction.'

'Moose Malloy!' we chorused.

He grinned at me. 'I've never met a woman who was a Chandler fan.'

'Really?'

He shrugged sheepishly. 'I don't tend to go for brainy types, if you know what I mean.'

I pictured a long line of pert blondes fanned out in front of him like a deck of mildly erotic playing cards. 'That doesn't surprise me,' I said ruefully.

'Hey, you can't have it all. Have you watched the films?'

I nodded. 'Most of them.'

'Who's your favorite Philip Marlowe?'

I considered this as we turned left and towards a row of neatly kept houses. 'Everyone always says *The Big Sleep*, and of course you can't argue with Bogart and Bacall—'

He shook his head and took a sip of his coffee. 'Can't argue with that at all.'

'But I think the best Marlow is Elliott Gould—'

'In *The Long Goodbye*!' he chimed. 'He's amazing, isn't he?'

I found myself beaming. No one ever knew about Elliott Gould. 'Totally!'

'That movie is so weird and 70s-trippy, right?'

'Those girls living across the hall from him . . .'

'And that scene in the house in Malibu!'

We nodded at each other like a couple of those bobble-headed dolls you could get in cheap souvenir shops around Leicester Square. Just then, a scraggy-looking dog bounded up to us, tongue out, tail wagging. I took a step back – when I was little, my mother had warned me not to pet strange dogs because they could 'bite my face off' – but Jackson was on his knees in an instant, scratching the dog behind its ears while it thumped its tail happily on the ground. I watched as the dog rolled over and showed him its belly. 'Good dog,' he cooed, getting right down on the ground beside it.

'Jackson,' I cautioned, 'be careful. That might be an attack dog or something.'

He took the dog's face in his hands and held it up for me to see. 'This dog?' The dog looked dazed with happiness, a thin thread of drool hanging from the corner of its mouth.

241

I took a cautious step forward. 'I'm just saying, you don't know what kind of dog it is.'

Jackson took the dog's cradled head and stared into its eyes. 'What kind of dog are you, huh? Are you a bad dog, like the mean lady says?'

'Jackson!'

'Or are you a good dog? I think you're a good dog, yes I do.' A brief bout of play wrestling commenced, and it was difficult to tell who was having more fun – Jackson or the dog.

It was amazing, really. I spent my whole life calculating risk, weighing up the options, and following the rules, and here he was, just ploughing through like a bull on a bender. And I still couldn't decide if he was a genius or an idiot because of it.

Just as I mentally debated the point, a frazzled-looking middle-aged woman with a bouffant of light blonde hair tore across the park towards us. 'Max!' she shouted, 'Max!' The dog momentarily stopped licking Jackson's face and gazed quizzically at the woman, who arrived by our side huffing and puffing like she'd just won the 400-meter hurdles. 'I'm so sorry,' she said, grabbing for the dog's collar. 'She was there one minute and when I turned around – whoosh! – she was off like a bloody rocket! Pardon my language.'

'No need to apologize,' Jackson said, getting to his feet and dusting down his knees. 'Max and I were having a good old time, weren't we, girl?'

'She's such a tart,' the woman said, shaking her head. 'I'm Marjorie, by the way.' Jackson and I introduced ourselves, as Max rolled around in a patch of grass. 'Fox poo,'

Marjorie said, pointing at the dog, wriggling merrily on her back. 'She can't get enough of it. Disgusting, really.'

'My dog was just the same,' Jackson said. 'He'd find a foxhole and go nuts for it.'

'Dogs are strange creatures, aren't they? Really, I don't know why I put up with her.' The indulgent smile on her face told a different story.

'They're crazy all right,' Jackson agreed. 'That's what I love about 'em.'

'Well, I don't want to take up any more of your time,' Marjorie said, producing a leash from her jacket pocket and bending down to secure it to Max's collar. 'Lovely meeting you.'

'You too,' I said, reaching down to give Max a tentative pat on the back. Her fur was thick and coarse, like horse-hair, and the smell of her lingered on my hand.

'Say,' Jackson said, getting back down on the ground and gathering Max in his arms for a hug. I was starting to wonder if we should leave them alone for a while. 'I don't suppose you could do us a favor? My friend and I here were looking to talk to someone who saw that fire at the cobbler's place up the road. I don't suppose you know anyone who might be willing to have a chat with us?'

I shot him a look. He was being way too upfront. There was no way this woman was going to—

'Of course!' Marjorie trilled. 'Now, I saw the smoke from my house – I live on Wellington Row, just over there – but I didn't see much else. Betty Cranfield, though – she'll have seen it. That woman sees everything around here. I swear, she must have been a member of the SOE during the war.'

'She sounds like our gal,' Jackson said, beaming up at her. 'Could you tell us where we could find her?'

'Let's see,' she said, consulting her wristwatch. 'It's ten to four on a Friday, so she'll be having her hair set in Daisy's just up the road.' This was impressive knowledge of Betty Cranfield's schedule. Marjorie must have clocked my surprise because she laughed and said, 'I know that makes me sound mad, but I always take Max for a walk at the same time every day, so you get used to seeing the same people in the same places. And every Friday, Betty's under the blower at Daisy's. You'll find her there, I'm sure.'

'Thank you so much,' I gushed.

'No bother! It's always a pleasure to meet a fellow dog lover.' She addressed this to the top of Jackson's head, and by the look on her face, I was pretty sure it wasn't just his appreciation for canines she was admiring. 'Just tell her Marjorie sent you, and tell her I'll be round in the morning with the papers once I'm finished with them. Saves her a trip to the shops,' she explained.

'That's very sweet of you,' I said.

She straightened her shoulders. 'It's a small community around here. It may be all posh bloody cafés and fancy boutiques on the street, but most of us have been here for ages. We look after each other.' I picked up a slight defensive tone in her voice, and wondered if she wasn't just talking about bringing Betty the paper. Maybe she knew more about the fire than she was letting on. 'Right then,' she said, tugging on Max's lead. 'Come on, you, let's get you back to the house. She'll be dead on her feet after all this excitement.'

Jackson gave Max a final scratch and reluctantly

climbed to his feet. 'A pleasure to meet you, Marjorie,' he said, taking her hand in both of his. Marjorie swayed slightly under the weight of his charm offensive, and I had to physically restrain myself from rolling my eyes.

'Lovely to meet you, too, Jackson. Maybe I'll see you again around the park . . . ? I know Max would love that.' Yeah right, I thought. Max is the one who'll be pining away.

'I hope so, too,' Jackson said, dipping his head and giving her a little wink. Jesus, the guy was really laying it on thick.

'Nice to meet you, too, Janice,' Marjorie said, giving me a cursory wave before turning to leave.

We watched her and Max make their way across the park, Max stopping at every bush, rock, bench, and fellow dog to have a sniff, while Marjorie tutted and tugged on her leash. It took me a few seconds to realize Jackson's shoulders were shaking with laughter.

'What's so funny?'

'Oh, nothing,' he said, a grin spreading across his face. 'You ready to go, Janice?'

'Shut up,' I hissed, but soon I was laughing, too. 'What about you, Casanova? You were practically clutching a rose between your teeth while doing the tango back there. I don't know who was more taken by it – Max or Marjorie.'

'Marjorie, I reckon.' I reached out and smacked him on the arm. 'What? It worked, didn't it?'

I rolled my eyes. 'We'll see about that. Come on, let's see if you can work your magic on Betty, too. Something tells me she's going to be a harder sell than poor Marjorie.'

Jackson interlaced his fingers and cracked his knuckles. 'Sweetheart,' he said, 'I'm just getting started.'

In the end, we were both right. Betty was indeed a tricky customer, all sidelong looks and tuts and sighs, and Jackson was indeed up for the challenge, all winks and grins and ma'ams. In fact, he basically ma'amed her into submission. No one could have withstood the tidal wave of ma'ams he unleashed, regardless of their suspicion of outsiders or the state of their bunions or their overall abiding sense that these two Americans were trying to pull a fast one.

We found her just where Marjorie said we would, her white hair neatly sectioned and pulled tight around a set of bright pink curlers, the tang of ammonia and the floral scent of her perfume heightened by the heat of the hood dryer that hummed above her head. Daisy's itself was set in time as tightly as Betty's perm, with its black bucket seats, checkerboard floor, and photos of elegant women displaying the latest hairstyles from 1963 tacked up on the wall. I wondered how this place had survived the transition into hipsterville, but the steady stream of nicely turned-out ladies of a certain age clutching rolled-up umbrellas and pulling check-printed shopping carts into the salon quickly answered my question.

So, after much cajoling and charming and downright flirting, Betty told us about the fire.

Well, she told Jackson about the fire, while I tried to make myself as inconspicuous as possible. Betty had taken one look at me in my Zara trousers and my court shoes and my trench coat and had decided that I was not trustworthy in the least. Worse – that I should be ignored at all costs, like a lunatic singing Abba tunes on the 134 night bus.

'I'll tell you what I saw,' Betty said, peering at Jackson above her bifocals, 'though I don't know what good it will do you. I was sat at the café across the street – you know, that trendy one that does the croissants with chocolate in them – and I was having a cup of tea – they do do a nice cup of tea, mind – when I smelled a funny sort of smell.'

'What kind of smell?' I asked. She ignored me.

'So I said to Sophie – she's the girl who runs the café, lovely girl even if she has ruined her face with that piercing – I said, can you smell that? And she said, yes, I can, it's a sort of acrid smell. I think it's coming from out-side. So the two of us went outside and there was smoke coming from the front of Ed's shop. Great thick black clouds of it.'

My mind whirred. Electrical fires usually produced white smoke. It was flammable liquids – like gasoline – that produced black smoke.

'I said to Sophie, quick, call the fire brigade! She went off to phone them and I stood outside and shouted up to Ed, in case he was home. "Ed!" I shouted. "Ed, your shop is on fire!" But there was no response. So I started worry-ing that maybe he couldn't hear – he's a lovely man, Ed, but deaf as a post – but then there he was, scuttling up the street fast as anything. The look on his face – well, I'd never seen anything like it.' She shook her head at the memory. 'Just horrible. He'd spent his whole life in that shop, and he'd only recently lost his Vicki . . .'

Jackson glanced at me. 'Vicki was his wife?'

She nodded. 'An absolute gem, she was. They were childhood sweethearts, you know.'

My heart softened at this. 'Have you seen Mr Bryant since the fire?'

'Oh no,' she said. 'As soon as the flames were out, he up and left. We haven't heard from him since.' She gave Jackson a beseeching look. 'You're not here to tell me he's dead, are you? I don't think my poor heart could take another shock.'

Jackson looked at me, and I shook my head. 'No, ma'am,' he said, reaching out and covering her hand with his. She visibly softened at his touch. 'We're not here to tell you anything bad has happened to Ed. My friend here is just trying to get to the bottom of how the fire got started, that's all.'

'Does Mr Bryant have any debts that you know of?' I asked. 'Any trouble with the shop?'

Betty bristled. 'He's an honest, hardworking man, if that's what you're asking.'

'I'm sure he is,' I said, 'but if he was struggling, or having trouble . . .'

'There's no trouble,' she said, 'the man is a saint.' The firm set of her mouth indicated that our nice little chat was now finished.

Jackson must have sensed it, too, because he pushed back his chair and got to his feet. 'Can we get you anything before we go? I could run across the street and get you a cup of tea?'

'That's fine, dear,' she said, patting the back of his hand. 'I'm all right for the moment, but thank you.'

'Thanks for speaking with us,' I said, offering her my card. 'If you think of anything else, please give me a call.'

She batted the card away and fixed me with a gimlet eye. 'I don't know what you think you're up to, but I can tell you this: you won't find any snitches around here, so it's no good you coming around here asking questions. I can promise you that no one around here has a bad word to say about Ed Bryant – you can be sure of that. Now if you'll excuse me, my curls are starting to singe.'

And with that, we were dismissed.

We walked out of the salon and headed down the street towards the cobbler shop, dejected. 'Did you have to go in so hard back there?' Jackson asked.

'I was just trying to get to the point!' He was right, though – I'd blown it. Subtlety had never been my strong suit conversationally, and I lacked Jackson's charm to finesse my way through it. The thought of his superior skill in the situation made me unnaturally angry.

'Man, you would have made a terrible salesman,' Jackson laughed. 'Did you see the look on her face?' He let out a low whistle. 'If looks could kill, I'd be ordering a cold cut platter for your funeral right now.'

'Thanks for the sympathy,' I spat. 'Shit. What am I going to do now? That woman was like the Columbia Road Mafioso, right? She's going to spread the word that a nosy American is poking around where her nose doesn't belong and – bam! – the doors will slam shut.' In my panic, I'd reverted to talking like Jeremy. 'I'm going to be left high and dry,' I sighed.

'Aw, it can't be all that bad, can it? I mean, how important is this whole thing, anyway? The man's shop burned down. He had insurance, you're the insurance company, so you pay out the money. Right?'

I tried to hold my temper. 'It's not that simple,' I said tightly. 'I have to prove that the fire was an accident, and so far there are a few things that suggest that it wasn't. Like Mr Bryant skipping town, for one.'

He raised an eyebrow. 'You really took those Chandler novels to heart, huh? Next thing I know, you'll be smoking a cigar and complaining about a dame that done you wrong.'

'Just be quiet and let me think, will you?'

He tipped an imaginary hat. 'Take your time, gumshoe.'

My mind whirred. What did I know so far? I knew that Edward Bryant had lived in the shop for years. I knew that we'd paid out life insurance following his wife's death, but that money hadn't materialized in his bank account. I knew that the shop was meant to have burned down in an electrical fire, but the smoke was black rather than white. And I knew that there was a safe hidden somewhere inside the boarded-up shop. An idea began to form.

'Come on,' I said, tugging on Jackson's arm.

'Where to now, PI?'

I glanced up at him as we hurtled down the road, past a shop selling bespoke Moroccan tiles and another selling expensive kitchenware. My heart thudded in my chest, knowing what I was about to do. 'How opposed are you to a little bit of trespassing?' I asked. It was madness, really, but I didn't care. My whole life seemed mad at this point. I might as well take a page out of Jackson's book and throw caution to the wind . . . particularly if there was the potential to be productive in the process.

He grinned and threw me one of his patented winks. 'Why, Jenny Sparrow, you are full of surprises.'

Breaking and entering was surprisingly easy. The front of the shop was boarded up, but if you went through the alley adjacent to it, you found yourself in a trim little garden that backed onto the building. And if you pushed the back door a little harder than one usually would, you were inside the burned-out shop quicker than you could say 'intent to commit a felony'.

'Right,' Jackson said, clapping his hands together. A pile of desiccated leather tipped to the floor. 'What are we supposed to be looking for again?'

'I'm not sure,' I admitted as I peered around at the charred walls. 'Proof that the electrics really did cause the fire, I guess.'

'I thought that was what the fire department was for.' He picked up a tool and brandished it in the air. 'What the hell is this thing?'

'An awl,' I said, 'and yes, the fire department did a full report and concluded it was an electrical fault, but I just need to double-check.'

'Because our good friend Eddy has disappeared?'

I nodded. 'That's part of it, but really it's just about being thorough. I like to be thorough.'

'I'm guessing that's how you knew this thing was an awl?' he said, waving the tool at me.

'I researched cobbler tools before I came, in case anything stuck out as strange.'

'Yeah, the thing that would be strange about this situation would be finding a tool that didn't fit.' He was about to put the awl back on the table when he stopped in his tracks and turned to me, eyes lit up like a pair of disco balls. 'Hang on a minute. Does that mean you were planning on breaking in here all along?'

I gave him a sly smile. 'I wouldn't say I *wasn't* planning on it . . .'

'You little devil! And here I was thinking you were a rule-follower.'

'I am a rule-follower!' I said, indignant. 'I love rules. It's just . . . sometimes to catch a rule-breaker, you have to be willing to slightly bend them yourself.'

'You call this,' he said, gesturing towards the pried-open back door, 'rule-bending?'

I nodded decisively. 'Yes.'

'Whatever you say, boss. Now, where do you want to start?'

'Over here, I think.' I stepped past a low stool and ducked behind what had once been a workbench. The smell of sulfur and damp paper and the oaky smell of charred wood filled my lungs. I stopped and stared.

In the far corner, just below the grime-smeared windows, a tangle of wires peeked out from a hole above the trim. I crouched down for a closer look. Sure enough, the protective coating had worn away on parts of the wires and the ends were all frayed. A fire hazard if I'd ever seen one. All it would have taken was one little spark to catch the curtains, and – whoosh! – the whole place would have lit up like a Christmas tree.

'Found something?' I looked up to see Jackson looming over me. I pointed at the wires and he let out a low whistle. 'Those are some dicey electricals right there. You think that's what caused the fire?'

I nodded. 'That's what it said in the report, and this looks like it matches up . . .'

'Huh. Well, at least you know the guy was telling the truth now, right?'

'Maybe . . .' I stood up and dusted down my knees, my eyes scanning the room until they snagged on the scrap of curtain I'd seen in the photograph. I hurried over and pushed it aside, revealing a stretch of soot-blackened wall, and – the hairs on the back of my neck stood up – a safe. I tried the door, assuming it would be locked, but it opened easily. I peered inside and my heart sank. The safe was empty. If there had been any evidence inside, Ed Bryant had made sure it was long gone by the time we turned up.

Jackson, on the other hand, had a different interpretation of events. 'Well,' he said, slapping the wall with the flat of his hand, 'looks like you hit the jackpot.'

I scratched the back of my neck and stared inside the empty safe. 'It doesn't prove anything,' I said finally.

He shot me a look of incredulity. 'What do you mean, it doesn't prove anything? The guy has a safe in his shop, the place burns down under suspicious circumstances and – poof! – the safe is empty and someone's covered it up! Feels like an open and shut case to me.'

I shook my head. 'All we've done is find an empty safe.

That doesn't prove anything other than that Mr Bryant was cautious about where he kept the store's cash.'

Jackson scrunched his face up. 'Then what the hell are we doing here?'

'Barking up the wrong tree, I guess. Sorry I've led you on this insane wild goose chase.'

'Don't worry about me,' he said, nudging me with his shoulder. 'Believe it or not, this isn't my first wild goose chase, nor is it the first crime I've committed.' He clocked the look on my face and laughed. 'No need to look so shocked, my dear – it wasn't anything serious, I promise. I'm not about to tell you that you're married to an axe-wielding murderer.'

'Thank God for small favors,' I grumbled. I looked around the room, suddenly despondent. 'God, what am I going to tell my boss?'

'Tell him the truth. You tried your best, but you couldn't find anything that incriminated the guy. Who knows – maybe the fire really was an accident.'

I shook my head. 'My boss definitely doesn't think so.'

He looked at me. 'What do you think?'

I considered this. 'Honestly, I don't know what to think. All of this stuff – the safe, him disappearing – it all seems to point to something bad. But for some reason, I can't bring myself to believe he did it. It was his home for forty years. His wife's, too, before she died. Why would he just burn it down?'

He let out a long sigh. 'Grief makes people do crazy things. Makes them strangers even to themselves some-times.'

I looked up at Jackson, willing him to say more, but his mouth was drawn tight.

I thought of my mother. If my father hadn't left her and broken her heart, would she be a different person now? Or was it always inside of her, and the grief had just unlocked it?

'I don't know about you,' Jackson said, breaking the dark silence that had descended on the room, 'but I sure could use a drink. I saw one of those fancy-looking gastropubs on the corner – why don't you let me buy you an overpriced beer?'

I hesitated. It was only five o'clock – I should really go back to the office and type up my notes, see if there was a piece of the puzzle I was missing. And I still hadn't sorted out a B&B for the weekend ... But the Tube would already be packed with early rush-hour commuters, and the look on Jackson's face was practically beseeching. Maybe a pint wouldn't be such a bad idea.

'Okay,' I said, picking my way through the detritus to the back door. 'But only one.'

'Sure,' Jackson grinned at me. 'Just the one.'

'Another round?' Jackson lifted his empty pint glass and waggled it at me. One had already turned into two after the first round disappeared in a matter of gulps – our adrenal systems still on high alert after all the criminal activity – but three felt ... incendiary. I checked the time on my phone: 6:45. Christopher would be home by eight at the latest, and I still hadn't booked anywhere for our weekend away.

Jackson saw the hesitation on my face and rolled his eyes. 'I'm asking if you want another pint, not a bunch of ketamine.'

'I'm just a little worried about the time,' I said. 'Christopher—'

'Christopher will cope if you're out past seven. C'mon, just one more. Particularly as you're leaving me high and dry this weekend.'

News that I was going away for the weekend had not been well received. There was cajoling. There was hectoring. There were even thinly veiled threats about husband's rights and the difficulty of procuring a divorce in the state of Texas. (Not true: I'd looked it up when he'd gone to the bathroom. For the low price of $139.99, you could get a divorce in Texas in less than twenty-four hours.) But finally, there'd been a nod of his head and a raising of his hands. 'I know when I'm beat,' he'd said, though he hadn't shown any evidence of that to date.

'Fine,' I said eventually, 'but just a half.'

He reappeared with a half-pint glass filled mainly with gin, only the faintest splash of tonic floating on top. I took a sip and winced. 'This wasn't really what I had in mind.'

He winked at me. 'I know it wasn't.' He clinked his glass – filled with a tawny brownish liquid – to mine. 'Bottom's up, sweetheart.'

The gin hit my stomach just as I realized I hadn't eaten anything other than a meagre Pret sandwich that day. 'I think I need some nuts or something,' I muttered as the heat from the liquor warmed my esophagus. The adrenaline from the break-in – I still couldn't believe I'd instigated something that could be described as a break-in – had deserted me, and I felt jittery and slightly giddy. I took another sip and felt my nerves begin to steady.

'Salted or dry roasted?'

The nuts didn't do much to mitigate the booze, and by the end of the glass, my head was fizzing pleasantly and I was lolling slightly to the left.

'Right,' Jackson said, pushing the little triangle of folded up paper across the table at me. 'Your turn.'

'Get ready,' I said, balancing the triangle on the table. He pointed his index fingers at the sky. 'Hang on, your goalposts are closer together than mine were!'

'They are not. Now are you going to shoot or what?'

'Not until you move the goalposts further out.' I reached across the table and pulled his hands further apart. 'There.'

'Are you kidding me?' He regarded the distance between his two fingers, which admittedly was now quite considerable. 'You're such a cheat.'

'I'm not a cheat!' I cried, indignant. 'You're the cheat!'

'That's real adult of you.'

'Cheat, cheat, never beat,' I chanted.

'For Chrissakes, will you just shoot already?'

I lined up the triangle and flicked. The bit of paper sailed across the table, through his upstretched fingers, and landed squarely in the middle of his chest. 'Goooaaaaaaaaaaaaaaaaaaaaaaal!' I shouted. A few of the other patrons turned and looked at me crossly, but for once I didn't care. Let them stare, I thought. I'd just won a game of flick football.

'Best out of three,' he said, pushing the triangle back towards me.

I shook my head. 'I'm officially retired,' I declared. 'I will never again play flick football.'

'For God's sake – you know, you're a real piece of work.'

'Takes one to know one,' I said, sticking out my tongue.

He shook his head. 'Man, I should have turned up with a flask that first day outside your office. You're a fun drunk, you know that?'

'I'm not drunk!' But I was. That much was obvious. More drunk than I had been since . . . I felt myself blush. Oh yeah. Since I married him.

'You were a fun drunk in Vegas, too. Do you remember the first thing you said to me in that bar that night?'

'I think we've established that I don't remember much from that night,' I said, but something at the back of my mind was pushing its way to the front, like a little kid who really, really has to pee. 'Wait, was it something about being an heiress?'

He nodded. 'You told me you were the great-great granddaughter of the man who invented the toilet-roll holder.'

Of course I had. As Isla would tell you, it was classic early 20s'-era Sparrow. She and I had spent pretty much the entirety of our twenty-second year cavorting around New York making up stories about ourselves while chatting up strange attractive men (strange in that we didn't know them, not in that they were weird. Though some definitely were weird). The toilet-roll holder one was a favorite.

'Did I also tell you that Isla was a princess whose family owned half of Peru?'

His eyebrows disappeared into his hairline. 'So you do remember! Yes, you tried that one, too, but I quickly sussed out that a Peruvian princess was unlikely to be named Isla. Call me crazy.'

A snort of laughter escaped from somewhere deep inside of me. 'Oh God,' I moaned, hiding my face in my hands, 'I can't believe I said those things to you.'

'Don't be,' he said, waving it away, 'it was hilarious. Like I said, you're a fun drunk.'

I thought back to my time with Isla in New York. We hadn't just been fun drunks, we'd been fun sober people, too. We'd crashed gallery openings, taken paper-wrapped subs from Peppino's to Prospect Park to watch the sun set, splashed through open fire hydrants on muggy August afternoons. We'd lived fast and loose with our time. I had work, sure, and Isla had school, but still the days and nights seemed to stretch before us as huge, endless expanses.

And then it had changed. I'd changed.

'Hey, you okay?'

I looked up to find Jackson studying me, his mouth pulled down. I forced myself to smile. 'Fine,' I said brightly.

'You were on a different planet there for a minute. What had you so lost in thought?'

'Nothing,' I said, shaking my head quickly. 'It's not important. So how long did it take you to figure out I wasn't a toilet-roll holder heiress?'

He leaned forward in his chair. 'Are you telling me you're *not* a toilet-roll holder heiress?' He whistled. 'Well then, what the hell am I doing here? I had big plans for that money, I'll tell you.'

I laughed. 'What makes you think I'd share any of my toilet fortune with you?'

'Alimony, sweetheart,' he said with a wink. 'I intend to be ruthless.'

'Well, I'm sorry to say the most I can offer you is a half a toaster and a couple of bonds I still haven't cashed from my graduation.'

'I thought the insurance racket was a good one,' he said.

'It's not bad.' I felt suddenly defensive of the payslip that arrived in my inbox each month. 'But London isn't particularly conducive to saving money.'

'I hear that. I pretty much only ate baked beans when I lived here, and I walked everywhere because I couldn't afford the bus, never mind the Tube. Best way to see the city, though, so I don't regret that.'

I paused before saying what I said next. 'You mean when you lived here with your ex?'

He nodded but didn't say anything more. And really, that should have been the end of it. He clearly didn't want to talk about it, and it wasn't any of my business, but I couldn't help myself. It was like trying to ignore a mosquito bite – eventually you were going to tear into the skin like a rabid dog with a chicken.

'What happened between you two?' He caught his breath as if I'd punched him in the gut, and I felt instantly, horribly embarrassed. 'Sorry!' I said hastily. 'Honestly, just ignore me.'

'No, it's fine.' He took a deep breath and let it out slowly. 'She died.'

I felt my face fall. 'Oh my God,' I gasped. 'I'm so sorry.'

He shrugged. 'It's okay.' He shook his head and corrected himself. 'I mean, it's not okay' – he let out a little half-laugh – 'of course it's not okay, that she died. But it's okay that you asked.'

'We don't have to talk about it.'

He took a sip from his pint, placed the glass back down on the table, and stared into it, as though an answer might be conjured from it. 'It's okay. Really. Her name was Anna. She was English – a real East London girl, all blonde hair and long legs and attitude.' I felt a twinge of jealousy and shooed it away. I had no right to be jealous of any girlfriend of Jackson's, and I sure as hell didn't have the right to be jealous of a woman who was dead. 'We met when I was backpacking through Europe,' he continued, rolling his eyes at the cliché. 'In Greece. I was off my face on ouzo and was walking back to the hostel when I ran into her. Literally. I physically ran into her. Almost knocked her over. I actually did fall over, right at her feet.' He shook his head at the memory. 'I remember looking up at this – this *goddess* towering above me, and thinking someone must have slipped something into that last glass because there was no way someone that beautiful could be anything other than a figment of my imagination. And then she opened her mouth and said, in the most incomprehensible cockney accent, "Fucking hell, watch where you're bloody going, you fucking idiot!"' He looked up at me and smiled. 'And that was it. Love at first sight.'

'I met Christopher the same way,' I said.

'You did?'

I nodded. 'I tripped running for his cab. He had to scrape me off the pavement. Though there was less cursing, and I'm pretty sure the word "goddess" didn't enter his mind when he was doing it.'

He shot me a weak smile. 'You never know. There must have been something to make him fall for you.'

'Maybe it was the way the light hit the asphalt,' I said. 'So you guys met in Greece, fell in love, and then you moved to London to be with her?'

'Pretty much.'

'How long were you together before . . .' I couldn't bring myself to finish the sentence.

He didn't hesitate. 'Two years, three months, and eighteen days.'

'That's a long time,' I said. 'Especially when you're that young.'

He shrugged. 'Yeah, well. Not long enough.'

Silence fell at the table. I picked up a beer bottle and started peeling strips off the label.

'You're wondering what happened to her,' he said finally. It wasn't a question. I nodded. 'A car accident.'

'Jesus.'

'She was on her way to some reclamation yard in Dorset. She loved going to those things – the more junk, the better. I used to call her Oscar the Grouch – obsessed with garbage.' His eyes creased fondly at the memory. 'She was good at it, though. Our flat was filled with stuff she'd found. "My gems", she called them. Anyway, she'd been wanting to go to this one place in Dorset for a while, so she convinced her father to lend her his van – he was in construction – and off she went.' He shook his head, just once. 'I was supposed to go with her. She'd been on at me about it for weeks, but the day before we were supposed to go, I got a call about a job. We needed the money, so I took it. And she went on her own.' He picked up his pint, swirled the liquid around. 'It should have been me that was driving. I'm a bad passenger, I would never have let her drive. She must have got distracted or something, taken her eye off the road. She went too fast around a sharp corner and—' He took a long drink from his pint and set his glass back down on the table.

'After she died, I couldn't handle it. I just cut and ran – packed a suitcase and caught the first flight back to Texas. I didn't even stay for the funeral.'

'You were in shock,' I said.

He shook his head angrily. 'I was a coward. I knew I couldn't stay in London – everywhere I looked, I saw her.' He smiled sadly. 'I still do. But I should have stayed and faced it with her family like a man, rather than running off like that. I'll never forgive myself.' He looked desolate. 'I've been running ever since, I guess.'

My heart thudded in my chest and I realized I'd been holding my breath. 'It wasn't your fault,' I said, in one long, rushed exhalation.

He looked up at me, the corners of his eyes crinkling at the edges. 'You said that the first time,' he said sadly.

'What do you mean?'

'I told you about Anna that night in Las Vegas. I thought you might remember but . . . it doesn't matter.'

I clapped a hand over my mouth. 'I'm so sorry,' I said, 'I can't believe I don't remember. I'm such an asshole.'

He put up a hand. 'It's fine.'

'It's not fine!' Shame shot through me like a hot flush. 'God, I can only imagine what sort of wisdom I was spouting in that state. I can't believe you ever wanted to see me again.'

He stared down at the table and rubbed at a water ring with his thumb. 'Actually, you were great.'

I studied his face for a minute. 'I was?'

He nodded, but wouldn't meet my eye. 'You were the first person I could talk to about it. It was strange – I mean, I never talk about it, about . . . her, but something about you . . . It was like I couldn't *not* tell you or something.'

I struggled to make sense of this. 'Sometimes it's easier to talk to a stranger,' I said, floundering.

He opened his mouth and I saw the hesitation on his face. 'You told me about your mother, too,' he said quietly.

I froze. 'What did I tell you about her?'

'About her breakdown. Her condition. About how you had to look after her after your father left.'

'Oh.' I wasn't sure what to say. I never, ever talked about my mother, but apparently I'd told a total stranger on a night out in Las Vegas. The realization brought the familiar terror with it. Maybe this was how it would start. Maybe I was finally losing control.

'Hey,' Jackson said, giving me a nudge. 'It's okay. We all need someone to talk to sometimes.'

I shook my head. 'I'm sorry I offloaded on you like

that,' I said. 'You must have thought I was . . .' I swallowed, hard. 'Crazy.'

He shook his head decisively. 'No. I definitely didn't think you were crazy.' He lifted his eyes to meet mine, and an electric current ran through me. 'I thought you were amazing.'

Jackson looked bemused as my gaze flicked around the room like a startled bird. I was definitely flustered. There was no chance of hiding that. What had he meant by 'amazing', exactly? That I was amazingly easy to talk to? Isla always said I had a 'responsible mom' vibe about me – that even when we did crazy and/or stupid things in our twenties, she knew she could count on me to have correct change for the bus, or tissues tucked away in my bag. Was this the same thing? Maybe, even in the depths of drunken oblivion, I'd tapped into those reserves. Maybe I'd offered him a shoulder to cry on, or sourced some soothing warm cocoa. Honestly, who knows?

I knew, deep down, that it was possible that he wasn't referring to my aptitude for packing tissues or proffering comforting beverages. There was some kind of connective undercurrent running between us. I raised my eyes to his, just for a minute. He was watching me with an intensity that was downright unnerving.

'Thanks,' I said finally, the words just managing to edge their way past my lips.

He opened his mouth to speak just as his phone started to buzz on the table. He looked down at the screen and his face fell. 'Shit,' he said, 'I have to get this.' He stood up from the table, picked up his phone, and walked to the far end of the bar. But not before I saw the name that had flashed up on his phone: Colette.

Colette. That was a pretty name.

I watched him as he spoke into the phone, head bowed, fingers running through his hair. He caught me looking and turned his back to me.

I tried to work my way through what Jackson had told me. He'd had a girlfriend called Anna, who he'd loved, who'd died. She was beautiful. He blamed himself for her death. He'd told me about this that night in Vegas – how could I not remember? – and I'd said something that had helped him. What had I said? How could I have helped?

I looked back towards where Jackson was standing, still deep in conversation. He'd turned back to face me now, and when I looked up his eyes met mine. He forced a smile, but his eyes looked pained.

I felt suddenly, irrationally, angry. Who was this Colette person, and what was she saying to make him look that way? A girlfriend, probably. I've never even asked if he was single. It's an odd question to ask your husband, admittedly, but it would have been useful to ask in this case, before . . . before what? I was engaged to Christopher. It was none of my business if he was seeing someone. Even if her name was Colette. God, she was probably French, which meant she was gorgeous and rake-thin and smoked roll-ups, and had one of those blunt fringes I'd always wanted but could never pull off. She probably wore leather trousers and looked good in them. Man, I hated Colette.

'Sorry about that.' Jackson had rematerialized and was settling back down at the table.

'No problem!' I said brightly. Do not ask who it was, I chanted to myself, do not ask who it was. 'Who was that?' I asked.

He shot the phone a treacherous glance. 'No one important,' he said. 'Just a work thing.' So beautiful French Colette was just a colleague. I did my best to ignore the relief that flooded through me. 'So,' Jackson continued, 'where were we?' My mind flashed back to the look on his face when he'd told me about that night in Vegas. What had he said again? 'I thought you were amazing.' No one had ever said anything like that to me before. And then the feeling that ran through me when I'd met his eyes, that fizzing electric heat.

'I can't remember,' I mumbled.

He leaned forward in his chair and brushed the back of my hand with his fingertips. My skin felt hot beneath his touch. 'I can,' he said gently. 'Jenny, I have to tell you something.'

'Oh, I'm sure you don't,' I said nervously.

'I lied when I said I'm in London for work this week.'

I looked at him. 'What?' What did this mean for French Colette?

'I mean, I'm here for work, but that's not the real reason.'

'Oh.' I could feel what was coming and gripped the arms of the chair as though preparing for take-off.

'That night in Vegas . . . the way we talked . . . I haven't been able to talk to anyone like that since Anna.'

'Jackson . . .'

He held up his hand. 'Let me finish. I've spent the past

ten years thinking I would never feel that kind of closeness with anyone ever again. Hell, I didn't want to feel it – I knew how much it hurt when it was taken away. But then I met you. Even that night in the casino, when you had that awful sunburn and you got so pissed off at the roulette table – do you remember? Even then, I felt like we had a connection.'

I raised my hands to my face. My cheeks felt hot to the touch. 'I was a mess.'

He smiled. 'Even when you're a mess, you're a good one.'

'Please,' I said softly. 'Stop.'

'After you left that morning, I realized I had to see you again. Obviously there was the whole matter of us being married by Elvis, but it was something more than that. You had this . . . hold on me. And then when this job came up and I knew I'd be in London . . .' He shrugged. 'It felt like fate.' He looked across the table at me, his green eyes clouded with uncertainty. 'Was it?'

'I should go,' I said, scraping back my chair.

He leaped to his feet. 'Please, Jenny. Don't run off like this.'

I shook my head. I needed to get out of there. I couldn't sit across from him one more minute – it was too much. Part of me was desperate to hear what he had to say, but another part of me – the same part that had worked so hard to build this life for myself, to tick off item after item on my list, to form myself into the person I felt I should be – couldn't stand to listen to another word. It was too dangerous. It felt . . . incendiary. As if my whole life would go up in a flash as soon as he opened his mouth again. 'I've got to write up these notes when I get home,' I gabbled, 'and Christopher will be wondering where I am, and—'

'Jesus, will you stop wondering about what Christopher wants for one second?' he spat angrily.

The breath caught in my throat. I'd never heard him speak like that. 'I do,' I spluttered. I felt my cheeks grow hot. 'I mean, I don't. I don't think about what he wants all the time.'

He folded his arms across his chest. 'That's bullshit.'

I was angry now, too. 'You know what? You're right, I do think about what Christopher wants. You know why? Because he's my fiancé, that's why. Because we have a life together. Because I love him.'

He shook his head. 'You don't have to waste your energy convincing me,' he said. 'You need enough of it to keep convincing yourself. How long have you been engaged now? A month? And you're still not wearing a ring. When are you going to stop pretending that you want to marry him?'

I gripped the edge of the table to stop my hands from shaking. 'You don't know what you're talking about.'

'That's the thing,' he said, reaching for my hand. I batted it away. 'I do know. I know you're not happy with him. I know he's not right for you. That night in Vegas, you told me—'

'Will you stop talking about what happened that night? Don't you get it – I don't remember any of it! It didn't mean anything to me! I was drunk, and stupid, and—'

'You told me that you never made him laugh.'

My mouth clamped shut. The truth of it pierced through me. It was true, I never made him laugh. I saw him laugh with his friends – a big, booming laugh, all teeth and belly – but with me, he never did. Maybe it was the whole British sense of humor thing – maybe we didn't match up. Maybe I just wasn't funny.

And then, as though he could hear my thoughts, Jackson said, 'You're funny, Jenny.' I looked up at him, and he nodded, just once. 'You are. And if Christopher can't see that, he's a fool and he doesn't deserve you.'

'You don't know him,' I said quietly.

He smiled sadly. 'But I know you.'

Silence settled around us. I could hear my heart thudding in my chest, the blood rushing through my ears. I thought of Christopher, the way he looked like a little boy when he came in from a run, bright-eyed and flushed. The solid warmth of his body beside mine when I slept. The years of long-distance phone calls and transatlantic flights. The look on his face when he picked me up from the airport when I finally moved to London, the way he'd held my hand and said to me, 'This is where our lives begin.' All the plans I had. The little house with the lilac bushes in the front yard (Number 34). The pink upturned faces of small children, a boy and a girl (Numbers 38 and 39). The vacations to Sardinia and Provence and Santorini (Number 43). The tiny white villa someplace hot where we'd retire (Number 51). It was all there for us, plotted out on a map that I held in my hands. And here was this stranger sitting opposite me, telling me I should scrap the whole thing and start again.

The air inside the pub suddenly felt muggy and cloying, and all I could smell was stale beer and the scent of roasting meat wafting through from the kitchen. My breath started to come in short, staccato bursts. I had to get out. I grabbed my bag and stood up. Jackson reached for my wrist, but I dodged him and ran out the door and onto the street.

The streetlamps had just switched on, casting a yellowish glow onto the pavement. Young couples walked arm in arm, peering in windows of boutiques that were now shut, heads tucked in towards each other as they murmured plans for the weekend. I pushed past them and set out at a run. I had to get away from all of them.

I heard footsteps behind me, and then a hand tug on my arm. 'Jenny, for God's sake, stop!'

I shook him off and spun around on my heel. Jackson was bent double, panting from the exertion. 'Jesus Christ,' he said in between gasps, 'I didn't realize you were part cheetah.'

'I did track as a kid.' Number 14 on the list: Make the varsity cross-country team. Tick. I took in his broad shoulders and lean torso. 'I didn't realize you were so unfit.'

He put a hand to his chest and patted it fondly. 'I did Marlboro Reds as a kid.'

I put my hands on my hips. 'What do you want, Jackson?'

'I want you to tell me why you ran out like that, to start with,' he said.

I sighed. 'Because I want to go home. Because I don't want to talk about that night in Vegas ever again. Because you have no right to sit across from me and judge the way I live my life. And that's just to start with.'

He shook his head, and, infuriatingly, smiled. 'You really are a pain in the ass, you know that?'

'Takes one to know one,' I said.

'Ah, there's that refined wit of yours.'

I rolled my eyes. 'Shut up, will you? Please, for once in your life, just shut up.'

He took a step closer, and then another. I could smell the faint trace of soap and aftershave lingering on his skin, along with something deeper, almost musky. Heat seemed to radiate from him. I took a step back onto the road, but he reached out and pulled me back onto the pavement.

What happened next seemed to unfold in slow motion. The Friday-night revelers streaming past, on their way to restaurants and pubs and house parties and evenings in with a takeaway and Netflix. The way Jackson raised his hands, tentatively at first, and then quickly, as though he was about to catch a firefly in his cupped palms rather than my face. The feel of his fingers on my cheeks, the softness of them, the surprising lightness of his touch, and then his face coming towards me, his hazel-green eyes open and staring straight into mine, and then the warm pressure of his mouth on mine.

It only lasted a second before I came to my senses. But not before I found myself kissing him back.

I pushed him away. 'What the hell are you doing?' I hissed.

He took a step back and ran his hands through his hair. 'I don't know,' he said, 'I just thought—' He gave me a searching look. 'You can't tell me you don't feel something between us.'

'I don't feel anything!' I shouted. An elderly man who was passing us stopped and asked gently if I was all right. The pity in his eyes made me want to weep. 'I'm fine,' I said hurriedly, waving him away. 'I was just going.'

'Don't go,' Jackson said, putting a hand out to stop me.

'Don't touch me,' I seethed. I saw the hurt look on his face and softened. 'I'm sorry. It's just – this is my life,' I said, gesturing around me. 'And here you come swooping into it and telling me to blow it all up.' I shook my head. 'And I can't.'

He bowed his head. 'I don't want you to blow your life up,' he said quietly.

'I have to go.' I moved to leave, but he blocked my way. 'I'm going away with Christopher this weekend. I have to pack.'

'Meet me on Monday morning.'

I looked at him. 'What?'

'Meet me on Monday morning halfway across Westminster Bridge. My flight isn't until the afternoon, I could take you for a coffee, or breakfast if you want, and we could . . .'

'What, Jackson? What could we do?'

'Talk,' he said gently.

'I can't,' I said curtly. 'I have work. I have a fiancé.' I threw my hands in the air, exasperated. 'I have a life!'

'I want to have a life with you.' His gaze remained steady, and I felt myself wilt under its intensity.

I looked away. 'This isn't real life, Jackson. You know

that, right? You and me, we never should have even met. I shouldn't have got drunk, I shouldn't have said whatever it was I said to you, and I sure as hell shouldn't have married you. Now please, I have to go home. Will you let me go?'

'Monday morning, nine a.m., Westminster Bridge,' he repeated. 'If you don't come, I'll go back to America and I'll give you your divorce.'

'You will?'

He nodded. 'I promise. If you don't show up, I'll send you the papers and you'll never have to see me again. But please, just promise me you'll think about it.'

'There's nothing to think about.'

'Maybe not,' he said. 'But think about it anyway.'

I nodded and pushed past him. I could feel his eyes on my back as I headed towards Hackney Road, but I didn't turn back to see.

'Something happened.' I was pressed against the side of a pub a few blocks away from the flat, phone clutched to my ear, breathing ragged and irregular. On the other end of the phone, I could hear Isla's footsteps as she rushed down the corridor, and the faint bleep of a far-off heart monitor.

'Okaaaaaay. You're going to have to be more specific.'

I'd managed to get most of the way home in a dull, shocked haze. I sat on the Northern Line, staring at my yellowed reflection in the train window, and willed myself not to think. A man next to me ate McDonald's French fries out of a grease-stained bag, and the woman opposite me made an O-shape with her mouth as she applied mascara. I wondered, briefly, why everyone made that face – it genuinely did nothing to aid the mascara application process – before the rising sense of doom chased the thought away. My life was literally disintegrating before my eyes. Who cared why people made that face when applying mascara?

At Camden Town, a hoard of teenagers wearing backpacks covered in badges and too much black eyeliner pushed on, clutching plastic bags filled with cheap T-shirts they'd bought at the market. They jostled and swore and cajoled and flirted with each other, while the rest of us seethed at their youthful exuberance, before finally, mercifully, the train reached Tufnell Park and I was deposited unceremoniously on the platform.

That's when the breakdown started in earnest.

Thankfully, Londoners are used to people having breakdowns on Tube platforms – and on buses, and in taxis, and on those death-trap rental bicycles, and probably on those gondolas to Greenwich no one uses – so everyone politely averted their eyes as I blubbed indecorously next to a pile of discarded *Metro*s.

I had kissed another man. Technically, he had kissed me – I pictured myself on the witness stand, jabbing an accusatory finger at Jackson's stupid, handsome face – but technicalities weren't particularly pertinent when I knew in the blackest depths of my heart that I'd kissed him back. Even for a second. I'd kissed him back and, worse, I'd enjoyed it. Even now, I could still feel the pressure of his lips on mine. A current ran through me.

The judge banged his gavel on the desk. Guilty!

And now, I was huddled against a brick wall down an alleyway, hoping that Isla would have some words of wisdom that would get me out of this.

She had words, but I wasn't sure how wise they were. 'Don't tell Christopher.' That was the first thing she said. And then, 'What was it like? He struck me as a tongue-thruster. Was he a tongue-thruster?' And then, most insanely, 'Maybe this is a good thing.'

'A good thing? How can kissing a man who is not my fiancé be a good thing?' I cried.

'For starters, the man you kissed is your husband, so technically it's more kosher for you to be kissing him than for you to be kissing Christopher.'

'Not helpful.'

'Second, and I'm going out on a limb here, but I'm guessing maybe you enjoyed it?'

I screwed up my face in disgust even as the current zinged through me again. 'I did not!'

'Come on,' she coaxed. 'Maybe just a little?'

Jackson's warm lips on mine, the smell of his skin, the pressure of his hand on the back of my neck . . . No! I shoved the thought down into the vault, where I kept other forbidden memories, like the time I let one fly during a particularly vigorous dodge ball session in seventh grade.

Isla took my silence for consent. 'I knew it!' she crowed.

'I'm telling you,' I said, balling my fingers into a fist, 'I did not enjoy it!'

'Ah, the lady protests too much,' Isla laughed delightedly.

There are times when I have to dig deep into the rich history of our shared friendship to prevent myself from absolutely clobbering her. 'Isla,' I said in my calmest kindergarten teacher voice, 'will you please listen to me? This isn't a joke. I seriously fucked up here, and I don't know what to do about it.'

'I'm sorry.' Her voice dropped an octave as she went into crisis-management mode. That's why I loved her – just when she was about to drive you around the bend, she put on her hero-doctor hat and sorted out a solution. 'Okay, let's assess the situation. What happened after the kiss?'

'I pushed him.'

'You pushed him?!'

'Yes, I pushed him. And then I yelled at him.'

'A push, then a yell.'

I nodded at the collection of cigarette butts scattered by my feet. 'That's right. What else was I supposed to do?'

'I don't know . . . talk about it?'

'Well, he did come out with this whole crazy speech about how we had a connection and how I shouldn't marry Christopher.'

I heard Isla take a long drag on her cigarette. 'Wait. Are you saying there was a declaration?'

'I wouldn't call it a declaration . . .'

'The man said you shouldn't marry another man because the two of you had a connection, correct?'

'Correct,' I said weakly.

'And this came directly after him kissing you?'

'Yes . . .'

'I would definitely call that a goddamn declaration.'

'Well, I don't care what it was.'

'So how did it end?'

I filled her in on his Westminster Bridge proposal. (The irony of receiving a proposal involving one of London's iconic bridges, but from the wrong man, and not of the sort I'd been after in the first place, was not lost on me.)

'Is this guy being played by Ryan Gosling or what?' Isla cried. 'The next thing you're going to tell me is he carries a pug under his arm and is really into capoeira.'

An image of Jackson petting the dog in the park earlier flashed into my head. 'I don't think he's into martial arts,' I said uncertainly.

'So what are you going to do?' she asked breathlessly (though I wasn't sure if the breathlessness was due to excitement or the third cigarette I heard her lighting).

'What do you mean, what am I going to do?'

'I mean, who are you going to choose? Ryan Gosling or . . . hmm, who would play Christopher in this? Oh! Who was that guy in *Love Actually*?'

'Hugh Grant?' I suggested.

'No, not him. The one who ends up with the Portuguese waitress . . . you know, the boring one.'

'Hey!'

'Colin Firth! God, he's so fucking boring I forgot his name.'

'Christopher is not boring,' I insisted.

'When was the last time you guys had sex in a non-missionary position?'

'Isla!'

'I rest my case! Soooooo . . . who's it going to be? Ryan "Hey Girl" Gosling, or Colin "Lockjaw" Firth?'

'I really think you're being unfair to Colin Firth,' I said. 'And to Christopher!' I added hurriedly. 'Anyway, this is crazy. Of course it's Christopher! He's the person I'm meant to spend the rest of my life with!'

For once, Isla had been reduced, at least momentarily, to silence. 'Are you sure?' she asked finally, gently.

'About what?'

'About you and Christopher. When I saw you in Las Vegas . . .'

'Jesus Christ!' I shouted. A passing dog walker stopped and peered at me down the alleyway and I conjured up a manic smile and a thumbs-up to keep him moving. 'I do not want to hear another thing about Las Vegas,' I hissed. 'Taking that trip was the biggest mistake of my life. If I hadn't gone, none of this mess would have happened.'

'Thanks a lot,' she said. 'I could have spent those Air Miles going to Ibiza, you know. That fact that I've never been to Pacha is practically criminal.'

'You know that's not what I meant. It's just, ever since that trip, my whole life has been completely turned upside down.'

'Is that such a bad thing? I mean, it worked for the Fresh Prince of Bel-Air.'

'Of course it is!' I cried. 'And can you please be serious for once?'

She sighed. 'I am being serious. All I'm saying is that maybe you should look at the situation not as a mess that needs to be cleared up, but as an opportunity to broaden your horizons.'

'Oh,' I snapped, 'my horizons have been broadened all right. They're so broad they couldn't fit sideways into an airplane hangar. That's the whole point – I don't want my horizons broadened. I want them narrowed down to a very finite number of things that are currently printed on a laminated list in my bag.'

'Oh God,' Isla groaned. 'Will you stop with the list already?'

'No, I won't stop! The list has got me where I am today.'

'Crying down the phone to me?'

'You know what I mean. I'm on a path, Isla,' I said firmly. 'Christopher and I have been together for six years. We love each other.'

'I spent all of 2001 wearing Juicy Couture tracksuits,' Isla said. 'Just because you do something for a long time doesn't make it right.'

'What's that supposed to mean?' I fumed.

'What if Christopher isn't the man you want to marry?' She heard my sharp intake of breath and hurried to explain. 'I'm not saying you didn't want to marry him at some point. Of course you did! He's a nice guy, he has a sexy accent, and he has very good hair. I get the appeal.'

'Exactly,' I said, triumphant.

'No, you're not listening. Maybe that was right for you when you first met him and decided to tick that box on your list, but that doesn't mean he's right for you now.'

'Of course it does.'

'Are you telling me that you're exactly the same person now as you were when you were twenty-five?'

I thought about this. 'I get better haircuts now,' I admitted.

'It's not just your hair!'

'. . . and I'm more responsible about dental hygiene.'

'Yes, I'm sure those things are true, and I'm glad to hear you're taking your dental hygiene more seriously, because gingivitis can lead to major health problems, but do you think you might have changed on a deeper level?' I didn't respond. 'Because I can tell you're a different person, even if you can't. A smarter, more interesting, more nuanced person. Do you know why?'

'Because I finally learned how to pronounce the word Sauvignon?'

'No! It's because literally everyone is a smarter, more interesting, more nuanced person at thirty-one than they were at twenty-five. Do you know why? Because twenty-five-year-olds aren't adults. They're people who wear adult clothes and pretend to go to adult jobs, but really they're just fifteen-year-olds who've been given access to credit!'

I thought back to my twenty-five-year-old self. True, I had been consistently surprised when a paycheck arrived in my bank account every two weeks. And sure, despite this, I hadn't managed to return a single library book without having to fork out a whopping late fine. And of course, there was the time I fell asleep on the subway and ended up in Yonkers. She may have a slight point.

'Jenny, you have to stop boxing yourself in like this. I know that after the day of the flying ants—'

My stomach dropped. 'I don't want to talk about that.'

'I know you don't, but I don't care. I was there. I know what you went through.'

'It was fine,' I said quietly.

'No, it wasn't. No kid should have to take on what you did.'

There it was. The phrase I'd heard so many times over the course of my life. It didn't change anything, though. I did what I did because I had to. My mother had needed help, and no one else would give it to her.

Sure, at first there were loads of people offering to help out. My aunt came by every week to check on us before a new job meant she had to relocate to a different state. Friends would stop by with casseroles and looks of concern, and most of the time my mother would conjure up a grateful smile and invite them in for coffee. But then there were too many flares of anger, too many curses shouted and doors slammed in faces, and they eventually stopped coming. There were social services, of course, but they were the people I feared the most. I was scared they'd try to take her away from me, or me away from her. Every time they turned up, I made sure she took her meds in the morning and I'd give her my little pep talk. 'You have to try to be good, okay?' I would coax. 'Just stay calm and it'll be over before you know it.' We would invite them in and show them around – look at our well-stocked fridge! Our freshly scrubbed bathroom! – give them a cup of tea and shove them out the door as quickly as possible. And then, after a year of successful visits, they stopped coming, too. And then it was just the two of us.

Most of the time it was fine. She took her medication, she went to therapy, she tried her best. I could see that in her – that constant fight against the tide of her condition. But sometimes she would lose, and I would come downstairs in the middle of the night to find her cleaning out her desk drawers or rearranging the canned goods alphabetically. Other times, she'd tell me she was going out to buy groceries and return three days later with a strange man in tow. And then, every once in a while, her anger would return, and I'd come home to find the kitchen destroyed, and I'd have to slope off to Walmart to buy a new set of dishes.

It never felt like a burden, though. No, it was different to that. It felt like my birthright. Like something I deserved. Deep down inside, in the cavernous recesses of my brain, a voice would tell me that, one day, the same thing would happen to me. It was only a matter of time. The dark thing that lived inside her lived inside me, too, and it was only a matter of time before it showed its face and began its work of systematically destroying me.

That's why I made the list. To my thirteen-year-old mind, the only way to keep it at bay was to remain completely in control at all times. My mother had been fine until my father left, and the plans she'd made for herself had fallen apart. I wouldn't let that happen to me. That's why the list was so important. It was my lifeline.

'All I'm saying,' Isla continued, 'is that you should just think about whether this is really what you want before you go through with it.'

That phrase again— 'just think about it'. Why did every-one keep imploring me to think? As if I was some kind of mindless automaton wandering through her day making vague bleeping noises. Didn't they know that I spent every single minute of every single hour thinking and planning and analysing my next move? 'I don't need to think about it,' I spat. I could hear the harsh edge in my voice, but I couldn't stop myself.

'But—'

'I don't need to take some time out or think about things or do anything that would further screw up my life. I know what I want, and what I want is to spend this week-end with my fiancé, planning our wedding, safe in the knowledge that when I get back, Jackson will be on his way back to America, and I'll never have to see him again.'

'What about the divorce?'

'He promised he'd send the papers regardless of my decision.'

'And you believe him?'

I paused to consider this. She had a point – there was a chance that Jackson would refuse to file the papers. I could sue him for them, sure, but not without a long, pro-tracted battle, one I might not be able to hide from Christopher. Still, something told me he'd be true to his word. 'I do,' I said softly. 'I know he would do it.'

I heard Isla take a deep breath. 'You know I'll support you whatever you decide. If Christopher is the man you want to marry, I promise you I will be the happiest god-damn maid of honor you've ever seen. I'll wear whatever disgusting lime-green monstrosity you want me to, I'll wear one of those stupid monogrammed terrycloth robes while we're getting ready – hell, I promise I won't even sleep with the best man, at least not until the reception is finished. But I want you to be sure that this is what you want.'

'It is,' I said firmly. 'I'm sure of it.'

14

Christopher and I were careening through the country-side, the wind whipping through our hair, the verdant rolling hills of Somerset stretched out before us like a plush carpet, the air filled with birdsong and lavender.

Wait, that's not true.

In reality, we were stuck in traffic on the M4, inhaling exhaust fumes while horns bleated mournfully and the carload of children next to us (really, it was like a god-damn clown car – they were packed in like little jam-smeared sardines) pulled faces at us and stuck boogers to the windows.

In other words, a typical Saturday morning journey out of London.

'We should have left earlier,' Christopher fumed.

'I know,' I said sheepishly. 'Sorry I overslept.'

The truth was, I'd been up until the early hours of the morning, trawling the Internet for a free room any-where in the vicinity of the wedding venue. Who were these people, taking up the rooms of every hotel, B&B, inn and coach house in the greater Farmborough area? Judging by the complete lack of availability, there were huge hordes of people cavorting around Somerset that weekend, though God knows what they were doing. Walking through fields ringed by electric fences? Getting too hot next to a roaring fire? Secret S&M parties? It was a mystery.

Finally, just as I was about to crawl into bed and admit defeat, a room popped up on TripAdvisor at a place called the Red Lion. It looked nice enough from the photographs, and the reviews were decent, though there was a surprising number of complaints about the paucity of their gravy servings. Still, beggars can't be choosers, and I've never been much of a gravy woman myself, so I entered in my credit card details, clicked reserve, and tried not to think about the extortionate price. Mental note to self: if ever in need of a quick buck, become an innkeeper in Somerset.

'Oh for fuck's sake!' Christopher cried as an articulated lorry began an elaborate nineteen-point turn on the slip shoulder, but my spirits couldn't be dampened. The further from London we got, the clearer my head seemed to become, and the more certain I was about my decision.

After I got off the phone with Isla, I'd pulled the dog-eared list out of my bag and read it again for the thousandth time. The clarity, the order, the clear sequentialism of a life well-led . . . I tucked it back in my bag confident that I was on the right path. It was the life I'd chosen for myself, and I was going to follow it to the very last stop (Number 87: Die peacefully surrounded by loved ones).

Four and three-quarter hours, two thermoses of coffee, one can of Diet Coke, and a Snickers bar later and we finally saw a sign for Farmborough. 'Thank Christ,' Christopher muttered. 'Now, do you want to check in first or go straight to the wedding venue?'

I checked the time – it was a quarter to one. 'Let's go to the venue,' I said. 'Maybe we can have lunch there.'

He punched the coordinates into the satnav. We followed the slightly frosty woman's voice down a series of increasingly narrow and dilapidated roads until we emerged into a clearing marked out by a stone wall. In the center of a gently rolling field of wildflowers sat a tall barn built of pale stone. The slate-tiled roof peaked towards a suddenly cloudless blue sky, and the enormous arched doorway was propped open to allow a glimpse of the bare-brick walls and vaulted ceilings inside.

'Holy shit,' Christopher muttered, and I nodded silently in assent.

It was, in every visible way, perfect, like something snatched directly from the endless Pinterest boards I'd assembled before we got engaged. There was even a vintage Range Rover parked outside, a plume of white ribbons tied to its back bumper.

Christopher held out his hand. I entwined my fingers with his, and together we proceeded with stunned caution towards the barn. Through the pretty little wrought-iron gate, up the stone path, through the small garden in first bloom.

We peeked our heads through the door and saw the full scope of the place. The beamed ceiling must have been at least twenty feet high, and the light pouring in through the high windows took on a particular golden cast through the tempered glass. At any minute, I expected an angel to appear and start singing down at us, but instead we heard a door open at the back of the barn, followed by clipped footsteps on the flagstone floor. A middle-aged woman with a bob of glossy brown hair and an open smile appeared.

'Hello!' she called. 'Can I help you?'

'We – uh – we were . . . I mean, we might . . .' I trailed off and shot Christopher a helpless look.

'We're getting married,' Christopher announced, his tone slightly defiant, as though he expected her to tell us off for it.

Instead, her face broke into an even wider smile, and she clasped her hands together. 'You are? How lovely!' she said with an enthusiasm usually reserved for close relatives or people who owed you money.

'Yes,' I declared, suddenly emboldened. 'We are!'

The three of us beamed at each other, and I wondered briefly if I'd slipped into a Richard Curtis film. I hoped I had.

'Well,' she said, bustling over to us. 'You'll have lots to sort out. Did you want to take a tour of the grounds?'

I gestured around the room. 'This isn't it?'

'Good heavens, no!' she laughed. 'At least, not all of it. This is Tillbury Barn, where some of our couples choose to marry. There's also Tillbury Hall, and Tillbury Mill.'

'There's a mill?' I said weakly. I'd had a whole board dedicated solely to mills.

'Of course there's a mill!' she said, as if it would be absurd – almost criminal – not to have a mill. 'Come on,' she said, taking us by our elbows and leading us back out the door. 'I'll give you the grand tour, and then we'll sit down and have some lunch and talk things over.'

Over her head, Christopher and I exchanged a

disbelieving look. (She was very small.) Had we fallen into an alternative space-time continuum? Was this *actually* a Richard Curtis film, and had this very convincing character actress mistaken us for the leads? Or was this some kind of elaborate trap that would lead to our body parts being sold on the black market?

The woman must have noticed the shocked looks on our faces, because she stopped and let out a tinkling little laugh. 'Gracious,' she said, 'how rude you must think I am! I'm Deborah, and I'm the events coordinator here at Tillbury Manor.' She held out a tiny hand, which we both shook while we introduced ourselves.

'There,' she said, satisfied that we were no longer appalled by her bad manners. 'Shall we go?'

Tillbury Hall was a squat, hulking sandstone structure capped with the crenellated teeth of a medieval castle. Christopher and I gazed up at it in silence.

'Did anyone die in it?' I asked finally.

Deborah's head snapped towards me. 'What do you mean?'

I felt myself blush. 'It's just . . . it seems like a place where people would be killed.' It was the parapets, I decided. I remembered them from fifth grade history class, and associated them with people getting lanced through the eye.

She laughed. 'No, at least not intentionally,' she said. 'It was only built in the late eighteenth century. The architect had a penchant for Arthurian legend, so built it according to an artist's rendition of Tintagel.'

'Oh.' I couldn't believe it. I'd loved all of that King Arthur stuff as a kid – I'd watched *The Sword in the Stone* so many times the tape wore out – and now I was being offered the chance to get married in a replica of his castle. 'It's very nice,' I added lamely.

'There's a formal dining room inside that seats one hundred and fifty,' she said, 'plus a ballroom for the reception.'

'Right,' Christopher nodded. 'And is there a bar?'

'Of course!' she trilled. 'Fully stocked and licensed. Shall we take a look?'

Tillbury Hall was, without a doubt, the grandest place I'd ever set foot in. The vestibule alone was the size of the house I'd grown up in. The floors were laid with jewel-colored tiles, the tall windows hung with plush red draperies, and the walls lined with expensive-looking oil paintings. The formal dining room was all elegant wood paneling and long trestle tables decorated with ornate brass candlesticks and huge vases of flowers. But it was the ballroom that took my breath away.

It was octagonal, and absolutely enormous. The floor was shiny, pure-white tiles, and the walls were painted duck-egg blue and trimmed with gold. If I listened hard enough, I was sure I would hear a string quartet playing as hoop-skirted women and top-hatted-and-tailed men swooped across the floor.

Christopher tugged at my sleeve and pointed towards the ceiling. I craned my neck and looked up to see an elaborate fresco depicting a man and a woman, both in the nude save for carefully-placed fig leaves, wrestling around a tree.

Deborah followed our gaze and smiled. 'The Garden of

Eden,' she murmured. 'Very fine work, though I've always thought the snake looked a bit too pleased with himself.'

She was right, the snake did have an unsettling air of self-satisfaction as it watched Adam and Eve writhe around in shame.

'He was a bit of a bastard,' Christopher pointed out.

'Very true,' she agreed. 'Now, enough about Satan — would you like to hear about our tasting menu?'

We heard about the tasting menu, and the canapé options, and the local florists, and the honeymoon suite located in one of the turrets. She showed us around Tillbury Mill — all craggy stones and candlelight and quaint rustic charm — and then led us back to Tillbury Hall for lunch.

'Let us know if it's too much trouble,' we begged, but she waved away our protests.

'None at all! Now, why don't the two of you sit in here,' she said, gesturing towards a cosy snug tucked behind the formal dining room, 'and I'll just run down to the kitchen and see what the cook has for us today. Any special requests?'

'No,' we chorused, 'Anything at all! We'll eat garbage if that's what you have!'

She laughed her funny little laugh and then disappeared, leaving Christopher and I to goggle at each other in bewilderment.

'Well,' he said nervously.

'Yes,' I agreed. 'Well.'

It was perfect, that much was obvious. How could it not be perfect? It offered every possbile variety of idyllic English countryside wedding. If we wanted quaint, it had quaint. Grand, it had grand. Rustic? No problem. And yet the pit of my stomach roiled with anxiety.

'It'll cost a fortune,' Christopher muttered, and I felt myself sag with relief.

It was strange. Here I was, touring the wedding venue of my dreams with the man of my dreams, but I couldn't bring myself to feel excited about it. It felt unreal, like planning an exotic holiday you know you'll never actually take, or envisioning telling your boss to go take a hike the next time he asks you to work late when you know you'll just smile and nod. This is your life, I reminded myself. This is what you planned. But Isla's voice kept ringing in my head.

'Yes!' I said. 'It will definitely cost a fortune.'

'We'll have to give them our first born,' he said, picking up an ashtray and weighing it in his hand.

'Probably,' I nodded. Poor little Number 38.

'Feel this,' he said, handing me the ashtray. 'It feels like it's made of solid gold!'

I took it from his hand and nearly dropped it. It weighed a ton. 'I think it might actually be made of solid gold,' I said, placing it with some difficulty back on the table.

'There's no way we're going to be able to afford this place,' Christopher said.

I looked over at him. Was it just me, or did I see a glimmer of relief on his face? 'Maybe not,' I agreed. 'And we definitely shouldn't go over our budget.'

'No,' he said, shaking his head gravely. 'Definitely not.'

Deborah returned holding a tray groaning underneath the weight of a full tea set. 'I'm afraid we're too late for lunch,' she said apologetically, 'but we should have enough for a nice afternoon tea.' She set the tray down on the table and proceeded to unload a truly insane number of silver teapots, jugs, dishes, bowls, spoons and strainers. 'The rest is coming,' she assured us, misreading the shocked looks on our faces.

A mousy young woman with a tangle of blondish hair appeared in the doorway. 'Here you are,' she said, quietly depositing two enormous tiered stands on the table. One was stacked high with a selection of cakes, scones and petit fours, the other with delicate little slivers of crustless sandwiches bursting with different fillings.

'Shall I play mother?' Deborah asked, holding the silver teapot aloft. Christopher and I nodded mutely and she poured the tea in a smooth stream into three bone china cups.

The three of us made polite conversation as we picked at the sandwiches and cakes – all uniformly delicious – but I was aware of the silent tension building in the room. Deborah had been so nice and had gone to so much trouble, and now she was going to tell us that we would each need to sell a major organ to afford a wedding here. We'd then have to extract ourselves awkwardly from the situation by nodding sagely and pretending we needed time to think before making a decision, while really making a break for the getaway car, Benny Hill music trumpeting in our wake.

'So,' Deborah said when the plates had been removed and the crumbs whisked away. 'I expect you'll be wondering about costs.'

'Oh, yes, I guess so, hmmm,' we murmured, as though

the thought hadn't occurred to us and indeed we were unfamiliar with the concept of financial transactions altogether.

'Well, I've got our brochure here, complete with pricing lists.' She slid it across the table and averted her eyes as we opened it, like waiters do in fancy restaurants when you're entering your PIN.

Christopher was the first to look, and by the way his eyebrows sprung up into his hairline, I was sure we were in for a shock. How much could it be, I wondered? Twenty thousand pounds? Thirty thousand pounds? Really, it's absurd how much people were willing to spend on weddings these days. It was just one day, in the end. There were so many more sensible things that money could be put towards, like a down payment on a house, or a nest egg for a pension, or an emergency fund in case one of you ends up a vegetable. Not romantic, I know, but you had to consider these things—

'Here.' Christopher shoved the pamphlet towards me with trembling hands. God, it must be worse than I thought. My eyes scanned down until I found the price list. And then my hands started trembling, too.

'Is this including food?' I asked.

Deborah nodded. 'Of course!'

'And drink?' Christopher asked.

'No—'

'Ah!' Christopher crowed triumphantly, as though she was Mrs Peacock and he'd just discovered her with the lead pipe in the Billiard Room.

'—but we charge at cost, and we're happy to keep the bar open for the entire night.'

'Right,' Christopher said, clasping his shaking hands together. 'Right.'

It was under our budget. Way, way under our budget. So far under our budget, I started to wonder if we were secretly signing up for one of those reality wedding shows, and the catch would be that the whole thing would be planned by a bunch of pre-schoolers. Or maybe it was a cult, and we were actually volunteering to be part of a mass wedding where we all wore clothes made out of burlap sacks and chanted to the Moon God Zoltan during the ceremony.

Finally, the speculation was too much for me to bear. 'What's the catch?' I asked, narrowing my eyes suspiciously.

Deborah looked taken aback. 'There's no catch, my dear, though if that price is too high, I'm sure we could negotiate on a few points. Some people forego the harpist, for instance, though I do think it adds to the atmosphere.'

A goddamn harpist. Could you believe it? Next she was going to tell me that a flock of doves would be released when we went in for the big kiss.

'And there's also the matter of the doves,' Deborah continued.

Unbelievable. 'What about availability?' I crowed triumphantly. 'I'm sure you're booked up through the year!'

'Let me see,' she clucked, whipping out a leather-bound calendar. 'It looks like we have weekends free in June and July.'

'That's too soon,' I said hurriedly. 'We'll never get it organized in time.'

'I can help with all that,' she said, smiling indulgently. 'But if you feel it's too much of a pinch, we have slots free all the way up to Christmas.' She closed the book and beamed at us both. 'I have to say, this is a lovely place to have a winter wedding.'

'Right,' Christopher said again. The needle was stuck in his groove.

Deborah must have sensed the uncertainty, because she got up from her club chair and smoothly excused herself. 'I've just got to check in on the stables,' she said. 'I'll leave you two to discuss.'

I watched her back retreat down the corridor. 'They have horses?' I said weakly. 'I love horses.'

'Right,' Christopher said, and I resisted the urge to slap him on the back to unstick him. 'What do you think?'

'It's perfect,' I said.

He nodded. 'And cheap.'

'And we could choose the date based on when the most people could come.'

'With the rooms in the Hall, we wouldn't have to worry about where most of the guests would stay.'

'And there are horses,' I added.

'Yes. There are horses.'

We looked at each other, each trying to read the other's mind. Finally, I opened my mouth. 'Let's do it.'

He looked at me carefully. 'Are you sure?'

'Of course I'm sure!' I cried. All of my dreams for this wedding – every single one of them – were fulfilled by this place. How could I not be sure? The memory of Jackson's lips on mine popped, unwelcome, into my head and I swatted it away. Yes, I was sure. 'September would be nice,' I murmured.

He gave me a tight nod. 'September it is.'

Deborah's perfectly coiffed head appeared at the door. 'Any decisions?' she asked brightly.

'We'd like to put down a deposit for the first weekend of September,' I said. I looked down to see that my hands were still trembling slightly, and I moved to still them.

'Lovely!' Deborah sang. 'But no need to put down a deposit now. I've met you, so I know I can trust you. I'll just pop your names in my book and you can give me a bell when you're ready.'

Christopher and I exchanged an incredulous look. It was too good to be true, and yet here was our new best friend Deborah beaming at us like a beatific angel.

'Okay,' we said cagily. 'If you're sure . . .'

'Of course,' she said. 'Now, if you don't mind, I should probably be getting on with the day. Not that I wouldn't love to spend it with the two of you!'

'Of course!' We sprang out of our chairs as if there were flames beneath them. She shepherded us out of the hall and back down the little pathway past the barn and out to our car. 'It's been a pleasure spending the afternoon with you. You're a lovely couple.'

'Thank you,' I blushed. 'We really appreciate you taking the time.'

'Not at all,' she said. 'And if you have any questions or concerns, just give me a bell on this number.' She handed me a card with her name and number written on it in embossed gold.

Christopher stuck out his hand and shook hers. 'Thank you again,' he said. 'We'll be in touch.'

'I certainly hope so!' Deborah said, giving us a little wave before turning and walking back up towards the Hall.

'What a nice woman,' I sighed as I buckled in.

Christopher nodded. 'Incredibly so.' He turned the key in the ignition and revved the engine. 'It's all working out, isn't it?'

'Yes,' I agreed. 'Perfectly.'

The Red Lion was perfect, too. Downstairs, it was a cosy little pub with an open fire, walls covered in pictures of ye olde people, and a stack of board games. Our room upstairs was positively palatial, with beamed ceiling, a four-poster bed and a basket full of those little individually-wrapped cookies I loved so much. Once again, we marveled at our luck.

'It's a turn-up for the books,' Christopher said as he surveyed the claw-footed tub.

'It really is,' I agreed as I fell back on the down comforter.

We chucked our bags on the bed and headed swiftly downstairs to the pub. It was nearly five o'clock, but the place was empty save for an elderly couple and their decrepit greyhound. I love decrepit greyhounds.

'What do you want?' Christopher asked as I settled down in a beaten-up old armchair.

'Gin and tonic,' I called. He looked surprised – I almost never drank spirits, and definitely not first up – but my nerves were all over the place and I needed something strong to settle them.

'Good idea,' he said, pulling out his wallet and making a beeline for the bar.

I watched him as he waited for the bartender, his back turned to me. I'd always loved his back. In those three long years we were apart before I moved to London, I'd ask him to turn around when we Skyped so I could see it. There was something reassuring about his broad shoulders and slim, narrow waist. Something secure.

He returned with two gin and tonics (each with a single ice cube floating in it) and a pack of salt and vinegar, which he tore open with his teeth. The decrepit greyhound caught the scent and lumbered over to us. I gave him a scratch behind the ear while Christopher sneaked him a crisp.

'Sorry about him!' the elderly man cried from across the room, but we told him not to worry and kept petting the dog and feeding him crisps until he collapsed in a satisfied heap at our feet.

'Well,' Christopher said, raising his glass to mine, 'to Tillbury Manor.'

'To Tillbury Manor,' I said, clinking merrily. 'It really is perfect, isn't it?'

He took a long slug of his drink. 'It is,' he agreed.

'And so reasonably priced.'

'Very reasonable.'

'It's good to have it booked,' I said. I took a sip of my drink and winced. Christopher had ordered doubles. Still, the warmth of the alcohol was nice as it made its way down my throat. 'Now that we have a date and a venue, we should look into invitations.'

'I meant to mention that to you,' Christopher said, pulling out his phone. 'A woman I used to work with – Becky, you remember Becky? – well, she's started a letterpress company.'

'Becky has a letterpress company now? I thought she was on the partner path.'

He shrugged. 'She got passed up for promotion last autumn and just thought, sod it. She's some sort of Instagram star now.' He swiped on his phone and tapped something into the search engine. 'I'm sure this is the name of the company . . . Ah! Here we are!' He held out the phone to me and I took it from him.

'Oh,' I said quietly. The page was full of beautiful images of stationery. Notecards printed on thick card stock, the letters embossed so deeply you could practically feel the ridges. Elegant invitations printed in silver and gold, the edges artfully frayed. All straight from my Pinterest board. Again. 'They're gorgeous,' I sighed.

'I thought you'd like her stuff,' he said, taking another sip from his drink. 'She said she'd give us a discount, too.'

'Seriously?'

He nodded. 'I helped her out on a big case once.'

'Wow. That's the invitations done, I guess.'

'I guess.'

We drank in silence for a minute, the decrepit greyhound snoring peacefully under the table.

'Fancy a game of Monopoly?' Christopher said, leaping to his feet.

'Sure.' I was grateful for the offer of a distraction. 'But only if you promise not to stockpile property on Bow Street.'

'I promise nothing,' he said, leaning down and giving me a quick peck on the lips. 'Another round?'

'I'll get it.' I reached under the table and felt for my wallet, but found a decrepit greyhound's snout instead.

'Nah, you stay where you are,' he said, waving me away. 'I don't want to upset our friend down there.'

I peered under the table at the sleepy dog. 'Do you think his owners know we've stolen him?'

He shot a quick glance at the elderly couple, who were both wrist-deep in thick paperbacks. 'I think we've just about pulled it off.'

We spent the rest of the evening playing board games (despite my protests, Christopher built three houses and a hotel on Bow Street AND I was sent to jail six times) and drinking gin and tonics. Eventually, the bartender called last orders, the elderly couple reclaimed their dog, and we decided it was time for bed.

'We're going to feel this tomorrow,' we said as we weaved uncertainly up the narrow staircase to our room.

But we didn't. Both of us woke up the next morning feeling positively jaunty. 'It must be something about the country air,' Christopher remarked as he hopped into the shower. 'Do you want to go down to breakfast?'

'Actually,' I said, 'I think I might go for a walk in the village. I'll bring you back a scone or something.'

'Sausage roll, please!' he called.

I pulled on my sneakers and headed out onto the sidewalk. The village consisted of a single street lined with sweet little shops, rising to a beautiful sandstone church topped with a soaring spire. It was Sunday morning, and the church doors had just flung open, releasing a chattering group of parishioners onto the street. They bustled down side streets and into shops, calling out to each other as they went. I smiled shyly at the locals as they passed and they rewarded me with hands raised in greeting and the occasional hello. The whole place was so friendly, so chocolate-box perfect, that it was mildly unnerving. It was like being in an Agatha Christie film before the body turned up.

I was peering into the window of a vintage homewares shop when I saw it in the reflection of the glass.

I spun around on my heel and hurried across the street. The shopfront was painted a cheery yellow, and the sign above the door read 'Jenny's Bridal Suite'. The shop was named after me! It must be a sign. And sure enough, there in the window hung my perfect wedding dress.

Snow-white, sweetheart neckline, vintage lace. I could tell you what it looked like from behind, even though I couldn't see it – low-backed, with a row of tiny pearl buttons leading down to the just-fitted-enough skirt. I held my breath as I cupped my hands around my eyes and peered into the window. There was a price tag dangling from the neck of the mannequin and I squinted to read it.

My heart dropped. It was eye-wateringly expensive. Way, way beyond my budget – in another dimension, in fact. I sighed and leaned against the window. I guessed we'd already exhausted our wedding luck, what with booking the perfect venue on the cheap, and Becky's gorgeous discounted stationery. I couldn't expect it all to work out so seamlessly.

I heard a knock on the window and looked up. A brassy-haired woman in a tightly buttoned shirtdress waved at me from inside the shop. I looked around to see if there was anyone else she might be waving at, but the street had cleared and I was the only one standing on the sidewalk. 'Come in!' she mouthed, smiling broadly. I really didn't have a choice.

A little bell above the door chimed as I pulled it open. My stomach was heavy with dread. I was going to be trapped in this boutique with a crazy woman – presumably Jenny – and she was going to hoist dress after dress on me until I was forced to admit that I couldn't afford any of them, and then I'd have to slink shamefaced back onto the street.

'I saw you standing out there and thought you might like a cup of tea,' the woman said, ushering me into the store. 'We're usually shut today, but I came in to do a stocktake.'

'Oh,' I said, backing towards the door, 'I don't want to intrude . . .'

'Don't be silly. It's nice to have the company – I hate being in here on my own. Do you take milk and sugar?'

'Oh – uh, just milk please,' I stuttered. She disappeared into the back of the shop and left me standing there, stunned, surrounded by the most beautiful wedding dresses I'd ever seen. None of them could compare to the one in the window, though. I approached it gingerly, careful not to get too close in case I accidentally sneezed on it or somehow set it on fire. It was my dress, all right. There was the long line of pearl buttons trailing down its back. It was more perfect than I could ever have imagined.

'Lovely, isn't it?' I spun around to find the woman

holding out a steaming mug of tea. 'Careful,' she warned, 'it's hot.'

'Thank you,' I said, taking a tentative sip. I normally wasn't a tea drinker – not in my DNA – but this was delicious. Warming and comforting and just perfect.

'I'm Jenny, by the way,' the woman said, patting me gently on the arm. 'Very nice to meet you.'

'Me too,' I said. 'I mean, my name's Jenny, too. And it's nice to meet you.'

'So have you set a date?'

I looked at her in surprise. 'Yes. Early September.'

'Ah, a wonderful time of year for a wedding. And the venue?'

'Tillbury Manor.' It was strange letting these details roll off my tongue, and it struck me how much had come together over the weekend. It was all sliding neatly into place, just like I'd planned.

'Lucky you! Such a lovely place for a wedding. Deborah is an old friend of mine – she'll take good care of you.'

I nodded and took another sip of tea. 'She seemed great.'

'It's beautiful, isn't it?' She gestured towards the dress in the window and smiled. 'I couldn't help but notice you admiring it.'

'It's my dream dress,' I said, looking at it longingly.

'Well then, what are we standing here for? You'll have to try it on!'

I sighed. 'There's no point. I can't afford it. I'm sorry – thank you for inviting me in here, and for the cup of tea, but I should probably be going. I don't want to waste your time.'

'You're not wasting my time at all, dear,' she said, smiling kindly. 'I always love hearing about a bride's wedding plans, even if she doesn't end up buying her dress here. But,' she added, a twinkle in her eye, 'have I mentioned we're having a bit of a sale?'

My heart leaped. 'You are?'

'I am! That's why I'm doing the stocktake today.'

'What sort of sale?' My mind raced. Even if it was twenty per cent off, it would still be out of my price range, and there was no way she would discount it for more than that—

'Fifty per cent off!' she declared.

My jaw dropped. 'Wait – you're having a half-off sale?'

'I am!' She gave me a sly look. 'Would you want to try it on now?'

I'm pretty sure I left scorch marks as I ran for the fitting room. It fitted perfectly, of course. Like a dream. Jenny even teared up a little when I came out to show her.

'It was made for you,' she said, clasping her hands in delight. 'I can't imagine it on anyone else.'

After I'd gleefully handed over my credit card and begged Jenny to hold the dress for me in her stock room until I could come back and get it taken up a bit, I strolled back to the inn to find Christopher in the pub with a coffee and the papers. 'Nice walk?' he asked as I settled down beside him and snatched the review section.

'I bought a dress!' I announced.

'That's nice,' he said, face buried in the paper.

I tugged on the page. 'I mean, I bought a *dress*. A wedding dress!'

306

His eyes widened. 'Are you serious?'

I nodded. 'I found it at a boutique in the village. It's perfect.'

'God.'

'I know.'

'Well,' he said finally, 'it seems we have a wedding on our hands.'

'Looks that way!'

We laughed nervously.

Even the drive back was easy, and we made it in record time. By five o'clock, we were back in the flat and unpacked, Chinese food on its way.

It was like as if the stars had aligned, and all of the plans I'd made were clicking seamlessly into place.

Just . . . perfect.

15

So, of course, I didn't meet Jackson on the bridge. When the clock hit nine as I was crossing Green Park, I felt a little twinge when I thought of him standing there, alone, waiting, but then I pushed it out of my mind. He probably wasn't even there, I reasoned. He'd probably forgotten all about it. Even if he was there, it didn't matter. Jackson wasn't real life. He was a distraction – a speed bump. Christopher was real. This wedding – now more than ever – was real. I wouldn't let myself get rattled again.

Monday morning passed uneventfully at my desk, a haze of coffee and post-weekend chatter and deleting a weekend's worth of spam emails. Ben swept in at a quarter to ten, cheeks flushed and eyes giving out that telltale glow.

'You spent the weekend with Lucy, huh?' I said, as he deposited his bag under his desk and threw himself down in his chair.

He looked pleasantly surprised. 'How did you know?'

'Because you look like a man who's just spent two days having more sex than he ever thought possible.'

'Jenny!'

'Well, it's true, isn't it?'

He gave me a sly smile. 'Maybe.'

'I knew it. Tell me everything. Wait – no, not everything. Just the G-rated, lovey stuff.'

He beamed. 'She's amazing.'

'Really?'

'Absolutely, positively amazing. It's like she was beamed out of my brain or something.' He looked like a cat that had just been presented with the world's largest bowl of cream.

'So you saw her on Friday . . .' I prompted.

He nodded. 'We went to dinner, and then for drinks, and then we walked and talked for hours.'

'Aw.'

'And then we just holed up at my flat for the weekend and watched movies and ate takeaway and . . .' The sly smile made another appearance.

'I get it!' I cried. 'No details necessary!'

He shrugged happily. 'She's just brilliant. I feel like I finally know how you and Christopher feel, you know?'

I laughed nervously. 'Sure.'

'What about you? Good weekend? You went to the countryside, didn't you?'

I nodded.

'Shoot any pheasants? Hunt any foxes?'

I was horrified. 'Of course not!'

'That's what people do in the countryside, isn't it?' Ben grew up in Clapham.

'Actually,' I announced triumphantly, 'we found a wedding venue.'

'Hey, that's great!'

'And invitations, and a dress.'

'Bloody hell.' He shook his head. 'If Napoleon had been half as efficient as you, we'd all be speaking French right now.'

'*Mais oui*!' I said. 'Do you want to see it?'

He pulled a face. 'What, your dress? Look, we're mates and everything, but let's not push it too far.'

'The venue, not the dress,' I chided. 'The dress is a secret.'

'Go on then.'

I pulled up Tillbury Manor's website address, and Ben dutifully made vague approving noises over my shoulder as I clicked through the photographs. Seeing it again filled me with a vague sense of unreality. Was I actually looking at the place where we'd get married? Or had it all been some strange fever dream?

No, I chided myself. It was really happening. Somewhere, in the depths of Somerset, there was a dress hanging in the back of a shop to prove it. It was all going to work out exactly as I'd always planned.

An idea struck me. 'Why don't you and Lucy come over for dinner?'

Ben looked at me strangely. 'I'm not sure if we're ready for a public outing . . .'

I rolled my eyes. 'Don't go all weird on me now. You like her, right?'

He nodded.

'Well, eventually you're going to have to introduce her to other humans, and Christopher and I are the perfect guinea pigs. We don't have any embarrassing childhood photos of you, we don't know any awful stories about you throwing up a bottle of Aftershock in the middle of the university bar, and we can't moan about how much we liked your previous girlfriend, not least because she doesn't exist.' Ben still looked doubtful. 'Plus,' I cried, 'we'll make pies!'

Ben's eyes lit up. 'Pies?'

I nodded. 'Christopher loves a pie. You name the pie, we'll make it.'

'Sold! I'll ask Lucy for a few dates. God,' he said, shaking his head. 'A dinner date with another couple. What the hell has happened to me?'

'Just go with it.'

We worked through until noon, steadily typing away, with the occasional hot beverage break. I say worked, but every time I turned around, Ben was tapping out a text message on his phone, or swiping moonily through Lucy's Instagram feed. The guy had it bad.

At lunchtime, I headed out for my usual combo of sad Pret sandwich and sneaky Diet Coke. A little voice in the back of my head wondered if Jackson might be out there waiting for me, but when I pushed through the revolving door, the only person on the sidewalk across the street was a street cleaner prodding at an Irn-Bru can with his collecting stick.

I ignored the vague sense of disappointment, and headed for Pret.

It was a beautiful day. The sky was a clear cornflower blue, and the sun was strong enough to warm my shoulders. It would be summer soon. The city would be thronged with tourists and school groups and runners chugging up the Mall. There would be ice-cream vendors and great bursts of flowers, and the days would suddenly be long and filled with that ineffable summertime sense that anything is possible.

I bought my sad sandwich and my lukewarm Diet Coke and headed for St James's Park. There was a free bench by the little swan lake and I nabbed it, settling my jacket down first to protect me from the inevitable globs of old gum and bird shit. I tilted my head towards the sun and tried to relax. It was over now. Jackson would be boarding a plane for Texas, and in a few weeks I'd have the divorce papers. He'd be true to his word, I knew that. And then Christopher and I would get married, and then Number 27 would be ticked off and I could move on to the next thing on the list.

I'd beaten it. I'd had a moment of uncertainty, a little flicker of the chaos that I was sure was buried deep inside of me, but I'd overcome it. I wouldn't be like my mom. I wouldn't let myself go like that again.

I waited for the weight to lift from my shoulders, but it stubbornly wouldn't budge. Maybe after the papers arrived, I reasoned. Maybe after I'd walked down the aisle.

I ate the rest of my sandwich and hurried back to the office. This time, I didn't look across the street before I went inside. I knew he wouldn't be there waiting for me.

16

The rest of the week passed by uneventfully. Ben continued to stumble into the office starry-eyed, and spent his days exchanging messages with Lucy. I tried to keep Jeremy at bay despite his frequent 'Knock knocks!' followed by casual probes into my progress on the Bryant case. Christopher went out with his running group. I looked at my wedding Pinterest boards for the first time in months. We chose the invitations. We booked a tasting at Tillbury Manor for June, and I made an appointment with the other Jenny for a dress fitting.

I didn't hear from Jackson.

Life, in other words, returned pretty much to normal, and I reminded myself every night to be grateful for it.

It was late on Friday afternoon, shortly after another 'Knock knock' from Jeremy, and I was flicking through the photographs from the cobbler's shop for the hundredth time. Ben was looking at a recipe for slow-cooked lamb. 'What the hell is a tagine?' he called over his shoulder. 'Lucy's obsessed with it, so I want to make it for Sunday lunch, but from the look of this it's just a load of meat with some dried apricots thrown in.'

'That's pretty much it,' I replied.

'Eurgh.' Then he copied the link to the recipe and sent

it to himself. 'I guess it doesn't hurt to give it a go,' he shrugged, 'if it'll make her happy.'

'Man, you are whipped,' I said, tossing a close-up of the cobbler's workbench onto the pile. I made a couple of *whah-pssh*! sounds for good measure, but he just smiled.

'Guess so,' he said, turning happily back to his screen.

I glanced at a few more photographs, but nothing had changed from the first ninety-nine times I'd studied them. 'I think I'm going to head out,' I announced. I started stuffing the photographs back into the file. One of them slipped out of my hand and fluttered to the ground.

I reached down to pick it up. That's when I saw it. 'Holy shit,' I muttered.

Ben spun around in his chair. 'Find something?'

I nodded and held the photo out for him to see. 'Bottom left corner.'

He leaned over. 'What is that – a bin?'

'Look what's in the bin,' I said, tapping a finger on the print.

He squinted at it. 'Is that what I think it is?'

'I think so.'

Our eyes met. 'Holy shit,' he muttered.

'I've got to go.' I quickly shut down my computer and stuffed the file into my bag. 'I'll see you Monday,' I called as I rushed out of the cubicle.

'Where are you going?' he shouted after me.

'Columbia Road!'

I sent Christopher a text message on my way, warning him that I'd be working late. It was nice to be able to say it without lying.

My heart thudded in my chest as I made my way down Hackney Road. If what I'd seen in that photograph was still there — if my hunch was right — I was about to prove that Mr Bryant's place didn't burn down because of an electrical fire. A person — not a fuse — had caused that fire.

Columbia Road was fairly quiet when I got there, but the first signs of Friday-night reveling had begun to appear. Clusters of men in rolled-up shirtsleeves stood outside the Royal Oak clutching pints, foreheads tinged red from the sun. People strolled down the road in twos and threes, stopping to peer into shop windows. A couple walked ahead of me, heads tilted towards one another, deep in conversation. I could only see his shock of blond hair and her long tangle of red waves, but the familiarity was enough to knock the breath out of me.

How had it only been a week since Jackson and I had stood on this sidewalk together? A week since he'd told me how he felt. A week since he kissed me. A week since I kissed him back.

A mix of emotions flooded through me. Sometimes, a week can seem a lifetime. Anyway, it was over now. Ancient history.

I passed by Daisy's and quickly peered in to see if Betty was under the dryer, but the place was empty except for a sullen-looking girl pushing a broom around the floor. It was probably best I didn't run into her anyway. She'd made it clear she wasn't a fan of mine, and without the one-man charm offensive of Jackson by my side, I didn't think she'd even acknowledge my presence.

It didn't matter, anyway. I had a burned-out wreck to break into.

By the time I reached the shop, my nerves were so bad that the back of my mouth tasted metallic. It was one thing breaking into a place in the middle of a sleepy afternoon, but the street was filling up fast, and I was sure to get a few suspicious glances. I stood outside for a minute and leaned up against the brick wall, trying to look casual. Now, I thought to myself, would have been a good time to smoke. Instead, I took out my phone and pretended to study something extremely interesting while I waited for a group of Danish tourists to pass.

Finally, the coast was clear. I ducked down the alley next to the shop, picked my way through the detritus-strewn garden, and shouldered the back door open.

I crept into the shop, my phone in hand, with the camera switched on and at the ready. The smell hadn't changed. Acrid-stale smoke still snaked its way into my lungs, and I could feel the damp in my bones. My footsteps sounded absurdly loud, echoing off the charred walls.

There was the wall where the safe had been, still covered by the scrap of tattered canvas. There was the workbench with its set of blackened tools. There were the fragments of a leather apron, still hanging from its hook. But there was no sign of the wastepaper basket anywhere.

My heart sank. Of course he would have destroyed the wastepaper basket and whatever was inside it. I felt like a fool. All this effort, and still nothing to show for it. I would have to tell Jeremy that I hadn't found anything after all.

And then I heard it. At first, I thought it was a rat, its claws scuttling across the floorboards above, but then there was a thud and a sigh. Someone was upstairs.

I froze. Oh fuck. I was going to get caught. I was going to get arrested! What the hell was I doing here, anyway? Why was it so important that I solve this case? Why couldn't I have just told Jeremy to pay out the money and end it, like a normal person?

I could see the headlines now: Insurance agent breaks into charred remains of elderly client's home. Maybe they'd deport me. Maybe they'd have me committed. Maybe this was it. Maybe I really was going crazy.

The footsteps were getting closer.

'Hello?' The voice was low and slightly trembling. 'Hello?'

I thought about making a break for it. How fast could I run? I gazed down at my feet. What had possessed me to wear these goddamn heels on today of all days? I could kick them off and take off barefooted, but then I'd have to get all the way home without any shoes on. I would definitely get tetanus, maybe worse. And my shoes would be here waiting to be found, like some deranged criminal Cinderella's.

I saw part of the wall open up and a small, white hand appear. Too late.

'Hello?' A man's pale face appeared. He was older – in his sixties – and wearing a plaid flat cap and a look of terror. He saw me and his face fell. 'Are you from the police?' he asked, taking in my dark Zara trousers and blouse.

'No!' I said, a little too quickly, and then I thought,

damn. Maybe I should have pretended to be the police. Though impersonating an officer is definitely a crime, too.

'Then who are you?' His hands were shaking slightly, and I could still hear the tremor in his voice.

'I'm, um . . .' No point in trying to hide it now. 'I'm from your insurance company.'

His face grew even paler. 'Oh,' he said quietly. He shuffled into the shop. I realized now that the part of the wall he'd emerged through was actually a doorway leading to a stairwell. The handle was missing and the grime had made it blend into the wall. The realization flooded me with relief: at least he wasn't a ghost.

'I was just checking a few things,' I said. I stood up straight and tried my best to look official, despite my soot-covered palms.

'It's fine,' he said, holding up his hands. 'I was expecting you.'

'You were?'

He nodded. There were heavy pouches of skin under his eyes, and deep lines carved along the sides of his mouth. This was a man who was suffering. 'Can I buy you a cup of tea?' he asked, moving towards me.

'You want to buy me a cup of tea?' I tried to keep my face neutral, but I could hear the incredulity in my voice. It wasn't every day that a man whose home you were currently invading offered to buy you a cup of English Breakfast.

'It's the least I can do,' he said, 'dragging you all the way out here.'

'But—'

'Come on, keep an old man company for a while.' He gave me a beseeching look. 'Please?'

I nodded. In for a penny, in for a pound. 'Where do you want to go?'

'There's a nice little caff around the corner,' he said, shuffling towards the back door. I remained rooted to the spot. 'Come on, love,' he called over his shoulder. 'I'm not getting any younger.'

We walked the short distance in silence, both of us ignoring the curious glances of people wondering what a pensioner and a woman who apparently looked like an plainclothes police officer were doing together and, more importantly, why they were both covered in soot.

The place was an old-school greasy spoon that looked as if it had been plucked from another era, all peeling Formica tables and brightly colored signs advertising egg and chips for a pound. We chose a booth at the back and settled in.

'You've got to go up to order,' he said, plucking a laminated menu out of the holder on the table and handing it to me. 'Used to be table service, but then Margie left and they didn't bother replacing her. Which is fair, to be honest – she was an awful waitress. Spilled more than she served.' He was talking at a rapid clip and in a cockney accent so thick you could stick a fork in it. 'Now, what would you like? Have anything you like – it's on me. They do a lovely sausage roll in here.' He sized me up from across the table. 'Though I expect young ladies like yourself don't eat sausage rolls these days, do you?'

'I'll just have a cup of tea, thanks,' I said weakly.

He nodded and slid out of the booth. 'Back in a jiffy.'

I sat there, stunned. The man had every right to call the police on me, but instead he was at the counter, ordering me a cup of tea. How had this happened? And what was I supposed to do about it?

'Here you are,' he said, depositing two large, thick-rimmed mugs on the table. Steam curled from each of them, and they were filled to the brim with murky mahogany-colored liquid.

'Is there milk in this?' I asked as he settled himself across from me.

He gave me an indulgent smile. 'That's a builder's brew.'

I took a sip. It was so bitter with tannins, I could feel the enamel being stripped from my teeth. I forced a smile. 'Delicious.'

He looked genuinely delighted. 'They do a proper cup of tea, not like most of these phony places around here. All style and no substance, that's what my Vicki used to say.' His eyes filled at the mention of his wife and I looked away. I couldn't bear to see his sadness, knowing I was potentially about to make it worse. 'So whereabouts in America are you from?'

'New Jersey,' I said, and braced myself for the Sopranos impression.

'Ah, lovely place,' he said. 'My wife and I went there on our holidays once. Walked the boardwalk, did a tour of the house that chap who invented the lightbulb lived in. Must be twenty years ago now.'

My jaw nearly fell into my tea. 'You went on vacation to New Jersey?'

'It's called the Garden State, isn't it? Besides, Vicki had a cousin out there at the time. Lovely holiday, that.'

He got that wistful look in his eye again, and my heart actually physically hurt. The man loved his dead wife and he loved New Jersey and I was trying to screw him out of his insurance money. Christ.

'So what brings you to London?' he asked.

'Work,' I said. 'And my fiancé.'

'You're engaged? Congratulations! Marriage is a wonderful thing. Nothing better.'

I squirmed in my seat. 'That's nice to hear.'

'Anyway, I didn't drag you over here so I could grill you on your personal life. I wanted to explain myself.'

'Explain yourself?' I stuttered.

He leaned back in the booth and sighed. 'I may look young for my age, but I wasn't born yesterday. I'm guessing you didn't come all the way down here to hand me a cheque for the insurance money.'

'Now that you mention it, there have been a few . . . discrepancies raised that I wanted to discuss with you.'

He wrapped his hands around his mug. 'Go on.'

'Well, there's the wastepaper basket . . . and one of your neighbors mentioned that the smoke was black, not white, which is what you'd usually expect with an electrical fire.'

He nodded. 'Sharp as a tack, aren't you?' His smile faltered, and suddenly he looked old. 'I was a fool to file that claim. I should have just let sleeping dogs lie, but my son . . .' he shook his head. 'It doesn't matter now. I suppose you'll be calling the police.'

I stared at him. His blue eyes were rheumy and

red-rimmed, the edges of his mouth sagging in defeat. 'Why don't you start by telling me what happened?'

He took a sip of tea. 'My wife, Vicki ... she passed about a year ago.'

'I know,' I said. He looked surprised. 'The insurance money,' I explained.

'Oh. Right.'

'I'm very sorry for your loss.'

He took off his cap and ran a hand across his thinning hair. 'She was sick for a long time. Cancer.' He shook his head. 'Horrible thing, cancer. Ate her alive. When she finally died, everyone told me it was a blessing. That she was in a better place now, away from the suffering. I tried to believe it – I promise I did – but the more I thought about it, the angrier I got.' His eyes met mine. 'All the pain she went through, all the years – how could that be a blessing? And even if she was in a better place, what about me? I'm still here, without her.' He stared down at the table and worked at a bit of congealed grease with his thumb.

I realized what he was about to tell me, and the breath caught in my throat.

'I tried for a year. I really did. I went to work, said hello to people in the shops, saw my kids.' He smiled sadly. 'I held my first grandchild – a little girl. Clara.' He shook his head in wonder. 'Beautiful. But,' he said, laying his hands flat on the table, 'it wasn't enough. Every single second of every single day with her not there ... and all I could see was all the days still in front of me.' He sighed. 'I went to see my kids on the Saturday. Gave my granddaughter a kiss. And then I came back to the shop.

'I wasn't trying to burn the place down – I swear it. I got home that night and it was exactly the same as it always was, only she wasn't there. The walls were covered with pictures of Vicki and me everywhere . . . I couldn't bear to look at them anymore. I started burning them in the bin. I don't know what came over me – the kids would have killed me if they'd known I was burning things of their mum's, but I was like a man possessed. I threw in a few of the rags from the workshop to get things going, and the flames got out of control and the place filled up with this thick black smoke and I thought . . . maybe it would be easier if I just lay down and went to sleep.' A tear slid down his cheek, and I reached out and took his hand. 'It was the sirens that woke me up. I looked up and I swear to you, my Vicki was there. She was standing above me, this funny little smile of hers she gave me when I'd done something stupid, and she told me to get up and run. So that's what I did. I went straight to my son's house and told him what had happened. I didn't want people thinking I was mad, you see. I didn't want their pity. He understood that, my son. He's a good boy. He went back there with me after the firemen cleared off and he pulled a bit of the wiring out of the wall. He's an electrician, you see. Said everyone would think it was a fault with the old electrics. He told me I should file an insurance claim to make it look like it was all on the up and up.'

'And the safe? Was your wife's insurance money in there?'

He shook his head. 'What was left of it, which wasn't much. We'd signed her up for this experimental treatment

323

that wasn't covered by the NHS. Left us with a mountain of debt, and didn't do her any good in the end.' He grasped my hand in his. I could feel the rough callouses on his fingers from years of working with his hands, and the warm blood that flowed beneath his skin. 'I wasn't in my right mind when I filed that claim. I was going to cancel it, but I didn't want to bring any more attention on myself. I hoped it would just sort of . . . go away. Stupid of me, really.' He tightened his grip, and when I met his eye, all I could see was desperation. 'I'm not bent, I swear it. Neither's my son – he was only trying to help me. Please, you have to believe me.'

'Mr Bryant . . .'

'Ed,' he said, 'call me Ed.'

'Ed,' I said gently, 'I'm not going to call the police.'

'You're not?'

I shook my head. 'It was an accident, that's all. But you should cancel the claim.'

He nodded. 'Of course. I don't know how to thank you.'

I remembered something Jackson had said to me. 'Grief makes us do crazy things.'

He smiled at me sadly. 'It's not grief that makes you do crazy things, sweetheart. It's love.' His gaze drifted towards the window of the café, where the Friday-night crowds drifted past. 'All those people out there . . . I see them sometimes, young kids in love, holding hands, in their own little bubble. Like it's the two of them against the world. Do you know what I mean?'

I nodded.

'I see them, and I think, hold on tight, because when

they're gone, there's no replacing them. You remember that for you and your fellow, too. You tell him to hold onto you tight.' My eyes filled unexpectedly with tears, and they spilled over onto my cheeks before I could stop them. 'I'm sorry, love,' he said, hurrying to hand me a tissue. 'I didn't mean to upset you.'

'You didn't,' I said, waving him away as I blotted my face, but the tears kept coming. We sat in silence for a minute, and he handed me fresh tissues as I fought to control my shuddering breaths. 'I'm sorry,' I said finally.

'You've got nothing to be sorry for,' he said, mock-sternly. 'A lovely girl like you is allowed to have a bit of a cry every now and then without apologizing.'

'Thanks,' I smiled. 'What are you going to do next?'

He shrugged. 'Get on with the act of living, I suppose. Find a little flat somewhere. Spend time with my grand-daughter.' He patted the back of my hand as he climbed out of the booth. 'What about yourself?'

I shot him a startled glance. 'Me?'

'Do you know what you're going to do next?'

I was silent.

'Take your time, love,' he said, picking his cap up off the table and settling it on his head. 'It's a long life, full of twists and turns. Just promise me one thing.'

'What's that?'

He smiled as he headed towards the door. 'Be happy.'

17

One week turned to two, and then three. Jeremy had been thrilled when I'd told him that Mr Bryant had dropped the insurance claim, though I clammed up when he asked for specifics.

'Just so long as the sly dog doesn't try any more of his tricks,' he warned as he adjusted the cuffs on his floral shirt. One of these days, I was sure he was going to appear in a pair of polished wingtips and a black fedora.

'Don't worry,' I assured him, 'we won't hear from him again.'

He winked and told me I'd done 'a bang-up job'.

The wedding plans continued apace. A stack of invitations arrived and sat accusatorily on the kitchen counter, waiting to be stuffed and sent. Christopher and I made a shortlist of possible bands, exchanged long, torturous emails about the guest list, and made tentative enquiries into applying for a marriage license. I sent Isla links to bridesmaids' dresses, and she even admitted that one of them didn't make her want to pull out her eye teeth and swallow them. Progress, all of it.

When a large Manila envelope turned up on my desk at work with a Texas postmark in the upper-right corner, I didn't open it. I didn't need to – I knew what was inside. I promised myself every morning that I'd deal with it, and every night I left for home with it still unopened in my desk drawer.

Other than that, I didn't hear from Jackson. He was a man of his word – he'd sent the papers and left me alone. I tried to convince myself that I was grateful, but couldn't quite manage it.

Christopher and I settled back into our routine. He brought me tea in the mornings before heading off to work, and I made sure the house was stocked with pies in the evening. Friday nights we ate Kung Pao chicken on the sofa, and on Sunday afternoons we ate roast dinners in the Queen's Head. He went running. I read. Everything went back to normal.

Only I couldn't get Mr Bryant out of my head. To be that grief-stricken that you wanted to take your own life . . . I thought of my mother. I thought about what Mr Bryant had said, about it not being grief that made people crazy, but love. It began to gnaw at the edges of me.

Another week passed, and then it was Saturday night, and Ben and Lucy were due to arrive for dinner any minute. I had a chicken and leek pie in the oven, and a steak and kidney cooling on the side and I was now sprinting around the flat desperately cramming bits of clutter and detritus into cupboards and underneath beds.

'Where are my pants?' Christopher cried as he dashed down the hall, still naked from the shower.

'I put them in the wash!' I called after his retreating back.

He stopped in his tracks and turned around. 'Bollocks.' I wondered if he was being literal, until he added, 'They were my last pair.'

'Well,' I said, stuffing a pile of junk mail into the cutlery drawer, 'you'll have to go commando!'

He grimaced. 'I don't like the sound of that.'

'It's good for them.'

'Good for who?'

'Them!' I cried, waving towards his nether region. 'Your . . . wrinkly twins.'

'Oh Christ,' he muttered, before sloping off to the bedroom.

'Hurry!' I found a couple of loose screws languishing on the coffee table – where had they come from? Where? – and tossed them in the crack between the sofa cushions.

They were, of course, late. What had I expected? They were in their mid-twenties and in love. They were probably late to everything. It turned out to be a blessing, anyway, as it gave me a chance to sort through the cutlery to find four clean forks and light the fancy smelly candle I'd bought.

When they finally did turn up, a cool forty-five minutes late, Christopher and I had already sunk two glasses of wine each and were both a little unsteady on our feet when we answered the door.

'Hello!' I said, slightly too loudly. Ben immediately thrust a bouquet of tulips wrapped in brown paper and tied with twine into my arms (hipster flowers, of course). I stepped aside to let the two of them in.

Ben was wearing what I can only describe as his version of Sunday Best: a pair of black drainpipes, a white shirt buttoned all the way up, and polished brogues so pointy, my shins winced instinctively. I gave him a quick kiss on the cheek and pushed him out of the way so I could get to Lucy.

'Hello!' I cried. 'You must be Lucy!' It occurred to me that I was acting like someone's deranged great aunt.

Lucy looked like a modern-day wood nymph, tiny and slight, her blonde curls tumbling almost to her waist. She was wearing an outfit that would have had me committed, but looked achingly cool on her, all long layers and jangly jewellery and mismatched prints. She looked as if she should be living in a hollowed-out tree in a copse somewhere rather than a studio in Homerton.

'Hello,' she said, extending a minuscule hand. Her voice was much louder and deeper than expected, and both Christopher and I jumped.

'Should we take off our shoes?' Ben asked, finger already looped around the back of his brogue. His eyes darted around the flat, and I saw him take in the framed print over the fireplace, the patterned rug spread under the mid-century modern coffee table, and my fancy candle flickering away.

The realization struck me like a thunderbolt. He thinks we're grown-ups.

I glanced at his face, which was pale with nerves.

It was worse than that. He thought I was his mother. He was basically introducing his girlfriend to his work-mom.

'No!' I was shouting now, I could hear it. 'It's totally fine, we're not anal about that kind of thing.' Christopher shot me a sceptical glance. I was, in fact, anal about that kind of thing, hence us both being in socked feet. I ploughed on regardless. 'Come on in!'

I sat them down on the couch and dispatched Christopher to get them drinks.

'You have a lovely home, Jenny,' Lucy said in her peculiar, gravelly voice. It was nice, actually – sexy, even – but there was something unsettling about it coming from Tinkerbell's mouth.

'Yeah,' Ben added. 'It's, like, immaculate.' He was theoretically seated on the couch, but in reality he was hovering just slightly above the cushion, as though any contact between himself and the upholstery would be disastrous.

'It definitely isn't,' I said, eyes trailing treasonously to the pile of magazines I'd shoved under the sofa. 'It's basically a garbage pail.'

'You're crazy,' Ben said. 'If you think this place is a tip, you would genuinely have a heart attack if you saw my place.'

Lucy's eyes lit up. 'Did you know that his flatmate doesn't believe in sell-by dates?'

'Wait, what?'

She nodded. 'The first night I stayed at his place, I tried to make coffee in the morning, and the milk was basically cheese. When I went to chuck it away, Ben freaked out and was like, no! That's my flatmate's! He freaks out if I throw any of his stuff away! And I was like, Ben, the milk is off! But apparently it doesn't matter.'

'Ben,' I chided. 'That's gross!'

'It's not me!' he cried.

'And,' Lucy added, triumphantly, 'the walls of their bathroom are absolutely *covered* in mould.'

Ben threw his arm around her and pulled her close. 'Come on, it's not that bad.'

She nestled into the crook of his shoulder. 'It so is.'

'Well, at least my bedroom isn't covered in clothes. Jenny, you should see Lucy's place. It's basically a wardrobe with a bed tucked in the corner.'

'Hey!' She gave him a playful swipe.

'It's true!' He grinned at her. 'Just try to deny it.'

She shrugged. 'You can't criticize a girl for having too many clothes. Right?' She looked at me for reassurance.

I smiled at her. 'Absolutely.'

The two of them were so adorable, so completely and utterly crazy about each other, that just being in the same room as them made me feel like some kind of weird interloper. All this cutesy banter and snuggling into each other, and the way they kept appealing to me for approval . . . by the end of it, I wasn't sure if I was supposed to applaud or leave the room so they could be alone. When Christopher finally reappeared with the drinks, I fell on him like a starved hyena on a stray scrap of wildebeest meat.

'Let me help you!' I cried, vaulting over the coffee table and nearly knocking the tray of drinks from his hands.

'It's fine,' he said, shooting me a funny look. 'I've got it.'

We sat around the coffee table, Ben and Lucy taking up one half of the love seat and leaving the other cushion cold and alone, while Christopher and I perched in the two semi-uncomfortable chairs we'd bought because they looked nice but that we never actually sat in. I plucked a crisp out of the glass bowl we only used for this specific purpose – eating crisps with company – while Christopher tried to follow a story Lucy and Ben were telling that was meant to be about the two of them going to Brighton for the day but was actually about how adorable the other one was. I'd already heard Ben's version in the office – basically, they went to Brighton, ate fish and chips, came home – so I allowed my mind to wander.

Would the pies be any good? Did I have enough glasses for both water and wine? Had I remembered to take the bottle of Chablis out of the freezer? Would the mousse be set? And, finally, looking over at the occupied half of the sofa, where Ben was gazing at Lucy with a look of such abject wonder it wouldn't have surprised me if she was shooting fireworks out of her ears, had Christopher and I ever been like them?

And then it was time for dinner. The pies were good. (The chicken and leek was a little dry). The wine was chilled, and we had enough glasses. The mousse had set.

Ben and Lucy were the perfect guests – extremely appreciative and with fairly low standards. They *ooh*ed and *ahh*ed over every dish I brought to the table, thanked Christopher profusely every time he topped up their glasses, and marveled over the fact we had matching plates and a full set of cutlery. At one point, Ben spilled a bit of wine onto the table and offered to pay for the napkin he used to wipe it up, 'because it's cloth'.

I hadn't noticed it at work, but I was suddenly aware of how young Ben was. He was still in a world where cloth napkins seem fancy. He and Lucy went to parties where the host didn't serve food. They went to bars where the music was too loud for them to talk, and didn't complain about the fact that there wasn't anywhere to sit. They would stay out until 1 a.m. on a weeknight, and, not only would they be fully functional at work the next day, but they would describe themselves as not having had a late one. They were hangover-proof. They smoked cigarettes without worrying about how it would affect their mile time.

They were young, they were in love, and they were happy. So, so happy. They turned towards each other as though they were each other's North Star, seeking each other's light for guidance and assurance.

'Lucy and I are thinking about moving in together,' Ben blurted out over dessert, and I had to steady myself on the edge of the table.

'That's fast!' Christopher gave me a sharp look. 'I mean, that's great!' I stumbled. 'Congratulations.'

'It's not a definite yet,' Ben said, digging a spoon into his mousse.

'Yeah,' Lucy chimed. 'We don't mean, like, tomorrow or anything, but Ben's place really is rank, and my place is tiny, so we thought maybe it might be better . . .' She gave Ben a shy look.

I saw him reach under the table for her hand. 'Since we're together all the time anyway,' he said.

'We could get a really nice one-bed in Stoke Newington for what we're both paying at the moment.'

'Or around here, even,' Ben added.

I tried to keep the shock off my face, and failed. 'But you always say Tufnell Park is for corduroy-wearing, middle-aged *Guardian* readers,' I spluttered.

He shrugged. 'It's got a few nice pubs, plus the Heath is right on your doorstep . . .'

'We're thinking about getting a puppy!' Lucy beamed.

I was like a puppy myself, clinging stubbornly to a bone. 'But . . . you call it Tossers' Park, because only tossers live here!'

'Ben!' Lucy scolded. 'That's so rude!'

Ben held up his hands in mock outrage 'What?!' He laughed.

I shook my head in disbelief. 'I can't believe you're thinking about moving to Tufnell Park,' I murmured.

'Jenny, let it go,' Christopher cautioned quietly.

'Okay! Okay! I'll let it go! Move to Tossers' Park if that's what you want. Get a dog and then get married and then have kids and then grow old together and die in each other's arms! Okay?'

A shocked silence descended on the table. Lucy and Ben nudged their chairs closer together, as if proximity could protect them from the madness on the other side of the table. Christopher looked at me as if I were some lunatic who'd wandered off the street wearing a tinfoil hat rather than his fiancée. And I was starting to wonder if he might be right. (Minus the tinfoil hat.) (For now.)

'Sorry,' I mumbled, and then, conjuring up as much joviality as I could muster, 'Coffee anyone?'

After admiring the fact we had a French press rather than a jar of instant, Ben and Lucy gulped down their coffees and made their excuses. They had a party to go to, and if they left it any later, everyone else would be too off their faces for it to be fun.

We waved them off after pressing a spare bottle of wine and a bag of real coffee onto them, and then trudged into the kitchen to start clearing away the damage.

'Can you imagine going to a party at this time?' Christopher wondered as he scraped a half-eaten bowl of mousse into the trash.

I glanced at the clock: it was ten to midnight. 'I guess that's youth for you,' I said, slinging back the dregs of someone's glass of red. 'They seem so happy,' I said quietly.

Christopher nodded. 'They really do.'

We worked in silence, stacking the dishwasher and cleaning the pots and wiping down the table and placing the good wine glasses back in the cabinet.

Christopher was hanging the dishtowel back on the oven handle when he said it. 'I can't do this. I'm sorry.' He said it so quietly the first time that I thought I'd misheard him, so I asked him to say it again. I heard it loud and clear the second.

I could have pretended I didn't understand. I could have asked if he was referring to putting away the dishes, or decanting the leftovers into the Tupperware containers on the counter, but life was too short and we'd already wasted enough time.

'Me neither,' I said. His back was towards me, and I watched his shoulders rise and fall. That back of his, that strong, gorgeous back. Every part of me wanted to walk across the room and wrap my arms around him, press his body into mine, feel the warmth of him, the solidity. But I knew I couldn't. 'I'll move out,' I said, and he nodded.

'Take your time,' he said quietly. 'I'll help if you need money for a deposit . . .'

'I have money,' I said, a little too sharply. I didn't though.

Not enough for a deposit. I flushed with humiliation. 'Thanks, though. I might have to take you up on that.'

'All you have to do is ask.' He turned around at last, and the look on his face was one of such aching sadness that I thought my heart was going to burst out of my chest. 'They're so in love,' he said, his voice full of wonder.

I nodded. 'They are.'

'It just made me think . . .' He trailed off, shaking his head.

'I know,' I said quietly. 'Me too. You deserve that. I want you to feel that.'

He raised his eyes to mine, and I was surprised to see they were rimmed with tears. 'So do you.'

We stared at each other for a minute, our eyes locked onto one another, and it was as though both of us were watching the film of our life together run across an invisible screen. The cab in New York. All the late-night phone calls and transatlantic flights. The Sunday morning walks in the park, both of us still tingling from sex, our cheeks pinked from the breeze. All of the nights we'd spent curled into one another. I watched our hearts break at the same moment.

'We had a good run, didn't we?' he said finally, after the credits rolled.

I smiled and tasted tears. I hadn't realized I'd been crying. 'We sure did.'

'I love you, you know.'

'I love you, too,' I said.

I knew we both meant it. We would always love each other, in that way you always love your childhood best friend, even if you haven't spoken for twenty years. But that love was a ghost of what we'd once had, and both of us deserved to have something with blood still pulsing through its veins.

I'd been living in a world of ghosts for years. All of those items to be ticked off some arbitrary list I'd made as a kid . . . the absurdity of it struck me as I stood there. How much time had I wasted trying to live the life I thought I should be living, rather than letting life happen to me?

I thought back to Mr Bryant's words. 'It's not grief that makes you do crazy things, it's love.' All these years, I thought I was dodging my mother's fate, and really I'd fallen straight into it. It was a bright and clean and orderly sort of crazy, sure, but it was crazy nonetheless.

It was time to throw the list away.

The rest of the weekend was surprisingly bearable, considering it was spent with my now-ex-fiancé. Now that everything was out in the open, it was as if both of us had taken a deep breath of fresh air and relaxed. We called Deborah on Sunday and canceled Tillbury Manor – I'm pretty sure she was more upset about our break-up than we were, bless her – and I contacted the other Jenny and asked if I could sell her the dress back at half-price. She gave me a full refund. The wedding invitations went in the recycling, and Christopher phoned his parents to give them the news. I called my dad and my aunt, both of whom were great about it. And just like that, the wedding – the whole life – I'd thought about for so long, ceased to exist. You pull one thread and the whole skein unravels.

On Monday morning, I got to work early. Ben wasn't in yet – presumably still basking in the refracted glow of Lucy's love as he showered in his mouldy bathroom – so I had the office to myself. I got myself a cup of coffee, opened my emails, scrolled through the news. And then, finally, I took a deep breath and opened my desk drawer.

The envelope was where I'd left it. The edges were bent and furred from being shoved into the back of the drawer, and an uncapped pen had left an inky smudge on the front. I slit it open with my finger and inched the papers onto my desk.

The form was surprisingly simple. Just a couple of pages with some legal language declaring the marriage null and void – initial here, sign and date there. Jackson's signature was already there, his handwriting blocky and bold. I ran my finger over it, felt the impression his pen had made on the paper. And then I uncapped my pen and added my signature next to his.

That was it. We were divorced.

I breathed out a long sigh. I felt tired – deep, down to the bone tired – but relieved, too. Now I really could have a fresh start.

I was tucking the papers back into the envelope when I found it. There, at the bottom of the envelope, was a photograph. I reached in and pulled it out. I didn't recognize it at first. It was a close-up of my face tilted upwards. The camera had zoomed in on my eyes, their green obscured by the kaleidoscope of color dancing in them.

The lights around Westminster from that night. He'd taken a picture of me looking at them without me noticing. I stared at it. I looked so happy, so filled with wonder. And he'd seen that and captured it for ever.

My heart swelled.

Ben burst into the cube trailing a cloud of shower gel, the ends of his hair still damp. 'Sorry I'm late,' he called as he tossed his bag down on the floor. 'Thanks again for dinner on Saturday – it was really great. Lucy and I couldn't stop talking about how nice your flat is. Even if it is in Tossers' Park.' He threw me a cheeky smile, but I sat there, immobile. He saw the look on my face and faltered. 'Only joking. Lucy and I are seriously thinking about making a move over there. How much do you think the average rent is there for a one-bed?'

'No idea,' I mumbled.

'Oh, right – I forgot Christopher owns. Lucky bastard. I can't even think how much that place is worth now. Has he had it valued recently? Christ, Lucy and I are never going to be able to afford a flat. Not unless one of our relatives dies and we inherit some serious cash. Not that I want that to happen or anything,' he added hurriedly. He sat down heavily in his chair and stared at me. 'You all right? You look like you've seen a ghost or something. Old Jeremy hasn't been in here giving you hell, has he?'

I shook my head.

'Good. Anyway, tell Christopher I said thanks for the tip about that trainers shop in Covent Garden. Lucy and I popped down there yesterday after we had lunch with some of her mates and he's right, they have an incredible selection. I got a pair of limited edition Adidas that I swear were sold out everywhere.'

'Christopher and I broke up.'

Ben's head snapped so hard I worried for his neck in later years. 'What?'

I nodded. 'After you left on Saturday night.'

'Holy shit. But . . . why? You guys seemed great when we left. Did you get in a fight or something? Has he been cheating on you? That bastard. I swear to God, if he's been cheating, I'll shove my limited edition Adidas so far up his arse—'

'We didn't fight. He isn't cheating. It just . . .' I shrugged. 'It wasn't working.'

'But the wedding – you guys just booked that place in Somerset . . .'

'Canceled.'

'Fuck.' He looked genuinely devastated, and I was touched by how much he cared. 'What can I do?'

I shook my head. 'I'm fine, honestly. It was a mutual decision, and it's one hundred per cent for the best.' He looked so dubious that I had to laugh. 'Honest! It's a good thing. I promise.'

He eyed me warily. 'Okay, but if you want to, like, cry or whatever, I'm cool with it. I'll put my headphones in.'

'I don't want to cry.'

'Okaaaaaaay . . .'

'I don't! But there is something you could do for me.'

He nodded. 'Whatever you need.'

'Can you cover my cases for a little while?'

He tilted his head to the side. 'You going on holiday?'

'Sort of.' I hadn't realized I was until I'd said it, but now that I had, I was desperate to go.

'That's great. A bit of time off will be good for you. When do you leave?'

'Soon, actually.' My mind whirred. 'Tomorrow.'

'Christ, that is soon. Have you told Jeremy?' I shook my head. 'I'm sure he won't mind,' Ben said, trying and failing to look reassuring. 'You never ask for time off, and he still loves you because of the Bryant case. And I'll handle your cases, no problem. How long will you be gone? A week? Two?'

'I don't know,' I said, and admitting the uncertainty felt like clearing a great swathe of space in my head. My shoulders actually sagged with relief.

Ben shot me a strange look. 'Jeremy might have an issue with that.'

'I know,' I said. I glanced down at the photograph on my desk. The eye stared up at me, full of color. 'I'll risk it.'

18

Dallas is enormous – a never-ending sprawl of tract houses spreading out from the gouge of skyscrapers at its center. As the plane circled for landing, I peered out of the window and down at the city spread out beneath us. Its size was dizzying, humbling, and beyond its craggy, uncertain edges, a patchwork of golden fields stretched to the horizon, where it met with the biggest and bluest sky I'd ever seen.

'Flight attendants, take your seats for landing.'

It was only then that the nerves bubbled up inside me. It had all come together so quickly, I hadn't had the chance to consider what I was doing. When I asked Jeremy for the time off, he'd practically shoved me out of the office. 'Hey, after the way you put the screws on old man Bryant, the least I can do is let you get a break from the rat race.' I thanked him and backed out of his office slowly.

I didn't tell Christopher where I was going, only that I'd be gone for a while and that I'd hopefully have a place lined up by the time I got back. He told me that there was no rush, that I could stay in the flat for as long as I wanted, but I could see the relief in his eyes.

Isla thought I was crazy, but in a good way. 'Thank the Lord!' she'd howled when I told her that Christopher and I had broken up. 'Not that I didn't like the guy,' she added quickly, but I'd known what she meant. I was relieved, too. The more time passed, the more sure I was that it had been the right thing. When I told her what I planned to do next, she wished me luck and made me promise to swing by New York afterwards. 'I'm going to take you out for the biggest drink of your life!' she declared, before remembering what had happened the last time she had done that. 'No secret weddings, though,' she warned, 'unless I'm there as a witness.'

I bought the plane ticket with the refunded wedding dress money, threw a few things in a bag, and away I went.

The plane made a bumpy landing, my stomach flipping with every hop. We pulled up to the gate and my fellow passengers commenced unbuckling their seat belts and stretching their legs, and checking their phones, and nearly braining each other when pulling their unfeasibly large carry-on luggage out of the overhead compartments. I stayed put.

I was here. I was about to do what I'd come here to do.

I was terrified.

'Excuse me, miss.' I looked up to see the brassy-haired woman who'd been my loud-snacking seatmate for the flight staring pointedly at the still-gridlocked aisle. 'I need to get my case.'

I dutifully got up and did the standard half-stand/half-crouch in my seat until the passengers in front of us had shuffled off the plane. I grabbed my bag, checked that I had my passport, my phone, and the Manila envelope I'd tucked in the front pocket, and made my way to passport control.

It was true what they said about Texans: love them or hate them, they are unfailingly polite. By the time I was handed the keys to my rental car, I'd been ma'amed so many times I'd almost forgotten my real name.

I'd asked for the smallest car in the lot, but it was only with a modicum of surprise that I found myself in the driver's seat of a medium-sized tank. 'It's an SUV-hybrid, ma'am,' the man at the desk explained when I returned to ask if he had anything smaller.

'Don't you have a compact?' I'd asked pleadingly.

He shook his head. 'Ma'am, that *is* our compact.'

And so I set off in the SUV-hybrid, carefully edging my way out of the parking lot and onto the vast highway system that threaded through Dallas, feeling like I should be wearing a trooper helmet and peering out of a periscope rather than a windshield.

The route, according to the minuscule map on my phone, was a straight shot on US-82. Once I was clear of the airport and out on the road, I felt myself relax into the drive. In five hours, I'd have my answer. But for now, all I could do was point the car along the straight, sure line of the road and hit the gas.

It had been a long time since I'd driven in America, and I'd never driven through anywhere like this. The sheer vastness of it was overwhelming. I drove and drove, but the horizon stayed a fixed point in the distance. Occasionally I passed through a small town, with its diner and post office and red-brick school, but mostly it was just land. Every once in a while, I'd see a herd of cows milling around near a thin wire fence, their faces impassive as their mouths worked their cud, or a tall barn standing proudly at the edge of a field, but mainly it was just nothing. An endless stretch of nothing.

It was so beautiful, it made my heart ache.

I pulled into New Deal at around dinnertime. The street lights were on, but it was still light outside, and their pale beams were no match for the sun. I pulled the car over. There was a general store up ahead, the sign a shingle hanging above the door, which was propped open to let the air circulate. I went inside and walked up to the counter. A man in a blue button-down was sitting behind the register rolling change.

'Excuse me,' I said quietly, 'I was wondering if you could help me.'

He looked up at me and smiled. 'I sure hope so, sweetheart. What can I do for you?'

'I'm looking for a man,' I stuttered. 'He – I'm pretty sure he lives here.' The address listed on the divorce papers had just been a PO Box. I had no idea what street he lived on, or the house number. I'd turned up like Blanche Dubois, hoping to rely on the kindness of strangers. Ridiculous, really.

'Well, if he does, I'd know about it. New Deal is a small place. What's his name?'

'Jackson. Jackson Gaines.'

'Of course I know Jackson!' he crowed. 'I went to school with his daddy.'

Relief coursed through me, tinged with something else. Fear. 'Do you know where he lives?'

'Sure do, though I'm not sure if I should be going

around telling strangers.' He sized me up. 'Though I'm guessing Jackson wouldn't mind me telling a pretty lady like yourself. He's over on Monroe. Number 19, I believe. It's got a swing on the front porch, though I guess they all do. If you can't find it, come on back here and I'll take you over there myself.'

'Thank you!' I beamed. I hurried out to my car and threw it in reverse. I'd passed Monroe half a block back.

Jackson's house was small but perfectly formed. Weathered white clapboard with a generous front porch, with, as promised, a swing bench swaying gently next to the door. I walked up the flagstone path, Manila envelope crushed against my chest. I could feel the sweat pooling underneath my cotton T-shirt. I'd swiped on some lipstick in the rear-view mirror, but between the nine-hour flight and the five-hour drive and the now-almost-unbearable anxiety, it hadn't made much of an improvement. My nerve faltered, and I stopped in my tracks. What was I doing here? Had I lost my mind? But it was too late now. I was here, on his front porch. I could only keep going.

I knocked gently at first, and then took a polite step back from the door, as though I were a census-taker, or a Jehovah's Witness. No answer. I approached again and knocked harder this time. Waited. Still no answer.

I'd come all this way and I hadn't even checked if he'd be home. Embarrassment flooded through me. What had I been thinking? I knew he traveled all the time. I knew he was almost never home. What on earth had possessed me . . .

'If you're looking for Jackson, you won't find him here.'

I turned, startled, to see an old man sticking his head out of the upstairs window of the house next door.

Oh God. Now someone had seen me. There were witnesses. 'It's okay!' I shouted up to him. 'Never mind!'

'This time of day,' the old man continued, 'he'll be over at Bucky's with his pop.'

I gaped up at him. 'He's in New Deal?'

'Sure is. Saw him about an hour ago. You go down to Bucky's if you want to find him – he'll be there.'

'Okay!' I called. 'Thank you!' I was waving with both arms now. Soon I'd be doing a cartwheel.

The old man had his head half-pulled in when he remembered something. 'You know where Bucky's is, right?'

I froze. The man had a good point. 'No. Where is it?'

'Up the road, take a right. Look for the neon cowboy boot – you can't miss it!'

Turns out, Bucky's was right next to the general store. I'd got it right in the first place.

I sat in my car for a few minutes, heart thudding in time with the blinks of the neon cowboy boot above the door. There wasn't any other sign, or windows you could see into, or any sign of life other than the faint clack of pool balls clipping each other on their way into the side pocket.

I took a deep breath. I braced myself. I got out of the car.

The first thing that hit me when I walked through the door was the sour fug of stale beer mixed with the sweet scent of cigar smoke. I guess the smoking ban didn't apply to Bucky. The second thing that hit me was the wall of silence that descended as soon as my feet were over the threshold. It was so quiet, I could hear the man in the corner digesting the burger he'd eaten for lunch. The third thing, which I could only barely discern through the haze of smoke, was that Jackson wasn't there.

My heart sank. The man in the general store, the old man in the window . . . they'd led me on this stupid wild goose chase. But really, I'd got myself lost. And now here I was, in an unfriendly bar in the middle of Nowhere, Texas, without so much as a hotel reservation for the night. I was starting to be grateful for the spacious back seat of my SUV-hybrid. I might be sleeping in it that night.

I heard his laugh first. Deep, full-throated, inviting everyone along for the ride. A door in the back of the bar swung open and out walked Jackson, followed by an older, more sinewy version of Jackson. His father, presumably. My knees almost gave out.

He saw me straight away, presumably because he was wondering what everyone was staring at. Our eyes locked and I saw his mouth move. 'What in the world . . .' I tried to move towards him, to close the distance between us, but my feet were rooted to the spot. So he came to me.

Which, considering I'd already traveled 4,894 miles, seemed fair.

'Jenny.' It wasn't a question. It wasn't a statement. It was as though he was reassuring himself that his eyes weren't fooling him. That I was real.

I pulled out the envelope and handed it to him. 'All signed,' I said. 'We're officially divorced.'

His eyes trailed down to the envelope and then back up to mine. 'You came all the way to New Deal to give me these? We do have a post office here, you know.'

'I know,' I said. 'But there was something else. A question I wanted to ask.'

'Is that right?' He took a step towards me, and the familiar smell of him cut through the smoke. 'Shoot.'

'Do you want to go out sometime?'

He took another step towards me. I could feel the heat of him now, sense the magnetic pull of it. 'I thought you were engaged.'

'Not engaged,' I said, shaking my head. 'Not engaged *or* married.'

'So, you're saying you're free?' Another step closer. His hand brushed against mine and a thrill ran through me.

'As a bird,' I murmured. 'So I thought we could get a coffee or something. Talk.'

He tipped his chin down and frowned. 'I thought you weren't all that keen on talking. I waited on that bridge for three hours in the hope of talking to you.'

'I – I'm sorry,' I stuttered. 'I thought I knew what I wanted – Christopher, marriage, the whole thing – but then you turned up and . . .' I shook my head. 'I was scared.'

Silence stretched between us. The whole bar had gone quiet except for the faint twang of a country song on the jukebox, and I could feel everyone's eyes on us. 'I'm sorry.' I felt the hot flush of embarrassment run up my neck.

'God, I don't know what I was thinking, turning up here like this. You must think I'm nuts. And you'd be right! It was crazy of me, really. I just thought, maybe, if we could talk for a little while, if I could make you understand . . .'

He brought a hand to my face, traced my lips with his thumb. 'Sweetheart,' he said gruffly, 'I could talk to you for the rest of my life.'

He leaned down and touched his mouth to mine, and we melted into a kiss.

'Jenny,' he grinned when we finally broke apart, 'allow me to introduce you to the good people of New Deal.' He threw an arm around me and pulled me towards him. 'Good people of New Deal,' he announced, turning to address the room, 'this is Jenny Sparrow, my ex-wife, and the woman I one day hope to marry.'

The room burst into raucous applause. 'Bucky,' Jackson shouted, 'line them up! We've got some celebrating to do.'

Six months later

'Jenny, are you going to get dressed or what?'

I checked the time: 6.00. 'Shit!' The dinner started in forty-five minutes, and I was definitely not ready. I scooted off the hotel bed and started frantically pulling a dress over my hips while attempting to simultaneously apply lipstick.

Jackson was leaning against the mini-bar, a wry smile playing on his lips as he watched me try to wrestle my hair into something vaguely resembling a French twist. After two failed attempts, I gave up, tipped my head upside-down, and sprayed my roots with an ungodly amount of hairspray.

'Do I look like a member of Whitesnake?' I asked as I studied my reflection in the mirror.

Jackson appeared behind me and slid his hands around my waist. 'Nah ... though you do look a little like the woman in the "Here I Go Again" video, which is nicely fulfilling a teenage fantasy of mine.'

I whacked him on the arm. 'You were eight when that video came out.'

He ducked out of reach and grinned. 'What can I say? I'm an old soul. Anyway,' he said, leaning in for a kiss, 'you look gorgeous. The prettiest maid of honour I've ever seen.'

'Do you think I'm a matron of honour now? Since I'm a divorcee?'

'Say that word again,' he said, pulling me towards him.

'Which one? Matron?'

'No. The other one.'

'Divorcee?'

He kissed my collarbone and then moved up my neck. 'Man, you make that word sound sexy.' I felt his hands wander up towards the zipper of my dress. I could smell his cologne, something woodsy and crisp, and underneath it, the smell of his skin. I felt myself weakening. It wouldn't be the end of the world if we were ten minutes late . . . He nipped my earlobe with his teeth. Or twenty.

'Stop!' I forced myself to pull away. 'We can't be late – I'm giving a speech!'

He sighed. 'Fine,' he said, 'but I expect you to re-enact that video tonight when we get back here.'

I checked my teeth in the mirror for lipstick. 'Doesn't that involve cartwheeling across two Rolls Royces?' I tossed over my shoulder.

'I'm pretty sure I saw a Dodge and a Honda parked outside. What do you say?'

I pulled a face. 'Not quite the same effect.'

'No imagination,' he sighed. 'That's your problem. Shall we?' He offered me his elbow and I slid my hand through it.

'Let's.'

The venue was predictably bonkers. Usually, rehearsal dinners took place in staid restaurants with linen tablecloths and guttering candles. Isla had chosen an enormous concrete warehouse space in the depths of Queens. The theme, of course, was Up All Night.

I had already laid out a pair of Advil and a glass of water on the bedside table back at the hotel.

The cab pulled up and the cabbie shook his head. 'If you think I'm coming back here, you're nuts,' he called as he sped off into the night.

Wait, I should probably explain. Yes, Isla was getting married. No, I couldn't believe it.

She'd met him four months ago at an underground S&M club in the Meatpacking District. 'It was great, babe,' she'd said when she called the next morning (or, more accurately, the next afternoon, which is when she woke up). 'This guy in a mask came up to me and started spanking me with this bamboo cane.'

'That sounds awful!'

'No, it was totally hot. And I could tell by the way he was spanking me that he was really caring. You know?'

Not really, but it didn't matter. What mattered was that they were madly, insanely in love and had spent the past four months shacking up in his TriBeca loft. And now they were getting married.

Isla let out a scream when she spotted us walk through the door. 'You're here!' she cried as she launched herself at the two of us. She was, of course, wearing a silver body-suit, stilettos and body glitter. 'You look amazing,' she said as she squeezed me tightly in her arms. 'Like one of those video babes from the 80s.'

I shot Jackson a knowing glance, and he laughed. 'And you!' Isla said, turning her attention on him. 'You look like a sexy urban cowboy!' It was true, he did. He was wearing his battered old cowboy boots, with a dark, slim-cut suit, and one of those bolero ties I'd always made fun of until he put one on, at which point I found it insanely attractive. But then again, I found pretty much everything he put on insanely attractive. It was convenient, that.

'So,' I said, 'how's it going?'

'Pretty good,' Isla beamed. 'I mean, the space is amazing, and we have the DJ until 6 a.m., and enough MDMA to keep everyone happy until Tuesday.'

I spotted her parents huddled in a corner, her mother wearing a pink feather boa and her father sporting a jaunty top hat. Isla followed my gaze and laughed. 'Obviously all family members have been told that this thing ends promptly at 10.30,' she said.

'Well, that's a relief. I really didn't want your father coming up to me and stroking me with a feather duster.'

Isla laughed. 'I can't guarantee that won't happen, but I can promise you it won't be drug-related. Are you ready for the speech?'

I nodded nervously. Jackson threw a protective arm around me and pulled me towards him. 'She's been practising like a lunatic,' he said. 'She didn't want to leave anything to chance.'

Isla reached out and squeezed my hand. 'Some things never change. I've just got to check on the caterer – you guys go get yourselves a drink and mingle, okay? When I get back, I want to hear all about San Francisco.'

Jackson and I had moved to San Francisco a few

months ago. After I'd surprised him in New Deal, we agreed that we needed to at least be on the same continent if we were going to make things work. I'd always liked the idea of living on the West Coast – even though it hadn't been part of my master plan – and the insurance company in London had an office there and agreed to a transfer. For Jackson, it was the perfect base to get to LA or Vancouver for work, so we found a pair of apartments and signed the leases.

That's right, two separate apartments. We were taking things slow this time. Letting things happen when they happened. It felt good to let go of a timescale. It felt right.

Jackson fetched two glasses of bourbon from the bar and offered one to me. Across the room, I watched Isla wrap her arms around her fiancé and reach up on her toes to kiss him. They glowed with happiness.

We raised our glasses in a toast.

'To happy endings,' Jackson said, clinking his glass to mine.

'To happy endings,' I said, 'whatever road it takes to get there.'

Acknowledgements

This book wouldn't have been possible without the help of three people: Felicity Blunt, my agent and friend, who lobbed ideas at me fast ball-style, and fought my corner when I finally caught one; Simon Robertson, my husband, who listened patiently, offered advice, and took me to the pub when all else failed; and Katie Cunningham, my sister from another mother, who encouraged me to keep digging the clay and supplied me with a constant stream of dog photos as a distraction. You guys are great.

Thanks to Tilda McDonald, my editor at Michael Joseph, for her feedback and guidance, and to Maxine Hitchcock and the whole team at Penguin for their sterling work.

Finally, thanks to my family, both the Pimentels and the Robertsons, for their love and support. I'm a lucky gal to have you all in my life.